Praise for The Long Game

'A riptide of excitement, it totally swept me away!'
Daniel Godfrey, author of *New Pompeii*

'A great read for fans of space opera and criminal capers'
SF Crowsnest

'Big screen space opera at its most entertaining.
With a welcome hint of an updated *Stainless Steel Rat*,
Orry Kent makes for an engaging and savvy protagonist'
Gavin Smith, author of *The Bastard Legion*

'Imaginative world-building . . . a lively sci-fi romp'
SFX

'For those in need of a gallivant through space with a
bunch of mismatched chancers, *Shattermoon* should be
at the top of your list'
SciFiNow

'This book builds and builds with so much action that it kept
me entertained to the very end'
Dyslexic Reader

'[A] fast paced read from start to finish, a total page turner,
which I read almost in one go'
Bookish Outsider

'A fun and fast-paced heist novel'
I Should Read That

'An action-packed space adventure, Dominic's debut is a blast!'
Laura Patricia Rose

'An exciting read with a capable and cool-headed protagonist'
Blue Book Balloon

Also by Dominic Dulley

Shattermoon

Morhelion

DOMINIC DULLEY

Jo Fletcher
BOOKS

First published in Great Britain in 2019
This edition published in 2020 by

Jo Fletcher Books
an imprint of Quercus Editions Ltd
Carmelite House
50 Victoria Embankment
London EC4Y 0DZ

An Hachette UK company

A CIP catalogue record for this book is available
from the British Library

PB ISBN 978 1 78648 608 0
EBOOK ISBN 978 1 78648 607 3

10 9 8 7 6 5 4 3 2 1

Typeset by CC Book Production

Printed and bound in Great Britain by Clays Ltd, Elcograf S.p.A.

For Bea, who thought up the bubbles

CONTENTS

1

GYRE

'Hand me that bypass clip, will you?' Mender said, intent on the partially disassembled scrubber in front of him.

Orry Kent regarded the unfamiliar equipment spread across the table in the farm's kitchen module with dismay. Her father had taught her a lot of things, but bomb-making wasn't one of them.

'Come on, come on,' Mender muttered, flapping his hand.

'Um ...' Her fingers hovered over a short band of curved metal before she changed her mind and offered the old man a length of coiled wire.

He didn't look up as he took it and tried to attach it to the scrubber – then he frowned and peered at the object in his hand. Sighing, he rummaged through the junkyard on the table. 'This,' he growled, holding up a short cable, 'is a bypass clip.'

He connected the cable, then returned his attention to a set of schematics displayed on the databrane spread out beside him. The scrubber was a squat cylinder, one of several *Dainty Jane* used in her life-support systems. The old ship could easily spare it – she was rated for a crew of twenty, and with just Mender,

Orry and her fifteen-year-old brother Ethan living aboard, there was a lot of surplus capacity.

Don't forget to isolate the exchangers, the ship sent over the common integuary channel. She had set down a few hundred metres away, well clear of the network of plastic growing tunnels that surrounded the farm's hab modules.

I know what I'm doing, Mender sent back, and Orry smiled at her integuary's precise rendering of his long-suffering tone inside her head. He manipulated the schematic with a gesture, located an access panel on the side of the scrubber and picked up a long probe.

As he inserted it into the casing, *Jane* reminded him, *You need to drain the residual charge from the capacitors.*

His hand paused. *Do you want to do it?*

Just trying to help.

Well, don't. The probing resumed.

Give it a rest, you two, Orry subvocalised. *You're bickering like an old married couple.* She stood behind Mender and rested her hands on his shoulders as she peered inside the scrubber.

'What are you doing?' he grunted.

'Just watching.'

'Go and watch something else.'

She made a face at the back of his head, then wandered over to one of the worktops that ran around the curving walls, idly fiddling with the stainless-steel utensils sticking out of brightly painted ceramic pots. Everything on the farm was well used, but it was clear the unknown residents took pride in their few possessions. A bowl of colourful rock fragments the size of little sweet tomatoes caught her eye and she picked one up. It was porous, lighter than she'd expected, and shot through with tiny crystals that sparkled like miniature prisms as the light struck them.

'I wouldn't touch that,' Mender said from the table.

'Why, what is it?'

'Scorite.'

She looked at the chunk of rock with interest. This job couldn't succeed without scorite, but she'd never seen the mineral before. 'It's pretty,' she said.

Mender rose from the table with a grunt and stretched, working out the kinks in his back before limping over and taking the scorite from her. When he held it up to the light, spots of reflected colour danced in his artificial eye.

'You know why this stuff is so valuable?' he asked, then before she could answer he whipped round and hurled the fragment at the far wall. It struck with a sharp *crack* and ignited instantly, flashing into incandescence as it dropped to the floor, burning with a white light so intense that Orry had to look away, afterimages ghosting her vision. A smell of melting plastic and scorched metal filled the module and she began to worry that the stuff might burn clean through the floor. When the flame did finally sputter and die, it left a nugget of glowing slag in a circle of melted floor covering and blackened metal.

'Very dramatic,' she coughed, waving smoke from her face.

'There's a lot of energy bound up in those rocks,' Mender said, obviously pleased with himself. 'It's a delicate business, digging out the stuff without losing some part of you you'd rather keep attached.'

She stared at the scorch mark, thinking of the vast strip-mines that scarred Gyre's barren surface. Outside of a few larger settlements like Charter City the place was all open-cast mines and agro-stations like this one.

Mender returned to the table and Orry checked the local time. *Still hours to go.* She needed something to keep her hands occupied.

'Anything I can do to help?'

He pointed at a plastic tub full of small sachets. 'You can start emptying that lot into a bowl.'

She examined one of the packets curiously. 'Desalination crystals?'

'Hope so – I bought a hundred of 'em. Now do me a favour and shut the hell up. I need to crack this bloody thing.'

She found a suitable bowl under the sink and began tearing open the sachets and pouring out the crystals. By the time she was done, Mender had got the scrubber's casing open and extracted an oval reservoir of viscous liquid.

'Put these on,' he said, handing her a pair of gauntlets.

She wrinkled her nose at the acrid smell as Mender carefully emptied the gelatinous contents of the reservoir into the bowl of crystals and stirred it gently with a metal spoon.

'Baggies,' he said, snapping his fingers.

'Shouldn't we be wearing respirators?' she asked as she picked up the roll of self-sealing food bags on the table, tore off the first one and held it open beside the bowl. The smell was lining the back of her throat now, leaving a viscid residue.

Ignoring her, he spooned half the contents of the bowl into the bag.

You'll be fine as long as it doesn't touch your skin, sent *Jane*.

Orry sealed the bag and laid it carefully on the table before tearing off another. Once it was filled, Mender set the bowl and the remains of the scrubber aside and cleared a space for the spherical object he pulled from his pocket. It was painted with yellow and black warning stripes and covered with danger symbols.

'A mining charge?' she said, alarmed.

'Uh-huh,' he grunted. He reached for a roll of tape, bit off a length and secured one of the baggies around half the charge.

'Isn't that a little powerful?' she asked.

'Nope.' He reached for the second baggie.

'Lefevre isn't going to buy a hole in the ground.'

'Relax, girl. I know what I'm doing. Do you?'

She looked sharply at him. 'What's that supposed to mean?'

'Just that we've been on this rock for three weeks and this con of yours has burned through all but the last of our cash.'

She hesitated, suddenly very aware of the bulge in the small of her back, concealed by her coat. 'It'll work,' she assured him.

'It had better. You wouldn't like me when I'm starving to death. I get *tetchy*.'

She folded her arms. 'I don't like you now.'

He chuckled and turned the charge over in his hands, examining it carefully, before rising to his feet. 'Coming?'

'Right behind you.' She checked the time again, resisting the urge to get an update from Ethan; her brother wouldn't thank her for pestering him.

She was still fastening her jacket as Mender left the hab. The moment he was gone she reached behind her and pulled out the package. When she opened the door of the unit she'd chosen and saw the near-empty shelves she felt better about what she was doing, even if she was keeping it from Mender. She pushed the package onto the top shelf, then hesitated. What if things *did* go wrong? Did she really have the right to do this? She really wished her father was there. *What would he do?* she asked herself, then realised the answer was obvious: Eoin had always made sure the mark was the only one who suffered.

She closed the cupboard door, looked regretfully at the circle burned into the floor, then raised her hood and followed Mender outside.

Gyre's sky was the colour of amber, its distant sun made hazy by the dust high in the thick atmosphere. It was everywhere, a by-product of the constant mining that made the place taste like burnt coffee and coated the curve of *Dainty Jane*'s hull as she towered like the shell of a vast crustacean above the farm's growing tunnels. On the horizon a range of high peaks were blanketed in snow discoloured by the weird amber light.

Gyre was a small moon, which meant low gravity. Orry shrank deeper into her coat as she stepped carefully across the frozen ground.

'I've been asking around,' Mender said as she caught him up.

'About what?'

'You hear about the local firm?'

'Yeah, Uri told me about them. Don't worry – there's no reason for them to find out what we're doing here, so there's no point getting involved with them. We'll be gone in a couple of days.'

'Did you know they kick back to Roag?' His breath was steaming in the bitter air.

She tried to ignore the spike of hate the name drove through her chest. 'I didn't, but it doesn't surprise me; that bitch has her claws into everything. All the more reason not to get involved.'

'So this job has nothing to do with revenge?'

'In case you hadn't noticed, the Ascendancy is at war and Cordelia Roag started it. She's the most wanted person in human space, which makes her kind of difficult to locate. When I'm ready to settle things with her, you'll be the first to know. What we're doing here is purely business.'

'You expect me to believe that? She killed your old man.'

Orry stopped walking. 'You still don't trust me,' she said accusingly. 'After all that's happened.'

He held her gaze, then spat on the frozen ground and stomped away, muttering.

Of course he trusts you, Jane told her on a private channel. *He's just nervous.*

Orry snorted. *That old bastard doesn't* have *nerves.* She set off after him. *Nervous about what?* she asked as they approached the ramp down to the cavern.

We were alone a long time, he and I. He's used to calling the shots. Having you running things for a change is difficult for him.

Orry stared at Mender's back as he limped down the steep slope ahead of her. Perhaps she *had* been a little blunt with him – but putting this job together had taken a lot of effort. She'd never really realised how much Dad used to do behind the scenes; no wonder he'd always been grumpy in the run-up to a grift. Blinking hard at the memories, she followed Mender into the cave beneath the farm.

Gyre was riddled with caverns like this one. The voids made mining difficult, but the rewards were worth the risks. Scorite was vital to the starship industry and since the Kadiran attack on Tyr, the Ascendancy needed as much of the stuff as it could get to bolster the Grand Fleet.

Switching her integuary to low-light mode, she saw Mender fixing the mining charge to the end of a long cable dangling from the roof, suspending their homemade bomb at head height. As she looked at the size of the cavern she had to admit that his choice of the charge was probably a wise one; it would need a considerable blast to do the job.

The old man stepped back and looked up at the rough ceiling metres above his head. 'That should cover it nicely.' He looked at her. 'You want to blow it?'

She frowned. 'You're sure this will work? How can goop from a scrubber and some desalination powder fool a sniffer?'

'The chemical signature's identical to scorite,' he assured her. 'It'll work.'

She chewed her lower lip, not entirely convinced.

'All right,' she said eventually, 'give me the detonator.'

2

VILLANUEVA '28

Ethan had chosen the alleyway carefully. He and Uri waited in the frigid air a short distance from the main street like actors in the wings. *Is this how it feels before going on stage?* he wondered as his stomach churned with nervous anticipation.

Five seconds, Orry broke into his thoughts. *Four, three, two . . . and go!*

He handed Uri the gilt chip, wondering if he would ever see it again. The man wouldn't have been his first choice, but beggars couldn't be choosers when seeking out grifters in a strange town.

'Hey!' Ethan yelled as the other man took off as planned, heading towards the street. He gave Uri a couple of seconds' head-start, then set off in pursuit just as the banker, Simon Lefevre, passed the alley's entrance. 'Stop him!' Ethan shouted.

Uri cannoned into the startled banker – and dropped the gilt chip at his feet. Lefevre stumbled back, but before he could say anything Uri was gone, bounding away down the salted pavement in an ungainly low-gravity lope.

Ethan ran into the street, cursing, and skidded to a halt by

Lefevre as he stooped to pick up the chip. He let his mouth drop open at the sight of it.

'You stopped him!' Ethan said, taking the chip from the banker's unresisting hand and pressing a button on the side. Beaming, he showed the balance to Lefevre. 'It's all here,' he exclaimed with relief. '*Thank you!*'

The banker raised his eyebrows. 'That's a lot of money.'

Ethan laughed and clapped him on the shoulder. 'You have no idea how important this is. Thank you, so much!' he repeated.

'If it's that important, perhaps you should be more careful with it.' Lefevre peered down the street after Uri. 'Did he mug you?'

'Pickpocketed, actually,' Ethan explained. 'I felt something, but he was away before I could grab him.' He reached out and pumped Lefevre's hand. 'I don't know how I can thank you.'

'It was nothing, really.' The banker disengaged with difficulty, looking uncomfortable.

'Nothing!' Reaching into his jacket, Ethan pulled out Mender's empty hipflask, put it to his lips and grimaced. He upturned it, shaking his head sadly. 'At least you'll let me buy you a drink?'

'Aren't you a little young to be drinking?'

'I'm old enough,' Ethan protested, looking around. One of the reasons for selecting this particular alley was the Ruuz-style champagne bar across the street. He could see Lefevre's interest spark when he followed Ethan's gaze. 'Well, I'm having one, anyway,' Ethan said. 'I think I might be in shock.'

The banker checked the time and smiled. 'Why not?'

Got him, Ethan reported as they crossed the street.

The bar was a better-than-average rim world rip-off of an upmarket Fountainhead drinking establishment; the décor wasn't bad, for a start. And Lefevre was clearly pleased when Ethan ordered a decent bottle.

He paid cash, using the last of their local currency. *This had better work*, he thought, plastering a smile onto his face to hide his concern. 'We haven't been introduced,' he said cheerily. 'I'm Abram.'

'Simon Lefevre.'

The banker was a big man who looked like he'd been in shape once but was now running to fat. His curly hair was slicked back with too much product and he sported a pencil-thin beard in a futile attempt to re-establish his jawline.

He leered at the pretty waitress who brought their champagne over. 'What time do you get off?' he asked as she opened the bottle with a muted *pop*.

She smiled uncomfortably. 'Would you like me to pour?' she asked.

'That's not all I'd like you to do, sweetheart.'

Ethan felt desperately sorry for the poor girl as he watched her fill two glass flutes; she recoiled when Lefevre reached out to caress the bare skin of her arm.

'Will that be all?' she asked stiffly, putting the bottle down.

'For now.' He stared at her legs as she returned to the bar, then rolled his eyes lasciviously at Ethan. '*That*,' he pronounced, 'should not be allowed.'

Arsehole, Ethan thought as he raised his champagne and grinned. 'I'll drink to that!' He drained half his glass, then grimaced.

'Something wrong?' Lefevre asked.

'Not really,' he replied, aiming for weary nonchalance. 'I'm just looking forward to getting back to somewhere I can get a

11

decent drink.'

The banker sniffed his glass and tasted the contents. 'Tastes all right to me.'

'It's fine, I suppose. The Villanueva '28 just doesn't travel well. You should taste it on Tyr.'

'You've been to Tyr?' Lefevre sounded interested.

'I was born there.'

'Really?' The banker looked at him a little doubtfully. 'What brought you here?'

'My father.' Ethan finished his glass, trusting the alcohol inhibitors he'd taken to keep a clear head. Allowing a slight slur to enter his voice, he continued, 'He invested heavily in Ghent-Masson, then when things started to go badly he dragged us all out here so he could oversee the mining operations personally. It didn't work, and the company went belly-up.'

'What did he do?'

Ethan stared into his empty glass. 'He put a laser in his mouth and pulled the trigger. I was eight.'

'Rama – that's tough.'

'He left us with nothing but the family name, and what's that worth out here? Marta – she's my sister – had to take a job to support us. A *job*!'

Lefevre topped up Ethan's glass. 'What *is* your family name, if you don't mind me asking?'

'Grekov. It's a minor house, but we're a cadet branch of House Marquardt. Not that those bastards lifted a finger to help.'

'Why not?'

'Father's investments were *vulgar*, they said, *bourgeois*. They were glad when he came out here; not so embarrassing for them.'

Lefevre looked sympathetic.

On the hook, Ethan thought happily. He took another gulp. 'We'll show them though, when we go back to Tyr with a fortune.'

'Two thousand imperials is hardly a fortune.'

Ethan waved the gilt chip dismissively. 'I'm not talking about this. Anyway, drink up and have another – without you, we wouldn't be going anywhere.'

'Glad I could be of some small assistance.' The banker drank, watching him curiously.

'Damn it all, but I wish I could thank you properly.' Ethan put his glass down with some force. 'Honour means everything to a Grekov.'

'Perhaps you could spare some of that fortune you mentioned,' Lefevre suggested lightly.

'You're right,' he said decisively.

'I am?'

'I should give you a reward.'

'Really?'

'Yes, yes – and I know just how I can. What are you doing right now?'

'Well, I have a meeting—'

'Cancel it.'

'Why should I do that?'

Ethan finished his drink. 'I can't give you anything now, but if you can spare me half an hour I'll show you just how generous a Grekov can be.'

The banker narrowed his eyes. 'How?'

Ethan smiled. 'Come with me and find out.'

He held his breath as Lefevre considered. Eventually the man smiled and shook his head as if he couldn't quite believe what he was doing.

'All right then, my lordling. Where are we going?'

3

HARPER'S PULLED OUT

While ostensibly an Ascendancy colony, Gyre was owned and governed by the Empyrean Development Company. Clearly quality of life for the miners and the farmers who supported them wasn't high on EDC's list of priorities, Orry thought, looking at the Brutalist architecture of Charter City. The land registry office on Tenth Street she was waiting outside was a case in point: the block was the same reddish-brown local rock as every other structure in the city, apparently the only raw material available to the construction printers.

The street was almost empty, even at noon; the cold and dust did not provide a conducive environment for a lunchtime stroll. She'd been on worse worlds, but not many. Spotting Ethan approaching in conversation with the mark, dead on time, she took a breath and prepared herself.

'Who the fuck is this?' she demanded before her brother could open his mouth.

Ethan looked genuinely surprised. 'Simon Lefevre ...' he began formally, 'may I present my sister, Lady Marta Grekov. I'd like to say she's not always this rude, but that would be a lie.'

Lefevre sized her up, taking in the poor condition of the padded jacket over her thermal coveralls. 'Look,' he said, 'I should probably go.'

'Yes,' she agreed with feeling, 'you should.'

'No,' Ethan said, 'this man has done our House a great service. Without him we wouldn't have enough.' He held up the gilt chip.

She grabbed him by the arm and dragged him aside. 'Are you *insane*?' she hissed, just loud enough for Lefevre to overhear. 'Who the hell *is* he?'

'He's all right. He saved me.'

She glared at him. 'What happened?'

'I was attacked by a street tough – Simon put his own life at risk to recover our investment.'

Orry thought he was hamming it up a little, but Lefevre didn't appear to notice anything suspicious. He probably just thought Ethan was drunk.

'Have you been drinking?' she asked.

'No. Well, a little.' Ethan waved it off. 'The point is, our House owes this man an honour debt.'

'*Our House?*' Orry snorted. 'There is no House. Just us, and this.' She held up her own chip, loaded with all that was left of their gilt.

He stiffened. 'I don't care what you say. I am going to pay our debt to this man.'

'What if he's' – she glanced at Lefevre and lowered her voice a little more, just audible to straining ears – '*in the Corps?*'

Ethan snorted. 'Hey, Simon, are you an arbiter?'

'What? No! I told you, I work for a bank.'

'There you are,' her brother said triumphantly. 'If he was an arbiter he'd tell us. They have to, you know, or it's entrapment or something.'

'Will you *shut up*—'

'He's a good guy,' Ethan interrupted. 'I'll vouch for him.'

'You don't even *know* him.'

'I'm a good judge of character. Besides, he saved me and we owe him. Look, I'm just going to give him a bit of my share, okay? It's my money. I still care about our family honour, even if you don't.' He shook his head. 'Look at us: what have we let ourselves become? If we don't pay an honour debt, this place has beaten us. Is that what you want?'

She glared at him, thoroughly enjoying herself. It felt good to be back in the game. 'Fine,' she said eventually, 'you can do what you like with your share. But if we end up in a Company gaol, it's on you.'

'We won't – I promise.'

She held out a hand for his chip and saw Lefevre sidle closer, curious, as she transferred Ethan's two thousand to her own chip. His face changed when he glimpsed the balance.

'*Twenty thousand imperials?* I thought you were destitute?'

'It's taken years to raise that much,' Ethan told him.

'What are you going to do with it?'

'Mind your own business,' Orry snapped. 'I'll be back in a minute.'

She walked into the registry building and spent a few minutes studying the claim maps on the walls. The bleak and soulless interior matched the outside. A clerk watched from behind a counter.

'Can I help you?' he asked eventually.

'No thanks.' She pulled out the databrane Ethan had prepared for her and strode back out to the street.

'Did you get it?' her brother asked.

She grinned and held up the brane. He whooped and gave her a high-five.

'Is that a land deed?' Lefevre asked. He was edgy now, but Orry could tell he was intrigued. An honest man would have made his excuses and left at this point, but Simon Lefevre was not an honest man.

'Never mind what it is,' she said.

'Not long now,' Ethan reassured him. 'Just a quick walk over the street.' He led the way into the lobby of a mid-scale hotel used by visiting managers and mining company execs.

Uri? Orry sent. *All set?*

Yeah, all ready for you.

Good. We're on our way up now.

In the lift she could tell the banker's nerves were getting the better of him, but reassuring him was not her job. She was about to give Ethan a mental nudge when he piped up, 'Do you remember that place we stayed at on Halcyon? I was only, what, five? I still remember it. Better than this shithole. Have you ever been to Halcyon?' he asked Lefevre, who shook his head. 'Amazing place. We'll have to go back there, Sis. After . . . you know.'

She gave a non-committal grunt, pleased with him, and the doors opened.

Uri was barely recognisable when they entered the room Orry had sweet-talked the concierge into letting her rent for a couple of hours. He might be a short-con merchant but there was no doubt the man had a talent for disguise, she reflected. There was no way Lefevre would recognise this smooth, booted and suited executive as Ethan's shabby pickpocket.

The suite was comfortable, with a view over the city's industrial sprawl. A metal case rested on a ceramic-topped coffee table.

There were no introductions, no pleasantries. 'Do you have it?' Uri asked peremptorily and Orry pulled out the forged deed and handed it to him.

'And the survey results?'

She produced a second databrane and he studied the two carefully. 'Well, this all looks satisfactory,' he said at last, rolling up both branes and slipping them into his pocket. He bent to open the case on the table and she could feel Lefevre's tension when he saw the layers of currency. 'Sixty thousand imperials, as agreed,' Uri said. 'Would you like to count it?'

Bottom row, third from the left. She picked up the only stack not padded out with blank sheets, held it up and examined it, then riffled through it before replacing it and closing the case. 'That won't be necessary. Thank you.'

'No, thank *you*,' Uri said, moving to the door. 'The suite is booked for the night if you want to make use of it. The account has been settled in advance. Good day.'

Ethan waited for him to leave before clapping his hands and running to the table. He hugged Orry, then opened the case and stared at the money.

'What just happened?' Lefevre asked.

She picked up the bundle of genuine notes and counted out six thousand imperials, which she handed to Ethan.

'Four thousand profit,' he said. 'Not bad for ten minutes' work.' He peeled off ten hundred-imperial notes and handed them to Lefevre, who stared dumbly at them. Orry could almost see the cogs turning in his head. 'I told you honour is everything to a Grekov,' Ethan told him, grinning broadly.

'You're giving him a grand?' she objected.

'So? Relax, Marta; tomorrow we'll be spending more than that on breakfast.'

She shot him an angry look that Lefevre must surely interpret as an instruction to shut the hell up, walked to the door and opened it. *Now, Uri*, she sent. 'It was nice meeting you, Mr Lefevre,' she said aloud, 'and I thank you for your service to my brother, but I'm sure you're a busy man.'

The phone she'd lifted earlier that day rang. Still holding the door open, she took it out and thumbed it on. 'Marta Grekov.'

'Good luck,' Uri said, and rang off.

'You're fucking kidding me,' she said into the dead phone. 'The deal is set for *tomorrow*.' She waved Lefevre impatiently towards the open door and walked away from him. 'Where the hell am I supposed to find someone in twelve hours? No, I can't, you idiot. I'm not a damned cash dispenser.'

The banker was still loitering by the door. *Good.*

'Let me explain this one more time, as simply as I can.' Her voice was getting icier by the second. 'It *has* to be tomorrow or the old man will put the place up for auction. So no, I think that attitude is less than helpful. Fuck you, too.'

She hurled the phone across the room, then rounded on her brother. 'Harper's pulled out.'

'Oh *shit* – so what do we do now?' He sounded panicky. *Perfect.*

It took a moment, but eventually Lefevre cleared his throat. 'Uh, why don't you tell me what's going on?' He stepped away from the door and closed it. 'Perhaps I can help?'

4

SCORITE SEAMS

'You said you're a banker?' Orry waved Lefevre to a sofa and started pacing the room. 'How much do you know about scorite?'

'A bit.'

She studied him for a moment, as if deciding whether or not he could be trusted. 'Well, I *work*' - she loaded the word with disgust - 'as a mineral surveyor for the local factor's office, which means I spend my life driving around this shithole of a moon looking for scorite seams. When I find one, I report its location, and for that I receive a modest finder's fee, then the factor auctions the land rights to the highest bidder. Generally, it goes for tens of thousands of imperials.

'The Company treats me like crap and the money I get isn't enough to support one Grekov, let alone two of us, so I decided there must be a better way. Two years ago, when I found a small deposit under some unclaimed land, I borrowed enough cash to purchase the plot myself and found someone - the man who just left - to buy the claim from me. Doing the deal direct meant he paid a fraction of what it would have cost at auction, while I trebled my investment.'

'Who is he?' Lefevre asked, but Orry was already shaking her head.

'Not something you need to know, Mr – Lefevre, was it? I'll just say he works for an interested party.'

'You mean for one of the mining concerns.'

She ignored him and went on, 'I have been exceptionally careful to stay under the radar, building my nest-egg and waiting for the big one – which I found a week ago.' She gave him a glowing smile. 'It's the richest vein I've ever seen – you should see the spectrometry results. The sniffer practically blew a fuse. This deposit will be worth *millions*.'

He looked sceptical. 'So what's the problem? Just buy it and go back to Tyr.'

'The *problem* is the person who owns the land.'

'Ah.'

'Precisely. Eighty per cent of this godforsaken rock is unclaimed, but *my* vein just happens to be under a farm run by a crazy man.'

'Will he sell?'

'He will, but he wants a hundred grand for it, even though the land isn't worth even a quarter of that.'

'How much do you have?'

She gestured at the case. 'Half. I had a partner who was going to put up the rest, but as you heard, he's pulled out. It's taken me a lot of time to put all this together and the old coot is getting impatient. If he doesn't get the money by midday tomorrow, the deal's off. And I'm worried he's starting to get suspicious. The last thing we want is him commissioning his own survey.'

'Why does he think you want the land?'

'I told him the concern I represent wants to build a relay-transmitter and his farm happens to be ideally positioned for our triangulation needs.'

'You should have fluttered your eyelashes, fed him some sob story – that way he might not have jacked up the price,' Lefevre said unhelpfully.

'Thanks for that,' she replied sarcastically.

'So you need fifty thousand before tomorrow?'

'It looks that way. Why are you asking?'

Lefevre regarded her for a moment, then stood up to leave. 'It was nice meeting you both.'

'Whoa, whoa, whoa!' Ethan exclaimed, practically falling over a chair in his haste to reach the banker before he got to the door.

Leave it, Ethan, Orry warned, but her brother ignored her.

'*This* is how I properly repay you, Simon – you could come in with us – this is *totally* safe! You bring your fifty thou to the farm tomorrow morning and walk away with a hundred: double your money in a matter of hours!'

Lefevre considered this. 'I want two hundred.'

'I don't think so,' Orry told him in disgust.

He continued towards the door.

'But—' Ethan started.

The banker stopped and turned to look at him. 'Take it or leave it,' he said. 'You said it yourself: this deposit will be worth millions. And you're desperate.'

'Marta?' Ethan prompted.

She clenched her jaw and reluctantly met Lefevre's greedy gaze. It was perfect; this way he felt like he had the upper hand. She sighed. 'Very well: two hundred.'

'I'll need to see the survey reports.'

'Not a problem.'

He walked over to her; she took his proffered hand and they shook.

'We're going to make a lot of money together,' Ethan said happily.

Once Lefevre was safely gone, Ethan dropped into a chair and let out a deep breath. 'Rama! I really thought we'd lost him there.'

'We still might,' Orry said. 'Did you hook into his phone?' And when he nodded, 'So shouldn't you be keeping an eye on it?'

'Nah, *Jane* let me repurpose one of her ancillary processing modules to use as an interpolator. It's monitoring his signal: it'll intercept any searches related to us and send back a bunch of results I set up earlier to corroborate our story.'

Ethan was the tech in the family so she ignored the temptation to tell him to monitor anyway and instead asked, 'What about a vehicle?'

His cocky look slipped. 'Um . . . all in hand . . .'

'You forgot, didn't you?'

'No!' He dropped his gaze and muttered sheepishly, 'Yes. I'll get on it.'

'Something *mid-range*,' she called after him. 'We're broke.'

5

FELIKS

As their subverted all-terrain buggy crested the crater wall, Orry saw the neat lines of plastic growing tunnels spreading like spokes from the farm's hab modules. Around them, the frozen ground had been partially thawed by the heat leeching through the cheap insulation. She was relieved to see *Dainty Jane* was no longer towering over the farm.

Ethan guided the ungainly vehicle down the rough road, Lefevre's buggy bouncing along behind them. The driver, the banker's 'assistant' Clovis, was clearly less a PA and more a bodyguard hired to protect his investment. Orry wasn't surprised, but Clovis was bound to be armed and weapons made her nervous.

They drew up in front of the modules and as she climbed down from the buggy's high cab, the cold brought tears to her eyes and made her exposed nose and cheeks ache.

Mender limped out of a doorway and scowled at the four of them. 'Didn't expect you to bring half the friggin' moon with you. You got the cash?'

Ethan promptly opened the metal case and showed Mender the notes.

He picked up the real pile, flicked through it and grunted, then turned to Lefevre. 'You the one with the rest of it?'

The banker smiled and indicated the similar case Clovis was holding. 'Indeed I am – but first I'd like to see what I'm getting in return.'

'I'm not a fucking tour guide.'

'You misunderstand me: I mean the deeds.'

Mender hawked and spat. He eyed Lefevre, then reached into his coat and produced a databrane which he shook into rigidity and held up.

'Perhaps you would permit my assistant here to examine the document more closely?' the banker asked. 'Inside, perhaps?' He held out his hand and Clovis passed him the case. 'While you do that, I'll take a look around.'

'Go with them,' Orry told her brother.

Mender glared at Lefevre, but he stumped to the door, followed by Clovis and Ethan. As soon as they disappeared inside, the banker turned to Orry.

'What a charmer. Now, before we proceed, there's something I need to do.' He opened his case to reveal not cash, but a high-grade chemical spectrometer. The gear looked far more expensive – and far more sensitive – than she'd expected.

'If the old man sees you with that he'll suss us in an instant,' she said, worried.

'Clovis will keep him busy,' Lefevre said dismissively as he began to set up the equipment with what looked suspiciously like practised ease. 'A contact of mine works for Praxis Minerals; he owed me a favour,' he explained as he worked. 'He let me borrow this and showed me how to use it. Took a look at your survey results, too.'

Orry threw up her hands in genuine dismay at his words. 'You were supposed to keep your fucking mouth *shut* about this! Who else have you told?'

He finished erecting the scanner on its tripod and started its calibration routine. 'No one,' he assured her, 'and I didn't tell him a thing. Like I say, he owed me. The survey results were fine by the way. Very promising.'

'That much I know,' she said tartly. *One less thing to worry about, I suppose.*

The machine chimed and he set it running. It oscillated in its gimbal, creating a chemical picture of the ground beneath their feet. The spectrometer chimed again and Lefevre examined the screen.

Resisting the urge to gnaw on a fingernail and desperately hoping Mender had got the chemistry right, she waited until, finally, Lefevre looked up and gave her a thin smile.

'It appears you were right, Lady Grekov.'

Ethan and Clovis rose from the kitchen table when Orry and Lefevre entered and stood either side of Mender, who had remained seated, the databrane containing the deed in front of him.

The banker placed a different case on the table, before sitting facing Mender. 'The price was one hundred thousand imperials, I believe.' He opened the case. 'Here it is . . . *all* of it.'

Orry turned her smile of delight into an angry scowl. 'What the *fuck*, Lefevre?'

It took Ethan a moment longer to work out what he'd just said. 'Simon?' His voice sounded uncertain.

Mender frowned. 'I thought you were splitting it? Half each.'

'The deal has changed,' the banker informed him. On the other side of the room Clovis adjusted his jacket to reveal a hefty pistol in a shoulder holster. 'This charming young lady can give you only fifty thousand, whereas I am prepared to offer the full asking price of one hundred thousand imperials. What do you say?'

Mender looked from him to Orry and then at the case open in front of him. He licked his lips and chuckled. 'Looks like you've been given the shaft, girly.' He stood and extended one hand, holding the deeds in the other. 'The farm is yours, and I can get the fuck off of this shithole.' They shook and Lefevre took the databrane.

'You backstabbing bastard!' Orry spat with relish, then rounded on her brother. 'This is all your fault, you – you – *idiot* – I *told* you we couldn't trust him—'

Ethan was doing a great job of looking completely stunned.

'Hey!' Mender said, slamming the case shut, 'take it outside. I have packing to do.'

'Be gone by tomorrow,' the banker told him, pocketing the deeds. 'Clovis, I think we can leave them to it.'

'Lefevre!' Orry yelled, thoroughly enjoying herself, 'you bastard, you won't get away with this!' She stormed outside after him, only to pull up short at the percussive thump of distant engines rolling across the crater floor.

Lefevre, standing next to his vehicle, stared up at the amber sky.

Using her integuary, she zoomed in on a dark speck that was growing rapidly larger.

Orry, said *Jane* in her head, *I'm tracking a medium-sized contact heading in your direction. No transponder.*

'Friends of yours?' Lefevre snarled at her. 'I *knew* you were planning to rip me off.' He climbed in next to Clovis, the engine hummed to life and Orry was forced to jump back as the buggy lurched into a tight turn before heading for the crater wall.

'I don't like the look of this,' Mender said, coming up behind her.

'Arbiters?' Ethan asked, but the old man shook his head.

'Not without a transponder.'

Orry stared at the approaching craft. *How fast can you get here, Jane?*

Six minutes.

Get moving, Mender told her, studying the incoming craft, a hulking atmospheric transport that looked like a black slab with four engine nacelles. The craft suddenly stopped and dropped down in front of Lefevre's buggy, blasting away small rocks and chunks of permafrost with its downwash. The buggy made a panicked U-turn and fled back towards the hab, pursued by the transport. It might have looked ungainly, but it hunted its prey like a raptor, swooping low, making the vehicle swerve wildly into a growing tunnel, which promptly collapsed on top of it.

The black craft steadied, lowered its landing gear and settled noisily in front of the hab modules; almost before it was down, six armed men had emerged and were running to the collapsed tunnel. Clovis was struggling as he and Lefevre were hauled from their buggy, until one of the men relieved him of his pistol.

The newcomers approached them, pushing their captives ahead of them.

Now would be good, Mender told *Jane*.

Four minutes, the ship replied. *Almost—* Her transmission cut out.

29

Jane? Orry sent, then, '*Mender?*' But he was shaking his head. Their integuaries were dead.

The men were a motley mix of mercenary, bandit and city mobster, and the weapons they were brandishing with deceptive casualness were similarly eclectic but uniformly lethal. The largest of the men, a chimera genetically sculpted to resemble a lion, wore a leather jacket over a thermal bodysuit and held a pimped-out assault rifle as if it were a toy. The pupils in his startling yellow eyes were vertical slits; metallic whiskers sprouted from downy skin and his shaggy mane of brown hair was streaked with blond highlights.

He stepped forward and smiled. 'If you're trying to call for back-up, you needn't bother,' he said. His cultured accent was distinctly at odds with his appearance. 'We're jamming you.'

'Who are you?' Orry demanded. 'What do you want?'

He moved closer, nostrils flaring as he drank in her scent. 'My name is Feliks.' Resting his rifle casually over one shoulder, he stepped up to Mender and held out a hand.

Scowling, Mender handed him Lefevre's case.

Behind the chimera, the banker began a slow hand-clap. Feliks turned with leonine grace and stared at him. 'Oh, well *done*,' Lefevre said. 'All very elaborate.'

'Shut up,' Orry told him, a terrible sinking feeling in her chest.

'So it was all a con? You really had me going there for a minute. And what happens now? These "gangsters" take my money and I'm so scared I don't go to the arbiters?'

'Seriously,' she said, 'you really need to be quiet now.'

'Oh, *please*! Am I supposed to believe these guys are for real?' He stepped up to Feliks, who was a good head taller than him.

'Look at this poor fruit: he looks like a reject from some low-rent production of *Roaring Lions*—'

'For the love of Rama,' Mender growled, 'will you shut the hell up?'

'Admit it was a scam!' the banker demanded angrily. When no one spoke, he grabbed the case's handle and tried to pull it from the chimera's grip.

Feliks looked down at him and sighed. He gestured to one of his men.

'No!' Orry yelled, starting forward, but the shot was already ringing out and Clovis crumpled to the icy ground, the back of his head a bloody ruin.

Lefevre stumbled back, staring at the body in disbelief, then doubled over and vomited noisily.

'Let's go,' Feliks said.

6

SALAZAR

Orry looked up as the cell door opened and Feliks announced, 'It's time.'

She, Mender and Ethan rose to their feet, but Lefevre remained huddled in the corner of the featureless cell, his head drooping, his eyes dull. He'd said barely a word since they'd been brought here from the transport.

'Time for what?' she asked. Their integuaries were still blocked.

The chimera just smiled. 'Come on. Bring him.' He pointed, and one of his men dragged the unresisting banker to his feet.

The metal-lined tunnels were furred with crystalline growth; that, together with the close air, made Orry think they were underground, probably in one of the subterranean cave systems that riddled Gyre. They were led into a warehouse of some sort, stacked with crates and shipping containers, and herded up a flight of corroded metal steps to an office above their heads.

Feliks opened the door at the top and announced, 'I've got them, boss.' He stepped to one side and motioned for them to enter.

Inside, a middle-aged man wearing clothes far too youthful for him was seated behind a cheap desk. A woman with short, tightly curled blonde hair stood at his shoulder, her formal, high-collared frock coat cut in the latest Fountainhead style. Behind them was another man, lurking by the wall, suited but jacketless, his shoulder holster plain to see. The man at the desk leaned back in his chair and waited for the four of them to line up in front of him.

'Do you know who I am?' he asked.

'Should we?' Orry responded, cold-reading him. She didn't care for what she saw. His clothes might have looked ridiculous but it was all designer gear and very expensive. She suspected this man, whoever he was, had risen from Charter City's street gangs; the mere fact he'd survived to middle age, let alone to the boss's seat, was a good indication of both his ruthlessness and his intelligence.

'Tell them, Irina,' he said.

The blonde woman surveyed them with a look of distaste. When she spoke it was with a cold, high-born accent. 'This is Viktor Salazar. Nobody engages in criminal activity around Charter City without paying him tribute.'

Orry wasn't sure whether to be happy she'd worked that one out. She hoped Salazar was a reasonable man, but she had her doubts. 'How did you find out about us?' she asked.

'Nothing goes down in this city without my knowledge.'

'It was Uri, wasn't it?'

Salazar smiled. 'You can't blame him. If he hadn't told me, I would have asked Feliks to show him what his insides looked like.'

'We're new around here,' Orry said. 'If I'd known, of course

I would have cut you in. In fact, let me do it now – what's your normal percentage? You can take it out of the case.'

Salazar stared at her, then began to laugh. Beside him, Irina smiled thinly.

'Did you hear that, Irina? The girl has balls.'

'So it appears,' the blonde said.

'I'll be keeping *all* the money,' he told Orry. 'Is that all right with you?'

She clenched her teeth. 'Of course.'

'Now, the question is, what should I do with you?'

Lefevre dropped to his knees. 'Please,' he begged, 'I had *nothing* to do with this. Just let me go – I won't say a word, I swear. The money's mine – take it all! I can get you more—'

A look of disgust crossed Salazar's face. 'Get that out of my sight,' he told Feliks, who gestured at one of his crew.

'*Please!*' the banker moaned as he was dragged away.

'What are you going to do to him?' Orry asked. Lefevre was an odious, greedy man but she didn't want his death on her conscience.

'That depends on if he's telling the truth about laying his hands on more money,' Salazar answered. 'I'd be more concerned about what I'm going to do to *you*.' He took his time studying the three of them. 'You know, Irina, these three look familiar somehow.'

'Indeed.'

'You say you've just arrived on Gyre?'

Orry nodded, unsettled by his smile.

He snapped his fingers. 'Of course! You' – he pointed at Orry – 'are Aurelia Kent, so this must be your brother Ethan and the infamous Captain Mender.'

'Oh, shit,' Mender muttered.

Salazar beamed. 'I couldn't have put it better myself. What a lovely surprise this is. Cordelia Roag *will* be pleased when I tell her I've found you all.' He tilted his head in a quizzical look. 'You *did* know I work for Roag, didn't you?' His face fell. 'Oh dear, Irina, I don't think they knew.'

'I imagine they did not.'

'And I've just remembered: I've *already* told her about you! She was delighted – in fact, she was *so* delighted that she's on her way here as we speak. It must have slipped my mind.'

'You prick,' Mender growled.

Salazar's smile slipped and for a moment Orry was afraid he was going to leap over the desk and kill Mender where he stood.

After an obvious struggle with his inner thug, Salazar leaned back in his chair and waved a hand laden with gold rings. 'I'm bored now. Take them away, Feliks.'

As the lion-headed man stepped towards them, Salazar smiled at them. 'But don't worry,' he reassured them mockingly, 'I'll be seeing you again very soon.'

'You look like a right twat in that get-up,' Mender informed him as he was shoved towards the door.

Salazar's eye twitched. 'I'm very much going to enjoy watching Roag go to work on you.'

The door closed behind them and they were herded back down the stairs to the warehouse floor.

Orry tried not to see the hopeful looks Ethan was giving her, wishing with all her heart she had a plan, or any idea, however tiny, she could use to reassure him.

Unfortunately, she didn't.

7

VIRIDIAN CARPET

A couple of hours after being returned to their cell, the overhead lights changed from white to dim red. Orry only realised she'd fallen asleep when she was jerked awake by the squeal of the door being dragged open.

A guard entered, followed by Salazar's blonde lieutenant, Irina. 'Stand up,' she ordered.

They rose slowly, Orry searching for an opening, but the guard looked alert and was standing far enough back for his scattergun to easily take out all three of them.

Irina produced a slender, long-barrelled pistol. 'Salazar wants them cuffed,' she told the guard.

He propped his gun against the wall and produced a bundle of plastic restraints. 'You first, old man,' he said to Mender, stepping forward.

As he lowered his head to wrap a tie around Mender's outstretched wrists, Irina pressed her pistol into the guard's back and pulled the trigger. The gun made hardly any sound, just a soft percussive *thump* that Orry felt rather than heard.

The man collapsed just as silently.

'Where's your ship?' Irina asked.

Orry, still processing what just happened, asked, 'What is this?'

'I can get you out of here, but I don't have a ship. Where's yours?'

For a fleeting moment Orry considered the possibility that this was an elaborate ruse to get hold of *Dainty Jane*, but the neat hole between the guard's shoulder blades and the twitchy irritation in Irina's face were all too real.

'He's dead,' Irina confirmed, 'and we'll all be joining him if you don't get a grip.'

'We can't contact our ship with our integuaries jammed,' Orry pointed out, but she'd already made her decision.

'We need to get out of these caves then. I can do that, but I have one condition: when we get to your ship, you take me where I want to go.'

Mender grimaced at that, but they didn't have much of a choice. 'Agreed,' he muttered.

'Good,' Irina said. 'Follow me – and for Rama's sake, keep quiet.'

'What about Lefevre?' Orry asked. 'He really wasn't in on it—'

'What about him? He doesn't have a ship – you do. Now *come on*.'

Orry didn't move. 'No, it's our fault he's here. We can't leave him.' She glanced at the others. 'Right?'

'Absolutely,' Ethan agreed, but Mender was already at the door.

'I'm good with it,' he said. 'Let's get the hell out of here—'

Orry's glare silenced him, and after a moment he relented. 'Fine, whatever.'

'It's out of the question,' Irina said.

'Then you don't have a ship,' Orry told her. She sat on her cot and indicated the dead guard. 'Good luck explaining that.'

'You're bluffing.'

'Try me.'

Irina set her jaw, then uttered a few well-chosen expletives that clearly impressed Mender. 'All right,' she said. 'I just hope that useless bastard's worth all our lives.'

She led them along the passage until signalling a halt just short of a corner. 'Wait here,' she whispered, then put her gun behind her back and stepped out.

'Come to keep us company, Irina?' a deep voice said, followed by a high-pitched giggle. 'You can sit here if you like . . . on my face.' Wet mouth-sounds followed.

'Sit on *this*.' Irina's pistol spat twice, then she reappeared and beckoned Orry forward, rounding the corner into an open area. The two dead men, one of them broad with a bald head, the other a boy not much older than Ethan, were sprawled across the floor.

Irina was going through the bald man's pockets until she found a keycard. 'This is what we need. Come on, he's in here.'

Orry tried not to look at the caved-in ruin of the guard's face as she followed Irina to the door.

'No more, *please*,' Lefevre wailed from within as the door opened. 'You can have everything, I told you!'

'Keep your bloody voice down,' Irina snarled, pointing her pistol at him. Orry stepped past her to see the man, bruised and bleeding, was cowering against the back wall.

'Come with us,' she said soothingly. 'We're getting out of here. It's going to be fine.' *I hope.*

'Wh-what?' The hope on his face was pathetic.

She held out a hand. 'Come on, Simon. But you have to keep quiet, understand?'

He rose unsteadily to his feet. 'This is all your fault,' he said accusingly.

'We can discuss that later,' she said.

He walked cautiously into the passage, moving like a hunted animal.

They followed Irina as she set off back the way they'd come through the warren of corridors dimly illuminated by red light. The metal cladding soon gave way to natural rock, until eventually they reached a substantial hatch set into the ground. Irina unlocked its genetic lock with a touch of her finger, and the hatch hissed open on pneumatic struts to reveal a ladder leading down. Orry followed her through the hatch, but she had descended only a few rungs when she stopped in amazement.

The ladder dropped some forty metres down through the centre of a colossal cavern, a natural cathedral bathed in a muted green glow emitted by a carpet of gently waving tendrils covering the ground like luminous grass. Columns of slick minerals surrounded her, and stalactites and stalagmites big and small grew from the ceiling or pushed up through the tendrils.

She resumed her descent, stunned by the cavern's beauty and wondering how many of Gyre's other natural wonders had been destroyed by the strip mines. When she finally reached the ground she knelt, pulled off a glove and brushed a hand across the softly waving tendrils, which wafted towards her skin as if sensing her. Rising to her feet, she tried to contact *Dainty Jane* on the private channel.

Irina noticed her glazed expression and said, 'We need to get clear of the caves before your integuary will work. It's the scorite in the rock, it kills the signal. It's not normally a problem here – very few people on Gyre have brainware.'

'Who *are* you?' Ethan asked, joining them, but Irina was already moving again.

'Later – we need to keep going. There are worse things than Viktor down here.'

'Like what?' Mender asked, stepping off the ladder.

'Some of the local wildlife has developed an unfortunate taste for human flesh.'

'Of course they have,' he said heavily, as if this were only to be expected.

'How much further?' Lefevre whined, bringing up the rear, but Irina ignored him and set off across the viridian carpet at a brisk pace.

A chattering howl was the first indication they were not alone. Orry was not happy to see Irina pale and increase her pace.

'What the hell was that?' Mender huffed, struggling to keep up.

'Pack-apes,' she told him unhelpfully, but Lefevre clearly understood, because he broke into a wheezing sprint.

'Oh, Rama,' he moaned, and put on a burst of speed for a couple of seconds before coming to a panting halt.

Irina dragged him back. '*Idiot*. We stay together. They're less likely to attack a group.'

'What are pack-apes?' Ethan asked, his head on a swivel as he ran.

Orry caught sight of shadows in the near distance, moving low and fast.

'They're scavengers,' Irina explained. 'When the miners drove them out of their natural habitat, they moved into these cave systems. The caves connect with the city, so they're good for access and shelter.'

The ape-things were quickly getting closer, scampering at breakneck speed in Gyre's low gravity, although they were still behaving cautiously – for now, at least. They were pure white, the size of the large hunting dogs beloved of Ruuz aristos, with powerful rear legs and prehensile fore-limbs. Their necks and shoulders were heavily muscled, but it was the curved fangs in their narrow, snapping jaws that made Orry shudder.

'Keep up!' she told Lefevre, who'd gone back to his normal shambling pace and had two of the pack-apes snapping at his heels. She dropped back to jog beside him, then turned and ran at the two creatures, waving her arms and shouting. The apes scattered briefly, but they quickly reformed, just a little further back. Passing a stalagmite growing from the cave floor, as thick as her arm at the base and tapering to a sharp point, she snapped it off and swung the metre-long piece of calcified stone, feeling its heft. It wasn't a great weapon, but it was a damn sight better than nothing.

Orry grabbed Lefevre's arm and dragged him onwards – just as a big white shape came barrelling in from her left.

She jabbed at it and missed, but at least she'd scared the ape enough to make it scamper away, snarling and chittering—

—and another immediately took its place. This time her makeshift spear glanced off its side, making it yelp. She readied herself for another pass when up ahead, Ethan cried out – then the cavern lit up, the soft thud of Irina's pistol sounded flatly in the huge space and in the flash Orry saw a huge ape beside her brother tumble and fall, white fur soaked red.

Without warning, Lefevre swerved and collided with her, almost knocking her down, but she clung to his arm and kept pounding along, even as a snarling pack-ape leaped past him, straight at her, jaws gnashing. Reacting instinctively, she thrust the stalagmite through its neck. Warm blood spattered her face but she didn't stop moving and Lefevre, still whimpering, somehow managed to keep up.

More shots came from up ahead, punctuated by yelping and snarling and cries of alarm. She could see Mender and Ethan both had their own stalagmite clubs now and were swinging them wildly, fending off any apes that got too close.

Suddenly the cavern roof vanished, replaced by a thin scattering of stars shining feebly through Gyre's enveloping dust-blanket. The ground steepened immediately and Orry realised they were climbing one of the innumerable spoil heaps that littered the moon, cones of rock fragments rejected by the mobile processing plants that roamed the strip mines on giant crawler tracks. As she struggled up the side, shoving Lefevre ahead of her, she could see the pack-apes were spreading out to encircle the base of the mound. Despair tugged at her. They were like a tide of white, washing around their island in a swell of snapping jaws and glinting, evil eyes.

Irina finally stopped when she reached the flat top of the mound, hardly out of breath. Below them, the beasts were massing around the spoil heap.

'Oh, well done,' Lefevre gasped. 'Now we're fucking trapped—'

'That's it,' Mender spat, 'I have *had* it with you—' He lunged at the banker, but Ethan took his arm and held him back.

'Everybody calm down,' Irina snapped.

Orry stared down at the apes. Most were still prowling around the base of the mound, but a few had started slowly climbing towards them.

Irina slipped the magazine from her pistol and examined it. 'Two rounds left,' she said grimly. She looked at Lefevre. 'Stay in the middle.'

Without being told, Orry, Ethan and Mender took up position at the edge of the slope, spacing themselves around the perimeter. The gaps between them felt alarmingly wide. At least twenty of the apes were approaching cautiously, and there were plenty more down below.

Orry held her stalagmite like a short spear. Sweat was running down her back despite the freezing night air. On the horizon an eerie bow of blue light heralded the rise of Hecate, the gas giant around which Gyre orbited. She didn't have much time to appreciate the planetrise, because two of the creatures rushed at her. She thrust wildly at one, grazing its flank, but the other cannoned into her and she fell back, too winded even to scream, and stabbed blindly upwards.

In some disbelief she felt her weapon sink into yielding flesh. A howl split the night and she pulled her spear back just in time to block a pair of ferociously snapping jaws. Thanking Rama for those endless self-defence classes her father had insisted on, she kicked out, sending the ape flying, and scrambled back onto her feet to see its companion circling warily. This time when it charged, she swung the stalagmite like a club and connected firmly with its jaw. It flopped to the ground and, steeling herself, she plunged the point into its throat before staggering back, panting.

No time for a pat on the back, she told herself, even as someone behind her screamed. She whirled round to see an ape's jaws locked around Ethan's calf and another about to pounce. Her heart froze as she realised she and Mender were too far away to help—

—then a muffled shot sounded and the ape with its teeth in Ethan's leg fell dead.

Still shouting, her brother stabbed the other creature and stumbled back towards Irina, blood sheeting his leg. Mender was retreating too, swinging his stalagmite wildly to keep at bay the snarling creatures stalking him.

There were more apes climbing the slope too, and Orry, worrying that they would get separated and picked off one by one, fell back until she was standing with the others at the centre of the mound's flat top.

'Huh. Never thought I'd end up being eaten by a damned snow monkey,' Mender commented, and Orry managed a wry smile. She tried her integuary for the hundredth time, but it was still dead, so she went charging forward, just a few steps, screaming, and the apes did back off – but not far, and not for long.

Reaching for Ethan, she clasped his hand.

He squeezed back, so tight it hurt. 'I hate this bloody moon,' he said.

As if at some unseen signal, the pack-apes charged.

8

IRINA

Laserlight flickered suddenly in the night, green beams piercing the charging apes, scorching fur and meat, melting bone, and Salazar's lumpen transport roared overhead, its downwash throwing up pebbles and ice-crystals. The remaining apes fled, racing howling down the slope. The transport slowed and banked steeply, returning to hover ten metres off the mound's edge, level with its flat top. The rear ramp dropped to reveal Salazar, with Feliks standing beside him. Behind them they could see the hold was crammed with gun-hands.

'I've seen some useless escape attempts in my time,' Salazar said, his voice booming from the transport's external speakers, 'but this is just embarrassing. Irina, if I wasn't about to kill you *very* slowly, this lack of planning and poor judgement would reflect badly in your next appraisal.'

Irina gave him the finger and he grinned nastily.

Orry snatched her gun from her and pointed it at him, enjoying the flicker of uncertainty that crossed Salazar's face before he rallied.

'You really think you can hit me with that little thing from all the way over there? Lay it down or I'll have Feliks put one in your knee. I'm sure Roag will forgive me a few extra bullets in you, just as long as you're not actually dead.'

'What are you doing?' Irina whispered. She'd just noticed where Orry was aiming: not at Salazar but at an outcrop of distinctive glittering rock at the base of the spoil heap.

Orry said nothing as she fired.

At first nothing happened, then she detected a red glow deep within the outcrop. The glow spread quickly – and the scorite suddenly ignited, sending a blinding flare shooting twenty metres into the sky. The transport tilted violently away, but the burn, however bright, was brief, and a few seconds later the flare dimmed then died, leaving nothing but a blackened mess of bubbling stone in a puddle of meltwater.

The transport stabilised after its frantic movement and Salazar's voice boomed from the external speakers. 'Pathetic. That was nowhere near us.'

'I wasn't aiming at you,' Orry said, desperately searching the sky, but it was Ethan who spotted her first. He let out a great whoop as a familiar shape came screaming over the ridge. Dainty Jane's dorsal turret lit up briefly and one of the transport's nacelles exploded. One side of the ungainly vessel dropped, and they could hear the howling from the other three engines as they failed to compensate. After a moment, the injured transport slewed away, skimming the rocky ground until it disappeared into a deep crater.

After chasing off the enemy, the starship returned to the mound and settled at its base. Orry and Mender helped Ethan down the slope and she realised her integuary was finally working again.

Nice of you to drop by, Mender told the ship drily.

Are you all right? asked *Jane. I've been worried sick.*

Ethan needs the medbay, Orry told her, *and we need to get off this rock. Cordelia Roag's on her way here.*

Oh dear. Very well . . .

The cargo ramp closed and she felt the ship lift.

'Where are we going?' Lefevre asked.

She'd almost forgotten about the banker. 'It's up to you,' she told him, pausing at the door leading to the crew spaces and medbay. 'We can drop you in the city, or offworld somewhere.'

'Offworld?' His voice rose. 'I don't want to go offworld! I have a job here, a life—'

'Your life won't be worth much if Salazar catches up with you,' Irina pointed out.

He paled at the thought. 'But what about my money?'

'Your money's gone, you dumb fuck,' Mender informed him. 'Or haven't you been paying attention?'

Lefevre slumped into one of the seats lining the bay and put his head in his hands. 'This is all your fault,' he sobbed. 'Why did you have to pick on *me*?'

'Says the man who tried to double-cross us,' Orry retorted angrily, 'or had you forgotten that? My father always said you can't con an honest man. It's rule number one.'

'And that's supposed to make me feel better, is it? You've ruined my life.'

'Actually, I think you'll find *you* tried to ruin hers,' Mender reminded him. 'Deal with it.'

'*Ow*,' Ethan said pointedly, hopping awkwardly on one leg. Blood was pooling on the deck at his feet.

'We'll drop you wherever,' Orry told the banker again, 'within reason, but right now, Ethan needs to get to the medbay.'

'You're not very nice people,' Lefevre yelled after her. 'Not nice at all!'

'My name isn't really Irina.'

'No shit,' Mender said. 'What is it, then?'

'Irina will do – I'm just telling you because I want to be honest.' She looked around the cramped galley below *Dainty Jane*'s cockpit, then back at Orry and Mender. The ship had already left Gyre's atmosphere and was heading for the nearest egress point outside the moon's gravity well at a comfortable 1g. Ethan was still in the medbay and Lefevre back in the city, presumably packing for a major life change.

'I need you to take me to Morhelion.'

'What's that?' Orry asked. 'A planet?'

'Yes.'

'Why do you want us to take you there? Who are you?'

Irina loosened her high collar and allowed herself to slump a little; that small change in her posture made her look suddenly weary. Orry wondered where the woman had learned to be so guarded.

'I know who you are,' Irina said, 'and I know what you did for the Ascendancy last year, which is the only reason I am trusting you with this. We owe you a great debt.'

'"We"?' Orry asked.

'I work for the Administrate. My job is to gather information and report back.'

'She's Seventh bloody Secretariat,' Mender said, throwing up his hands in disgust. 'Well, that's just fucking great.'

'*Seven?*' Orry said. 'Bullshit. If you're a spook, what are you doing on a shithole moon way out in the rim, working for some jumped-up street hood?'

'I'm not going to tell you that,' Irina – or whatever her name was – said calmly, 'but I will say that I am on the trail of information of vital importance to the war effort.'

'Fan-bloody-tastic,' Mender commented with a scowl.

'And that trail leads to Morhelion?' Orry asked, ignoring him.

'Precisely.'

'Morhelion is a long way from here,' the old man said. 'What's in it for us?'

'I just saved your lives,' Irina pointed out.

He barked out a laugh. 'Don't give me that crap, girly. You'd have let us rot if you didn't need our ship. I've met your kind before.'

Our *ship*? *Dainty Jane* sent archly on the private channel.

Orry noted that she hadn't revealed her sentience to Irina.

'Is he always like this?' Irina asked.

'No,' Orry answered, 'sometimes he's downright rude.'

She quirked her lips. 'I'd like to see that.'

'Trust me, you wouldn't.'

Ignoring Mender's snort, she said, 'I can offer you ten thousand imperials for the charter. On arrival, of course.'

'Fifty,' Mender said immediately.

'Twenty. Whatever my motivation, I did save your lives.'

'Thirty, and that reflects any life-saving that may or may not have occurred.'

'Very well, thirty. Agreed.'

Mender spat in his palm and Orry grimaced when he offered it, but to her surprise Irina spat in her own hand and shook without hesitation.

The old man stood. 'I'll plot the collapse.'

'I like him,' Irina said, watching him climb the ladder to the cockpit. 'He's blunt. It's refreshing.'

'*You* don't have to live with him.'

She smiled. 'That was clever, what you did back there with the scorite flare. I can see why the Imperator thinks so highly of you.'

'He does?' Orry had only met the Imperator Ascendant twice, and the first time he'd thrown her in gaol. The second meeting had gone a little better.

'That's what I hear.' Irina's long fingers idly rotated a silver signet ring she wore on one hand. 'Can I ask you a question, Aurelia?'

'It's Orry, but go ahead.'

'You're a capable woman. Humankind is at war. Why are you hiding out here committing petty crimes?'

'Everyone has to eat,' Orry said tightly, wondering why she felt so defensive. She'd always hated everything the Ascendancy stood for and the Kadiran could burn the whole imperialist structure to the ground, for all she cared.

'You do realise it's not just the Fountainhead systems that will suffer if the Kadiran win this war,' Irina went on. 'Several of the rim worlds have already fallen.'

'That's because the Grand Fleet won't protect them,' Orry said angrily. 'There aren't enough Ruuz on those colonies to make them worth defending.'

'You're right,' Irina admitted, 'but only to an extent. The Grand Fleet is large, but we've suffered some disastrous losses and we're being pushed back on every front. There simply aren't enough ships to defend every world. So it's true that difficult decisions have had to be taken.'

'*What* losses?' Orry asked, taken aback. 'There's been nothing on the newsfeeds.'

Irina looked disappointed. 'We're *at war*, Orry. Do you really believe everything you hear on the feeds?'

Her cheeks flushed. In truth, she hadn't been paying much attention. The terror and excitement of the foiled attack on Tyr had been followed by the jingoistic fervour surrounding the deployment of the Grand Fleet, and since then she'd assumed things had settled into a tense stand-off. Apart from the loss of a couple of outer colonies and a few skirmishes, nothing much had been reported. Now she felt like an idiot for believing the propaganda she and the rest of human space were apparently being spoon-fed. The Administrate probably had a department specially for this kind of thing. Her father would be spinning in his grave.

After a moment, she asked, 'So what's really going on?'

'It's bad,' Irina admitted, 'and if what I've discovered is true, it's going to get a lot worse. You really should think about returning to Tyr. We could use someone like you.'

'That's not going to happen, so save your breath.'

'But you're happy to let others fight and die to protect you.' Irina's tone was sharp.

'Screw you,' Orry snapped, rising to her feet. 'I didn't ask for their protection.'

Irina regarded her with distaste. 'In that case, just take me to Morhelion. I'll make sure you get your money.'

'You'd better,' she said angrily. 'You don't want to know what Mender did to the last person who tried to stiff him.'

'I can see why you two get on so well,' Irina told her. 'You're very similar: all you care about is yourself.'

Orry walked away.

Dainty Jane's cockpit had four mesomorphic acceleration shells in a free-floating transparent sphere. Mender, sitting in the commander's shell, glanced up when Orry came in and threw herself into the seat to his right.

'I don't like spooks,' he complained before returning to flicking switches on the old-school instrument panel curving around the front of his shell.

'I've never met one before,' she told him, still angry, 'but I have to agree. Let's just get our money and get rid of her.' She used her integuary to hook *Dainty Jane*'s navigation core and saw that Mender had already programmed the collapse to Morhelion. Her stomach turned over at the thought of using the postselection drive, which always played havoc with her insides.

'Pre-collapse checks,' Mender said, handing her the ancient checklist. Although she'd never admit it, she was beginning to enjoy the antiquated procedures he insisted on.

'Disengage mass-inversion drives,' she read from the old screen, frosted with decades of tiny scratches.

The rumble of *Dainty Jane*'s drives died and she felt the gel lining of her acceleration shell grip her as she became weightless.

'Drives off,' Mender confirmed.

'Retract radiators.'

'Vanes retracted.'

'We'll skip the stabilisers,' she murmured. 'We still need to get them fixed.'

Mender grunted, as he always did at this point in the checklist, and she ran through the rest of the items with a smile. 'Acceleration shell clear and functional,' she finished, checking her own shell.

'Clear and functional,' Mender replied, then switched to his integuary. *Prepare for collapse into Morhelion,* he told Ethan and Irina on the shipboard channel. He turned to Orry. 'Ready?'

She held up her sick bag. 'Let's get it over with.'

He grinned, and her mind fractured as their wavefunction collapsed.

A week's vacation at the fancy spa out near Highridge had left Jackson Fitch relaxed and in good humour. He hadn't even realised the Farmers' Collective ran a monthly draw until the transmission had arrived informing him he'd won, but with Oliver's birthday coming up and their limited gilt needed for new seed stock, the timing couldn't have been better.

His good mood evaporated the moment his old truck bounced over the crater wall.

'What in hell's happened here?' he said, seeing the collapsed end of one of the growing tunnels. As they rumbled down the crater wall he spotted a crashed buggy under the tangle of plastic. Another vehicle was parked in front of the hab. Jackson engaged the autodrive and reached into the back of the cab for his shotgun, while Oliver opened the tool chest and after rummaging around, produced a wrench as long as his forearm.

He parked the truck behind the buggy and they both climbed out. The unknown vehicle was empty, so Jackson gingerly approached the front door and peered in. There were signs of someone having been in the kitchen, and a burn mark on the floor, but he couldn't see anyone now. Oliver followed him inside and they searched the place; it didn't take long to confirm it was empty.

'I can't see anything missing,' Jackson said, scratching the back of his head as he stood by the kitchen table. 'Reckon we should call the arbiters?'

Oliver was checking the kitchen cabinets, doubtless making sure his precious spices were still there. 'Way I see it, we've lost one tunnel and gained two vehicles,' he said. 'That puts us up on the deal. Joel can sell them on for us, no questions.'

'What if the owners come back?'

Oliver didn't reply but turned from the cabinet with a bulky, plastic-wrapped package in his hand. 'It's addressed to "The Owners",' he said nervously.

'Okay . . . so best open it,' Jackson told him.

Oliver tore the package open and whistled. He pulled out a wad of plastic notes and fanned them in his hands. 'There must be a couple of grand here.' He looked at Jackson, frowning. 'What the hell is going on?'

9

COMPANY GALLEON

Morhelion's swirling atmosphere filled the upper half of *Dainty Jane*'s canopy as the local sun crept beneath the planet's curve. Thick gases softened the star's harsh light into a vibrant spectrum and sent it rippling out through the layers of clouds. Orry had seen countless sunsets from high orbit, but this one took her breath away. She gazed, rapt, until the sun disappeared and a cloak of darkness spread over the planet below. As her eyes adjusted, she could make out twinkling points of light across Morhelion's night side, thousands of individual specks of varying brightness, separated by vast gulfs of utter blackness.

Those must be the habisphere communities, she thought, imagining the town-sized bubbles floating high above the rocky surface, which was a hellscape of crushing gravity and searing temperatures, according to *Jane*.

'Have you ever been here before?' she asked Mender.

'Nope,' he answered, his eyes locked on the head-up display showing their deorbit vector as his hands moved over the instrument panel, flicking a switch here, adjusting a dial there.

'And here I was thinking you'd been everywhere.'

He grunted. 'The galaxy's a big place.' He turned in his acceleration couch to address Irina, standing behind them. 'Where do you want to go exactly, now we're here?'

'There's only one port,' she told him, 'and it's in Hardhaven bubble.'

He activated the com. 'Morhelion Traffic, *Dainty Jane*.'

'Morhelion Traffic. Go ahead, *Dainty Jane*.'

'*Dainty Jane* is a merchant vessel inbound from Gyre with four persons on board. Request vectors to Hardhaven port.'

While Mender dealt with the formalities, Orry idly scanned the few other ships in orbit. She nudged him. 'There's a Company ship here.'

'What?' Irina said, leaning forward. 'Which one?'

Orry called up the metadata. '*Venturer*. She's a galleon out of Alecto.'

'Hail her.'

'Why?' Mender said.

'*Hail her*.'

'I don't want anything to do with EDC. They're worse than the damned Grand Fleet.'

'It won't be a problem,' Irina said. 'This is perfect; I didn't expect to see a friendly ship this far out. I have to speak to the captain.'

Orry and Mender exchanged a look. 'Company galleon *Venturer*,' he sent, 'merchant *Dainty Jane*.'

There was a distinct delay before a woman's voice replied, 'Pass your message, *Dainty Jane*.'

'We have a passenger aboard who needs to speak to your captain.'

Another pause. 'What is this concerning, *Dainty Jane*?'

Mender turned and raised a bushy eyebrow at Irina, who leaned forward and said, 'That's classified, *Venturer*. I'm not prepared to discuss it on an open channel.'

'Then I'm afraid you can't—'

'Article nine, paragraph two of the Empyrean Development Company charter requires any Company vessel in time of conflict to gather intelligence wherever possible, provided so doing will not unduly compromise the safety of the ship. I am in possession of such intelligence, and I pose no threat. I demand to see your commanding officer.'

'Uh, wait one, *Dainty Jane*.'

'There's no way they'll go for that,' Mender said, but Irina ignored him, her jaw set.

'*Dainty Jane*, *Venturer*. We're sending a launch.'

'I'll be damned,' Mender said. 'Wait a minute, what about my money?'

'Once I've spoken to the captain you'll be paid in full. You have my word.'

He gave a short laugh. 'I've heard that one before. You'll be safe over there with your pals and we'll never see a penny.'

'I'll go with her,' Orry said, and when Mender started chewing on his beard, a sure sign he was concerned, said reassuringly, 'It'll be fine. I'll get the money and come right back.'

'It's never that simple with the Company,' he told her. 'Be careful over there.'

The launch was a far cry from what Orry had expected: thick pile carpet, state-of-the-art acceleration couches and huge media screens. The luxury was ameliorated somewhat by the presence of three armed members of the Mercantile Defence Division,

EDC's private army. A taciturn sergeant named Lowson introduced himself and spent the rest of the twenty-minute transfer to *Venturer* in silence.

The vast galleon was in orbit above Morhelion, rigged for microgravity without her mass-inversion drives to provide thrust. The lieutenant awaiting them in the hangar used molecular hooks on the soles of his boots to hold him to the deck. Orry activated her own molly hooks, but Irina floated gracefully in freefall, effortlessly maintaining an upright position relative to the officer, a fresh-faced young man with neatly trimmed blond hair and the slightly bloated look of someone who'd spent too much time in orbit. His whiskers, very much a work in progress, had been teased with wax into precise points.

'I'm Lieutenant Krupin,' he said. 'Welcome aboard. I understand you have some intel for us?'

'For the captain,' Irina corrected him.

Krupin smiled disarmingly. 'Skipper's busy overseeing the loading. Why don't you tell me, miz? Then you can be on your way.'

'Major.'

The young officer's smile slipped a fraction. 'Excuse me?'

'My name is Major Yolkina and you will address me as such.'

Krupin cleared his throat. 'Aye, Major.'

'And stand to attention when you address a superior officer!' Irina snapped.

The lieutenant jerked up and instinctively tried to snap his boot heels together. Hampered by the clinging molly hooks, the result was less than impressive.

'Better,' Irina said. 'Now take me to the captain. At once.'

Krupin wavered, his eyes flickering to Sergeant Lowson.

'Is there a problem, Lieutenant?' Irina enquired.

'Uh, no, miz – I mean, Major. One moment . . .' Krupin's eyes glazed as he accessed his integuary. 'Captain Selidova will receive you in her quarters. It's this way.' He led them from the hangar with the sergeant bringing up the rear, darklight carbine held ready across his gleaming chest armour. Captain Selidova was clearly taking no chances.

Venturer was an enormous ship, evidently too massive for Morhelion's docking facilities; during the transfer Orry had watched streams of transports, each one dwarfing *Dainty Jane*, shuttling back and forth to fill the galleon's cavernous holds. The passageways they were floating down now reminded her of a cruise liner, a far cry from the cramped, functional interior of a military vessel. Crew uniformed in the distinctive purple and white of the EDC shuffled or drifted aside to let them pass.

They eventually arrived outside a door in the command spaces. Krupin knocked, and upon a shouted instruction to enter, he ushered them inside.

The captain's cabin was spacious and set with easy chairs and a substantial dining table, on which rested a formal tea set. Selidova was young for a First-Captain, but her cut-glass accent revealed the likely reason for her rapid advancement through the ranks. She rose from a desk surrounded by monitors and regarded her visitors coldly.

'Major Yolkina, I understand. Major of what, precisely?'

Irina brushed the question aside. 'Captain, what I have to say is for your ears only.'

Selidova fixed her with a stare. 'Sergeant Lowson, did you search these women before bringing them aboard?'

'Yes, ma'am. They're clean.'

'Very well, please wait outside my cabin. Krupin, you're dismissed.'

'Aye aye, ma'am.'

'Tea?' Selidova asked once he was gone. She crossed to the table and added a thick sludge of concentrate to a glass sphere, then pumped in flash-boiled water from a dispenser. 'What's this all about?'

'I need you to take a message back to Tyr,' Irina said.

'You want to use one of my dispatch pods?'

'No, I need *you* to deliver a message to the Trefoil in Usk, Captain. *Personally.*'

'Personally?' Selidova appeared to be having trouble deciding if Irina was serious. 'I have a ship to command,' she said at last, and Orry could hear her anger building. 'Why in Piotr's name would I abandon my vessel to travel back to Tyr?'

'You misunderstand me,' Irina said, 'I don't want you to abandon anything.' She spoke the next words slowly. 'I want *this ship* to fly back to Tyr so that *you* can deliver my message.'

Selidova stood there thoughtfully for a moment, then called, 'Lowson!'

The sergeant burst into the cabin. 'Captain?'

'Our visitors will be leaving now.'

'Aye, ma'am!' He indicated the open door. 'This way, ladies.'

Irina sighed and touched the silver ring on her right hand. Orry blinked as its plain face reformed into a coronet topped with seven stylised stars. Irina held it up to ensure Selidova could see it.

The captain paled.

'I think I will have that tea,' Irina said.

Selidova recovered herself. 'That will be all, Lowson.'

'Skipper—'

'Is there something wrong with your hearing, Sergeant? Get out!'

He frowned, then snapped to attention and left the cabin.

Orry was mystified.

'Shall I be mother?' Irina said, dispensing three bulbs of tea. She turned her hand a little to display the ring. 'So I take it you know what this represents.'

'It's the personal seal of the Imperator Ascendant,' the captain replied. 'Who *are* you?'

'Merely a humble servant of the Imperator.' Irina sipped her tea; the other bulbs floated untouched above the table. 'Will you deliver my message?'

'We need at least another week to finish loading, then we're due back at Alecto – I suppose we could divert to Tyr on the way but—'

'Today. Now. Abandon your transports and break orbit immediately. Make best speed and collapse as soon as you're able.'

'But—'

Irina held up her hand to display the ring again. 'This seal grants me the voice of the Imperator Ascendant. While I wear it, when you speak to me, you are speaking to him. Do you understand?'

'Yes.'

'And so I will tell you again – *he* will tell you again – abandon your transports and break orbit immediately. Now, what do you have to say to your Imperator?'

Selidova dropped her eyes. 'We'll begin preparations at once.'

'Excellent.' Irina winked at Orry. 'Oh, there's one more thing I need.'

The captain looked up. 'What?'

'Thirty thousand imperial sovereigns—'

Klaxons suddenly began blaring and Selidova jerked, her face blanking as she accessed her integuary.

'What's happening?' Irina asked, but the captain was already halfway to the door.

'Raiders,' Selidova answered briefly, opening the door to reveal Sergeant Lowson in the process of knocking. He looked tense. 'I'm afraid your request will have to wait, Major Yolkina. I'm needed on the bridge.'

Orry and Irina exchanged a glance, then followed the captain.

What's going on out there? Orry asked on *Dainty Jane*'s common channel.

All hell's breaking loose, Mender replied. *Get out – fast!*

Working on it, Orry said, really hoping they were. She had an uneasy feeling in her gut about this.

Red lights were flashing as well now, a counterpoint to the howling alarm, but the men and women sailing down *Venturer*'s passageways were showing no signs of panic, despite the racket. Orry knew Company vessels were well-armed and the entire crew would be trained to deal with opportunistic raiders, but the way the ship was shuddering was deeply worrying and Selidova's expression was less than reassuring.

The captain stopped a squad of troopers heading down through the vessel and snapped at the under-lieutenant leading them, 'Goddard? Sitrep.'

The officer saluted. 'Boarders in Bay Epsilon, Captain – they came in on one of our transports and they're spreading through the ship. We believe they're heading for the bridge and the drive spaces.' *Venturer* shuddered again and gas vented from trunking in the overhead. 'They're hitting us topside too,' he continued, raising his voice to be heard over the alarm and the hissing from the pipe. 'At least seven ships.'

The captain nodded curtly. 'Carry on, Lieut—'

A beam flashed past Orry and bisected Selidova from hip to shoulder. As her body separated into two halves, blood wept through blackened flesh to form elastic bubbles which stretched and warped in the recirculated air. The smell of charred meat coated Orry's nose.

More flickering beams were answered by a chatter and crack as Lieutenant Goddard's squad retaliated. Orry dragged her eyes from Selidova's remains to see raiders spilling into the lower part of the junction, spreading out to engage the defenders with a variety of weapons.

Irina grabbed her arm. 'Move – this way!'

Orry pushed off from a bulkhead, droplets of Selidova's blood bursting on her face as she shot after Irina. She felt the wind of a low-velocity round as it whipped past her ear to flatten itself against a brace with a metallic *spang*. A green beam of coherent energy swept towards her belly, then flicked off as the raider firing it was sent tumbling by a slug to the chest.

Irina had reached an exit and was clinging onto a wall-ring with one hand while gesturing with the other at a stylised escape pod glyph displayed above the opening. Most of Goddard's squad was down, she saw, and even more raiders were flooding into the chamber.

As Orry sailed towards her, the air around Irina's outstretched arm shimmered and her hand and forearm unravelled, skin giving way to slick muscle, then bone, and in less than a second the end of her arm was a cloud of red particles. Irina gasped, releasing the handle to clutch at the fresh stump, which had been neatly severed below the elbow.

Orry grabbed her and tugged and they tumbled into the passageway, Irina groaning as her injured arm left a trail of bloody globules behind them. Orry could see the escape pods up ahead, lining one wall. *So close . . .* She used her mass to stabilise their trajectory, then shoved off from a bulkhead to boost their speed.

Mender!

She reached the nearest pod and slammed her palm on the access pad to open it.

Kinda busy right now. Talk to your brother.

'Great.' She heaved Irina into the pod and floated in after her. A beam flashed down the passageway outside, but she was already hauling the hatch closed.

Ethan, we're bugging out, she sent, strapping Irina into one of the six seats. *Can you pick us up?*

Sure, he answered. *Where—*

No can do, Mender interrupted, then grunted. *Shit – that was close.*

Orry dropped into the seat next to Irina, her stomach sinking. *Trouble?*

You could say that. Mender cursed. *Three of these bastards have taken a dislike to us and it's getting hairy.*

Forget it then, she told him, fumbling to fasten her harness. *I'm in a pod – I'll be fine. Get yourselves clear and find me when it's safe.*

No way, Sis! Ethan objected. *It's a pitched battle out here – we're not leaving you.*

You have to—

She's right, Mender put in. *Good luck, girl.*

Orry tuned out her brother's protests as she disengaged the pod's safety and saw the launch button illuminate. *Venturer* lurched again and she flicked up the switch's cover and mashed her thumb onto it.

The seat punched her in the back as the pod hurtled from the ship. Through the viewports set in its conical nose she caught glimpses of laserlight playing off *Venturer*'s hull. A ship swooped past, little more than a quad cannon and thrusters mounted on an open frame. The larger ships were keeping their distance, visible only by the ordnance they were spewing.

A loud *clang* sent the pod spinning violently, making the view from the ports whirl. Orry fought the g-force to make sense of the screen above her seat. One of the pod's two engines was flashing red on the display: out of action. She hurriedly shut down the other engine and took manual control of the verniers, using the small thrusters to try to halt the vomit-inducing spin.

The pod's interior turned an eerie blue as Morhelion's roiling clouds filled the viewports. They were clear of the battle now, she realised, but heading down into the planet's crushing atmosphere rather than to the refuge of deep space. She stabbed at the touchscreen, trying to change course, but the little thrusters were no match for the relentless grip of Morhelion's gravity well.

'Hell's teeth!' she muttered. When she looked at Irina, the woman was completely still, her eyes closed. Orry hoped she was just unconscious.

Ethan? Mender?

But her integuary had fallen silent and there was no response.

10

SHAKE THE BASTARDS OFF

'We can't just leave her!' Ethan was trying to shout, but his words were coming out as more of a gasp as the mesomorphic lining of his acceleration shell stiffened, compressing his lungs to keep him conscious during *Dainty Jane*'s brutal acceleration.

'We got no choice, kid,' Mender wheezed. As if to underline his words a sparkling beam of energy flashed over the cockpit's clear canopy and *Dainty Jane* vibrated with the muffled thud of her chaff dispensers firing.

Ethan closed his eyes as his shell slammed shut around him. The mesophase gel flashed to fluid, which instantly filled the confined space. Once he'd forced himself to relax and drawn the oxygenated liquid into his lungs, the g-forces diminished, leaving him floating freely as *Dainty Jane* accelerated past 5g.

Later, ballbags, Mender sent happily.

The ship shuddered violently and the rumble of her mass-inversion drives faltered and died.

My ion shunt has been hit, sent *Jane*.

Can you reroute? Mender asked.

Not in orbit, the ship told him. *You'll need to perform a physical bypass.*

Hell and death!

Ethan hooked the avionics core and watched their acceleration decrease rapidly. The dispensers thudded again, creating a light show behind them as the strips of foil chaff dispersed the pursuers' beams, but the chaff-counter was ticking down with alarming speed.

What are we going to do? he asked.

Mender didn't answer, but *Dainty Jane* nosed over into a swift dive that took her directly towards the planet below. The swirling, multicoloured clouds grew rapidly closer.

Are we going to be able to stop? he asked.

One thing at a time, kid. Let's shake off these bastards first.

Their speed began to bleed away as Morhelion's upper atmosphere buffeted the ship. Mender twisted and turned, evading beams and hypersonic slugs. Ethan watched through the external lenses, the disconnect between the whirling view and relative stillness of his body in the acceleration shell making his stomach crawl up his throat. Only one of the pursuing ships appeared to be atmosphere-capable, but its heat shields were soon glowing cherry-red and it broke off the pursuit, transitioning from a plummeting descent into a gentle climb back to orbit. Ethan's acceleration shell drained and snapped open, the mesophase gel's residue evaporating quickly from his skin and clothes. He vomited up liquid from his lungs and gasped.

Mender's hands were still flying over the controls. Ethan could see the distant lights of habisphere bubbles rising quickly towards them – he'd found out the colonies floated at a carefully selected altitude above Morhelion's inhospitable surface, where the pressure was one standard atmosphere; if they ventured much below that, *Dainty Jane*'s hull would collapse spectacularly, crushing them all.

The lights of the habispheres came level, then rose above them.

'Uh, Mender?' He studied the external pressure in alarm. It was building fast; the indicator had already turned from green to amber.

'I know, I know. *Jane*, fire the verniers, we need to get out of this dive.'

'The verniers are too weak—'

'*Just do it!* We need everything we can get. Nacelles to forty degrees. Open the scoops – that should slow us.'

'We could use the emergency chutes for drag,' Ethan suggested, clenching his hands. Their angle of their descent had lessened, but not nearly enough.

'We're too fast and the atmosphere's too thick,' Mender told him. 'They'd just burst.'

The external pressure monitor was into the red and rising. Around them the hull was creaking and popping alarmingly. Ethan started scanning the canopy for cracks.

'I'm designed to keep from *exploding*, not imploding,' *Jane* pointed out. 'We don't have much longer.'

'If you have any suggestions,' Mender grunted through gritted teeth, hauling on the control yoke, 'I'm all ears.'

Ethan stared through the canopy. The clouds were darker now, and streaked with purple and brown. He was completely disoriented, unable to tell up from down, but the avionics core was telling him they were still descending, though at a shallower angle than before. *Still not shallow enough*, he thought with a stab of fear.

'*Jane*, deploy the chutes,' he said.

'I told you—' Mender began, but Ethan was shaking his head wildly.

'What have we got to lose? Try it!'

'Deploying emergency chutes,' *Dainty Jane* announced calmly, and they watched through the lenses as three enormous ovals woven from microfibre filament blossomed behind the ship.

They did slow their descent a little, which allowed Mender to reduce their angle of attack still further – then one of the chutes burst into tatters, quickly followed by the others.

'Shit.' The pressure readout was flashing red now.

'You bought us a minute,' Mender said, and Ethan wondered if that counted as grudging praise.

'Er . . . great?'

A shadow suddenly loomed through the whorls of thick gas, obscured by swirling particulates, and it took Ethan a moment to realign his senses. When his spatial awareness kicked back in, he realised the shadow was below them – and they were heading right for it.

'There!' he cried. 'Is that the ground?'

'No mountain is this high,' Mender snapped, then, as the shadow became more distinct, solidifying into a cratered brown landscape of ridges and valleys, 'Well, I'll be damned.'

'Land on it!' Ethan said urgently, but Mender was already aiming *Dainty Jane* at a shallow valley.

They came in steep, scraping a smooth ridge before hitting the valley floor with a surprisingly gentle impact. The ship bounced once, almost tipping over, then righted herself and skidded across the soft ground before coming to a halt on her belly just short of another fold in the terrain.

The pressure readout was still flashing red, but *Jane*'s hull was holding, for the moment at least.

Orry? Ethan sent. *Where are you?*

'I'm afraid she won't hear you,' *Jane* told him. 'Morhelion's atmosphere is a highly charged electromagnetic environment. It will severely disrupt integuary signals at anything more than very close range.'

'This trip just keeps getting better,' Mender grunted, levering himself awkwardly from his shell. 'I hate bloody spooks.'

'If it's any consolation,' the ship continued, 'Orry is very competent in a crisis. I'm sure she'll be fine.'

Mender stumped across the cockpit.

'Where are you going?' Ethan demanded. 'We have to find her!'

'We ain't finding shit until I get *Jane* working again.' He started down the ladder.

Ethan jumped from his shell and poked his head down the hatch after him. 'Is there anything I can do?'

'Yeah,' Mender said without looking up. 'Figure out what the hell we just landed on.'

After a violent descent and equally hair-raising deceleration, the escape pod was now bobbing gently below a ring of balloons. Orry slipped from her seat and turned her attention to Irina, who was looking deathly pale. The biomesh dressing she'd slapped on the wound was already saturated with blood.

The Seventh Secretariat operative opened her eyes. 'Where are we?' she murmured weakly.

'Somewhere in Morhelion's atmosphere.'

Irina licked her lips and Orry moistened them with water from a bulb. 'I want you to do something for me.'

'Save your strength,' Orry told her. 'Don't talk.'

'No, listen.' Irina grabbed her hand with surprising strength. 'You have to do something for me. You have to complete my mission.'

'*What?*'

'I know you don't want to get involved, but you *have* to. I got close to Viktor Salazar because of his connection to Cordelia Roag. My original mission was to find her and either apprehend or eliminate her, but then I heard something . . .' Her grip tightened. 'The Kadiran are planning to assassinate the Imperator.'

'That's hardly news,' Orry said, 'and the Imperator is well protected.'

'Not from this.' Irina's eyes burned into hers. 'They're getting information from someone close to him – information that makes this a credible threat. Roag is the conduit, passing secrets from the source in the Imperator's inner circle direct to the Kadiran.'

'What does that have to do with Morhelion?'

'I don't have all the details, but there's someone here who has the information I need. A Kadiran deserter—'

'You're shitting me.'

'No, he's an exile, hiding on one of the scoopers' deep rigs. You have to find him, Orry. Find out what he knows about the plot.'

'And then what?' She was horribly afraid she knew the answer.

'*Stop* them. Do whatever it takes. Here . . .' Irina lifted her arm with difficulty. 'Take my ring.'

Orry hesitated.

'Piotr is the only person keeping the Great Houses in line,' Irina said. 'If he dies, a civil war is inevitable – and there's no way we can fight ourselves as well as the Kadiran.' She gripped Orry's hand. 'You have to stop this. Promise me!'

'I . . .' She felt trapped. The last thing she wanted was to get involved, but she wasn't stupid: she knew that if the Ascendancy fell, the colonies would follow. She tightened her jaw. 'I'll do what I can.'

'Give me your word,' Irina hissed.

'I'm not Ruuz.'

'Promise me.'

Orry sighed. 'All right. I promise.'

Irina released her. 'Take the ring.'

It fell from Irina's hand into Orry's, and when she placed it on her right index finger the silver band adjusted to fit. Irina pressed a fingertip to its surface and her eyes clouded for a moment as she accessed her integuary. The ring vibrated gently in response.

'It's locked to your integuary now,' she told Orry, her voice barely audible. 'Just touch the ring and will the seal to appear.' She paused, struggling for breath. 'There's one final thing. When I die, you need to get rid of my body. I can't be found here. Let me fall.'

'Don't talk like that.'

Irina managed a weak smile. 'Let me fall. I won't feel a thing.'

Orry touched the ring and the Imperator's Seal appeared with a thought. 'What if I can't find this Kadiran exile?' she asked.

Irina didn't reply.

'Irina?' Orry picked up her hand and with a leaden stomach she checked her pulse, then gently closed her staring eyes.

She sat back, listening to the pod creaking as it drifted. She tried her integuary again, fruitlessly, then examined the pod's supplies. *Enough for six weeks, longer if I'm careful.* She really hoped she wouldn't be stuck here for anywhere near that long.

Once she had done everything she could do to postpone the inevitable, she turned her attention to Irina's body.

Some time later, after a meagre meal, she reclined on one of the pod's couches and slept.

11

LEVIATHAN

Ethan found Mender's legs protruding from an open access panel in *Dainty Jane*'s cargo bay. The high-pitched whine of a powerdriver emerged in short bursts.

'I know what we landed on,' Ethan said, barely able to contain his excitement.

'Good for you, kid.' Mender's voice was muffled and he sounded distracted. 'What is it?' The powerdriver started up again.

'It's an aeriform leviathan.'

The noise stopped and a moment later Mender wriggled out of the hatch.

'What else can it be?' Ethan continued. 'You said yourself: we're *way* too high for mountains. I thought it might be a wreck, but we're moving too fast for that – whatever we're on top of, it's going much faster than the surrounding atmosphere. So I recalibrated *Jane*'s protein tagger and pointed it straight down and guess what? We're resting on organic tissue – a *lot* of it.'

Mender grunted. 'Thought it might be that. Lucky for us.'

'Lucky it's shoaling season,' Ethan agreed. '*Jane*'s been telling me all about this place—'

'He has an enquiring mind,' the ship broke in.

'—and these aeriform leviathans? They normally spend their time so deep in the atmosphere we'd have been crushed *way* before we reached them. These things are crazy-interesting: the one we're on must be part of a bloom – that's what it's called when they swarm – so we could be surrounded by *dozens* of them.'

'Is it likely to go back down with us on its back?' Mender asked with a frown.

'They come up to mate, so it depends if it's . . . uh . . .'

'Had its oats already?'

Ethan grinned. 'Yeah.'

Mender slammed the hatch shut and rose stiffly to his feet. 'Then let's get the hell off this thing before it decides to disappear and take us with it.'

It was hard to believe that the barren landscape falling away below them was a living creature. Ethan remained glued to *Dainty Jane*'s external lenses until the drifting gases obscured the vast leviathan. If it was part of a bloom, its fellows were invisible in the murk. As Mender engaged the main drives and *Dainty Jane* fought her way up through the soup, Ethan caught a final vanishing glimpse of colossal tentacles moving ponderously before the gargantuan beast disappeared entirely.

'I've been modelling the possible trajectories of Orry's escape pod,' *Jane* said suddenly, 'and narrowed down the search area to a volume of fifteen thousand cubic kilometres.'

'Sounds doable,' Mender said. 'Should only take a couple of hours with your sensors at max range.'

'That would be true in open space,' the ship agreed, 'but

unfortunately my sensor range is severely degraded by the electromagnetic interference caused by Morhelion's atmosphere.'

'How long, then?' Ethan asked.

'Approximately four days.'

'Oh.'

'Don't worry, kid,' Mender reassured him, 'that pod she's in? It will have plenty to eat and drink. She'll be fine for weeks.'

'I guess.' He thought about being stuck in a tiny pod for that long and shuddered; it would drive him nuts – but Orry was made of stronger stuff.

'We'd better get started then,' Mender said. 'I'm going to get some rest. *Jane*, wake me if you find anything.' He limped away.

'I think I'll stay here a while,' Ethan said.

'I am more than capable of conducting the search on my own,' *Jane* pointed out.

Ethan shifted in his shell, scanning the sensor read-outs floating in front of him. 'I know, I'm just not tired yet.' He yawned.

'I understand,' *Jane* said.

12

JUNKDOGS

A *clang* reverberated through the escape pod, rocking it wildly and startling Orry awake. Heart thudding, she checked the time on her integuary and realised that more than five hours had passed. She raced to the nearest viewport and stared out at an extraordinary vessel floating nearby. It looked like a platform constructed from scrap metal and parts of defunct machines. A small wheelhouse rose from what she decided must be the bow, while amidships, the prehensile arms of a crane rose up and outboard, disappearing from view above her pod. A thin man in dirty coveralls and a respirator was hunched over the crane's controls, apparently being directed by the gestures of another man, similarly dressed but filling his coveralls rather more substantially.

'Junkdogs,' Orry muttered. 'Shit.' She'd come across their kind before, but never actually dealt with them. Her father had always been adamant that they couldn't be trusted, no matter on which particular world they were encountered.

Feeling a little foolish, she waved. The larger of the two men saw her – but rather than wave back, he turned to his companion and gesticulated angrily.

'Well, that's not good,' she said aloud as he started stabbing a finger repeatedly in her direction. She hadn't seen anything in the pod she could use to defend herself if things came down to it, but she still began re-checking the lockers she'd already investigated twice.

The pod rocked again as something thudded onto the curved hull above her head and a metallic screech set her teeth on edge. The port behind her darkened, covered by what looked like the claw of a giant grabber.

Sighing, she returned to the viewport.

The fat junkdog raised his arm and the pod went with it, hoisted up and then swung precariously in over the vessel's deck, which appeared to have been assembled from a patchwork of mismatched materials. The pod oscillated, pendulum-like, as it was lowered in brief, jerky motions, and by the time it came to rest with a solid thud, Orry's stomach was churning.

Boots clanged on the pod's hull and a sleeve wiped the viewport set into the hatch. A face peered in: the thinner of the two junkdogs, who she could now see was an old man. The features behind the respirator mask were wrinkled, and hair the colour of tobacco-stained fingers stuck out from under his greasy baseball cap like dirty straw. He grinned when he saw her and shouted something down to his comrade, then banged on the port and gestured for her to open the hatch.

She considered her options with a sinking feeling, for she had only two: open the hatch, or don't. If these men meant to harm her then opening up would make things easier for them, but if she didn't it would only prolong the inevitable; there was nothing to stop them burrowing through the outer shell to the oxygenator and flooding the interior with something that would drive her out – or worse.

Better to face things head on. *Hope for the best and prepare for the worst*, Dad always said. *Except this time I can't prepare for anything.*

She pulled a rebreather over her face and checked the air supply, then took a steadying breath and released the hatch. It let go with a thud and a hiss and she stepped back as the man outside hauled it open and squatted in the entrance.

'Hello, sweetcheeks,' he said, his voice slightly muffled by his mask. 'Why don't you come on out of there and let me take a look at you?'

'Who are you?' Orry asked, eyeing him warily.

'Never you mind that, honeybunch – just come on out. Ain't nobody gonna hurt you.'

Hoping to Rama that was true, she clambered out and followed the old man down the pod's curved side and onto the deck. A third member of the crew had appeared, presumably from the wheelhouse, and was standing beside the fat junkdog, whose patchy beard was doing little to conceal his double chin; up close, she saw this one was middle-aged, while the newcomer was a lanky boy in his late teens. He was staring wide-eyed at her from a face dotted with acne. His blond hair, so pale it was almost white, was cut in a harsh line straight across his forehead. Orry spotted a family resemblance immediately – and something else: the boy's ear had been replaced recently, and poorly, by the look of it. A vivid ridge of purple scar tissue ran around the new addition, which did not quite match the other one.

Reading these three was almost too easy: insular and poor, the patchwork vessel beneath her feet representing pretty much everything they had in the world. She'd seen the same story a hundred times in impoverished colonies far from the Fountain-head systems. Men like this were interested in only one thing: a route out of their poverty.

'What's your name, then?' the old man asked, going to stand with the others.

'Jade Flint,' she told him. 'And you?'

'They call me Sticky Pete. These are my boys: Janco and Rudi.' He indicated the fat man and the youth in turn. 'Where you from, then? We saw you come down all the way from Grampus bubble. That's an EDC pod, ain't it?'

'It is,' she confirmed, suddenly realising what she had to do. 'If you can take me somewhere I can get a message to a Company representative, there'll be a substantial reward in it for you.' If these men thought she was worth something, they were likely to treat her well – and if she could find a way to send a message, maybe she would be able to contact *Dainty Jane*.

Sticky Pete laughed at that, a hacking cackle that turned quickly into a violent coughing fit that sprayed the inside of his mask with brown moisture. When the coughing had subsided he managed to wheeze, 'Don't you know nothin', babydoll? The only Company reps on Morhelion are up in orbit.'

Even better. 'Can I get a message to one of them?'

Pete gave Janco a derisive nudge, as if to say, *This girl* really *don't know nothin'*. 'Transmissions can't go from bubble to bubble,' he explained, his patronising tone making Orry want to punch his respirator in, 'so they sure as shit won't reach orbit. Only place you could talk to ships up there is Hardhaven bubble, and that's only 'cause they strung a cable all the way up out of the aether.'

'The aether?'

He looked suspiciously at her, as though she was deliberately trying to wind him up, then rolled his eyes and indicated the drifting gases that surrounded them. 'The *aether*,' he said slowly.

'Oh, okay. So how do I get to this Hardhaven bubble?'

'Hardhaven's halfway round the planet, honeybunch. It'll take you weeks – if you can even find a smoker to take you.'

The clouds of pollution spewing from the vessel's engines saved Orry from having to ask what a smoker was.

'Can *you* take me?' she asked. Being cooped up on this heap of junk with these three creeps was not her idea of a good time, but she couldn't see many other options to get her back to *Dainty Jane*.

'To Hardhaven? Does this thing look like it'll make it that far? Nope, we're heading back to Grampus bubble – and we're keeping your pod to pay for the fuel what we've burned coming out to get you.'

'Grampus bubble? Is that your home?' The junkdog nodded. 'Could anyone *there* take me to Hardhaven?'

'Everyone's guh-gone,' the younger one, Rudi, piped up. His brother Janco glared at him and the boy stared at the deck, but after a few seconds his eyes drifted up to gaze doe-eyed at Orry once more.

'Boy's right,' Sticky Pete said. 'Spumehead's your best bet.'

'Spumehead? Is that another habisphere— I mean, bubble?'

'Yep.'

'But if everyone's gone, how am I going to get there?'

'Tyrell might tuh-take you,' Rudi ventured, then blanched and glanced nervously at Janco.

'Tyrell?' Orry asked, filing the name away.

Sticky Pete just snorted. 'Good luck getting *him* to leave Grampus.'

'Where would I find this Tyrell?'

'Anywhere there's booze and women.'

Orry didn't like the way he was looking her over, like she was a piece of meat. Janco was just glowering at her.

'Let's get you back to Grampus and you can go talk to him,' Sticky Pete said. 'But we get to keep the pod – deal?'

Orry briefly considered haggling for some local currency as well, but dismissed the notion; they had rescued her, after all, and Janco looked about ready to throw her overboard as it was. She would have to hope that this Tyrell character would buy her story about a reward from EDC. 'Deal,' she said.

As if picking up on her thoughts, Pete asked, 'And when you get back to the Company, you'll send the reward our way?'

'Sure – you did save me, after all.' She looked at him with suspicion; Sticky Pete did not look the trusting sort and she didn't like the smile he was giving her. 'How long will it take to get back to Grampus?' she asked.

'Be back by nightfall. You're welcome to come below. It ain't much but at least you can take your mask off down there.'

'Thanks, but I think I'll stay up here and admire the view.' The clouds were extraordinarily beautiful, and there was no way she was going to be trapped below with these three men. Rudi was looking distinctly love-struck – clearly they didn't see many young women around here – but Janco exuded hostility, and as for Sticky Pete . . . well, he made her skin crawl. And what was it with that *name*?

'Your choice,' he said with a shrug. 'Rudi, let's get going.'

He shoved the boy towards the little wheelhouse while Janco

strode to the stern to tend to the engines.

Orry gazed out over the clouds and wished she was anywhere else.

A few hours later she was thoroughly sick of her rebreather's stale, recirculated air. The junkdogs hadn't spoken to her again, doubtless too busy keeping their vessel from shaking itself apart, but now she saw Rudi emerge from the wheelhouse and start testing the tension on the cargo straps holding her pod to the deck. Every couple of seconds he glanced over at her.

She watched him, thinking about her promise to Irina. *Well, it's not as if I have anything else to do right now.* She walked over.

'Hello – Rudi, isn't it?'

'Uh-huh.' He blushed beneath his mask.

'This place we're going to, Grampus bubble – are there any . . . scoopers there?'

'Suh-scoopers?' he stammered, grinning shyly. 'What d'you want to know 'bout them cuh-crazy buh-bastards for? Talk your ear clean off if you luh-let 'em.'

'I need to find someone. On one of their' – *What was it Irina called them?* – 'deep rigs.'

Rudi shook his head. 'Ain't no suh-scoopers in Guh-Grampus. Spumehead, though, mebbe. Be all suh-sorts there right now, with the Royal Buh-Breach an' all.'

'The what?'

'*Rudi!*'

The boy jumped as if he'd been shot.

Sticky Pete stuck his head out of the wheelhouse and shouted, 'Stop bothering the girl and go help your brother.'

'Yes, Puh-Paps.' Rudi shrugged apologetically and hurried away.

Pete stared at Orry for a few seconds before returning to the wheel.

Shading her eyes, she searched out the bloated disk of Morhelion's sun getting lower in the sky and wondered how much longer the trip was going to take.

13

GRAMPUS BUBBLE

The voyage took several more hours, as it turned out, but finally, to Orry's immense relief, she made out a pale disk in the distance, glowing milky-white against the darkening clouds. As the disk grew nearer it resolved into a sphere and she realised it must be Grampus bubble, their destination.

The smoker lurched and as it shuddered closer, she could see the habisphere's translucent skin was streaked with grime, its interior coated in moisture that obscured whatever lay within. Directly ahead she could see a vast cylinder of machinery set into the bubble's surface. Wheels rotated and pistons extended, opening a pair of colossal doors within the circle. *An airlock*, she realised, as it swallowed them. The interior was cavernous, designed to cope with far larger vessels than even the sizeable junk platform. The doors closed heavily behind her and she watched the swirls of gas being sucked out before a matching pair of doors opened ahead to reveal an extraordinary sight.

An entire town hung suspended within the bubble, multiple layers of streets and buildings, the structures' original printed designs long lost beneath extensions and modifications, many of which were crumbling. Steep ramps joined the different levels, marked up for traffic although Orry could see no vehicles. In fact, she couldn't see *anything* moving, other than a handful of tiny figures scattered across the deserted town.

Hundreds of metres below her a disgusting lake of filthy water had gathered in the bottom of the sphere, its oily surface thick with floating detritus and garbage. A docking basin that took up a third of the habisphere's volume was filled with a multi-layered complex of wharves linked by ramps, ladders and lift shafts. But despite the basin's obvious capacity – Orry reckoned it could handle dozens of smokers like the one she was on – there was only a single lonely craft moored there: a small, cigar-shaped metal tube with stubby triangular wings.

Seeing the junkdogs remove their masks, she did the same, to find the air was warm and clammy, with an unpleasant hint of unemptied bins on a hot day. The high moisture content made it difficult to breathe and she felt a rising panic as the soupy air filled her lungs. She concentrated on breathing steadily, in and out, and after a moment her laboured panting settled down.

The smoker passed layer after layer of empty wharves as it traversed the basin, making for what turned out to be a private dock tucked away high on one side, in front of a dilapidated warehouse. The vessel slowed to manoeuvre alongside and Janco leaped ashore to catch a cable thrown to him by his father.

Finally, the rumble of the engines gave way to silence.

Janco assisted the old man onto the wharf and they both looked around the deserted basin, then in the direction of the nearest buildings. Only the topmost two levels were visible from here and Orry couldn't see a soul on either layer. The place was a ghost town. A chill of apprehension shivered down her spine. The sooner she was out of this place and on her way to Spumehead, the better.

Pete reached out to help her down to the wharf, his palm moist against hers. As she took it, she noticed his hands were as mismatched as Rudi's ears. She jumped down – and a pair of powerful arms immediately enveloped her from behind.

Janco! she thought in sudden panic, seeing Rudi watching wide-eyed from the smoker's deck. She struggled violently, but he was strong as well as fat and lifted her easily from her feet, squeezing until she feared her ribs would crack. She stopped moving, fighting to draw a breath, and his grip relaxed a fraction.

Pete stepped close and examined her face before nodding approvingly. 'You'll do just fine, honeybunch.'

Her arms were pinned, but her legs were dangling free. She kicked out as hard as she could, her boot landing squarely between the old man's legs, and he leaped back with a piercing shriek. Janco's vice-like grip tightened and she thrust her head back, but found nothing for her skull to connect with. Lungs bursting, she kicked backwards, driving her heel into Janco's shin again and again, finding his leg each time he tried to move it, until finally, as her vision began to cloud, he roared with frustration and threw her to the ground.

She barely felt the impact as sweet air flooded her lungs. An instant later she was up and running towards the town beyond the mounds of junk that were scattered all around.

She'd taken perhaps five steps when a harsh buzz-saw rip tore through the silence and a line of flechette darts appeared in the ground in front of her, driven up to their tiny flights into the wharf's ferroform composite.

Orry froze, suddenly terrified as she imagined the next salvo of darts tearing through her flesh, shattering bone. She turned slowly to see Janco aiming an ugly-looking fletcher at her. He gave a twisted grin. Behind him Pete was standing awkwardly beside Rudi, clutching his groin, his face drawn with pain.

'Get her in the fucking hole,' he snarled, limping to a pile of junk, one amid many. He stooped and tossed aside a few strips of twisted composite to reveal a metal hatch set into the ground.

Janco and Rudi approached her, the older brother hauled open the hatch and gestured towards it with his fletcher. As she got closer she saw a short ladder leading down into darkness.

She stopped abruptly. 'Are you kidding me? There's no fucking way I'm going down there!'

Pete and Janco exchanged a glance and the old man gave the smallest of nods. His son smiled nastily and promptly shot Orry in the thigh.

It was only a single flechette and she cried out more in shock than pain at the sight of the finger-long dart protruding a few centimetres from the leg of her flight suit. Blood started weeping out almost immediately, staining the material a darker red. She gritted her teeth and pulled the thin dart out.

'You bastard,' she hissed, but Janco just twitched his fletcher towards the hole. Sick with dread, she climbed down the ladder, her thigh throbbing with every step. Her boots clanged hollowly when she reached the bottom and harsh lights flickered to life, illuminating what turned out to be the interior of an old fuel tank. The metal walls and ceiling were lined with compressed foam soundproofing; the air was dry and scratchy in her throat. Fans suddenly hummed into action and the ceiling lights buzzed. In the centre of the room was a complicated-looking chair of pipes and pistons, topped with wipe-clean cushions fitted with wrist and ankle restraints. The gunmetal grey monolith filled her with terror – and then she saw the multi-armed bot bolted to the floor beside it: an ancient surgical model with dirty brown fluid leaking from its many joints. Smears of red on its white shell pointed to a half-hearted cleaning attempt, abandoned partway through.

She backed away – and received a heavy blow on the back of her skull. She staggered, seeing stars, and almost fell, until Janco's hands gripped her and dragged her to the chair.

'No!' she screamed, thrashing in his grasp. Rudi raised the fletcher, but the threat wasn't needed: Janco struck her hard across the jaw and before she could recover he and Pete had lifted her bodily into the chair and expertly snapped the restraints closed.

'You bastards!' she yelled, bruising her flesh on the metal bands. Terror had gripped her, driving out any rational thought, and she started screaming at them, 'Let me go! Let me *go!*'

Ignoring her, Sticky Pete picked up a handheld cellular scanner from a table.

With a supreme effort, Orry forced herself to calm down.

'Listen, please—' she began as Pete pressed the device to her neck. A sharp pain made her wince. '*Ow!*'

The little machine chimed and Pete examined its screen. His face broke into a wide smile and he studied her approvingly before gesturing to his boys. The three of them headed for the ladder.

'Stop!' she cried after them. 'You can't just leave me here! *You can't do this!*'

Rudi glanced back, but his brother cuffed him on the ear and sent him up the ladder ahead of him. Pete went last. At the top, he turned back and winked at her. The hatch slammed shut.

A moment later, the lights went out.

According to her integuary, almost an hour had passed – the longest sixty minutes of her life – when she heard the hatch open again. A moment later, white light flooded the chamber again, blooming painfully against her integuary-enhanced low-light vision. She squeezed her eyes shut, deactivated night mode and when she opened them again, she saw a pair of thick legs on the ladder. They descended slowly, followed by a corpulent frame almost too fat to fit through the hatch. Relief swamped her when the newcomer finally turned and she recognised a police uniform.

'Thank Rama!' she babbled. 'How did you find me?'

The enormously fat policeman was wheezing badly after his exertion. A bushy handlebar moustache compensated for the sparse strands of grey hair carefully combed over his glistening head. A silver name badge on one bulging breast read 'Purvis'. He looked her over with piggy eyes sunk deep in a fleshy face that was moist with sweat.

'My, you *are* a ripe one.'

Her momentary relief soured instantly to fear. 'Stay the fuck away from me!'

Sticky Pete descended the ladder behind the policeman, trailed by his two sons, Rudi still armed with the fletcher.

'Told you she was prime meat, Marshal,' the old junkdog said. He held up the cellular scanner. 'Gizmo says she looks as good on the inside as out. She pop up on the system?'

'Nope. Far as Hardhaven's concerned, she don't exist.' Purvis looked thoughtful, but Pete clapped his mismatched hands together.

'Dibs on her lungs.'

The marshal turned to him. 'Lot of buyers for fresh lungs,' he said, and the joy went out of Pete's face.

'I'll pay for 'em. Out of my share, like.' He coughed wetly.

'Damn right you will.' Purvis eyed the surgical bot. 'You fix this fucking thing? We don't want a repeat of last time.'

'Sure did!' Pete replied a little too enthusiastically. 'Rudi fixed it right up.'

Purvis spat on the floor. 'That's what you said last time.'

'It'll be fine, Floyd.' Pete reached for the marshal's arm, then thought better of it. 'The boy'll stay down here, keep an eye on it. Let's go get us a drink.' He gestured at the ladder.

Ignoring her churning fear, willing her voice to remain steady, Orry said, 'If you want money, I'm worth a lot more to you alive.'

Pete scowled at her, but the marshal looked amused. 'Ain't you been listening, love? Even if this reward of yours is real, which I doubt, d'you think the Company will be paying us shit once you told 'em what we got planned for you?' He turned away.

'I'm not talking about EDC,' she said quickly, and saw him hesitate. 'I have friends, *wealthy* friends, who would pay a lot to see me again – no questions asked.'

He turned back. 'What *friends*?' Doubt dripped from the word.

'Fountainhead friends.'

'Prove it.'

'How do you expect me to do that? Get me a channel to orbit.'

The marshal thought for a moment, then grunted out a laugh. 'You're full of shit, girly.'

'I'm serious! You're throwing away a fortune!' she yelled as he waddled away. Pete gave her a triumphant look and followed. '*Shit*. Marshal? *Marshal!*' But his head was already out of the hatch and Janco was close on his heels.

Pete paused at the foot of the ladder. 'Don't. Fuck. This. Up,' he told Rudi, punctuating each word with a jab of his bony finger in the boy's chest.

'I-I won't, Puh-Paps.'

'Hey!' Orry yelled, close to losing control, 'you can *buy* a new set of lungs – just let me prove it!'

Pete's face twitched with irritation but he said nothing, just climbed the ladder. A moment later, the hatch clanged shut.

Avoiding Orry's gaze, Rudi crossed to a metal table and picked up a slim, transparent tablet. Its screen lit up as he touched it.

Her stomach clenched, nausea filling her throat as the surgical bot's arms began to move.

Each of the limbs terminated in a different instrument – scalpel, needle, syringe, bone saw – and now they were all in motion. 'Please,' she said, unable to tear her eyes from the lethal ballet being performed beside her, 'please, just *listen* to me—'

'It's okay,' Rudi said, trying to soothe her, 'you won't feel a thing, I puh-promise.' His finger touched the screen and the syringe swung into position above her left forearm.

She'd just spent an hour trying to release herself and she knew it was useless, but she still couldn't stop herself struggling, trying in vain to pull free of the restraints. Two more of the bot's limbs swept in: one gripped her arm while the other cut a neat square in the red fabric of her flight suit.

'No!' she screamed. Her forearm was held perfectly still, even as the rest of her body heaved and thrashed. 'Don't you fucking dare!'

Rudi didn't reply but kept his eyes fixed on the screen.

The machine's grip on her forearm suddenly tightened, making her cry out – then its crippling hold on her released completely.

'Shit!' he muttered as the lethally tipped limbs all whirred into motion, gliding about in a flurry of random activity. Two of them collided with a clang and there was a screeching scrape of metal on metal. Rudi was now stabbing frantically at the tablet.

'What are you doing?' Orry yelled, ducking her head as best she could to avoid a glittering scalpel blade sweeping over her scalp. 'Shut it down!'

'I'm tuh-trying!' Rudi's fingers were still flying over the screen, but nothing was stopping.

An arm slammed into the chair just centimetres from her head, badly denting it.

'Hurry up,' Orry shouted, 'or there'll be nothing left of me to butcher—'

He looked at her for the first time, his face white. 'Nuh-nothing's wuh-working!'

A blade came out of nowhere and Orry felt a cold line drawn across her cheek. A moment later came the pain, the burning accompanied by a warm wetness.

'Get me out of this fucking chair!'

But Rudi was frozen with indecision as he stared at her face and the blood dripping onto the seat.

'*Rudi!*' she screamed, trying to break through his paralysis, 'what is the marshal going to do to you if you mess this up?'

That did it. He dropped the tablet and ran to the chair,

ducking under one sweeping limb and fumbling to release her left arm. As the restraint popped open, a blade slashed across his chest, parting his shirt to expose the sallow flesh beneath. He swore and leaped clear, then looked down to see blood welling from the long incision.

Without a word, he turned and fled.

Swearing, dodging scalpels and saws, Orry fumbled with the restraint on her other arm and at last got it free. She was about to sit up so she could reach her legs, when a swinging limb only narrowly missed her, forcing her first to dodge and then to hunch back down. She wondered briefly why Rudi wasn't already on the ladder, then caught sight of him on the other side of the room, scrabbling behind one of the freezers. He reappeared with a rusty meat cleaver in one hand.

She saw a gap in the arms' movement, sat up again and started scrabbling to free her legs. She'd just managed to unbuckle the first restraint when Rudi raised the cleaver and brought it down sharply.

There was an explosion of sparks and the room plunged into darkness.

After a moment, emergency lights flickered to life and in the ghastly red glow, she saw the bot had finally stopped moving, its arms hanging limp and lifeless.

Rudi rose to his feet, looking stunned, and turned to her. Their eyes met – and they both surged into action: Orry pulling at the final restraint while Rudi racing towards her with the blackened cleaver still in his hand.

'No, you cuh-can't!' he cried, waving the cleaver ineffectually. Remembering what had happened earlier, he tried to grab her free leg, but she drew it back and kicked out, *hard*. Her boot thudded into the centre of his chest and he dropped the cleaver and staggered back, gasping for breath. He picked himself up just in time to see her open the last restraint.

He turned and ran for the ladder, still panting for breath.

He'd got halfway up it when she grabbed him around the knees and yanked him back down. She lost her grip as he landed and he kicked out wildly, sending her staggering into the wall. As he tried to regain his feet, her fear flashed into boiling rage and she leaped on his back, driving him back to the ground where he squirmed beneath her until he managed to roll onto his back and land a stinging blow on her wounded cheek. She was straddling him now, though, and punched down hard on his chest where the bot had slashed him open, feeling a savage satisfaction as he cried out, bucking under her and trying to throw her off. She punched him again for good measure, then grabbed his mismatched ears and slammed the back of his head into the ground once, twice, three times, until finally he lay still.

His eyelids were fluttering, so he wasn't dead. Yet.

Orry rocked back, shaking with adrenalin. Pain came rushing back in, but this wasn't the time to worry about it. *Get it together*, she told herself sternly, and forced herself to her feet.

She dragged her aching body up the ladder to the hatch and stopped at the top. She couldn't hear anything outside, even using her integuary's enhanced audio detection, but that didn't mean the junkdogs hadn't posted a guard. Steeling herself, she eased the hatch open a fraction, but when she peered out, the yard looked empty. She could hear muffled laughter coming from inside the warehouse.

She crawled out, lowered the hatch silently back into place

and slowly slid the heavy bolt home, wincing at every metallic squeak.

Keeping low, using the piled junk for cover, she set off towards the town.

Ethan stared out at the streamers of multihued gas whipping past *Dainty Jane*'s cockpit. He'd finally given in to the ship's entreaties and retired to his cabin, where he had drifted in fitful sleep disturbed by dreams of Orry and their father, and their old freighter, *Bonaventure*. After a couple of hours he gave up and returned to see how the search was progressing.

'This is pointless,' he said. 'We're never going to find her like this.'

'You got any better ideas?' Mender grunted from the commander's seat.

'Actually, I do.' After a moment's hesitation he manoeuvred himself into the shell beside the old man, which was Orry's usual position. 'So, I've been reading up on this place. All these little bubble communities? They're supposed to be independent, but really the whole place is run by the Whaling League. They've got their headquarters in this big habisphere cluster called Hardhaven.'

'The one with the spaceport?'

'Yep, that's the one. Anyway, I figure if Orry's pod is recovered she'll be sent to Hardhaven to be returned to *Venturer* – if it's still in orbit.'

Mender looked at him. 'So you want to go to this Hardhaven place? What if she's not been picked up?'

'Then we come back and carry on looking. But it's worth checking, isn't it?'

Mender stroked his whiskers thoughtfully. '*Jane?*'

'If Orry has been picked up, she might not have given her real name,' the ship pointed out.

'So I'll try some aliases,' Ethan said breezily.

Mender gazed out of the canopy. 'She's your sister, kid,' he said eventually. 'It's your call.'

Ethan grinned with relief. 'Then I say we try.'

14

THREE-CARD SHAFT

The Rampant Cat was a real dive, a few groups of desultory punters scattered around dingy booths. It was an ugly, one-storey building a couple of levels down from the junkdogs' yard and a little way back from the basin, but it was the first barroom Orry had found that wasn't boarded up. *Anywhere there's booze and women*, Pete had said, before he'd tried to carve her into her component parts, and this place satisfied the first criterion, if not the second. She wondered how long it would be before Rudi was discovered. Or perhaps he had already been found . . .

The man behind the bar wore his dark hair short. His tight black T-shirt showed off a torso a little too muscular for Orry's taste. He looked terminally bored.

'What's your poison?' he asked.

'I'm looking for someone – a man named Tyrell. Do you know him?'

'Maybe.'

Excellent. 'Can you tell me how to find him?'

'This is a bar, lady, not a dating service. You gonna to buy a drink or not?'

After everything that had happened recently, a drink sounded pretty good . . . but she had no gilt. On the other hand, when had that ever been an obstacle for Eoin Kent's daughter?

She smiled. 'So what do you drink round here?' she asked.

He looked at her with a spark of interest. 'That depends.'

'On?'

'On whether you want to go blind or not.'

She grinned. 'I'm quite attached to my eyes.'

He smiled back. 'They're very pretty. The good stuff, then.'

'The good stuff.'

He busied himself preparing a generous measure of red liquid from a bottle that was either hand-blown or printed to look that way. Swirls of yellow streaked the red as he added a mixer of some sort, then ice. He topped it off with a rather sad-looking green leaf.

'One Aether Sunrise.'

'Impressive,' she said, and took a sip. It wasn't half bad: fruity, with a bitter aftertaste. She drank some more.

'Seven notes,' he told her, wiping his hands on a bar towel then flipping it over one shoulder.

She nodded, looking around the place. The few patrons were seated in small groups, all of them playing either cards or a game Orry didn't recognise that used small ceramic tokens. 'People like to gamble around here?'

'Sure. Not much else to do in Grampus bubble.'

'Is that right?' She placed her glass on the bar and rotated it idly by the stem. 'And are you a gambling man?'

He gave her a sardonic smile. 'Seven notes.'

'How about this?' she said, looking up. 'I will bet you this drink, and two more like it, that I can flabbergast you.'

'*Flabbergast* me?'

'That's what I said.'

He sighed and said ruefully, 'Go ahead then: flabbergast me.'

'I knew you were game,' she said with a grin. 'Now, I shall need two items from you: a glass full of whatever rotgut you sell most of here, and a glass of purest H2O.'

Grinning now, the barman placed two glasses on the bar and filled them.

'Excellent,' she said. 'What's your name?'

'Sheng.'

She extended her hand. 'I'm Amber. Now then, for the *three* drinks as previously discussed, I bet you that I can transfer the water into the rotgut glass and the rotgut into the water glass.'

He thought about this. 'You mean without using a third glass or container or whatever?'

She sighed, as if disappointed in his lack of faith. 'Would that flabbergast you?'

'I guess not. What about your mouth? Could you maybe hold the water in your mouth, pour the skullburst into the other glass, then spit the water out again?'

'Skullburst? Sounds delicious. No, my mouth would count as a third receptacle.'

He studied the two glasses thoughtfully. 'All right. I haven't seen this one before, so I reckon it's worth a couple of drinks to find out how you do it.'

'I knew I liked you, Sheng.' She reached along the bar and plucked a dog-eared laminated cocktail menu from its stand. She placed it over the top of the water glass to prevent it spilling, then upended the glass and menu and balanced them carefully on top of the skullburst. 'Are you ready to be flabbergasted?'

she asked.

'I can barely contain myself.' Despite his dry tone, Sheng was watching with obvious interest. Orry's father had never paid for a drink, not when he'd been a veritable encyclopaedia of bar tricks.

She carefully eased the menu back a fraction, allowing the water to leak down into the glass below. A couple of bubbles rose, followed by the brown skullburst swirling up into the top glass as the water travelled down into the bottom.

Sheng rested his arms on the bar as he watched the liquids slowly switch glasses.

'Very good,' he admitted, 'but I'm not sure I'm flabbergasted.'

'What? This is practically sorcery!'

He chuckled. 'Okay, okay. You can have your drinks. How does it work?'

'Chemistry, my friend,' Orry said cheerfully. 'Or is it physics? I never did quite work out the difference. Anyway, water is heavier than alcohol because the atoms are more densely packed, so the water displaces the skullburst, forcing it up into the top glass.'

'Very clever.' He began fixing two more drinks.

'So, about this Tyrell person . . .'

He looked up. 'What do you want with him, anyway?'

'A lift.'

The barman grunted. 'You know anything about him?'

'Nope.'

'Then take my advice and get a lift with someone else.'

'Why?'

'Vance Tyrell is not a nice man.'

'Does anyone else around here have a smoker for hire?'

Sheng stared at her for a moment, then said, 'I guess not.

He's sitting over there.' He pointed at a handsome, dark-haired man in a nearby booth who was carefully laying three playing cards face-down on the table. The man sitting opposite him was sipping unsteadily from an elaborate layered cocktail, apparently not noticing that it was slopping onto the bundle of brightly coloured bank notes in front of him. The man Sheng had pointed at started moving the three cards over the table top as the drunk struggled to keep track.

Orry snorted; she'd played more than her share of three-card shaft as a child. *So, Tyrell is a grifter*, she thought. *That should make things interesting.*

'Just watch yourself,' Sheng said as she picked up her glass and slid off the stool.

'Thank you, but I think I'll be fine.'

He laughed. 'You know what? I think you just might.' He grinned, and thanked her when she pushed her last drink back towards him.

Orry wandered further along the bar, watching Tyrell and his mark. The card-sharp wasn't bad, switching the position of the money card with some expertise as his hands moved deftly over the table. When the cards stopped moving, the drunk pointed in triumph at the wrong one.

Tyrell flipped it with a smile and scooped up the wad of cash.

'God dammit, you cheated me!' the mark protested, slamming his glass down on the table.

Tyrell's smile vanished. 'I'm sorry,' he said quietly, 'I didn't quite hear you.'

The drunk's indignation faltered under Tyrell's cool gaze and his eyes dropped to a large metal hook honed to a vicious point and fitted with a handle of what looked like yellowing bone that was dangling from the card-sharp's belt. Sweat broke out on the mark's brow.

'What was it you just said?' Tyrell enquired lightly.

'Uh, nothing, nothing.' The drunk rose unsteadily to his feet and lurched away. The card-sharp shook his head and started counting his winnings.

Orry studied him for a moment longer before making her way over to the booth. She landed heavily on the seat opposite him and took a large gulp from her drink.

'Whatcha doing?'

He glanced up, an amused look on his unshaven face. Tyrell turned out to be a good decade older than her, and he was even more good-looking close up. His mane of black hair and dark stubble gave him a piratical air, strengthened by the shabby jacket he wore over a shirt that might once have been white. The jacket was made from some thick animal hide that Orry had never seen before, oily and glistening where it wasn't scuffed with use.

'Vance Tyrell, at your service.' When he extended a hand bedecked with rings, she noted a slender antique watch strapped around his wrist.

'Amber Sphene.' She clutched his hand and giggled like a schoolgirl.

'You look like a capable young woman, Amber Sphene. Tell me, do you enjoy a wager?'

'What sort of wager?'

His face split to display a set of perfect teeth gleaming white against his weathered skin. In another life he could have been a highly successful politician, she decided. He was possessed of that rare, ineffable quality so valuable to grifters: people *liked* him. She could feel it herself. She made a mental note to be on her guard.

'It's a simple game,' he told her, flipping the three cards over to reveal the queen of hearts and the jacks of clubs and spades. 'All you have to do is follow the lady. Do you think you can do that?'

'Sure I can!' she said enthusiastically.

'Okay, so let's see.' He scooped up the cards and showed her the red queen before tossing it back, face down, followed by the others. His hands moved swiftly, but not so fast that she couldn't easily follow the money card. He shuffled the cards in a graceful flow and stopped. 'Where is she?'

Orry pointed at the queen and he flipped it over.

'Hey, you're good at this!'

It was as much as she could do not to burst out laughing. It was lucky for Tyrell that he was so charismatic; he was skilful enough with his hands, but his patter was worse than Ethan's. She suspected he was used to working alone.

'Let's try it again, shall we?' He showed her the queen again before repeating the performance. After she'd found the money card three times in a row, he finally got down to business. 'Actually, you're so good I'm not sure about this wager any more.'

She let her face fall. 'Oh.'

He gazed into her eyes as he appeared to consider. 'Ah, go on then. I can't resist those big green eyes of yours. Tell you what: one'll get you two – how does that sound?'

She creased her forehead. 'You mean, if I can find the card again you'll give me twice what I bet?'

'That's it.'

She looked doubtful. 'I don't know. I've heard about games

like this . . .'

He leaned back and opened his arms, inviting her in. *Playground stuff.* 'Hey, it's no skin off my johnson.' He managed to look disappointed in her. 'I just thought you had something about you, is all.'

'I *do* have something about me!'

He looked away, unconvinced.

She clapped her hands and giggled again. 'All right,' she said, 'let's do it. I'll take your wager.'

He returned to the cards with a grin, fully engaged once more.

I'm going to enjoy this, Orry thought when Tyrell nudged his bundle of cash forward and looked expectantly at her.

'Oh,' she said, sounding disappointed, 'I just realised – I don't have any more money on me.' As his brows lowered, she continued quickly, 'but . . . um . . . what about this?' She pulled off Irina's silver ring and placed it on the table in front of him, hiding her anxiety as he picked it up. But after a cursory examination he merely grunted, unimpressed. 'Nothing else?'

'Not on me.'

He thought for a moment. 'Okay, you know what? If you find the lady I'll give you twenty notes, and if you don't, I keep this trinket.' He rolled his eyes. 'And I'm only doing this because I like your face.'

She smiled sweetly. 'That ring is worth way more than twenty and you know it. If I pick right, I want that.' She pointed at the bundle of notes. 'All of it.'

Tyrell guffawed, then looked thoughtfully at the ring. 'Maybe it is worth that much, and maybe not.' He pursed his lips. 'All right, I'll bet it all. But if you lose, I get the ring . . . and a kiss.'

Oh Rama . . . She looked coyly at him. *'Just* a kiss?'

He grinned broadly and Orry was surprised to find herself wondering what kissing this man might actually be like. She dragged her mind back to the job at hand with a flush of irritation. *Focus.*

'The ring, and a kiss,' she agreed.

He rubbed his hands together and picked up the cards once more. When the hype came, she was ready for it. He showed her the red queen in his left hand, but actually tossed one of the jacks face down onto the table in its place. It was expertly done, and if she hadn't performed this trick hundreds of times herself she would never have spotted the switch.

But she had.

Tyrell stopped moving the cards. 'Well?'

She frowned for a good few seconds – it was only fair he got his money's worth of anticipation – then she reached out and flipped the queen over.

Vance Tyrell's face was a picture as she scooped up his money and replaced Irina's ring on her finger.

'You should really get yourself a crew,' she told him as she counted the notes. 'If you had a capper playing as well, he could've outbid me when I picked the right card. Marks do that sometimes, you know, just by dumb luck.'

She tensed as Tyrell's confused expression gave way to anger. That hook of his looked nasty, but she didn't think he would use it on her, not with Sheng watching from the bar. Once she'd left, though – that was another story. But if things went to plan, that wouldn't be a problem.

'You cheated,' he said sourly.

She just raised an eyebrow. 'Really? Is *that* how you want to play this?'

He licked his lips and changed tack. 'I need that scrip.'

She folded the plastic notes and slipped them inside her flight suit. 'My father always told me never to gamble what you couldn't afford to lose.'

'Your father sounds like a right laugh.'

'He's dead.'

Tyrell met her gaze. 'Am I supposed to say I'm sorry?'

She shrugged. 'Also, if you want to make money you'd be better off sticking to something you're not so shit at.'

He laughed at that and sat back in the booth, spreading his arms. 'And you could do better, I suppose?'

'I just did.'

'You got lucky.'

'If that's what you want to believe, go ahead.'

He leaned forward. 'I need that money,' he repeated.

'For what?'

He glanced at the door. 'None of your damn business, is what. You have to give me a chance to win it back.'

'Why?'

'Call it professional courtesy.'

'Maybe we can help each other out. I need to get to Spumehead.'

He snorted. 'Good luck with that, sister.'

'What do you mean?'

He eyed the front of her flight suit, but he was clearly more interested in the money than her body. 'Are you going to let me try to win that back?'

'Maybe, but right now we're just talking. Tell me about Spumehead.'

His mouth tightened with frustration. 'You know what a Royal Breach is?' He laughed as she shook her head. 'No, of course you don't. Okay, so every fifty or sixty years the drifters come up in their hundreds, whole blooms of 'em. The 'casters reckon there's one due any time now, and Spumehead is the nearest port. Soon as the news reached this place, every sod with a smoker lit off for there, hoping to get in on the action. There's not a working boat left in Grampus except that old shit heap Sticky Pete and his boys use for scavenging salvage, and *that* wreck wouldn't make it as far as Hannagan's End, let alone Spumehead.'

'*You* have a smoker.'

His eyes narrowed. 'Who are you?'

'Just someone who needs a ride.'

'No way, sister. I'm happy right where I am.' He picked up the cards and began to shuffle. 'Now, what about my money?'

She pulled out the bundle of scrip notes and laid them on the table. 'You can have it all – *if* you take me to Spumehead.' She reached across the table and picked up one of his hands. 'Please.'

He glared at the cash, then pulled his arm away and stood abruptly. 'You know what? Keep the damned money. There are plenty of other suckers in this bubble.' He glanced around the bar, now entirely bereft of suckers, and his jaw tightened. He stalked away.

'Shit,' Orry murmured. She quickly examined the watch she'd lifted from Tyrell's wrist, then slipped it into a pocket. *Why can't people just do what I want them to in the first place?*

The door to the street slammed as Tyrell left the bar. Orry scooped up her winnings and hurried after him, pausing only to slap a few notes on the bar in front of Sheng.

'Be careful!' he called after her as she ran out into the street.

15

ZEPHYR

Tyrell was already halfway down the deserted street that wound back towards the docks. She walked briskly after him, only breaking into a run when he disappeared around a bend.

As she rounded the corner, strong hands grabbed her from behind and pulled her into a narrow alley between two buildings. Tyrell raised a finger to his lips and turned away from her, pressing his back against the rough wall where the alley met the street and raising his hook in one hand. His face looked strained.

Now she could hear footfalls, moving fast, and as a figure ran past the entrance of their alley. Tyrell lunged, sweeping the hook into the man's shoulder and yanking him into the wall. The stranger yowled in pain and Tyrell quickly shoved his hand over the young man's mouth to stifle his cries.

'Shut up!' Tyrell hissed, pressing the hook harder. The man's eyes bulged but his muffled screams reduced to a whimper. 'Search this bastard,' he told Orry.

'What – why? Who is he?' Things were moving too fast; she felt like she needed a moment to adjust. 'What the hell are you doing?'

'Search him!' Tyrell twisted the hook, drawing a sharp hiss of pain.

'*Rama* – okay, okay!'

She patted the young man down and found an antiquated handgun tucked into his belt. She pulled it out and showed it to Tyrell, who grunted.

'You working alone?' he demanded.

Orry realised the young man nodding frantically was little more than a boy, but she busied herself with the pistol, sliding out the magazine and checking its load so she wouldn't have to see the pain in the kid's face.

'Bet you thought you'd shit out a whalestone when you saw me, huh?' Tyrell said. 'How'd you hear about the bounty?'

'A-at the copshop. Spent the night there for . . . drunk and disorderly. Marshal Purvis had it on his desk. Dead or alive, it said, but twice as much alive.'

Orry gripped the pistol tighter at the mention of the marshal. Judging by the expression on Tyrell's face, he felt much the same way.

'That fat fuck Purvis knows? When was this?'

'This morning. Please . . . it hurts.'

Without warning, a ragged-looking girl burst into the alley. 'Let him go!' she screamed, her voice high-pitched and wavering with panic. The little gun she gripped with both hands trembled.

Orry whipped up the old pistol and pointed it at the girl's face. 'Okay, just relax,' she said calmly, somehow managing to keep her voice steady. 'We'll let him go, but you need to lower your gun first.'

'Like *fuck* we will,' Tyrell snarled, yanking the hook and making the boy on the end of it howl.

'Stop it!' the girl screamed, taking a step towards him. 'I'll shoot you – I swear!'

'Shut up, Tyrell,' Orry snapped, then softened her tone. 'If you shoot him,' she told the girl, 'I will shoot you, understand? And I really don't want to have to do that.' She waited a beat for that to sink in. 'Now, what's your name?'

The girl glanced at her. 'Mari.'

'Good, I'm Amber. And who's that?'

Mari's eyes were streaming. 'H-Henry,' she gulped.

'And is he your sweetheart?'

The girl nodded frantically.

'Okay, so Henry wouldn't want to see me shoot you, would he? Just imagine that.'

The very thought made Mari wail.

'But that doesn't have to happen,' Orry continued quickly, 'if you just put down your gun. I promise that Tyrell here will remove his hook and you and Henry can be on your way.'

'R-really?'

Tyrell looked about to say something, but had the sense to clamp his jaw shut.

'Really,' she assured her. *And if he doesn't remove that hook I know who I am going to shoot.*

Mari thought about this for several seconds, then tossed her pistol to the ground.

'Nice work,' Tyrell said. 'Now shoot the bitch.'

'Like hell I will. Let that poor kid go.'

'Poor kid? These two pricks were aiming to kill me.'

'I know the feeling. Let him go.'

Tyrell glared at her, then smiled abruptly. 'No problem at all.'

Henry gasped as the hook slid out of his shoulder and he

sank to the ground. Mari was already running to him and Orry lowered her pistol in relief – but the moment she did, Tyrell darted forward, scooped up Mari's fallen weapon and pointed it at the teenagers. The girl shrank away from the gun, trying to shield Henry's bleeding body with her own.

'What are you doing?' Orry demanded.

'What do you mean?' Tyrell looked genuinely puzzled. 'These arseholes tried to kill me. I'm not the forgiving type.'

'Leave them alone! Look at them: they're terrified.'

He turned his head to stare at her. 'Who the fuck *are* you, anyway? Piss off and tell some other poor bugger what to do.'

Orry had had enough. She raised her gun but he turned quickly to face her, putting the two of them into a stand-off as they each stared down the other's barrel.

'Leave them alone,' she repeated firmly.

He chuckled. 'Are you really prepared to die over these two bottom-feeders?'

'Are you?'

They stood there for what felt like an eternity. A bead of sweat rolled down her temple. Tyrell wore a quiet smile, as if he got into this sort of situation every day, but she could see the tension beneath his feigned nonchalance.

'Well, well, well,' a horribly familiar voice said from behind her, 'what *do* we have here?' As she started to turn the harsh *ch-chack* of a shotgun's action made her freeze. Tyrell's confident smile bled away as he stared over her shoulder.

'Now, you know me, Tyrell,' Marshal Purvis' voice continued easily, 'so you will believe me when I say that this shotgun I'm holding is loaded with enough discarding sabot to turn everyone in that alley into mincemeat. Am I bullshitting you?'

Tyrell's face was strained. 'I believe you, Purvis.'

'That's *Marshal* Purvis, you son of a bitch. Now drop that fucking piece. You too, girly.' When Tyrell hesitated, the marshal added, 'Beeto's offering twice as much if you're still alive, so don't make me kill you, son. It would piss me off.'

The card-sharp met his gaze, then slowly placed his pistol on the ground. He motioned for Orry to do the same and she did, a cold dread settling over her.

'Now kick 'em away,' Purvis ordered.

The guns clattered to the side of the alley and Orry turned slowly to face him. He smiled widely.

'Well, lookee here: a twofer,' he said, running his eyes over her, letting them settle on her chest.

'That's an interesting bulge you've acquired since we last met. Care to show me what you're hiding in there?'

Slowly, she lowered the zip of her flight suit and extracted a fistful of her winnings. Purvis' eyes sparked with interest as he gazed at the money and Orry's pulse quickened as an idea formed in her mind.

'You know what that is, girly?'

'Yeah,' she answered. 'Mine.'

He chuckled. 'That there is what we in the law business call *evidence*. Hand it over.'

She stepped cautiously forward, stopping a metre from his shotgun. 'You want it, Marshal?' she asked, fanning the notes out.

'Don't fuck with me,' he growled.

'Here, then,' she said. '*Have it!*' She flung the money into the air, letting it fall like leaves over him.

His head went up instinctively and she lunged for the

shotgun, grabbing its barrel and forcing the weapon upwards. Purvis cursed and the weapon went off, blasting a large hole high in the alley wall, but she had her arm between the shotgun and his flabby chest and now she heaved. Purvis lost his grip and staggered back into the wall as the gun clattered across the ground. Tyrell took off, haring out of the alley, and Orry saw her only chance of getting out of this bubble disappearing with him. Purvis lunged at her, wheezing, but she dodged easily and dashed after the card-sharp.

She spotted him immediately, pounding towards the docks, and set off in pursuit. He was heading straight for the solitary smoker she'd seen earlier, the cigar-shaped tube with stubby triangular wings resting in a docking cradle. The craft had an antique quality that appealed to the engineer in her; the bare metal hull showed every rivet and as she drew closer she could see where dents had been beaten out over the years. Small windows formed a windscreen at the front and round portholes ran down the fuselage to a door above the short wings, which she now saw were in fact only the tips; the rest had been retracted into the lower hull. A tall tail rose above a blackened exhaust nozzle at the stern. Tyrell had leaped onto a wing and run to the door in the vessel's curving side before he realised she was following.

A look of annoyance appeared on his face, but after a moment's indecision he yelled, 'Release the cradle!' and gestured towards a lever on the dockside before disappearing inside the craft. She ran to the lever and hauled it back. Clamps around the smoker released with a hiss of hydraulics and she hurried to the door – only to find it locked.

'Oh *hell* no,' she muttered, looking around.

Marshal Purvis appeared at the far end of the dock and spotted her immediately. He shouted something she couldn't catch, then set off towards her at a waddling run. She hopped onto the cradle and ran nimbly around to the craft's nose, where she could see Tyrell sitting behind the cockpit windows.

She banged on the windscreen but he just grinned and continued flicking switches and turning knobs. 'Let me in, you backstabbing bastard!' she shouted.

He cupped his ear and held up his hands in a helpless gesture. Thrusting her hand into her pocket, she pulled out the slender wristwatch she'd lifted from him earlier and dangled it in front of the glass by its strap. Tyrell's smug face turned furious. Trying to ignore the marshal's wheezing yells, which were getting closer by the second, she held the watch out over the oily, litter-strewn water sloshing like junkyard broth hundreds of metres below. Tyrell's lips formed a curse, but he left his seat and Orry got back to the wing just as he opened the door.

'Give it,' he said. His jaw tightened as she shoved the watch inside her flight suit and zipped it up.

Shot clattered nearby as Purvis fired. *Out of range*, she thought, *but not for long*. Tyrell must have realised the same thing because he moved aside. She fell through the door and he slammed it closed behind her. The smoker rang as Purvis' next shot hit the hull.

Inside, the craft was cramped and musty. Two rack-like beds were bolted down, one on either side of the narrow cabin, and a small table folded down from one curved bulkhead opposite what looked to be a pretty primitive galley. Tyrell ran to the end of the cabin where an open door led to the cockpit. Orry followed him, picking her way carefully through all manner of junk.

The smoker's controls were primitive: a stick and pedals, and banks of switches and buttons. The instrument panel appeared to be made from yellowing bone and was edged with the same lustrous leather as Tyrell's jacket; it made *Dainty Jane*'s obsolete cockpit look bleeding-edge.

He dropped into the pilot's seat and reached under the panel. There was a solid *clunk* and a hum filled the cockpit. Lights illuminated across the panel.

'What the hell was *that* all about?' she demanded. 'Why is Purvis after you?'

'A misunderstanding.'

'Really? Because it sounded to me like you have a bounty on your head – dead or alive.'

He threw a series of switches. 'That is possibly technically correct.'

'Why? What have you done?'

'Can we get out of this goddamned bubble before we swap life stories?'

The lights flickered, then died and the hum faded away. He cursed and rammed a fist into the side of the console. The hum resumed and the lights relit, strong and steady.

'That-a-girl,' he crooned.

'Is this thing even going to make it to Spumehead?' Orry asked.

'Hey!' He whipped round in his seat, raising one finger. 'If you don't like *Zephyr* I can drop you off any time.' He turned back to the controls and muttered, 'Preferably in open aether.'

Outside the cockpit windows they could see Purvis, standing on the dockside and aiming his shotgun at Tyrell. When he fired,

Orry couldn't stop herself flinching at the shower of impacts which left the window even more scratched.

'We really should go,' she said.

'I concur.' Tyrell flicked one more switch, then reached down and pumped a handle several times. His finger hovered over a worn red button for a second or two, his lips moving as if in prayer, then stabbed down on it. The whole smoker shuddered and Orry gripped the back of his seat in alarm.

'What's happening?'

An explosion sounded from the stern, followed by a coughing, gurgling roar. Oily black smoke drifted past the windows, making Purvis choke and cover his mouth.

'Just starting her up,' Tyrell said happily, checking a bank of dials. 'Listen to that purr.'

Personally, Orry thought Zephyr sounded like a Mendulonian buffalo coughing up a lung, but each to their own.

He nudged the throttle and the smoker began to move surprisingly smoothly out of its cradle and away from the dock. Another rain of metallic clatters peppered the hull, but Zephyr was already picking up speed and heading for the exit lock in a wide, descending curve.

Tyrell punched a code into a keypad, a green light illuminated above it and ahead of them giant fans creaked into life as the lock doors swung ponderously open. The airlock cycled and they sailed out of the other end.

He extended a hand. 'Watch.'

'Are you going to behave yourself?'

'Don't play with me, sister.'

'Don't call me sister, dickhead.'

He scowled. 'Just give me my watch. Please.'

'What about our arrangement?'

His eyebrows shot up. '*What* arrangement?'

'Passage to Spumehead.'

'You're really beginning to piss me off—'

'I'm here now. Just point this thing at Spumehead and when we get there you'll get your money.'

He glowered at her. 'I want my watch before we go anywhere.'

'Okay.' She hesitated, judging how far to push things, and decided to risk it. 'There is one more thing: when we get there, I want you to help me find a scooper.'

'Now why the hell would I do that?'

'Because I'm a stranger around here and I need your help. And if you do, you'll never see me again.'

Tyrell barked out a humourless laugh. 'Half the money up front and I'll think about it.'

'Agreed.'

He ran his fingers through his hair, considering, then held out his hand. They shook, and she extracted the remaining notes and split them roughly. She passed half to Tyrell, but as she tucked the rest away it occurred to her how vulnerable she was on his craft.

Seeing her eyes drop to the bloodstained hook at his belt, he grinned. 'You're wondering if I'm going to kill you in the night and take the rest of it.'

'Are you?'

'We shook. I may be many things, but I never break my word.'

'Good to hear.' She would still be sleeping with one eye open, just in case. She reached into her flight suit and handed Tyrell his watch. He checked it for damage before carefully strapping it back around his wrist.

'How did you know?' he asked.

'That it means so much to you?' She shrugged. 'You make it pretty obvious.'

'I do?' He turned back to the controls. 'It was my mother's.'

'She's dead?' she asked, and he gave a non-committal grunt.

Orry stared at the clouds whipping past; *Zephyr* turned out to be every bit as fast as her rocket-like appearance had suggested.

'How long until we get there?'

'Long enough. Grab a rack' – he jerked his thumb towards the rear compartment – 'and get some rest.'

'What about you?'

He reached down and held up a half-empty bottle of a viscous blue liquid. 'Don't worry about me, sister. I'll be fine.'

16

BROAD-SPECTRUM ALGORITHM

Ethan's integuary woke him at four in the morning, Hardhaven time, and he lay on his bed for a moment, staring blankly at the overhead before remembering where they were, and why.

Dainty Jane had been docked at Hardhaven bubble – which turned out to be a cluster of twelve variously sized habispheres that reminded him of a tightly packed molecule – for more than a day. Everything about the place felt archaic, and that included the tech. It had been disappointingly easy for him to subvert the public systems and collate a list of all the escape pods recovered from the EDC galleon, and since none of the occupants had matched Orry's description, he'd set a broad-spectrum search algorithm running. Six hours later, it appeared to have finally come up with something.

He skimmed the report. Shouting, 'Yes!' he leaped from his bunk and hurried across the passageway to Mender's cabin.

The old man opened the door with a scowl on his face. 'It's four in the fucking morning, kid. This had better be good.'

'You know I set this search running?' Ethan gabbled. 'Well, it's come up with something – I think I've found her.' He knew he was talking too quickly and forced himself to slow down. 'There's this backwater bubble called Grampus, not too far from where we thought she'd come down. The search found a report from a local marshal there – name of Purvis – to somebody called Notable Beeto. Sounds like the marshal almost caught some fugitive that this Beeto guy is looking for, but he got away.'

'What does this have to do with your sister?'

'The fugitive had someone with him, a girl: early twenties, orange hair, wearing a red flight suit. Sound familiar?'

Mender rubbed his face wearily. 'You get that, *Jane*?'

'I've already laid in a course for Grampus,' the ship replied.

Mender's face was grim. 'Then let's go and have a chat with this Marshal Purvis.'

17

CLOSE ENCOUNTER

Tyrell joined Orry in *Zephyr*'s rear cabin a couple of hours into the voyage. The consumptive gurgle and cough of the engines was stopping her from sleeping and she was grateful for some company, even his.

'Are you going to tell me about this bounty now?' she asked as he collapsed onto the rack opposite. 'If I'm locked up in here with a wanted man I think I deserve to know what you did.'

'I never asked you to come.'

'I saved your life back there and you tried to abandon me, so frankly, I think you owe me.'

He shifted onto his side in the rack, cushioning his cheek on his bent arm to gaze across the narrow cabin at her. 'How about this?' he said. 'You tell me why you're so keen to get to Spumehead – and why you want to find a scooper – and I'll tell you about Notable Beeto.'

'Notable Beetle? Is that a name?'

'Beet-*o*! Beeto is. Notable is a title. He's a high-up in the League.'

'What league?'

Tyrell frowned. 'Seriously? Where are you even from?'

'What league?' she repeated.

'The *Whaling* League,' he said incredulously. 'They kind of run things round here? And by "run things", I mean they control *everything*.'

'Sounds like this Notable Beetle is a powerful man.'

'Very.'

'So what did you do to him?'

A faint smile appeared on Tyrell's face. 'It wasn't what I did to him that was the problem, more what I did to his wife.'

'I see,' Orry said coldly.

'I don't think you do.'

'Then tell me.'

He chuckled. 'You first.'

She plucked at a loose thread in the worn bedding. 'There's really nothing much to tell. I'm looking for someone and apparently he's holed up on one of the scoopers' deep rigs. Trouble is,' she admitted, 'I don't even know what a scooper is.'

'Looking for who?'

'Just someone.'

'And why do you want to find him?'

'Tell me about Beetle's wife,' she said, changing the subject.

'Ah, Meliflua.' He rolled onto his back and put his hands behind his head. 'She was a beauty, that one. His second wife, half his age – he married her after his first wife died.'

'What did she die of?'

'A skiing accident, according to Beeto, not that anybody believes that. Rumour was she'd found out about what he was doing with Meliflua on the side and was planning to divorce him, which in her eyes meant taking him for every damn penny. You can draw your own conclusions.'

'You think he had her killed? Wasn't there an investigation?'

He gave a bitter laugh. 'Beeto's a whaling nabob. He owns one of the largest flotillas in the aether – and that's not all he owns.'

'So if you're rich enough, you can do as you please around here?'

'Now you're getting it. Does that surprise you?'

'I come from the Fountainhead,' she said, 'so no, it doesn't surprise me.'

He grunted. 'I'm a simple man,' he continued. 'As long as I've food in my belly and fuel in the tank, I'm happy as a scooper with a new hat. I do have one weakness, though.'

'You amaze me.'

He waved a hand airily. 'I fall in love too easily.'

'Love, or lust?'

'A little of both, perhaps. Is that such a bad thing?'

'It is when it's someone else's wife.'

He sighed wistfully. 'She was something to see, Meliflua. Covered in golden down as soft as silk.'

'In *fur*? Like, all over?'

'Pretty much. She came from Falgex, you see, like Beeto. It's a godforsaken ball of ice somewhere out on the edge of this system and it's so damned cold, Meliflua told me, the original colonists decided to tweak some deactivated monkey genes or some shit.'

'Okay, so you fell head over heels in lust with this hairy chick?'

'I did. She was unhappy with Beeto, but she was scared about what he would do to her if she asked for a divorce.'

'I can see why.'

'We were going to run away, you see, start a new life together

124

somewhere Beeto would never find us.'

Orry might have just met Tyrell, but she didn't think he was really the sort to settle down. She wondered how much of his tale was true. 'So what happened?'

'Beeto found out about us.' Tyrell's oil-stained finger picked at an exposed rivet. 'He burst in on us – he was supposed to be away for the night. I only escaped by jumping out of Meliflua's bedroom window – naked as the day I was born, I might add.'

'What about Meliflua?'

'Last I heard, he'd locked her away. I doubt I'll ever see her again.'

Orry's silence was telling.

'What?' he asked, looking over at her.

'Oh, nothing.'

'No, you obviously have something to say. Go ahead.'

'All right. It's just, you say you're in love with this woman, but you give up at the first obstacle, so I have to wonder if you're really as in love with her as you think.'

'Well, that shows how much you know! Notable Beeto is quite an obstacle.'

'Don't get upset,' she said guilelessly. 'I'm sure you love her dearly.'

'I do!'

'That's what I said.'

He swung his legs off the rack and sat on the edge, glaring. 'Now, look here—'

She waved a dismissive hand. 'I'm tired. I'll think I'll get some rest before we arrive.'

'But—'

She rolled over to face the bulkhead, leaving him spluttering.

After a few seconds she heard him laugh ruefully. 'You're pretty good at reading people, aren't you?' he said.

She rolled back to him again. 'I get it from my father.'

'I really did love her. Once.'

'But not any more?'

He cocked his head to one side. 'Does that make me fickle?'

'It depends,' she said. 'Have you got your eye on anyone else?'

He gazed at her. 'I might.'

She returned his look for a few seconds and was surprised to find that her heart was beating faster. Then she burst out laughing.

The rhythmic roar of the engine skipped, making the smoker shudder, and Tyrell got to his feet, looking worried. The engine hiccoughed again, then faded and died.

'Problem?' she enquired.

'No problem,' he told her, 'it's probably just the exchange manifold. I'll have it fixed in a jiffy.' He headed for a door she presumed led to an engineering compartment in the stern.

'You want a hand? I know my way around an engine.'

His patronising laugh made her want to strangle him. 'Why don't you go up top? Sun's going down; there's nothing more beautiful.' He paused to toss her a respirator from a hook on the bulkhead, then disappeared through the door.

Well, if he doesn't want help . . . She stood and pulled the respirator over her nose and mouth. A short ladder led to a hatch in the overhead. She climbed cautiously out onto the gentle curve of *Zephyr*'s upper hull, listening to fans kicking into life as the swirling gas drifted into the smoker, then let the hatch fall shut behind her.

Through the strata of clouds, the vast disk of Morhelion's

sun burned brightly just above the hazy horizon. Tyrell was right: it was a breath-taking sight. The sun sank slowly and as it met the horizon, fire raced through the clouds, illuminating cascading rainbows of exquisite beauty, until at last the colours started slowly withdrawing, sucked back into the disk as it vanished, leaving only a gentle glow above the horizon.

The drifting aether was mesmerising. Orry sat cross-legged on the cold metal hull to enjoy the last of the dying light. Morhelion was an odd world, she decided, even by the standards of the rim, and what little she had seen of it intrigued her.

A haunting cry broke her reverie. Clambering to her knees, she shuffled closer to the edge of the hull and looked over. Some distance below, a vast shadow moved beneath the aether, although it was difficult to make out details in the crepuscular light. She watched, hardly breathing, as the shadow grew larger, rising from the depths of Morhelion's atmosphere.

The colossal creature drew level with *Zephyr* and simply hung there, twenty metres away. It reminded her of an enormous jellyfish, although it was covered in gnarled, pitted hide that looked more like tree bark than skin. Moving carefully on the slippery metal of the hull, she edged forward and slid down onto one triangular wing. Taking her life in her hands, she leaned out; when she peered down, she could make out dozens of thick tentacles dangling in the soupy clouds below the creature.

She stared at it, staggered by its sheer scale. The squat oval thing was huge, at least two hundred metres in diameter, far larger than *Dainty Jane*. Fronds fluttered along its flanks – then her breath caught as she saw an eye the size of a house blink languidly. The haunting sound repeated, sending shivers down her spine, and she felt oddly drawn to this vast, alien creature.

Time stood still as the eye regarded her – and then, with a final echoing hoot, its pocked hide sank back into the depths.

'You're lucky,' Tyrell said from behind her, making her start.

'Don't sneak up on me like that!'

He grinned and came to stand beside her, watching the creature's shrinking shadow. 'Not many people see one up close like that – not without looking down the sight of a harpoon, at any rate.'

'What *was* it?' she breathed, still completely overawed.

He looked oddly at her. 'You really are new around here, aren't you? That was a drifter – or an aeriform leviathan, if you want to get fancy about it.'

'It was *enormous*.'

'That? That was just a juvenile. Wait till you see the adults.'

She stared at him, trying to judge if he was serious. 'It was beautiful – ugly, but beautiful, you know?'

He nodded. 'There are fewer of them every season. It won't be long before the League's hunted them to extinction.'

'They *hunt* them?' The notion of hunting the placid creature she had just seen filled Orry with anger.

'The League licences the flotillas,' Tyrell explained, 'and the flotillas kill the drifters and sell the gases they have inside them back to the League, together with their hide and oil and bone and everything else. The bastards have the whole thing sewn up.'

'You don't sound as if you like them much.'

He snorted. 'They take everything and give nothing back. *Everybody* hates them.'

'So why don't you do something about it?'

'Like what, exactly? You have any idea how much leviathan products sell for in the Fountainhead? Anyone disrupts that trade and we'll have Company warships collapsing in.'

Orry looked at the drifter's departing shadow, feeling a familiar anger tight in her chest.

The shadow faded.

'Anyway, engine's fixed,' Tyrell said cheerily. 'You'd better come back inside.'

As she followed him in, Orry thought she heard a final, plaintive cry echo back from somewhere deep below her.

18

RED TAPE

Grampus was a provincial bubble, lacking the facilities to deal with even smaller starships like *Dainty Jane*; it was apparently able to cater only for the odd-looking craft that Ethan had seen puttering around Hardhaven bubble amid clouds of pollution. He could see why the locals called them smokers. Since docking at Grampus was impossible, Mender was forced to bring *Jane* to a halt a few hundred metres from the habisphere's lock and simply wait to be noticed. He insisted on trying the comms, despite *Jane*'s repeated assurances that the signals wouldn't penetrate Morhelion's atmosphere over even such a short distance, then lapsed into a disgruntled silence.

After a couple of hours, the impressive-looking lock mechanism opened and a vessel emerged.

'Rama,' Ethan said, 'look at that heap of crap.'

Mender groaned. 'Junkdogs.'

Ethan studied the approaching craft. It looked like a floating collection of junkyard parts with a crane folded up halfway along its length. Spewing oily black smoke, the vessel juddered to a halt nearby and two men in respirators and filthy coveralls emerged from a booth-like wheelhouse.

'Kid,' Mender said, 'go fetch my little lady, will you?'

Deciding that finding his sister was more important than objecting to being treated like an errand boy, Ethan hurried down to the old man's cabin and located his Fabretti Model 500. The pistol with the ridiculously oversized barrel gleamed among the detritus of Mender's life.

When he arrived back at the ladder up to the cockpit he found the old man waiting for him.

Mender checked the Fabretti carefully before strapping on its holster, then handed Ethan a snub-nosed sneakpiece. 'Here,' he said.

He looked from the miniature pistol to Mender's hand-cannon and raised his eyebrows.

'If people see too many guns, things tend to get difficult,' the old man explained. 'Tuck that away and only use it if you need to. Don't worry, it'll do the job if you're close enough – just don't expect it to get through body armour.'

Ethan started to tuck the pistol into his front pocket, but Mender held out a hand to stop him. 'Not there – that's the first place bad guys will look. Stick it down the front of your trousers, right down by your balls.' He gave a rare, twisted smile. 'You *do* have balls, don't you?'

'Inappropriate,' Ethan muttered, but he did as the old man advised. The pistol nestled uncomfortably in his groin, but Mender was right, it couldn't be seen through his baggy cargo trousers.

He followed Mender to *Dainty Jane*'s dorsal airlock, fixed a respirator over his nose and mouth, sucked down a couple of breaths of rubbery air, then made an *okay* sign with his fingers.

'Don't go anywhere, *Jane*,' Mender said.

'I won't,' the ship replied. 'Please be careful. I don't like being out of contact with you.'

'We'll be fine.' Mender pulled on his own full-face rebreather before cycling the airlock and leading the way up a ladder onto *Jane*'s upper hull.

The junk platform drifted closer, conned by a wiry man in the wheelhouse. The other two crew waited on deck until they were within hailing distance.

'Too big to fit through the lock?' yelled the smaller of the two. Ethan couldn't guess how old he was: dirty blond hair poked out from under his cap and his voice was muffled by his respirator, but he was hunched over like an old man.

'Can you take us in?' Mender bellowed back.

'Can do. You got business in Grampus bubble?'

'Wouldn't be here otherwise.'

When it became clear that further details would not be forthcoming, the man on the smoker yelled, 'Hundred notes each for passage. Same again to bring you back out.'

'How much is that in real money?' Mender muttered, and when Ethan told him his face hardened. 'Goddamn leeches.' He raised his voice again: 'A hundred for us both – in *and* out.'

The junkdog laughed. 'This ain't no negotiation. Ours is the only smoker in the bubble right now. You want in or not?'

Mender let loose a string of curses under his breath. 'All right,' he shouted at last, 'we're coming aboard. You first, kid.'

The larger of the crewmen extended a narrow gangway, which Ethan eyed with dismay as it rested against *Dainty Jane*'s hull. The junkdog pilot had manoeuvred as close as he dared, but there were still several metres to traverse. *Jane* was rock-steady relative to the habisphere, but the smoker was drifting a little as the pilot in the wheelhouse made constant adjustments. If Ethan lost his balance, he would disappear into the swirling gases below.

'You going or what?' Mender prompted, and Ethan gritted his teeth and started to run quickly across the gangway. He was halfway there when the junkdogs' platform suddenly lurched upwards and his feet left the narrow plank. He came down off-balance and desperately hurled himself forward, landing heavily on the rusting metal plates of the smoker's deck.

He looked back at Mender, concerned about his bad leg, but unlike him, the old man was as sure-footed as a Mimosan crag goat, shuffling easily across despite the jerking motion.

When the hunched junkdog who'd spoken earlier came closer, Ethan could see his lined face had a sickly pallor, with skin flaking off amid bristly stubble. His fat companion had an ugly scowl as he hauled in the gangplank.

'They call me Sticky Pete,' the older one said, 'and this here is my son, Janco. That there's my other boy, Rudi.' He pointed at the wheelhouse where a spindly runt of a young man who didn't look much older than Ethan waved through the cracked window. His hand was bandaged and he sported a black eye.

'I'm Mender. The kid's called Ethan.'

Sticky Pete shaded his eyes and regarded *Dainty Jane*. 'That's a big ole ship you got there. How many crew does a craft like that need?'

'Enough,' Mender said vaguely, and the old junkdog grinned a little too broadly behind his mask.

He looked his passengers over, eyes lingering for a moment

on the Fabretti and for even longer on Ethan. When he moistened his cracked lips, Ethan felt horribly uncomfortable.

'So, what brings you to Grampus bubble in such a fine vessel?'

Mender eyed him, considering, then said confidentially, 'Got some business with a Marshal Purvis. You know him?'

Sticky Pete narrowed his eyes for a moment. 'Might do. Could arrange an introduction, for another fifty.'

'I think I'll find him myself.'

The junkdog shrugged and held out a hand. 'Two hundred for the passage.'

Mender looked at how close the bubble was, then grimaced as he handed over several of the Whaling League scrip notes they'd picked up in Hardhaven.

'Nice doing business,' Pete said with a grin, tucking the money away. He gave a thumbs-up to his son in the wheelhouse and the smoker's spluttering engine coughed out a great gout of black smoke, lurched forward and clanked towards the lock gates.

Ethan looked around, fascinated, as they passed out of the lock and into the habisphere's interior.

'Place is an armpit,' Mender commented as they traversed Grampus bubble's deserted basin. He sniffed the muggy air. 'Smells like one too.'

Ethan had to agree; even Mender's socks were fragrant by comparison with this place. He was about to ask Sticky Pete why the basin was empty when something caught his eye. He gripped Mender's arm, his heart beating suddenly faster, and they both stared at the battered, blackened escape pod as they drew alongside a wharf.

This thing working? Mender sent, and the sudden voice in

Ethan's head made him start.

Yeah, he replied. *The habisphere must be shielded – not sure how effective it'll be, though. We might still lose contact if we get too far apart.*

Good enough. Stick to me like glue, then. And don't mention that pod – let me do the talking.

You got it.

The smoker pulled alongside the wharf with a thump and the engine coughed to a ragged stop. Pete and his sons hopped ashore and Ethan and Mender followed them – but the moment they set foot on the wharf, a corpulent man in a dark blue police uniform stepped into view, holding a brutal-looking shotgun.

'Welcome to Grampus,' he said as he approached, sweat glistening on his jowls. 'I'm marshal for this here bubble. Name's Purvis.'

Mender didn't look happy. 'You greet every visitor personally, Marshal?'

'Only the ones with a starship. What's your business here?'

'We came to see you, actually,' Ethan said.

'You did? Well, ain't that nice. But before we go any further, there's a couple of things I need to ask – red tape, you understand. First off: have you got a permit to carry that cannon you've got strapped on there?'

Mender looked down at his Fabretti. 'This old thing?' he said lightly. 'Didn't know I needed one.'

Marshal Purvis smiled nastily. 'Afraid you do. Luckily, I can fix you up with one, for a reasonable fee, naturally. Until then I'm gonna have to ask you to hand that firearm over – nice and easy, like.'

I fucking knew it, Mender sent. *It's a goddamn shakedown. Get ready.*

For what? Ethan replied, alarmed, but Mender was already reaching for the Fabretti.

'Ah, ah, ah,' Purvis chided, raising his shotgun, and Mender's hand froze.

Janco reappeared holding an ancient fletcher and went to stand next to the marshal.

'Two fingers, my friend,' Purvis continued, 'and lay it on the ground.'

Mender did as he was ordered and Sticky Pete moved in, picked up the Fabretti and handed it to the marshal, who examined it with interest while Pete searched Mender for other hardware. Ethan's heart sank when the junkdog gestured for him to raise his arms. It took just moments to find the hard edge of the sneakpiece nestling in his groin.

'What do we have here?' Pete crooned, and beckoned with his hand. 'Nice and easy.'

Ethan extracted the weapon and handed it to the junkdog, who tucked it into his belt.

'What do you want?' Mender growled.

'Anyone else on that ship of yours?' Purvis asked.

'What's that got to do with anyth—' Mender stopped and looked incredulous. 'You have to be kidding – you're after the *ship*?'

'You'd better hope whoever else is on board likes you,' Purvis replied, 'which seems doubtful. But don't worry, I'm a reasonable man. I aim to give 'em a choice: hand over the ship, or we start cutting bits off you.'

'You're crazy,' Mender said. 'We're not talking about one of your piece-of-shit smokers here – this is a *starship*. Where the hell d'you think you're going to sell it?'

'You let me worry about that,' Purvis answered. 'Now shut the fuck up and get moving.'

'Where are you taking us?' Ethan asked.

The marshal's answering smile made his skin crawl. '*You* ain't going anywhere, pretty boy.' He turned to Pete. 'You think you can manage to keep a hold of this one till I get back? Your retard kid ain't gonna let him escape this time?'

Annoyance twisted the old junkdog's face. 'Sure can, Floyd. You can trust me.'

Purvis snorted, and revulsion churned Ethan's stomach. *Is this what happened to Orry?*

Mender, beside him, had tensed at Purvis' words, but the marshal was clearly expecting a reaction and took a cautious step back, aiming his shotgun at Mender's face. 'Don't worry, old man,' he said, 'ain't no one interested in anything a withered bag of bones like you can provide.'

Mender got hold of himself with a visible struggle, then took a moment to gaze at each of the men in turn. Rudi paled under his steady glare, but the others just stared back.

'If you touch this boy,' Mender said quietly, 'I will kill every one of you.'

The simple, stark statement of intent sent a shiver down Ethan's spine and wiped the leer from Pete's face, but Purvis just laughed.

'I can see us two're gonna get on *real* fine,' he said, a hard edge beneath his humour. 'I do love a comedian.' His laughter stopped. 'Now move.' He gestured with the shotgun and after a final concerned glance at Ethan, Mender limped reluctantly away.

Don't let these twisted bastards touch you, kid, he sent, but the transmission was already beginning to break up as the distance between them increased. *And whatever you do, don't—*

His words cut out.

Don't what? Ethan sent desperately. *Don't what?*

19

SPUMEHEAD

Spumehead turned out to be a group of five huge habispheres, much larger than Grampus bubble. Orry stared out of a porthole at the bewildering variety of craft packing its basins as Tyrell squeezed *Zephyr* into a narrow mooring between the bulging sides of two enormous smokers.

'Are they freighters?' she called to him, her voice sounding unnaturally loud in the metal tube as the rumbling, hissing roar of the engine died away.

'Whalers,' he answered, emerging from the cockpit. 'Every ship is a whaler right now, but those two were designed for it. This lot will be joining the other flotillas soon.' He shrugged his jacket over his white shirt and looked around the cabin to make sure he hadn't forgotten anything.

'That jacket's made from leviathan skin, isn't it?' she asked, looking at the distinctive oily sheen of the leather. Now she knew what it was, the garment repulsed her.

He held it open for her to see. 'Finest whalehide,' he said proudly. 'I won it in a card game. Well, I took it from somebody who accused me of cheating in a card game. Same thing really.' He headed for the door.

She watched with cold eyes as he passed, then followed him out of *Zephyr* and into the shadow of the whaler beside them, its hull towering above the wharf. She stood and stared up at the bulging wall of corroded metal that seemed to go on for ever.

'So these leviathans live down deep, right?' she said. 'I mean, deep enough to crush a smoker?'

'Yeah, it would flatten that thing to the size of a whalestone.'

'So if you can only hunt them when they come up to this part of the aether, why do they come up?'

He started walking. 'They come up to mate. Don't ask me why, I only know it's something to do with the composition of the gases up here. The League employs forecasters who predict where the blooms will breach. They're wrong more than half the time, far as I can tell, but if they're right and if a smoker can get there in time – *and* if it manages to cable a drifter without getting its back broken – then the crew make a fuck-ton of money.'

'How do these forecasters know when and where the leviathans will rise?' Orry asked.

'Best you ask one of them that. I know they have some pretty powerful tech in Hardhaven bubble.'

They passed plenty of gangs of mechs making hasty repairs and crew busily loading crates on to ships before they reached the end of the wharf.

'It all sounds like a lot of "ifs",' Orry said.

Tyrell led her towards the nearest lift. 'Yeah, the whole thing's a gamble, with the odds stacked against you every step of the way.'

'Then why does everyone do it?'

He shrugged. 'It's a living. If it weren't for the drifters, this colony would have died centuries ago.'

They reached the lift, but while they waited for it to arrive, a bear of a man dressed from head to foot in leviathan hide passed them – then stopped abruptly and backed up.

'Vance Tyrell? As I live and breathe! You've got a pair on you, to be showing your face back here.'

A grin split Tyrell's face. 'Lindqvist, you fat fucking arsehole! How you doing, shipmate?'

The big whaler pounded Tyrell on his back, making him stagger, as Orry watched with amusement. 'I'm good,' Lindqvist rumbled, then threw his arms open to encompass the whaling vessels all around them. 'The 'casters are saying this will be the biggest breach in a century – we're all gonna be rich!'

'Rich or dead,' Tyrell said drily, making the man bellow with laughter again.

'Still the same old Handsome Vance. I'm surprised to see you here, boy, considering. That arsepiece Beeto has raised the bounty again – you'd better watch your back.'

'Don't worry, mate, I'm not stopping. Just dropping something off.'

The whaler's eyes followed his to settle on Orry, and he chuckled. 'Pretty young thing,' he observed.

'Hello,' she replied, smiling. Somehow, it was difficult to be offended by Lindqvist.

'You want to watch this one,' he advised her. 'Girl in every port. Boys too, I hear.'

Tyrell spread his arms: '*Mea culpa.*'

'I'll be careful,' she assured him.

Lindqvist turned back to Tyrell and punched him good-naturedly in the arm. 'So, you coming to get rich with me? There's still room on *Voyager*'s killing floor, even for a weedy streak of piss like you.'

'As tempting as it sounds to be violently killed in any one of a hundred gruesome ways,' Tyrell replied, rubbing his arm ruefully, 'my whaling days are behind me.'

His friend shrugged. 'Your loss. I'll buy you a drink when I find my whalestone.'

'I won't hold my breath.'

'Excuse me,' Orry interrupted, 'but do you happen to know if there are any scoopers in Spumehead at the moment?'

Tyrell shot her an irritated look, but Lindqvist just dragged dirty fingers through a dirtier beard as he thought. 'Heard one of 'em came in a couple of days back for supplies. I think Vigo's been trying to relieve him of his funds.'

Tyrell groaned.

'What?' Orry asked.

'Vigo Vestergaard owns the Whalestone Crown Casino,' Lindqvist explained with an evil smile. 'Let's just say your man here has some history in that place.'

'She still working there?' Tyrell asked, and when the whaler nodded, he sighed. 'Maybe I will come whaling after all.' The lift doors ground open and he turned towards them.

Lindqvist guffawed and punched him again, before slinging his kit bag over one shoulder and giving an airy salute. 'Good luck with Giselle. You'll need it.'

'Try not to die,' Tyrell shot back.

The whaler winked at Orry and walked away.

She stepped into the battered metal cage, which smelled of sweat and oil. As they descended, she said, 'So you used to be a whaler?'

'Not by choice.'

'There's always a choice.'

His eyes remained fixed on the interwoven wires in front of him. 'That may be true in the Fountainhead,' he said tightly, 'but not out here.'

'I—'

'I don't want to talk about it.'

'Fine, whatever. Will you at least show me where this casino place—'

'The Crown.'

'—where it is?'

'I'll show you. We had a deal and I won't go back on it. I'll find your scooper, then I'm out of here – *with* the rest of my money.'

'We do have a deal and you'll get your money.'

The lift juddered to a halt and they stepped into a wide tunnel leading out of the basin and through an open seal into a neighbouring habisphere. As they passed the seal, Orry saw a wall of people engaged in what appeared to be the biggest party she had ever seen.

'It's not normally like this,' Tyrell said, his eyes suddenly alight with excitement. 'I was born here – the place is dead for most of the year.'

She could feel the heat of close-pressed bodies as Tyrell pushed his way into the crowd and found herself overwhelmed by the mass of humanity crammed in on every side. Revellers staggered past, clutching each other for support. A woman in front of her bent over, puked copiously, raised a bottle to her lips and continued walking, having hardly broken her stride. Orry stepped over the pool of greasy vomit.

The buildings were different to those she had seen in Grampus bubble. These were supported by yellowing beams that Orry now realised must be leviathan bone, and many of the walls themselves were sheets of shimmering, gnarled hide. As far as she could make out, a lot of the buildings in this part of the bubble were bars. As she examined one of them, she noticed a couple screwing against the wall, in plain sight, and looked away, flustered.

Tyrell saw her blushing and grinned. 'They know they might be dead tomorrow,' he explained, then pointed. 'Come on, it's this way.'

He led her across the street towards a three-storey building festooned with a multitude of flashing, multicoloured signs gaudily promising winnings beyond anyone's wildest dreams. The place was rammed with patrons and thick in smoke. The stink of old leviathan hide and cheap perfume fought with the underlying stench of vomit, thinly veiled by bleach. The roar of conversation all but drowned the music thumping from caged speakers near the ceiling.

'Give me some scrip,' Tyrell said, holding out a hand. 'A hundred ought to do it.'

'What for?' Orry asked, suspicious.

'Do you want to find your scooper or not?' He gestured with his outstretched hand and, sighing, she reached into her flight suit and pulled out a couple of notes. He turned without a word and shoved his way through the crowd to the bar, forcing Orry to hurry after him. Tyrell waved to attract the attention of the beleaguered barmaid who, even with a flushed face and black hair plastered to her forehead with sweat, was undeniably beautiful. Despite the dozens of patrons baying to be served, she crossed to Tyrell as soon as she saw him.

'Well, look what the rats dragged in,' she said, planting her fists on her hips.

'Evening, Giselle,' Tyrell said. 'Looking as bonny as ever.'

She slapped him, much to the hilarity of everyone at the bar.

'*Three months*, Tyrell! You said you were going out for a bottle!'

He rubbed his cheek. 'What can I say, Gigi? A man has to earn a living.'

'Hah!' she snorted. 'What would you know about that? You haven't earned an honest penny in your miserable life.'

'That's just where you're wrong, my love.' He dragged Orry forward. 'I happen to be in a paid contract at this very moment – engaged by this young lady.'

Giselle looked at Orry as if she were a pool of something unpleasant that needed to be mopped up. 'Engaged to do *what*? They're paying *you* for it now, are they?'

Orry shook off Tyrell's hand and glared at the woman. He leaned over the bar and tucked the notes she'd given him into the front of Giselle's black shirt, murmuring something that Orry couldn't catch. The woman considered him for a few seconds, then rolled her eyes.

'You're in luck,' she said. 'There's one of them upstairs right now.'

'Thanks, Gigi. You're my girl.' Tyrell snatched up her hand and kissed it.

Her face softened and she stopped him as he went to walk away. 'Vance,' she said, unexpectedly tender, 'be careful. He's with Vigo.'

Tyrell nodded solemnly. 'Look after yourself, Giselle. I'll be back to see you once I've finished this job.'

'Course you will,' she said, and gazed at him with such melancholy longing that Orry felt like hugging her.

For his part, Tyrell appeared oblivious to the emotional havoc he was wreaking. *Either that or he simply doesn't care*, Orry reflected as he grabbed her hand and dragged her away through the crowd. She wasn't sure which she disliked more.

Behind them, Giselle turned back to the clamouring patrons and bellowed, 'Right then, you miserable bunch of pricks, who's next?'

A broad flight of steps led to the second floor, where a large man squeezed into a small suit blocked their path. Tyrell pointed across the sea of heads to the bar and Giselle nodded at the bouncer, who grudgingly stepped aside.

A pair of doors opened into a smoke-filled room full of people, although it was at least marginally less packed than the downstairs bar. Men and women were clustered around tables, either playing games of chance or watching others do the same. At the far end of the room was another bar.

Tyrell nudged her and pointed at an outlandishly dressed man, his face covered in tattoos, sitting at a long dice table. Every item of clothing he wore clashed with everything else, a harlequin riot of primary colours that set him apart from the other gamblers. A baggy, multicoloured hat rested on his head, gelled spikes of hair protruding from under it, each one dyed a different shade. A pair of oversized novelty sunglasses with one arm clinging lopsidedly to the end of his nose completed the ensemble. As she was staring at the bizarre sight in astonishment, Orry saw him leap up and caper in a circle, raising lanky legs clad in bright leggings and shaking his cupped hands like a crazy man. He sang as he rotated, an ululating croon that ended in a canine howl as he released a pair of multifaceted dice onto the table.

They rattled down the cushioned table, watched by a shaven-headed man in a sombre suit, otherwise unremarkable, especially next to his companion, apart from a livid purple scar where his right ear should be.

'That's Vigo Vestergaard,' Tyrell told her quietly.

The dice came to a stop and the harlequin lifted his broken sunglasses to peer at them. His arms shot into the air and he danced a jig, elbows thrusting like pistons.

'Dando's on a *rooooll*!' he yelled, dancing up to Vigo. 'In your *face*,' he exclaimed, thrusting a finger at his nose. Orry noticed in passing that the harlequin was wearing surgical gloves, but she was too busy waiting for the one-eared man to flatten him to think much of it.

Instead, Vigo just smiled greasily and handed over a wad of cash.

The harlequin turned away and performed a series of elaborate steps, singing all the while, but Vigo's smug expression told her everything she needed to know.

Tyrell started towards the table but she caught his sleeve. 'This stinks,' she murmured. 'He's going to keep letting this guy win until he bets everything he has, then—'

'—switch the dice,' Tyrell finished for her.

She looked up at him, not really surprised. 'Either that, or he's rigged the table with some kind of field-manipulator.'

He shook his head. 'I've met this bastard before. Vigo's old-school.'

'Who's the mark?' she asked.

He shrugged. 'A scooper. They're all mad as a sack of weasels and half as useful – although with any luck, he'll be able to tell you what you need to know.'

'If you say so,' she commented doubtfully, watching the scooper's antics.

Dando added more money to his winnings and laid it on the table. He swept up the dice and capered wildly again before casting them the length of the table. His arms shot into the air and he whooped with delight.

'So what's the play?' Orry asked. 'Let him lose the lot and offer him a lift home?' It sounded like a solid plan to her.

Tyrell was silent for several seconds, watching Vigo.

'No,' he said eventually. 'Let's take this bastard to the fucking cleaners.'

20

WELCOME TO THE HOLE

Ethan watched Sticky Pete cross to one of the piles of twisted debris. The old man shifted a tangle of composite strips aside and hauled open a hatch set into the ground.

Janco was holding his fletcher casually, as if Ethan posed no threat, but those darts would shred him in seconds if he gave the fat junkdog any reason. When Janco thrust him forward, he saw a short ladder leading down to what looked to be a soundproofed space beneath the yard. He recoiled at the musky scent of sweat and fear edged with a metallic tang. Sticky Pete and his boys followed him down the steps, the old man pulled the hatch closed after him and it slammed shut with a dreadful *clang* that made Ethan shudder.

'Welcome to the hole,' Pete said. 'Now get in the fucking chair.'

The fletcher being pointed at him left him little choice. Ethan eyed the beaten-up surgical bot beside him with unease as his wrists and ankles were secured. The chair was clearly designed to reconfigure into a bed, but it didn't appear to have any inte-guary capability.

149

The bot, however . . .

'Last chance, Rudi,' Pete said. 'Damn thing don't work this time, you're going off the wharf.'

This time? Ethan felt sick. *Was Orry down here – in this chair?* He eyed the surgical bot's numerous blades. *And if she was, what happened to her?*

Rudi scooped up an old tablet from a nearby table and ran a finger over the screen. 'Weren't my fuh-fault last time, Puh-Paps. It's working just fuh-fine now, though—'

His father snatched the tablet from his hand. 'Pray you're right, boy. Now go and help your brother unload. I'll deal with this.'

Rudi hesitated, his doubt clear on his face. 'I should suh-stay in case there's a guh-glitch—'

'A fucking *glitch*? Thought you said it was fixed?'

'It is, buh-but—'

'Is it fixed? Yes or no?'

Rudi's shoulders slumped. 'Yes.'

'Then fuck off and help Janco.'

'Yes, Puh-Paps.' With a final, worried glance at the bot, Rudi headed for the hatch.

'Idiot,' Pete muttered, turning to Ethan. He touched the tablet and the bot initiated its bootstrap routine, which was what Ethan had been waiting for. He dropped his head in mock despair to hide the integuary dullness in his eyes – although he doubted this moron would even know what that meant – and as he did so, a neat square of fabric caught his eye. His stomach fell away. He'd know that particular shade of red anywhere.

He gripped the chair's arms, forcing himself to breathe steadily and clear the turmoil from his mind; he needed to be clear-headed for this. He felt for the bot's contact field and found it immediately. *Stock protocols*, he thought, smiling coldly into his chest. *Nobody's updated this thing in years.* But why would they, on a world where integuaries were as rare as a kettlehead's teeth?

A simple vulnerability sniffer found him an unsecured port and within seconds he had full control of the bot's low-level functions. While its bootstrap routine ran, he had a quick poke around the machine's core logic. *Well, that's not right*, he thought, spotting a couple of corrupted subroutines immediately. He restored them, then accessed the bot's senses.

Pete watched the bot wake up and grinned. 'What shall we start with?' he asked cheerily. 'Feet first and work our way up?' He touched the tablet and looked expectantly at the machine.

Ethan held its limbs still, observing through the machine's senses.

The heat-map of Pete's face formed a frown as he stabbed at the tablet. 'God dammit, Rudi,' he snarled.

'It's not Rudi's fault,' Ethan said, raising his head so Pete could see his eyes.

'What . . . ?' the old man began, then his own eyes widened. 'Shit!'

He lunged forward, pulling Ethan's sneakpiece from his belt, but Ethan already had the bot moving and used one of the limbs to pluck the pistol from Pete's hand, then rapped him sharply on the temple, sending him staggering away. Four more limbs released Ethan's restraints and he rose from the chair. He was a little surprised to find himself shaking with fury.

After stooping to pick up the scrap of Orry's flight suit, he marched over to Pete and pointing the lethal little pistol at him, shouted, 'What did you do with my sister?' He waved the cloth in the junkdog's face.

Sticky Pete paled even more, if that was possible, and Ethan took a step closer and held the sneakpiece to his forehead. 'Did you do the same thing to her as you were planning to do to me? Answer me, you sick bastard!'

'No, no!' Pete's eyes darted to the hatch. 'Your sister's just fine, I promise – she got away before . . .' His voice trailed off, then he snivelled, 'Please don't kill me.'

Ethan's integuary, reading the man's facial movements, his heartbeat and respiration and a slew of other biometric and non-verbal cues, suggested an eighty-four per cent chance he was telling the truth, but his relief that Orry had got away from these twisted scumbags by herself did little to alleviate his rage and disgust.

'Where is she?' he demanded.

'Took up with a fella named Tyrell – Vance Tyrell. They left Grampus together in his smoker, headed for Spumehead, I reckon. She wanted someone to take her there to find a scooper – didn't say why.'

Ethan relaxed a fraction. That did fit with the report he'd picked up in Hardhaven, but—

The harsh squeal of metal made him start and he quietly retreated a step, keeping the pistol trained on Pete. The hatch opened and a pair of legs appeared, then Janco descended the ladder with his back to Ethan and Pete.

'Problem with the load, Paps,' he said on the way down. 'That crane ain't gonna take the—'

His words died as he turned to see Ethan pointing a gun at his father.

'Shoot him, you idiot!' Sticky Pete yelled, but before Janco could go for his fletcher, Ethan fired. The report was followed by a shrill scream and the fat junkdog staggered back, clutching at his face as blood dripped from his fingers. The sneakpiece wasn't an effective weapon at range and Ethan didn't feel like hanging around to find out just how much damage he'd done. He raced to the ladder, pursued by shouting as Pete lambasted his son. Janco's cries of pain were already turning to roars of fury, but Ethan had hared up the ladder and heaved the heavy hatch closed before he'd recovered enough to give chase. It slammed into place with a satisfying crash, mercifully silencing both men.

Only after Ethan had shot the bolt home did he turn, and saw the youngest junkdog – Rudi? – staring wide-eyed at him. He flinched away when Ethan raised the sneakpiece and demanded, 'Where did the marshal take my friend?'

The young man hunched over, holding his bandaged hand protectively in front of his face and staring fiercely at the ground. 'The cuh-copshop,' he stammered, 'in tuh-town.'

'How do I get there?'

'I . . .' Rudi risked a glance up at him. 'I can tuh-take you.'

The hatch at Ethan's feet shuddered at a blow from below, but the bolt was heavy and that lid wasn't going to be moving any time soon. The shuddering was replaced by barely audible thuds.

'If you try anything,' he told the junkdog, 'I'll shoot you. Understand?'

Rudi nodded vigorously.

Grampus bubble's copshop turned out to be a blocky building wedged between a shuttered chandler's store and an equally derelict casino. Casing the place, Ethan found the rear was a featureless wall backing onto an empty yard – so the only way in was through the front door. He pulled Rudi into an alley opposite and kept the pistol trained on him, even though he was pretty sure the vacant young man was too terrified to try anything.

Mender? Can you hear me?

The reply was thick with interference, but understandable. *You got out, then, kid? Thought you might screw things up.*

Ethan rolled his eyes. *Where are you? Where's Purvis?*

I'm in a cell out back. Bag of shit looks about ready to leave, so you better keep out of sight until he's gone.

He was right; a moment later the door opened and Marshal Purvis appeared, whistling merrily. He locked the door and waddled off towards the docks. Once he had turned the corner and was out of sight, Ethan gestured for Rudi to precede him across the street.

'Stand there and don't move,' he ordered, before turning his attention to the lock.

The copshop looked ancient, just as decayed and badly maintained as everything else he'd seen so far in Grampus bubble. The composite walls were chipped and yellowed with age and the biometric scanner on the keypad next to the door was so old that Ethan had never even seen the model before. He guessed it would be ludicrously easy for his integuary to crack, assuming he could rig up an interface node – but there was the problem. The electronic lock was clearly broken: the screen was cracked and the buttons were coated in the accumulated grime of years, and in its place the security-conscious marshal had sealed the door with a simple mechanical padlock.

Checking that Rudi was still where he should be, he knelt

and retrieved his picks from the compartment in the heel of his right boot. He set to work on the padlock.

A few seconds later it sprang open with a satisfying *click*.

He grinned.

'That's cuh-clever,' Rudi commented.

Ethan replaced the picks and eased the door open. 'Mender?' he called.

'Back here.'

A reception counter divided the room in two. Behind it were three desks, but only one of them appeared to be in use, the softly glowing screen of an old-fashioned terminal an island in a sea of disposable food cartons and coffee cups. The other desks were piled with boxes and assorted junk, while hardcopy prints of wanted posters surrounded a door standing ajar in the back wall.

Ethan hurried over to the door – then stopped and turned back to Rudi, hovering by the entrance.

'Come in and close the door,' he said, and when the young junkdog meekly obeyed, he decided he could risk leaving him alone for a moment. Beyond the open door was a row of five cells stretching the width of the building. Mender was the only occupant.

'What did you do to the junkdogs?' he asked.

'The young one's out there,' Ethan told him. 'I locked the other two up at their yard. I know where Orry is: she's gone to a bubble called Spumehead.'

Mender looked worried. 'Purvis is heading back to the yard. As soon as he finds 'em they'll be coming back here, and this time, they'll be loaded for bear. Hurry up and get me out.'

Ethan examined the lock in the cell door. It was a more

robust version of the front door keypad, but this one was in working order. Annoyingly, he couldn't see any interface ports in its thick casing.

Better get started then, he thought, and turned back towards the office.

'Where are you going?'

'This lock's so old it doesn't have an integuary node, so I'm going to have to rig one, and because there aren't any external ports, I'll have to crack the case to get into it. It's pretty heavy-duty, so I'm going to need a lockprise or something like it to get the damned thing open.'

Mender scowled. 'And how long is all that going to take?'

'A while,' Ethan admitted.

'Did Purvis take my Fabretti with him?'

'No.' The hand-cannon would have been impossible to hide.

'Then it must be out there somewhere. Go find it, kid.'

Ethan sighed and returned to the office, where Rudi was obediently waiting. It took him a moment to find the metal gun locker in one corner, secured with an electronic lock, but taking out his picks again, he quickly prised off the plastic casing and examined the circuitry within.

Too easy, he thought thankfully; he'd cut his teeth subverting locks way more complex than this one. Crouching, he retrieved his node kit from his other boot heel, extracted the extender from the little case and attached the leads. The molecular hooks in the tip of each cable held them in place while his integuary confirmed it had found a new node. Three seconds later the lock's LED turned green and the arms locker sprang open to reveal a netgun, two pistols, and Mender's hand-cannon.

He carefully repacked the kit, grabbed the Fabretti – which, despite its size, was as light as his sneakpiece – and hurried back to Mender.

'Give it here,' he said, thrusting a hand between the bars. It took some careful manoeuvring, but eventually Ethan got it through the gap. Mender checked it was still loaded before activating it. A high-pitched whine filled the air.

'Get back out there and find something to hide behind,' he said. 'And cover your ears.'

Ethan ran out and dragged Rudi behind one of the desks.

'Ready?' Mender yelled.

'Ready!' Ethan covered his ears and Rudi did the same, a fearful expression on his face.

The entire building shuddered as an explosion tore through it. Fragments of melted composite rained down, leaving scorch-marks where they bounced off exposed skin. Smelling burning hair, Ethan frantically brushed away a smouldering fragment, then raised his head slowly, his ears ringing, and stared at the ragged hole torn through the rear wall. The blackened remnants of wanted posters fluttered to the ground.

Mender peered out at him through a matching hole in his cell where the lock had been, the bars around it bent outwards like twisted claws. He looked slightly stunned as he shook his head to clear it. He pushed the cell door open and walked unsteadily into the office.

'Why are you standing around like a spare prick at an orgy?' he said, walking to the front door. 'You said your sister was headed for another bubble? So we need to get back to *Jane* pronto.' He looked at Rudi. 'And this asshole is taking us.'

'What about Purvis?' Ethan asked.

Mender hawked and spat. 'I truly hope that fucker tries to

stop us.'

Another rapid journey through near-deserted streets left Ethan wondering just how many people remained in Grampus bubble. Certainly, no one had come to investigate the noise of the Fabretti ravaging the copshop, and from what he'd seen of Marshal Purvis during their fleeting acquaintance, he suspected if anyone *had* heard the explosion, they would rather not get involved.

Now he crouched with Mender and Rudi at the edge of the junkyard wharf, sheltering behind the carbon-scored hull of Orry's escape pod as they watched Purvis wandering through the piles of junk, calling in increasing irritation for Sticky Pete and his boys.

'Just you keep that mouth of yours shut,' Mender growled at Rudi. His eyes fixed on the Fabretti, the junkdog swallowed and nodded rapidly.

Mender rested the pistol on one of the pod's blackened thrusters and aimed it at Purvis.

'What are you doing?' Ethan asked quietly.

'What d'you think I'm doing, kid? I'm going to trim some blubber off that fat fuck.'

Ethan was horrified. 'You can't just *murder* him!'

Mender snorted. 'You sound just like your goddamn sister.'

'He's a *policeman*,' Ethan insisted. 'Even if he is corrupt, he's the law here. If you kill him, they'll *definitely* come after us.'

The marshal disappeared into the warehouse, his voice echoing angrily as he shouted for Sticky Pete. Mender's hand relaxed a little on the Fabretti. 'I suppose you have a better idea?' he said quietly. 'Purvis ain't gonna just let us leave, you know.'

'Give me five minutes,' Ethan whispered, and slipped away before Mender could object further. He worked his way round the edge of the yard until he had enough cover to get within a few metres of the hatch. His plan had been to throw something onto it to attract Purvis' attention, but as it turned out he didn't need to; the marshal had reappeared and was marching straight for the hole, a furious expression on his face.

His heart thudding, Ethan circled around behind him. He was in the open now, standing between Purvis and Mender, and if the marshal turned . . .

The policeman placed his shotgun on the ground beside him and slid back the heavy bolt on the hatch. As he hauled it open, shouting erupted from below.

Purvis aimed his gun into the hole before peering down cautiously.

Now!

Ethan charged across the uneven ground and hurled himself at Purvis' broad back. The marshal cried out as he pitched forward, his chest slamming against the far edge of the opening. The shotgun went off as he fell, drawing a scream from below. Purvis grabbed for something to stop himself, but there was nothing; he just rebounded and disappeared down the hole. There was another scream of pain as he landed on someone below.

Ethan heaved desperately on the hatch and slammed it shut, then scrabbling with shaking hands, slid the bolt home.

He turned to Mender with a triumphant grin, but even as he performed an elaborate bow, a muffled shot made him leap forward in alarm. He turned to see a cluster of tiny holes in the hatch: Purvis was firing up through the metal.

Lucky he doesn't have Mender's Fabretti, he thought with a shudder.

The marshal's muffled voice rose through the pierced hatch. 'Goddamned sons of bitches!' he raged. 'I'll fucking *gut* you, you bastards—'

Another shot sent Ethan scurrying back to Mender, who appeared from behind the capsule, shoving Rudi ahead of him.

'Would've been easier to just shoot him,' he said. 'Now there's one more person wants to see us dead.'

'Are you planning on *ever* coming back here?' Ethan glanced nervously at the hatch as another shotgun blast punched through the metal. Purvis was clearly trying to shoot the bolt off. 'Because *I'm* sure as hell not.'

'Fair point,' Mender admitted. He prodded Rudi in the chest. 'What are you looking at? Go fire up that piece of shit over there and take us out to our ship – and when you get back here, you can tell those bastards how we went easy on 'em.' Another shot rocked the hatch. 'And hurry the fuck up,' he shouted after Rudi, who was already haring away across the yard.

Mender scratched his sparse beard and looked around with distaste. 'I hate fucking junkdogs,' he said.

21

CROOKED GAME

'Handsome Vance Tyrell! I heard Beeto's put a pretty penny on your head, though I reckon it's not your *head* he's really after.' Vigo Vestergaard grinned nastily. 'Maybe I'll cut off that famous member of yours and send old Beeto what he *actually* wants, see how grateful he is.'

'You're welcome to try,' Tyrell answered evenly. 'Maybe the quack will give you a discount when you ask her to grow back *both* your ears.'

Vigo scowled and as his hand slid into his jacket, Orry quickly stepped close to Tyrell and clutching his arm, '*Babes,*' she whined in her best approximation of what she thought a local doxy might sound like, 'I thought you said we was gonna play some dice.'

Vigo's hand reappeared, empty, and a smile spread over his face. 'Setting your sights a bit low, aren't you, Tyrell?' He chuckled. 'What's this one come as?'

Orry giggled idiotically, as if the insult had sailed over her head. 'Pleased to meetcha. I'm Amber.' She held out a hand.

'Vigo Vestergaard, at your service.' He kissed her proffered hand.

She smiled at him, eyes wide, and gushed, 'My darlin' Vance promised me a game of the dice, and we're going to buy me a whole new wardrobe out of the winnings – ain't we, Babes? I had to leave *everything* behind when we ran away together, you know?' She lowered her voice and whispered, 'This here' – she indicated her flight suit – 'is a *disguise*.'

'Oh, I see,' Vigo replied with a knowing smile, no doubt envisaging a father or husband somewhere baying for Tyrell's blood. 'Well, little lady, if it's dice you're after, you've come to the right place. Everyone's a winner at my table, isn't that right, sir?'

This last remark he addressed to the harlequin scooper, Dando, who had been studying the light fitting above his head during the conversation. His head snapped down and he looked puzzled for a moment, before a grin split his tattooed face and he waved his winnings at Orry.

'Dando's a winner!' he announced, before thumping his wad down on the table.

'Honeybear,' Tyrell growled, addressing Orry but glaring at Vigo, 'I think perhaps we should try a different game—'

'But I wanna play *this* one,' she wheedled, enjoying herself.

'You heard the little lady, Tyrell,' Vigo said. 'You wouldn't deny her, would you?'

'*Pleeease*,' she begged.

Tyrell did a great job of looking disgusted. 'All right, fine,' he told Vigo, 'but I'm watching you.'

Vigo smirked – then smiled wider as Orry pulled the bundle of notes from her pocket. 'It appears I did you a disservice, Tyrell. You clearly haven't lost your eye at all.'

'Just get on with it,' Tyrell muttered.

'Will this be enough to play?' Orry asked innocently.

'The more you bet, the more you win,' Vigo told her.

'That's more than enough,' Tyrell growled, taking the money and laying some of it on the table next to Dando's.

'All bets down,' Vigo announced. 'Lady's turn to cast, if that's all right with you, sir?'

Dando gave an elaborate bow and Vigo passed her the dice. They felt normal to her, but well-loaded bones were near impossible to detect, even for those on the look-out. But these would be weighted in the mark's favour, so she was guaranteed to win for the time being. *We just have to watch for the switch.*

She closed her hand around the dice, offered her wrist to Tyrell for a good luck kiss, then tossed them inexpertly down the table.

'Whale's eyes!' Vigo exclaimed as they came up on ones. 'The lady wins!' He placed a pile of notes next to hers, did the same with Dando's stake, and picked up the dice.

'I won!' Orry squealed excitedly. 'I *won*! Babes, I really did it! I wanna do it again! Can I do it again, Babes?'

Tyrell shook his head and was opening his mouth to object, but she was already adding more money to the pile on the table.

'Dando's turn!' the scooper said. He emptied his pockets, almost doubling his own bet. There was a lot of money on the table in front of him, and her own pile of notes was not inconsiderable . . .

It's going to be now.

And as Orry surreptitiously watched Vigo under her lashes, she saw the hand containing the dice slip into his side pocket, just for a heartbeat.

There it is, she thought as he handed the dice back to Dando.

She ran her fingers up Tyrell's arm and pinched him and he pressed his elbow to her side to show he understood.

Vigo reached for his drink, a brightly coloured concoction loaded with fruit, complete with sparkly umbrella and straw.

'Oh!' Orry said. 'That looks nice. What is it?'

'It's a Spumehead Special,' he said, offering her the glass. 'Care to try?'

She released Tyrell and stepped over to Vigo. The man was doused in cheap cologne but she gave him a teasing smile as she accepted the glass. He edged closer as she sipped at the drink, which was every bit as revoltingly sweet as she'd expected, and gazed up at him through half-lowered lids. *Honestly, some men are so easy to manipulate.*

'What's a pretty little thing like you doing with a loser like Tyrell, anyway?' he asked, running a finger down her cheek.

She sucked on the straw and let the drink moisten her lips before returning the glass to him. Vigo's eyes were locked on her face and his breathing was getting heavier.

'Mmm,' she murmured, licking her lips. 'Tastes like sweeties.' She offered him the glass and, as her fingers lingered against his, her other hand slipped inside his jacket and closed around the winning dice.

'Get the hell away from him!' Tyrell snarled suddenly, grabbing her arm and tugging her back.

'Ow!' she cried. 'Stop it, Babes – you're *hurting* me! I was just being polite—'

Tyrell had manoeuvred her so that Dando, still holding the switched dice, was behind her, watching the altercation. She tried to pull her arm free of Tyrell's grasp but he was keeping a firm grip on it.

'Let . . . go!' she demanded, pulling away just as he released her, which sent her stumbling backwards into Dando, *accidentally* knocking the dice from his hand. She faked a trip and fell, following the losing dice to the floor, but she landed awkwardly, bruising herself on a table leg. Ignoring the pain, she scoured the floor and quickly spotted one of Dando's dice. She flicked it away, sending it skittering into the corner of the room. But the other was nowhere to be seen.

She dropped the winning dice just as a pair of strong hands helped her to her feet: Vigo, his face full of concern. 'Are you all right, my dear?' he began, but Tyrell inserted himself between them, glaring at him.

'I'm *so* sorry, Sweetness,' he said to Orry. 'It was an accident – are you hurt, Honeybear?'

She dusted herself down before turning a dazzling smile first on Vigo, then on Tyrell. 'I'm fine,' she told them, 'really – just embarrassed, is all.'

'No need to be,' Vigo declared. 'No need at all.'

Orry held her breath as he stooped and he reached under the table to retrieve the dice, waiting for him to notice the switch, but when he rose again he just glanced at the pile of money on the table and handed the dice to Dando.

'Your roll, sir,' he said.

The scooper performed his capering ritual again, Orry clapping in time, and let the bones fly.

She clapped her hands delightedly as they came to rest on ones again. 'I win again!' she cried. 'See, Babes – I'm your lucky charm!'

Vigo stared, bug-eyed, then a look of fury twisted his face.

'How the fuck did you do that?' he snarled.

'Do what?' she asked innocently, reaching for her winnings, but Vigo's big hand closed around her wrist.

'What are you going to do?' she murmured. 'They're *your* dice.' She gave him a pointed look and dropped her accent. '*Both sets.*' She saw his eyes flicker nervously around the crowded room. 'I imagine there are a fair few people here you've cheated tonight – I wonder how kindly they'd take to knowing they never had a chance?'

His mouth was a thin line of hatred, but he released her arm. She picked up her winnings and tucked them away, but Dando was still kissing his thick wad of notes. He pushed past Orry to wave the money in Vigo's face.

Oh shit, she thought.

'Dando wins!' the scooper cried, and Vigo's right eye twitched. He thrust the money under Vigo's nose, making him smell it, and started again, 'Dando wi—'

Vigo's fist smashed into the scooper's jaw, sending him crashing onto the table, which promptly collapsed. The wad of cash flew into the air, notes fluttering everywhere.

Enraged, Vigo lunged for Orry, who squirmed aside and found herself surrounded by a mass of people, all pushing frantically as they tried to grab the money.

He let loose a roar of fury and started shoving his way towards her.

Tyrell was lost in the confusion, nowhere to be seen, and Dando was lying motionless on the shattered ruins of the table and out for the count. Orry cursed. They were well and truly blown. Hopefully she'd get another opportunity – but first, she had to get out of this alive. She turned and started for the exit.

When she finally made it to the stairs she found them jammed with people pouring up from the lower bar area like a tide, the doorman helpless in the face of so many drunken, greedy patrons.

She risked a quick glance behind her and saw Vigo just metres away, brutally manhandling people out of his way to get to her, a murderous look on his face. Fights were already breaking out on the stairs and it would be a matter of moments before the place descended into a total riot.

She managed to squeeze past the doorman and climbed over the banister, making her way down the outside of the staircase until she was near enough to the ground to jump. She raced for the exit, not looking back until she got to the door. Vigo was still at the top of the steps, fists flying as he tried in vain to clear a path. She couldn't see Tyrell anywhere, but going back for him wasn't an option. She wasn't too worried, though: Vance Tyrell struck her as more than capable of getting himself out of a mess like this.

Giselle, still behind the bar, was calmly smoking as she watched the chaos, but she frowned when she spotted Orry. She flicked away her sweetsmoke stick, vaulted the bar and strode over, reaching the door just as Orry pulled it open.

'This is Tyrell's doing, isn't it?' Her dark eyes glared at Orry. 'Where is he?'

'Still upstairs, I think. We got separated.' Orry eyed the door anxiously. She didn't fancy a stand-up fight with Giselle, who looked like she could handle herself.

'So you thought you'd skip out on him?' she spat. 'What a *bitch*.'

'Whoa!' Orry said, raising her hands. 'Tyrell's a big boy; he can look after himself.'

'He's a bloody child. Come on.'

Orry stepped back as Giselle reached for her arm. 'Hey! What the hell do you think you're doing?'

'I'm going to save his sorry arse – and you're going to help me.' Those dark eyes bored into hers.

Orry considered that. Going back for Tyrell wasn't actually a bad idea – and with Giselle's help, maybe she could get the scooper out too.

'All right,' she agreed, 'just keep your hands off me.'

Giselle snorted and headed back towards the bar. Orry started to follow, until a drunken whaler with blood running from a cut on his forehead lurched out of nowhere and grabbed her arm. He stank like ethanol and she recoiled as he pulled her towards him, slack lips straining for hers.

Before she could sink her knee into his crotch he was wrenched away, a small but powerful fist connected with his jaw and he staggered back, crashing through a table to land sprawling on the floor.

'Stop dicking around,' the barmaid told her, and now Orry could see the knuckleduster glinting on one hand.

The barmaid opened a flap in the bar and led Orry through to a door in the back wall well camouflaged by rows of brightly coloured optics. As Giselle reached for the handle, the door opened and Tyrell staggered out, Dando's limp body slung over one shoulder. Behind him, Orry saw a staircase leading upstairs. He stopped abruptly when he saw Giselle, who glowered at him.

'Oh – hi, Gigi.'

The sound of a bottle smashing nearby made Orry flinch, but

neither Giselle nor Tyrell reacted. 'This isn't my fault,' he said with an easy smile. 'Vigo tried to cheat us.'

'Of course he bloody did! What did you expect?'

'Well, okay – but he's after my blood, Giselle. We really need to get out of here.'

The main door burst open to admit a stream of marshals. They started pouring in to the place, but Tyrell's eyes remained fixed on Giselle's face.

'*Shit*,' she muttered in disgust. 'Why do I always—?' She thrust a keycard into his hand. 'Go and wait at my place. I'll be there once I've cleaned up your mess.' She turned and waved the marshals spreading through the bar towards the stairs. As batons began to rise and fall, she reached down and hauled open a hatch in the floor beneath her.

'Thanks, love,' Tyrell said, brushing his lips against her cheek as he passed.

'Don't you *dare* "love" me, you bastard.'

He gave her an apologetic grin and after struggling to squeeze Dando through the narrow hole, started down the steep steps.

'Keep your damn hands off him,' Giselle hissed as Orry moved to follow.

'Believe me, you're welcome to him,' Orry assured her. 'And . . . thanks.'

She narrowly avoiding being knocked out cold as Giselle slammed the hatch closed above her. After a moment, lights flickered on to reveal a cellar with metal barrels racked against one wall and empties standing near a hydraulic case hoist. Boxes and packages were stacked everywhere in untidy piles.

Tyrell crossed to the hoist and grabbed its control box. The moment Orry joined him, he pressed a green button and the platform jerked and began a painfully slow ascent. A pair of metal flaps above them opened to allow the platform to emerge on the street. Streams of passing revellers parted around them, none of them sparing the unconscious scooper draped over Tyrell's shoulder a second glance.

He dumped his burden on the pavement and turned to her. 'There's your scooper, so hand over my money. Now.'

'What – *here*? What am I supposed to do with him like this? At least help me get him to Giselle's place – then I can talk to him when he wakes up.'

He took a step closer, anger sparking in his eyes. 'My money,' he repeated, thrusting out a hand. 'I mean it.'

Orry heard a commotion in the crowd some distance away, marking the approach of yet more marshals. Above her, the muffled sounds of brawling still came from the casino's top floor.

'I'll pay you extra,' she said quickly, eyeing the approaching police. 'You can have my share of what we got from Vigo – all of it. Just help me get this guy somewhere safe.'

Tyrell had obviously seen the marshals as well. He kept glaring at her until the crash of a shattering window sounded above them and a moment later, a body hit the pavement just a couple of metres away, flooring two passing revellers as it landed. Two of the cops changed course, heading right for them.

'This is *the last goddamn time*,' Tyrell informed her angrily, before hoisting Dando back onto his shoulders. 'Giselle's place is this way. Hurry the fuck up.'

22

GISELLE'S PLACE

Giselle's apartment was a compact, single-bedroom module on the third floor of a rundown residential block several streets from the casino. A kitchen ran along one wall of the living room and a small shower cubicle opened off the side. There were a lot of cushions.

Tyrell dumped the unconscious scooper on the sofa and crossed to a table sporting an impressive collection of half-empty bottles. 'You want a drink?' he asked, searching for a glass.

'No, thanks.' Between the excitement of what they'd just pulled in the casino, the booze she'd already thrown down her neck that evening and the reaction to their narrow escape, Orry was feeling decidedly queasy.

'Suit yourself,' Tyrell said. She heard the clink of glass on glass and a long gurgle of liquid from behind her.

She knelt by Dando and checked his breathing, wondering how long he'd be out – and what, if anything, he would be able to tell her when he awoke. If the scooper did have a lead on the whereabouts of Irina's exiled Kadiran, she would need a way to pursue it. Kneeling back, she looked at Tyrell, who was wandering around the edge of the room, idly examining items on the shelves and tables.

'You did good back there,' he said, 'swapping the dice. Where'd you learn to dip like that?'

'My father taught me.' The pain of his loss was suddenly sharp in her chest again, piercing the alcohol's cushioning haze.

'You're lucky. The only thing my father taught me was how to cheat at cards.'

'You didn't get on?'

He laughed bitterly. 'I guess not. Bastard took off when I was nine.'

'I'm sorry. Why?'

'He didn't think I was his,' Tyrell said lightly, but she could see the bleakness behind his eyes. He hesitated for a moment, then continued, 'Ma was a drunk. It got worse after he left. She didn't want to do much of anything, so I had to do anything I could to feed us and keep a roof over our heads. Shoplifting and petty theft, mostly. A little grifting.'

'At nine? That's tough.'

'Yeah, well . . . I was eleven when she died – I came home to find she'd choked on her own puke.'

She stared at him. 'Rama – what did you do?'

'The League stuck me in a home, but . . . let's just say it didn't agree with me. So I left.'

'How did you live?'

'Same way I always had. Every time the marshals caught me they sent me back there, and every time, I'd get out again. After a while they'd had enough, I guess, and sentenced me to ten years' indentured servitude in the whaling flotillas. *That* kind of made me miss the home.' He was silent for a moment, his shoulders slightly hunched, then he chuckled and the easy-going mask was back. 'Anyway, Vigo must be taking a big old shit right about now.'

Orry felt like giving him a hug. Instead, she asked, 'Will he come after us?'

'Of course he will. You should watch out if you're planning on staying in this bubble.'

That wasn't Orry's plan at all. 'Giselle is in love with you,' she said, to change the subject.

Tyrell guffawed. 'No, she isn't. It's just a bit of fun, her and me. She's incredible in the sack' – Orry grimaced, her sympathy for the man quickly eroding – 'but the woman is absolutely *insane*. Between you and me, she scares the shit out of me.'

'You're a pig, you know that?'

He ignored her and continued going through Giselle's possessions. 'Son of a bitch,' he muttered, and turned to face her holding a folded pocket-knife with a bone handle. 'This is *mine*.' He opened the knife, then looked around the room. 'What else has that mad cow had off me?' Folding the blade away, he hurried around the rest of the room, examining everything.

'It's just a keepsake,' Orry told him. 'Something to remember you by. Haven't you got anything of hers?'

'No!' Having finished casing the living room, his eyes settled on what Orry guessed was the door to the bedroom. He strode towards it.

'You sure you want to go poking around in there, Tyrell?' she asked. 'I don't think Giselle will like that much.' He ignored her and disappeared through the door, slamming it shut behind him. 'It's your funeral,' she muttered.

Dando groaned. She instantly stopped worrying about Tyrell and focused on the scooper as his eyes opened.

He jerked upright. 'Where am I?' He looked around, wide-eyed and confused, then clutched his head. 'Ow! Dando *hurts.*' He gingerly touched his face, where a bruise from Vigo's fist was colouring the tattooed skin purple. He worked his jaw from side to side experimentally. '*Ow,*' he said again.

'Just relax,' she said, trying to soothe him. 'You're safe with us.'

He squinted at her. 'You ... you were in that place.' His eyebrows shot up and he patted his pockets frantically. 'What happened? Where is Dando's money?'

'Vigo knocked you out,' she explained. 'You dropped your money and things got a little heated. We—' She glanced at the bedroom door. '*I* dragged you out of there.'

'The money ... is gone? *All* of it?' When she nodded sympathetically, he buried his face in his hands and groaned, 'Oh! *What has Dando done?*'

'Hey,' she said softly, rubbing his shoulder, 'it's only money. At least you're still alive.'

'You don't understand,' he moaned, looking at her with red-rimmed eyes. 'Dando was *entrusted* to get supplies for his rig. That money was all we had. It was supposed to last us until the end of the season – and now it's *gone.*'

She had to work hard to resist the urge to enquire why exactly, if the money was that important, he had thought gambling with it was a good idea. Instead she said, 'Which rig do you come from?'

He sniffed and wiped his nose. '*Goat Locker.*'

She decided not to ask. 'I hear these rigs can go pretty deep?'

'Yeah, but the *Goat* is shallow right now. We found a rich current of super-abyssal gases about three kilometres down. We've been harvesting for weeks. Three kay is nothing for a deep rig like us.'

'Sounds like a lot to me,' she said, shivering at the thought of the crushing pressure that deep in Morhelion's atmosphere.

'*Goat Locker* is rated to five thousand atmospheres,' Dando said dismissively. 'That's about fifty kay. We've taken her deeper, too. Mind, after a while the popping gets to you.' He leaned closer. 'It's been known to drive a scooper mad.'

'Really?' she said with a straight face. 'These . . . super-abyssal gases? The ones you're harvesting. Are they worth a lot?'

'Offworld, a fortune.' The scooper scowled. 'But the League controls the export rights, so they set the prices. We'll be lucky to cover our costs' – his face fell again – 'especially now Dando has lost the money they gave me for supplies.'

'How do you get the gases?'

'There's a couple of ways. Right now the *Goat* is in a current, so we just open the intakes and stream it right through the filters.'

'What's the other way?'

'We have a whale-whisperer. Most deep rigs do.'

'A whale . . . *whisperer*?'

'Yeah – some of us are born with a special link to our brothers and sisters of the deep. The ancient ones can be asked to disgorge particular gases they have stored in their bladders.'

She stared at him. 'You're telling me some scoopers can *communicate* with the drifters?'

'Of course.'

'So they're sentient? *Fully* sentient?' When he nodded sadly, she asked, 'But I don't understand: how are the League allowed to *hunt* them, then? There are laws—'

'*Ascendancy* laws,' he spat. 'When was the last time an exo-botanist came to study the drifters? Twenty years ago? Fifty? The League controls everything that enters or leaves Morhelion, and that includes the truth. Besides, where would the Ruuz get their whaleskin purses and whalebone canes from if hunting was stopped?'

'That's *terrible*,' Orry said, her resentment of the Ruuz, never far below the surface, boiling up with fresh intensity.

'That's Morhelion,' Dando said, then lapsed into morose silence.

'Do you like coming to Spumehead?' Orry asked, trying to connect with him.

'We take it in turns to do a resupply run. Some of us hate it, but Dando quite likes it up top. For a few days, anyway. Gets him away from the others.'

'So *Goat Locker* is your home? You live there all the time?'

'Dando was born there.'

'How many of you are there?'

'Eighteen. We're a collective.'

'How many families?'

'What do you mean?'

'You know, mum and dad, children. Families.'

Dando looked puzzled. 'We're a collective.'

'So no children?'

'Of course there are children. How else would we survive?'

She frowned. 'Do you get married?'

'No, we exchange mates with other rigs. To maintain a healthy gene pool.'

That made sense, if the scoopers were an isolated set of communities. The galaxy was filled with all sorts of social variance. 'Do *you* have any children?'

He stared at the floor and Orry could see his jaw working under his tattoos. 'The shepherd picked out a mate for Dando. He has to produce offspring with her when he gets back.'

She grinned, nudging him playfully. 'You're on a promise.' She looked at his glum face. 'You don't sound very happy about it.'

He looked her in the eye. 'Dando doesn't like girls. Dando is in love with Faisal.'

'Ah. Have you told the shepherd this?'

'Of course.'

'But they still want to pair you off?'

'Not exactly. Dando can still be with Faisal, but we both have to have children and help raise them.'

'So what's the problem?'

He sighed. 'Dando just wants to be with Faisal. We don't want children – we just want to be together.'

She nodded sympathetically. 'Would you ever leave your rig – the two of you?'

'And do what?' he said bitterly. 'Slaughter our brothers and sisters like the bubble-dwellers do? We are all children of the aether.'

'You sound like you're very close to the leviathans,' she said. 'It must be hard, seeing them hunted.'

'The bubble-dwellers say we're mad, but that's just so they won't have to listen when we tell them the drifters are sentient.'

Orry smiled sympathetically and held out her hand. 'I'm Orry, by the way.'

He stared at it for a moment, then gave a tentative shake. 'Dando Kink. Why did you help me?'

'Does there have to be a reason?'

'Yes,' he replied.

A clatter from the bedroom reminded her that Tyrell was liable to reappear at any moment. 'There's someone I need to talk to,' she told the scooper. 'I think he might be on one of your rigs.'

He frowned. 'Who?'

She weighed up her options, recalling Irina's insistence on discretion. 'You'd know him if you saw him,' she said at last.

Dando stopped massaging his temples and he looked at her properly for the first time. 'Big fella? *Unusual* looking?'

'You could say that.'

'Not from round these parts?'

She chuckled. 'Definitely not.'

He thought for a moment. 'Dando might know who you're talking about.'

Finally!

'Do you know where he is?' she asked.

'That depends – what's it worth to you?'

'I saved your life – isn't that enough?'

'No. Dando wants his money back – Dando *needs* his money back.'

Orry reached into her pocket and pulled out her winnings. It was a considerable sum. She glanced at the bedroom door, from behind which came the occasional thump and squeak of furniture being shifted. 'All right,' she said heavily, 'how much?'

He stared at the wad. 'All of it.'

She handed over the bundle of notes.

Tears sprang to Dando's eyes as he tucked the money away in his satchel. 'Scoopers don't get many visitors,' he said. 'Are you sure you know what you're getting yourself into?'

'No,' she admitted, 'but this is *very* important.'

He said slowly, 'The person you are looking for is on *Deep Six*.' Fumbling in his satchel, he came out with a notepad and pen. He scribbled for a moment, tore off the top sheet and handed it to her. Below the words 'Deep Six' were scrawled several strings of numbers.

'That is where *Six* is,' he said, 'but you should be quick; she might already have moved on.'

'Thank you,' Orry said.

The low-level sounds of merriment outside grew suddenly louder, taking on a more purposeful note. She peered out of the window to see the street was emptying. Most of the people were moving away towards the docks, leaving a few prone bodies lying in their wake.

The bedroom door banged opened and Tyrell emerged, carrying a handful of unlikely items. 'Something's happening and I don't like it,' he said. 'Give me my money – I'm out of here.'

Okay, Orry, how are you going to play this?

'I . . . er . . . I don't have it.'

His face went rigid. 'You'll forgive me if I don't laugh.'

'I'm serious.'

'I warned you once, didn't I? *Don't* try and pull this shit on me. I fulfilled my part of the deal and now it's your turn. So just give me my money and I'm out of here.'

'I'm sorry, Tyrell, I can't. It's gone.'

'*Gone?*' He was getting angry now. 'You had it when we left the Crown – so where the hell has it *gone*?'

'I gave it to Dando.' She held her breath.

He smiled dangerously and inclined his head a little, as if he hadn't heard her correctly. 'I'm sorry, I thought you just said you gave *my* money – to *him*?'

'Yes, I did.'

'Uh-huh, uh-huh. Um . . . *why*?'

'For this.' She held up the piece of paper.

'And what's that?'

'It's the coordinates for a scooper rig called *Deep Six*. I want you to take me there in *Zephyr*.'

He snatched the paper from her hand and stared at the numbers written on it, then chuckled wearily. 'And I suppose you'll pay me when we get there.'

'Yes. Look, Tyrell, I know I keep letting you down, but you will get your money, I promise. Just one more trip.'

He stared at the paper and said slowly, 'You're right, I *will* get my money.' He rounded on Dando and his free hand dropped to the hook at his belt. 'Give me my cash, you crazy bastard. *Right now*.'

The scooper shrank away from him, shaking his head violently from side to side. 'Dando needs his money to buy food. You can't have it!'

Tyrell loomed over him. 'Don't make me hurt you, you goddamn clown.'

Orry grabbed his arm and spun him round to face her. 'Don't threaten him – *I* was the one who gave your money away. If you're going to take it out on someone, take it out on me!'

His face was tight with rage. 'Don't think I won't, just because you're a woman! It doesn't make any difference to me—'

'No, I don't suppose it does!'

'What's *that* supposed to mean?'

'I mean that you treat women like crap. Look at poor Giselle!'

He threw up his hands. 'Oh, I *see* – you're taking the moral high ground. Except, oh yes, *you're* the one who's welching on our deal—'

'You'll get your bloody money!'

'When?'

The front door opened and Giselle entered, closing it quickly behind her. She eyed them both suspiciously. 'Am I interrupting something?'

Tyrell's anger vanished, replaced by a transparently false smile. 'Gigi, *sweetheart*! What's going on out there?'

She crossed to the window and lowered the blinds. 'It's the Royal Breach – dozens of blooms, apparently. The whole flotilla's on its way out.' She turned to look at him, a guarded expression on her face. 'Things will be quieter here with them gone. You could stay here for a while . . . if you want.'

Tyrell's smile was corpse-like. 'I would *love* that, Giselle, except . . . except, *I* have to go too.' As her face assumed a thunderous expression, he added quickly, 'Just for a while—'

'Go where?' she demanded.

Pathetic, Orry thought as she watched him casting about for an excuse. Eventually he looked down and saw Dando's note, still clutched in his hand. He pointed at Orry. 'I have to take her to a scooper rig,' he said, almost triumphantly.

Giselle snorted. 'You expect me to believe that? You're screwing her, aren't you? I knew it—'

'No, my love, I swear on *Zephyr*, and you *know* what *Zephyr* means to me. This is strictly business, I promise you.' He thrust the note out for her to read. 'See?'

Giselle's brow creased as she peered at it. '*Deep Six*?'

'Yes,' Orry said, deciding to save him, 'Tyrell's going to fly me there. It won't take long and I'll pay him well.'

Giselle's jaw was locked tight beneath her pale skin. 'Fine,' she said coldly. 'You know what: I don't give a shit any more. Get out, all of you.' She crossed to the kitchen area, poured herself a large drink and drained it before turning back to them. 'Well?' she yelled. 'What are you waiting for? *Get out!*' She hurled the glass which narrowly missed Tyrell, exploding on the wall behind him.

Dando leaped to his feet and fled for the door, Orry close behind him.

'Right you are, my love,' Tyrell said, backing away. 'I'll see you in a few days then—'

'Out!' Giselle screamed, and he ducked out of the door a moment before something solid struck the other side.

'She's a passionate woman,' he said admiringly, flinching at another loud thud. 'We'd better go before she finds her gun – it wouldn't be the first time she's taken a pot-shot at me.'

He followed Orry down to the street, deserted now apart from the occasional body – either drunk, unconscious or dead. Dando was already disappearing into the distance, his parti-coloured legs pumping like pistons.

Tyrell cursed. 'There goes my damned money,' he growled.

'I know you have no reason to believe me,' she said, 'but I *do* intend to pay you. Look, take me to *Deep Six* – what have you got to lose except a bit of time and fuel? And once all this is over I'll get you as much money as you want. That's a promise.'

He ran a hand through his tangled hair. 'You are a real piece of work, you know that? I bet you can make men believe anything you say. Well, not this man, sister.'

'I'm telling the truth. I *have* to—' She stopped herself, but it was too late.

His eyes narrowed. 'You have to *what*? Why is it so damn important that you find this rig?' He hesitated, then came to a decision. 'You tell me that – the truth, mind – and I'll take you out there.'

Her eyes fell. 'I can't.'

'Fair enough. Goodbye.' He began to walk away, but she grabbed his sleeve and pulled him back so they ended up only inches apart.

'There's someone on that rig that I need to find. Someone very important. I can't say any more than that.'

He looked down at her, close enough for her to feel the warmth of his breath. 'This person,' he said quietly. 'Is he rich?'

'Better than that,' she answered, her voice a little husky. 'He's worth a lot of money to the right people. A *lot* of money.'

Tyrell considered this. 'If you're lying again, then so help me—'

'I'm not lying.' She gazed up at him, heart thudding in her chest.

He stepped back and the moment was broken.

'I guess we'll see, won't we?' He walked away, leaving her breathless.

She groaned and hurried after him.

23

YOU CAN'T MISS IT

Spumehead's basin was as deserted as the one in Grampus bubble. *Does anyone actually live in these habispheres?* Ethan wondered as a small local smoker carried them towards an empty wharf.

'Is it always this quiet round here?' he asked the craft's driver, a dour man with a prosthetic arm and half his skull protected by a metal plate.

'It's the Royal Breach, ain't it?' he said, eyes narrowed as he judged the distance to the wharf. The smoker thudded gently against it and he killed the power. 'Every bugger's gone to kill drifters.'

'Except you,' Ethan pointed out. The man turned to face him with a scowl and tapped his skull plate. 'I wasted enough years chasing them fucking things. Don't get you nuthin' but hurt – or dead.'

'Have you lived here long?'

'All my life.'

'Do you know a man called Tyrell?'

The one-armed man squinted at him. 'Bounty hunters, are you?'

'No, nothing like that. Why? Is this Tyrell guy in trouble?'

The man snorted. 'You could say that. I heard he was here yesterday – caused some kind of ruckus over at the Whalestone Crown Casino. Gone now, mind.'

'Gone where?'

'What am I – missing persons? That'll be ten notes for the ride and ten more for the information.'

Mender paid the man, then held up another of the scrip notes. 'Tell me about this casino.'

The Whalestone Crown looked like it had experienced some lively times recently, but the only people currently in the building were busy repairing damaged walls and broken furniture.

Spotting a black-haired woman behind the bar, Ethan nudged Mender. 'That must be Giselle.'

He grunted in agreement. 'Leave this to me, kid.'

'What'll it be?' the woman asked as he reached the bar.

'Whisky,' Mender said, 'and one for yourself.'

'Don't mind if I do.' She fetched a bottle and two glasses. 'If you're here for the breach, they've all gone already.'

'Not for that, no. I'm looking for someone – a man named Tyrell. You know him?'

Ethan could tell from her expression that she did.

'What are you? Bounty hunters?'

'You're the second person to ask me that.' Mender pointed at Ethan. 'Does he look like a bounty hunter?'

'Then what's Tyrell done?' Giselle asked.

'Nothing – I hope. We're looking for a girl, about your height, orange hair. We heard this Tyrell brought her here. You see anyone like that?'

'Why are you looking for her?'

Ethan ignored Mender and jumped in, his voice urgent. 'She's my sister – if you know where she is, *please* tell us.'

Giselle studied his face. She must have seen some similarity there because her expression softened a fraction. 'She was here. She had a hand in all this' – she indicated the smashed mirror above the bar – 'but she's gone now. Tyrell took her out to some scooper rig in his smoker. What was that name now?' She tapped her teeth with her thumbnail. '*Deep Six*, that was it – somewhere out past the Royal Breach. I can't remember the exact coordinates.'

'Thank you,' Ethan said gratefully.

'Just send Tyrell back this way if you find him.'

Mender drained his whisky and set the glass back on the bar. 'This smoker of his: what's it look like?'

'*Zephyr*? Like a silver rocket ship. You can't miss it.'

'Much obliged, miz.'

'Good hunting,' she said, as they walked away.

'You think we can find them?' Ethan asked as they headed out to the street.

'I don't know,' Mender replied, 'but we have a helluva lot less area to cover now. Let's go try our luck.'

24

DEEP SIX

Orry saw the pollution, a spreading smear a hundred kilometres long muting the vibrant aether, long before she spotted the smokers. The flotilla was a huge, motley assortment of vessels, the smallest many times larger than *Zephyr*, circling a colossal processing platform or drifting idly on the periphery.

'That's the *Hardhaven Voyager*,' Tyrell told her. 'Lindqvist will be happy; looks like they cabled a big one.'

She peered at the distant platform, stationary above a humped shape barely visible through the clouds.

'Get closer,' she said tightly. 'I want to see.'

'You really don't.'

'Get closer.' She grabbed a respirator and climbed up onto *Zephyr*'s hull.

As the smoker neared *Hardhaven Voyager*, Orry gazed down on the platform's endless expanse of metal, where hundreds of tiny figures were swarming around large wells sunk through the deck. Below the wells, she could see the leathery hide of a captive leviathan.

On one section of the deck squares of hide the size of landing pads were laid out, exposing a layer of fatty tissue metres thick which was being scraped by hand and the fat dumped into great vats. The stench reached her even through the respirator's filter and she swallowed, her stomach churning. Thick pipes snaking across the deck and penetrating the leviathan's flesh led to enormous gas tanks fixed to the sides of the platform.

Zephyr drew to a halt and a moment later Tyrell appeared beside her. 'Seen enough?'

'This is *disgusting*,' she told him, watching a fresh square of hide being lifted clear by a crane. 'That's an intelligent being they're slaughtering.'

'What can you do?'

Far below, a crew was toiling to unhook a pipe from one tank and connect it to the next in line.

'What's in the tanks?' she asked.

'Drifters go deep, way below the crush-depth of anything we could make, even offworld. Their bladders are full of gases we can't get any other way.'

A superstructure rose beside the killing floor, dotted with windows and capped with a lush roof garden protected by a transparent dome. Inside it, a man was seated at a table on a verdant lawn, sipping from a teacup. It was an incongruous sight.

A bulky smoker dropped in behind them, its pilot visible beneath a bubble canopy. He flicked a switch and his voice came booming through external speakers. 'What's your business here?'

Tyrell cupped his hands around his mouth and bellowed, 'Just sightseeing!'

'This is restricted airspace – move along.'

'Restricted my arse,' Tyrell yelled back. 'This is open aether. I have every right to be here.'

'Move along.'

'Make me!'

A hatch opened in the vessel's side and a two-man crew manhandled a heavy multi-barrelled gun onto a mount. Lights illuminated on the weapon as it activated and one of the crew aimed it at Tyrell. Behind the cockpit bubble, the pilot smiled coldly.

'Moving along!' Tyrell shouted. He gave the pilot a bow, then bustled Orry back inside and hurried to the cockpit. 'Bastards think they own the damn sky,' he muttered, coaxing the engines back into smelly life.

She stared at the stricken leviathan, close to tears, as *Zephyr* rumbled away from the flotilla. It was a relief when the clouds finally closed around the poor creature.

Orry knew something was wrong the moment she saw the buoy. Its squat tower was listing, one of the envelopes at its base deflated. The fabric was flapping like a beached squid. Scorch marks scarred the tower's brightly coloured walls.

'Ah, *shit*,' Tyrell spat. 'There goes my fucking money.'

Glowering, he conned *Zephyr* closer, tendrils of greenish-tinged aether drifting past the portholes. The choking rumble of *Zephyr*'s engines died. Below the buoy, Orry could make out a thick cable that had been severed just a few metres down.

'Looks like someone beat us to it,' Tyrell said. 'Who the hell is this person you're after? It takes a serious amount of firepower to do damage like that.'

Orry stared into the depths. 'How do the scoopers get down to their rigs?'

'Survival suits – terrifying bloody things. Don't change the—'

'Do you have one on board?'

'Yeah, I—' His eyebrows shot up. 'You can't be serious.'

She shifted and looked at him. She needed him to understand just how serious she was about this. 'I have to get down there. The person I'm looking for might still be alive.'

'You surely don't believe that.'

'I have to try. I'll go down in the suit and check it out. Wait for me here.' When he looked at her doubtfully she pointed out, 'Finding him alive is the only way you'll get your money.'

He sighed. 'Okay, sister . . . it's your funeral.'

'Have you ever used anything like this before?' Tyrell asked half an hour later.

'I know my way around a spacesuit,' Orry said, beginning to think this was a bad idea. The survival suit was bulky and its thick armoured plates made movement difficult.

'You're not in space here. This will stop the pressure from killing you, but you won't have the freedom of movement you're used to. I hate the damn thing. Just find the rig and get inside as quickly as you can, okay?'

She nodded, concentrating on her breathing as he screwed the helmet into place. It was a sealed sphere, with no way of seeing out. Claustrophobia clutched at her chest and she had to fight to control her panic. A moment later a visual display flickered to life in front of her eyes and she saw Tyrell waving.

'Can you hear me?' The grainy display and tinny voice made her long for her integuary.

'Yes – and see you. Just about.'

'Good. Look, you'll see a whole lot of readouts in front of your face, yes? Just ignore them, unless they turn red.'

She nervously scanned the numbers and graphics that glowed around her external view. 'What do I do if they turn red?'

'Pray.'

'I'm not that way inclined.'

He grinned. 'If anything goes wrong, I'll see an alert and reel you in. It'll take a while, though, so chances are you'll be a corpse by the time I get you back up here. Are you sure you want to do this?'

'Yes,' she said, doubtfully.

'Ready, then?'

She took a breath and nodded, then realised he couldn't see the movement inside her helmet. She swallowed and said, 'Let's do it.'

It took a lot of straining by Orry and shoving by Tyrell to get her up onto *Zephyr*'s hull, but once there, he unshipped a telescopic boom from a concealed recess in the curved hull. The hook fitted with data ports dangling from one end was attached to the boom by a thick metal cable. It unreeled with a whirring sound as he carried the hook to her and secured it to an anchor point at the small of her back. She noticed a couple of cracked screens wired into the side of the boom next to a control panel – presumably to monitor the poor sod on the end of the cable. *Which is me*, she thought wryly.

'The controls are simple,' he told her, and quickly demonstrated the buttons in each of her gloves. 'Try it: extend a few metres of cable.'

She manipulated the switch he'd indicated and a loop of cable spooled off the boom.

'It'll take a while to get down, so try to relax, if you can,' he said. 'And remember: the aether can do weird things to your mind.'

'Got it.'

'Off you go then. Try not to die.'

He actually sounds as if he means it, she thought, then snorted. *Probably just worried about his money.*

As he manipulated the boom's controls, she felt a tug from the cable and it lifted her slowly until her heavy boots left the deck. The boom swung slowly outboard with Orry dangling below it until all she could see beneath her feet was swirling aether.

'All set?'

'I think so.' *What in Rama's name am I doing?*

He chuckled. 'I'm going to enjoy this.'

'Enjoy wha—'

A muffled *thunk* sounded from somewhere above her and suddenly her stomach was in her throat as her body plummeted downwards. She screamed as the aether whipped past, clutching desperately at the controls until her rate of descent slowed. When her breathing had returned to normal she gingerly increased her speed again, going faster and faster, until her helmet displays indicated she'd reached terminal velocity.

Tyrell was right: even pre-warned, the fall took a lot longer than she'd expected. Morhelion's atmosphere was a multi-hued kaleidoscope outside her helmet, a tunnel of colour that blurred at the edges. The clouds began to take on a darker aspect as she descended and she eyed the flickering readouts anxiously. The one indicating the external pressure was rising sharply and she had to force herself not to think about the stresses being put on her suit.

A dark shape appeared below her, growing quickly larger as she fell towards it. She braked again, decreasing her rate of descent so she had time to study the rig as she approached it.

Deep Six turned out to be a cluster of cylinders, interconnected within a tubular framework. As the airlock protruding from the top of the largest cylinder rose to meet her, Orry could see the other end of the buoy's cable was anchored beside its door, the severed end dangling down into darkness.

She slowed her descent to a crawl and landed lightly on top of the cylinder, only a few metres from the airlock. She walked to it carefully, then reached behind her to release the hook and clip it to a D-ring set into the rig's hull, as Tyrell had instructed her. It took her a moment to gather her courage, but finally she pressed her glove to the panel and the doors swung open to reveal a dark hole. There was no illumination within the airlock, but the harsh glare of the suit's exterior lamps provided enough light for her to climb inside and close the doors above her.

Deep Six was on emergency power, although the dim red lighting provided scant illumination. The airlock had enough power to cycle, but she had to open the inner doors with a hand crank hanging on the wall. They revealed a metal chamber filled with crates and containers, several of them smashed open and their contents strewn across the deck. According to her readouts, the atmosphere contained high levels of carbon and organic matter, but it was breathable. When she removed her helmet and set it carefully down beside her she realised the air smelled like seared meat.

It took some time to struggle out of her suit by herself, but she eventually lifted off the top half, leaving the bottom clamped upright to the metal deck. There were two exits to the compartment she was in, at opposite ends of the cylinder. She moved cautiously towards the nearest, the echoing silence and eerie half-light making her wish she'd brought a weapon.

She found the first body just beyond the door. It was a man, or had been. The top of his head was missing, sheared clean off above a pair of startled eyes. She swallowed and moved on.

More bodies were scattered through the rig, killed by bullet, beam and blade. There were children too, a boy and a girl, their bodies shielded in vain by a woman with deep cuts in her hands and a dinnerplate-sized circle of red on her chest from a shotgun blast. Orry forced herself not to look away, cold fury forming a knot inside her.

The scoopers had apparently made a stand in the rig's control spaces, which was where the charred smell was coming from. Blackened skin cracked open to reveal pink flesh beneath; bodies were contorted in agony. She guessed the damage had been done by a thermal grenade.

Covering her mouth with her hand, she began looking for Kadiran remains – until a low groan made her whirl, the stench forgotten, to see movement in the semi-darkness. She moved closer and found a young man lying on his side, flesh and clothing fused to the deck. Half his face was burned away. The movement had been made by his remaining arm, which was waving feebly.

She crouched beside him, already knowing there was nothing she could do.

'Elise?' he rasped, looking at her with his one eye. The other was a burst ruin. She didn't know how he was able to stand the pain.

'No, I'm Orry.' She took his hand, feeling his weakness as he tried to squeeze.

'I thought they'd killed you, El, like the others. There's just us left.'

'It's okay,' she said, stroking his hand, trying not to look at his face.

He coughed, and blood clotted at the side of his mouth. 'Harris was right: we should never have let him down here.' She said nothing, and after a moment he continued, 'This is all my fault.'

'No,' she soothed him, 'it's not.'

'It is – a *Kadiran*, for fuck's sake. Of course the League would come looking for him.'

'You couldn't have known,' Orry said, and then, hating herself but knowing she had no choice, 'What happened to him – the Kadiran?'

'They took him back to the flotilla. I heard them talking. Someone's coming to collect him.'

She felt tears on her cheek, but she left them as she crouched, just holding his hand. He didn't say anything else.

When his rasping, laboured breaths finally ceased, she realised she didn't even know his name.

She smelled burnt flesh all the way back up to *Zephyr*. It was in her hair, her clothes, choking inside the confines of the helmet.

The first thing she saw as she rose level with the smoker was the familiar, beloved shape of *Dainty Jane*.

The sight of the starship hanging off *Zephyr*'s stern, dwarfing the craft, filled her with such relief that tears pricked her eyes again, spilling over to trickle down her cheeks. She took a few short, sharp breaths. *Get it together, Orry. Do you want Mender to see you like this?*

Jane's cargo ramp was extended onto the top of the smoker's hull, where Mender stood, pointing his Fabretti at Tyrell, Ethan beside him, watching anxiously. When he saw her, Mender lowered his gun, allowing Tyrell to run over to help her onto the deck. The moment he'd released her helmet, he offered her a respirator, which she clamped over her face and thankfully sucked down clean, odourless oxygen.

'I told you,' he said, only turning to Mender when he was sure Orry was okay. 'She's perfectly fine.'

The old man shot her a questioning look and she gave him a thumbs-up, still too choked up to trust her voice just yet. The Fabretti whined as he deactivated it and slipped it back in its holster.

'Okay, Sis?' Ethan said coolly as he came over, but she knew him too well to be fooled by his feigned nonchalance.

'Yeah, I'm fine,' she said, suddenly very tired. 'It's good to see you.'

'Awww, that's so precious.'

Her lips twitched into a smile. 'You took your sweet time finding me,' she complained.

He grinned. 'Well, *I* just wanted to leave you here, but Mender got teary so we had to come.'

'Hilarious,' the old man growled.

'I see you've met Tyrell,' Orry said.

'Are all your friends so charming?' he enquired.

'She doesn't have any friends,' Ethan said.

She would have kicked him if it weren't for the suit. 'Will you help me get out of this thing?' she asked Tyrell.

Ethan watched as the suit was broken down around her and

finally asked, 'What were you doing down there?'

She glanced at Tyrell and decided he might as well know the truth now, or at least part of it. After all, she still needed his help.

'Let's talk in the cabin,' she suggested. 'This might take a while.'

Orry told them everything that had happened since leaving *Venturer*, omitting only the part about the Kadiran plot to assassinate the Imperator. She could tell *Jane* and the boys about that later, but she didn't feel comfortable with Tyrell knowing. Tears filled her eyes as she described the dead children down in the rig, and the nameless scooper dying in her arms. *Rama, what is wrong with me? I need to get some sleep.*

'Well, that's it, then,' Tyrell said when she'd finished. 'If this Kadiran of yours has been taken to the flotilla, he'll be on the *Hardhaven Voyager*, which means you've lost him. What do you want him for, anyway? He must be worth a lot to someone, the effort you're putting into finding him.'

She didn't respond. Her mind had been working as she talked and an idea was coalescing, although still only half-formed. As she stared out of a porthole at the whorl of clouds, it came into sharp focus.

'How would you like to earn twice what I owe you?' she asked him.

'Now wait one damn minute,' Mender objected. 'Why are we talking about paying this hick?'

'None taken,' Tyrell said drily.

'What can he do that I can't?' the old man continued.

'Tyrell has local knowledge,' she told him. 'And besides, I owe him.'

'Rama,' Mender muttered, 'you've got a bloody plan, haven't you?'

The familiar blend of nerves and excitement started squirming inside her.

'A *plan*?' Tyrell repeated slowly. 'To get that Kadiran off the *Voyager*?'

'Yep.'

'The processing platform we saw yesterday – the *really* big one?'

'It'll be fine,' she assured him. 'Look, Tyrell, the offer's on the table: if I can get him back, I'll pay you double.'

'Triple.'

Mender rolled his eyes.

'Deal,' Orry said.

Tyrell thought for a moment. 'Are we going there in this thing?'

'I'm sure nothing will happen to *Zephyr* if we leave her here for a few hours.'

He looked around *Dainty Jane*'s interior, clearly uncomfortable.

'What have you got against *Jane*?' she asked.

'I've heard about starships,' he replied. 'I'm not sure I want to be broken apart and put back together again. Seems like I wouldn't be me any more – maybe just *think* I am.'

'Piotr's withered balls,' Mender groaned in disbelief.

'Hey, screw you,' Tyrell shot back. 'What's his problem?' he asked Orry.

She smiled. '*Jane*'s postselection drive doesn't work like that. The whole idea messes with your head, to be honest. For a while you exist in two places at once: where the ship *is* and where she's *going*. It works using entanglement. Then you just exist at your destination. The really weird bit is that the navicom uses post-selection to pick where you should be from an infinite number of quantum outcomes – *after* you've arrived. That's what causes the wavefunction to collapse.'

Tyrell stared blankly at her.

'In any case,' she concluded, 'we only use the postselection drive for interstellar travel—'

'That means *between stars*,' Mender added slowly, as if speaking to an idiot.

Tyrell glared at him.

'—so you don't need to worry about it for a short hop to the flotilla,' Orry finished.

Tyrell considered this for a while.

'You sure I can't go in *Zephyr*?' he asked.

25

HARDHAVEN VOYAGER

'Not taking any chances, are they?' Mender said, as *Dainty Jane* glided smoothly towards one of two large landing pads on *Hardhaven Voyager*'s superstructure.

Three heavily armed smokers, each far larger than the one that had moved *Zephyr* on before, had intercepted the starship while she was still kilometres from the processing platform and demanded to know their business. They'd appeared satisfied by Orry's response, but still insisted on escorting *Jane* in.

The pad extending from the superstructure was big enough to accommodate vessels even larger than *Dainty Jane*. Mender set her down gently in the centre and ran through the shutdown checklist with Orry. As the rumble of the main drives died away, leaving only the faint whine of the auxiliary heat exchangers, she saw a tall woman hurry onto the pad, flanked by four armed guards.

'Five people are approaching,' *Jane* announced.

'Welcoming committee,' Orry said, and Mender grunted.

They made their way to the cargo bay, stopping only to collect Tyrell and Ethan from the galley. All of them were armed.

'Remember,' Orry told them, standing with her back to the airlock's inner door, 'think bad thoughts.'

'Way ahead of you,' Mender growled.

Keep your engines warm, Jane, she sent. *We may need to get out of here in a hurry.*

Please be careful, the ship replied. *And remember to put your masks on.*

They donned their respirators as the cargo ramp unsealed with a hiss and Morhelion's atmosphere swirled into the airlock. Mender led them down to the pad. The tall woman who awaited them had a pale complexion and a disdainful expression that reminded Orry of a Ruuz. Her outfit was predominantly leviathan hide: some high-end designer's twist on the practical work clothes of her guards.

'Your business?' she demanded.

'We're here for the Kadiran,' Mender told her.

'Roag sent you?'

There was no surprise in her voice; Orry guessed one of the escort smokers must have tipped her off.

'Where is he?' Mender asked.

The woman looked them over. 'Who are you?' she enquired of Tyrell, evidently noting his clothes.

'Local guide,' Mender said. 'Who are you?'

She was silent for a moment. 'My name is Notable Rayne.'

He barked out a laugh. 'My condolences.'

'And you are?'

'Jack Meredith. These are my associates.'

'They look a little young.'

'I'm sorry,' Orry said acerbically, 'perhaps you'd like to discuss it with human resources?'

Rayne met her gaze. 'How do I know Roag sent you? You could be anyone.'

It was Orry's turn to laugh mockingly. 'Yeah, anyone with their own starship who just happens to know that you have a Kadiran prisoner for whom Cordelia Roag is paying a high price.'

Rayne considered that. 'You have the money?'

'You have the prisoner?' Mender countered.

She pursed her lips and appeared to come to a decision. 'Your weapons.'

Mender's eyes were flint. 'You want them, you come and get them.'

The guards started to raise their weapons, but halted at a gesture from Rayne.

'I'm taking you to see the chief,' she said, 'and that isn't going to happen if you're armed. It's your choice: leave your guns or fly away.'

Hand resting casually on the butt of his Fabretti, Mender glanced at Orry, who shrugged. Sighing, he drew the pistol and handed it to a surprised Ethan. 'As the lady says,' he growled.

Orry handed Ethan her carbine and Tyrell did the same with his hook and the shotgun they'd loaned him. Her brother stomped up the ramp, loaded down with weaponry, and re-appeared a minute later, unarmed.

'Follow me,' Rayne said.

Her guards formed up around them and escorted them from the pad.

The superstructure's interior was exactly as Orry had expected: generic metal passageways lined with pipes and trunking, like pretty much every starship she'd ever been on, just with less padding.

The familiarity ended as Rayne led them through a nonde-script door with the word 'Private' stencilled on it. Beyond it, not only were the metal decks carpeted, but the bulkheads were covered in some kind of faux wood veneer and lined with real fabric.

They climbed a flight of grand stairs and passed through a pair of double doors into the verdant garden covered by the transparent dome Orry had seen from *Zephyr*. The air was filled with perfume; she tasted something sweet on her tongue and remembered the man she'd seen relaxing with a cup of tea while the leviathan was being mutilated below him.

Her boots crunched on fine white gravel as they were ushered past a wrought-iron table set with two chairs on the manicured lawn. Beds of blooming flowers were interspersed with trees. A gardener, a dark-skinned man in a white shirt and baggy trou-sers held up with braces, was toiling in one of the beds, a tray of seedlings resting beside him on the path.

To Orry's surprise, Rayne stopped behind him and announced, 'Roag's delegation is here.'

The man finished pressing down the soil around a freshly planted flower and turned to look at them. He reminded Orry of Mender in some ways, the same craggy face and hard eyes, but he was bald on top and his grey hair had been pulled back into a ponytail.

He stood and brushed dirt off his hands before extending one of them to Mender.

'I'm Guzman. I'm in charge around here.'

Mender shook, brief and firm. 'Meredith. This is my crew.'

'Welcome,' Guzman said, running his eyes over them. 'Roag must want this Kadiran a lot, the amount she's offering.'

'Don't worry, we have your money,' Mender said.

Guzman waved dismissively. 'It's a shame your boss couldn't come herself. I'm a great admirer of her work.'

'She asked us to present her compliments,' Orry said. 'She's a little tied up with other business at the moment and hopes you'll understand.'

He burst out laughing. 'You lie. Cordelia Roag doesn't know who the fuck I am, and why should she? But I can see who's the diplomat in your little crew.' He turned his attention to Tyrell. 'You're Morhelian. Have I seen you somewhere before?'

'It's possible,' Tyrell said smoothly. 'I get around a lot.'

'Local knowledge,' Mender explained, and Guzman nodded thoughtfully.

'And the boy?'

Mender rolled his eyes. 'The son—'

Guzman interrupted with a sharp gesture. 'Can he speak?'

'Yes,' Mender growled.

'Then let him.'

'My mother works for Cordelia,' Ethan said. 'They're friends. I'm learning the business.'

Guzman narrowed his eyes. 'I didn't think Roag had friends.'

'His mother's a whore,' Orry said bluntly, and was pleased with Ethan when he winced and stared at the ground. 'One of Roag's lovers.'

Guzman clapped her brother on the shoulder. 'Nothing wrong with a good whore,' he said. He turned to the rest of them. 'I'll have a feast prepared. We've had some luck, as you can see' – he gestured towards the killing floor – 'and you will be my honoured guests. You can tell me all about Cordelia Roag.'

'Appreciate the offer,' Mender said, 'but we need to be going. The boss is keen to talk to the Kadiran, so if you'll hand him over we can give you the cash and be on our way.'

'No, no, no,' Guzman said, 'I won't hear of it. You must stay the night, share meat and drink with me. Then, in the morning, we can do business.'

'Like I said,' Mender persisted, 'we need to be going.'

Guzman's light-hearted demeanour vanished. 'And like *I* said, you are staying the night. You're on Morhelion now, my friend, and we take our hospitality very seriously.' He turned to Tyrell. 'Isn't that right, um . . . I didn't catch your name?'

'I didn't give it,' Tyrell said with an easy smile. 'I'm Vaughan.'

'Well, Vaughan here will tell you, it's very poor form to turn down a man's hospitality in these parts.'

'I don't give a shit what he tells me,' Mender said, growing a little red. '*I'm* telling *you*: give us the prisoner now.'

The two men stared at each other, Mender glowering, and a thin, dangerous smile on Guzman's lips.

Orry stepped forward. 'We'd be delighted to accept your kind invitation,' she said, and shot Mender a pointed look. '*Wouldn't* we?'

'Roag won't like it,' he muttered, his eyes still locked on Guzman.

'She'll be fine. What's one more day?'

Mender appeared to consider this, then asked, 'What are we eating?'

Guzman laughed and the tension dissolved as quickly as it had arisen. 'I like you, my friend. I can see why Roag sent you. Rayne! Arrange a suite for our guests.'

'I'm not your servant, Francisco.'

A pained expression crossed his face. 'Just fucking *do it*, all right,' he hissed, before turning back to them with an apologetic smile. 'Notable Rayne here thinks *she* should be running the League' – his voice hardened – 'but she lost the vote – *didn't* you, Rayne?'

Stiffly, the tall woman gestured towards the exit. 'If you'll come this way.'

'See you tonight,' Guzman said, beaming, and returned to his seedlings.

'What a psychopath,' Ethan said as he gazed around their expansive suite. He had already scanned it for bugs, but found nothing.

'He knows,' Tyrell said.

'He knows fuck-all,' Mender growled.

'It's fine,' Orry reassured them, wishing she believed it. Ethan was right: Guzman was definitely unstable, which was not what you wanted in a mark, and particularly not when your life depended on things going smoothly. 'We'll just stay in our rooms for a couple of hours, make nice at the feast, go to bed and pick up our guy in the morning. As long as we keep cool, we've nothing to worry about.'

'You have no idea who you're dealing with, do you?' Tyrell said. 'We just met *Francisco Guzman*, the head of the Whaling League. If I'd known he was here I'd never have agreed to any of this – money or no money.'

'Why not?' Mender asked. 'What difference does one man make?'

Tyrell laughed bitterly. 'He might be one man, but he's the most powerful man on the planet. The League may present itself as a civilised trade organisation, but its leadership is all about dead men's shoes. Guzman came to power fifteen years back, after a cull that left half the board dead. He's a ruthless, bloodthirsty bastard.'

'He did have that look about him,' Mender agreed. 'I've seen it before.'

'What else do you know about him?' Orry asked.

'Most of the League nabobs are born to it – the whole thing is run like one big private club, members bringing in their families; there's rarely any new blood. But Guzman is different: he rose up through the ranks. Started when he was a kid and spent years on the smokers, doing every shitty job that came along. Then he spent more years on the killing floor before he went back to the ships, in command this time. From there, he worked his way into management – and ended up taking over the whole damn League. Don't let that humble gardener crap fool you: Francisco Guzman is one scary motherfucker.'

'Rayne doesn't like him much,' Ethan observed.

'I don't know her,' Tyrell admitted, 'but she looks like she's a primogeniture, and the prims all hate Guzman because he wasn't born to it.'

'Sounds familiar,' Orry said. 'Will he keep his promise?'

Tyrell's palm rasped over his stubble as he considered that. 'If he's onto us, we're dead. No question. If he *suspects* we're not on the level, we'll *wish* we were dead. Guzman has ways of finding out the truth – and once he does, he'll probably hand you over to this Roag woman, and from everything I've heard, she's even worse than him, which is saying something.'

Orry and Mender exchanged a glance.

'What a delightful picture you paint,' Ethan said cheerily.

'If I'm wrong and by some miracle Guzman believes you really have come from Roag, then he'll hand over your Kadiran, but not until he sees the money. You *do* have the money, don't you?'

Orry let her expression answer for her.

Tyrell stared at her. 'You have to be kidding me,' he exclaimed. 'Why the hell did I let you talk me into this half-arsed excursion?'

'Oh, man up,' Orry snapped, annoyed because she knew he was right. 'You're a thief, aren't you? There must be *stacks* of money on this platform. So you steal it tonight, we'll give it back to Guzman in the morning and be away from this godforsaken planet before he figures out what we did.'

'*You'll* be away from this planet,' he pointed out angrily. 'What about me?'

'We'll drop you off somewhere,' she told him. 'You can start a new life.'

'With *what*?'

'Steal something extra for yourself!' She was angry at herself, not him. This whole job was too rushed, too full of holes she simply hadn't had time to fill, and now she was taking it out on Tyrell. She'd put them all in harm's way – and for what? To possibly save the Imperator? Again. She hated the Ascendancy, so why did it feel like it was always up to her to stop the whole corrupt structure tearing itself apart? She took a deep breath, trying to calm down. They were here now, and admitting her doubts would only make things worse.

The angrier Tyrell got, the more measured his words became. 'This is my home,' he said quietly.

'It's a big planet—'

'And the League is *everywhere* – or did you not listen to a word I just said?'

'Well, I hate to say it, but you don't have much of a choice, do you? If we don't get that money, Guzman will know something is rotten. At least my way you get to stick it to him and the League. And when Roag finds out he let her prisoner go she's not going to be best pleased, is she? Going after you will be *way* down his list of priorities.'

'Unless Roag sends him after me to get to you.'

Shit – he has a point. 'I'm not a fortune-teller,' she said, avoiding his eyes.

Tyrell looked like he wanted to punch her. 'I wish I'd never met you.'

'She has that effect on most men,' Ethan said lightly.

Tyrell turned on his heel and marched to the door.

'Where are you going?' Orry asked.

He stopped at the door and looked back. 'Do you know how much Roag is offering for the Kadiran?'

'No . . .' she replied, defensively.

'Do you know where they keep the money round here?'

'No, I–'

'Then I'd better go and find out, hadn't I?' Snagging a bottle from the drinks cabinet, he walked out and slammed the door after him.

Orry turned to the others, hiding her dismay. 'I don't think he's very happy.'

Mender barked out a laugh and limped over to investigate the cabinet. 'You think?'

'You did kind of give him the shaft, Sis,' Ethan pointed out.

'You think I don't know that?' She didn't feel good about it. Tyrell might be a crook, but so was she. He was selfish and a womaniser, but did that justify the way she was treating him? She *would* make things right with him, one way or another – if they got out of this mess alive.

Mender picked up a lacquered wooden box, which he opened to reveal an elaborate bottle of pale green liquid nestled in a silk lining. He whistled appreciatively.

Orry plucked the box from his hand and handed it to Ethan, who examined it curiously. 'I'm sure there'll be plenty of booze at the feast,' she told Mender. 'At least *try* to keep your wits together, will you?'

He scowled at her. 'If I were you,' he said, 'I'd be more worried about your new friend Tyrell selling us out to Guzman.'

'He wouldn't do that,' she protested.

'Oh no?' He fixed her with a stare from his good eye. 'Are you willing to bet our lives on that?'

26

THE RIGHT THING

Guzman's feast was undoubtedly lavish, but it was an interminable affair. The theme had quickly become apparent as dish
after dish came to the table: leviathan broth, leviathan steak,
flaked leviathan hide. Orry couldn't bring herself to touch
any of it. When Guzman had finally noticed and asked why
she wasn't eating, she told him she was a vegetarian – which
caused much amusement among the gathering of whalers.
It was obvious from what she finally ended up with that the
platform's chef was not used to such requests. That was fine,
though; she was too worried about what Tyrell was doing to
eat anyway.

Guzman had invited six other nabobs to join them: all rich
and spoilt, all highly placed in the Whaling League. Thankfully, they had left her and Ethan alone for most of the meal,
delighting instead in Mender's lurid tales about Cordelia Roag
– Mender really had been her senior enforcer for many years,
although he rarely talked about that period of his life. Orry
suspected most of the stories were true; she didn't think he had
the imagination to make up stuff like that. She listened with

interest and not a little discomfort, especially when she realised Ethan was as rapt as the fawning prims.

Guzman, sitting beside her at the head of the table, drained his wine and waited for it to be refilled by a white-jacketed steward, then leaned in closer. He smelled subtly of cologne, but when he spoke, the stench of seared leviathan flesh turned her stomach.

'Your friend is an accomplished storyteller,' he said.

'He's had a drink.'

Guzman chuckled, studying her face. Feeling uncomfortable, she kept her eyes fixed on Mender. 'You know, when you first arrived I had my doubts about you,' he said, 'but I have to admit, if this guy doesn't work for Roag he's the best liar I've ever met – and I'm a whaler.' He paused, then changed tack. 'How did you enjoy your salad?'

'It was delicious.'

He laughed at that. 'We tend to be unapologetic carnivores in this business, I'm afraid. I hope that doesn't offend you.'

'Not at all,' she lied smoothly.

He drank, and when he returned his glass to the table his hand was resting against hers.

She resisted the urge to recoil. 'Can I ask you a question?' she said, turning to face him. When he inclined his head, she continued, 'You might not like it.'

He grinned, delighted. 'This is not the usual polite chitchat. Continue, please.'

'The drifters – you know they're sentient, don't you?'

'You must have a very low opinion of me, miz, to imagine that I would willingly slaughter intelligent creatures. Tell me, how long have you been on Morhelion?'

'Not long.'

'And do you know when this colony was founded? Three hundred years ago, during the First Expansion. And how have we survived for so long, in such an inhospitable place? The trickle of abyssal gases pulled up by the scoopers in their rigs?' He snorted. 'It's not worth the Company's fuel to come and get it. The *only* reason we are still here is the drifters, and the League. Without the export market, this colony would be dead in five years. There's simply no way we could possibly produce what we need, confined as we are to the bubble habitats.'

'So you're saying it's a matter of survival: you know the leviathans are sentient, but you don't care.'

'The drifters are *not* sentient. If they were, the Administrate would shut down all whaling operations under Article 2 of the Xeno Rights Act – and that would kill Morhelion.'

'And your golden goose along with it.'

'What is my personal wealth compared to the wellbeing of my planet?'

Guzman's noble tone made her want to grind her dessert into his face. '*Your* planet? I'm not sure how the governor would respond to that claim.'

He made a sour face. 'What governor? That drunken Ruuz boor sent here by his father as punishment for fiddling with one of the house staff? He's far too concerned with the inside of a bottle to do anything but accept the payments we send him every month.'

Orry said nothing. *Never let personal feelings get in the way of the job*, her father had always told her. Until now she'd never realised how difficult that could be.

Guzman shifted closer and indicated the other guests with a sweep of his glass. 'You know, any one of these people would cut out my heart without a thought if they weren't so shit-scared of me. They hate me because I'm where they want to be, and because of where I came from.' He set his wine down and brushed her hair with his hand. 'I find your company very pleasant. Why don't we go somewhere quieter, where we can talk more privately?'

She stood, a little too abruptly. 'Thank you for a wonderful meal, but I have a long journey tomorrow.'

A scowl, quickly controlled, and Guzman rose too. He bowed and kissed her hand, his wine-moist lips lingering against her skin. 'Of course.'

'Meredith,' she snapped at Mender.

He looked over, surprised, then he and Ethan made their apologies and followed her to the door.

'See you tomorrow,' Guzman said.

She forced a smile, and strode away.

Night had fallen but the work never ceased. From his vantage point near the top of the superstructure, Tyrell watched the bloody toil far below, illuminated by the harsh glare of arclights mounted on high poles. Lindqvist would be down there some-where, as well as others he knew, but he wasn't overly concerned about being recognised; the workers on the killing floor would never be allowed into the executive levels. To his right he could see *Dainty Jane*, a dark mound on one of the two pads extending from this part of the superstructure. The other pad was empty, patrolled by a solitary, bored-looking figure.

The woman raised her assault rifle as he walked onto the pad, then lowered it again when he waved at her with the bottle he was carrying.

'Hello!' he called cheerfully.

'This pad's off-limits,' she told him.

'Sure, sure,' he agreed, walking up to her and stopping to stare out over the killing floor. 'Wow, kind of a great view from up here, though.'

'What do you want?'

He gave her his most charming grin and raised the bottle. 'I found this, and I hate drinking alone.' He opened it and briefly moved the respirator away from his mouth to take a hit of the good stuff. The brandy burned its way to his stomach and he snapped the mask back in place, tasting the bitter tang of aether.

The guard eyed the drink greedily, then looked around. They were entirely alone. She grabbed his arm and dragged him to the shadows at one edge of the pad. He handed her the bottle and she adjusted her own mask before raising the brandy to her lips. She passed it back. 'You're one of Roag's crew,' she said, her voice muffled by the respirator. 'I saw you arrive.'

'I'm not really with them,' he told her. 'I'm just the local guide.'

She looked him over. 'Where you from?'

'Spumehead.' He lifted the bottle again, taking his time before returning it to her.

'What a shithole.'

He chuckled. 'You've been, then.'

'What's your name?'

'Vaughan Tyson,' he said with a slight bow. She was studying him with more interest now, a look he recognised.

'I'm Kas.'

He bowed again. 'I think I owe you an apology.'

'For what?'

'I'm guessing you wouldn't normally be out here guarding an empty pad at this time of night.'

'I don't follow.'

'Guzman must be keen to protect this prisoner – that's what all the extra security is for, isn't it? So how much is Roag offering for him? Nobody tells me anything.'

She laughed. 'I heard a cool million, but that's not why he's tripled security. You didn't hear?'

'Hear what?' he asked, before taking his turn with the bottle.

'Last night – they found a whalestone.'

Tyrell choked on the brandy, coughing half of it up, then sucking down a lungful of astringent aether, which promptly made the coughing ten times worse. 'You're shitting me,' he eventually managed to get out, eyes streaming.

Kas was watching, amused. 'It's the truth,' she replied. 'The guy who found it is still celebrating. Guess his days of wading through drifter guts are behind him. Says he's gonna buy a bubble with his share: his own little kingdom.'

Tyrell couldn't stop his hand from trembling when he handed her the bottle. Finding a whalestone? That was the dream of every whaler. The iridescent nuggets of solidified gases formed in the digestive tracts of fewer than one in ten thousand leviathans, and they fetched many millions at auction. 'And it's here? On the *Voyager*?' He looked around and lowered his voice. 'Right now?'

She nodded, her eyes alight with an excitement that mirrored his own, and Tyrell watched with admiration as she demolished a good quarter of the bottle in one go.

'No wonder Guzman hiked the security,' he said, trying to

keep his voice casual, then, 'I suppose he's keeping it with the rest of his loot?'

'That,' she said, pressing a finger to his lips, 'is the big secret.' She moved closer, gazing up at him from lowered eyelids. She wasn't unattractive, although there was a touch too much of the whaler's daughter about her for his taste. 'He's doubled the guards on the vault,' she continued, slurring slightly now, 'but he's also posted them in a load of other places so as not to give anything away.'

'That's smart,' Tyrell said, running a finger down the curve of her cheek.

She smiled and took another drink. The effects of the alcohol were beginning to show in her eyes. He knew he should be asking about the vault, but screw the Kadiran – this was a *whalestone*. 'So where d'you think it is?' he asked, slurring a little himself and staggering for effect.

'Heh.' She tapped the side of her nose.

He grinned and waggled a finger drunkenly. In his experience inebriation worked like that, getting a signal boost from those you were with. 'You know something, don't you?'

'Maybe.' She was enjoying this.

'Come on then, spill.'

'Okay,' she said, suddenly animated, showing off, 'so, this mate of mine was on duty when they found it, and an hour later he's detailed to escort Guzman, who was carrying a case—'

'What kind of case?'

A look of irritation crossed her face. 'I don't know, like a briefcase – but big enough to hold a whalestone.'

'So where did he take it?'

Her smile returned and she laid a hand on his chest, looking up at him. 'Now why would I tell you that?'

He leaned in until their respirators were almost touching. 'Because you want to,' he murmured through the plastic.

Her breath steamed her mask, hiding her mouth. 'The data store,' she said. 'I've been thinking about it: it's the perfect place. It's secure, and no one ever goes there unless there's an audit. And he hasn't even posted a guard.'

Tyrell thought about that. If he found a whalestone he'd put a dozen guards on it – but then again, where do you find a dozen people you can trust not to steal it? 'I suppose it's possible,' he admitted.

She slapped his chest. '*Possible*, my arse. It's there.'

He looked down. 'And a fine arse it is, too,' he said playfully, stroking it.

Her free hand was moving too, slipping inside his shirt. 'So,' she said seductively, 'you're here for the night?'

'Looks like it. Guzman wants to cosy up to Roag's crew.'

'Good,' she said, tugging at his chest hair.

He winced. 'I was kind of hoping it would be an in and out job, but now I'm glad we're stopping.'

'Me too,' Kas murmured. With a breathy giggle she added, 'Though I do like an in and out job.'

He ran his fingers through her hair, stroking her head. 'I've never seen an actual Kadiran. Where're they keeping him?'

'Security centre, deck three,' she said, closing her eyes and raising her face to his.

He wondered how this was going to work with respirators on.

A rumble of engines made her step quickly back and tuck in her shirt. A smoker was approaching the pad, clouds swirling beneath its landing jets. The vessel settled onto the pad and a hatch opened in its side. A man jumped down and hurried over to them, bent against the blast from the idling craft until it lifted, when the downdraught almost bowled him over.

The smoker banked and stuttered away.

Kas broke off and strode out to meet the newcomer, suddenly all business, but Tyrell saw her relax as the man raised his bowed head to reveal his face. They clasped hands and she led him back to the edge of the pad.

'This is Carpenter,' she said. 'We go way back.'

'Tyson,' Tyrell said. 'Drink?'

'Thanks, brother.' Carpenter accepted the brandy and did some damage to it.

'What brings you way out here?' Kas asked. 'Get bored with Hardhaven bubble?'

'Message for Guzman.' He returned the bottle to Tyrell. 'Roag's crew have arrived. They'll be here in the morning.'

Tyrell's heart stopped, but Kas just laughed. 'You're out of the loop, mate. They're already here.'

'No,' he said firmly, 'they're spending the night at Hardhaven.'

Her smile faded as her brandy-soaked brain tried to process this, but by the time she reached for her rifle, Tyrell was already swinging the heavy bottle, which shattered against the side of her skull and dropped her like she'd been poleaxed.

Carpenter was also slow to react, but as shock slowly registered on his face and he reached for the pistol holstered at his waist, Tyrell jammed his shoulder into the man's midriff and drove him backwards into the safety rail surrounding the pad. He bent double, gasping at the impact, and Tyrell flung his arms around the man's legs and heaved him up and over the barrier.

At the last moment, his flailing hands grabbed hold of Tyrell's

shirt and he hung there, dangling over the dizzying drop into Morhelion's clouds. He stared up, wide-eyed, his mouth moving silently behind his mask.

The top rail was digging painfully into Tyrell's ribs as Carpenter's weight dragged on him. He hammered at the man's fingers, locked into the fabric of his shirt, managing at last to prise one hand open. When Carpenter gasped and fell another half a metre, the jerk almost pulled Tyrell over the rail – but finally, he felt the fabric rip and the man's mouth fell open in a silent scream as he plummeted away from the platform.

Tyrell staggered back, unbalanced by his sudden release, then quickly returned to the rail. He watched his victim falling, his arms flailing, a ribbon of white cloth still clutched in one hand. He glanced quickly around, chest heaving, but everybody was too busy on the killing floor to have noticed a thing.

When he looked back over the rail, Carpenter was gone.

Shuddering, he returned to Kas' crumpled form and rolled her onto her back. Gripping her under the arms, he dragged her backwards across the pad to the rail. He looked at the blood coating the side of her face and wondered what Orry would do in his position. *The right thing*, he imagined: tie her up and hide her somewhere.

He shook his head scornfully. *Somewhere she'll be discovered – but hey, at least we'll all die with a clear conscience.*

He checked to make sure he was still unobserved, then crouched beside the unconscious woman, rolled her under the rail to the edge and pushed her over.

He didn't watch her fall.

27

YOU GO FIRST

Orry felt a huge rush of relief when she found Tyrell waiting in the suite after the feast, but her heart sank when he opened his mouth and announced, 'We're in the shit.'

'So what's new?' Mender grumbled, following her inside. Ethan, bringing up the rear, shut the door after them.

'Roag's crew are already at Hardhaven bubble,' Tyrell explained, 'and they'll be here in the morning.'

'Yay,' Ethan said, and collapsed onto the bed.

'Are you sure?' Orry asked sharply.

'Dead sure.'

Just bloody perfect. 'Well, at least we don't have to worry about getting Guzman's money now. Did you find out where the Kadiran is?'

'There are a couple of places he might be. You thinking of getting him out tonight?'

'I suppose *you* want us to run?'

He grinned. 'You have a very low opinion of me. I say let's go get him – I've never met a Kadiran.'

'You're not missing much,' Mender said.

Orry studied Tyrell's face, but he was giving nothing away. 'Okay,' she said, 'we'll give it a couple of hours to let the place get nice and quiet after the feast, then we'll go and rescue him. Ethan, do you have everything you need to bypass security?'

'Right here.' He tapped his boot heel.

'Anything you can do from the suite?'

'I thought you might ask that,' he said, extracting his lock-pick set. 'Pass me that chair, will you?'

She carried it over to him and helped him climb onto it, a multipurpose microtool in his mouth. He reached up to one of the conduits running across the ceiling and a minute later had it open and was stripping the insulation from several of the wires running inside. Standing on one leg, he extracted his node extender from his other heel and connected it to the exposed conduit cores. Then he climbed back down and sat on the end of the bed again. He gave her a wink and closed his eyes.

Orry smiled and left him to it, resisting the urge to join Tyrell in a drink while she waited. It was going to be a long few hours, but she wanted a clear head at the end of it.

'You said there wouldn't be any guards,' Orry hissed.

Tyrell glared at her.

Ethan had swiftly gained full access to *Hardhaven Voyager*'s antiquated network of cameras and from his makeshift command station in the suite, he had used the system to guide them through the remote passageways deep within the superstructure. Now they were staring at an armed guard standing outside a heavy door near the end of the passageway. He looked remarkably alert, considering the early hour.

Orry ducked back before he spotted her. *Ethan*, she sent,

grateful for the shielding within the superstructure that allowed integuary communication, *I need to get behind this guy. Any way to do it?*

Why? What are you planning? No, forget that – I don't want to know. There's a cable run under the deck, but I'm not sure you'll fit in there with your massive backside.

Funny. Where is it?

There's a grate behind you, centre of the corridor you're in, about five metres back the way you came.

She retraced her steps until she found it and levered the square of metal up, careful to make no sound.

'What are you doing?' Mender whispered.

She lowered herself into the crawlspace, which came up to her hips. 'I'm going to distract the guard. Don't let him shoot me.'

'And how am I supposed to do that with no gun?'

Did the old man look worried? She gave him a smile. 'You'll figure it out.'

Despite Ethan's sarky comment, there was ample room for her in the crawlspace, which had cabling running along both sides, gathered every metre or so with plastic ties. She made her way on her hands and knees to the junction where the tunnel split, turned right and passed silently under the guard, who she could see through the occasional narrow gaps in the deck plates above her. The crawlspace ended at a sheet of steel, with the cables feeding through it into the room beyond.

Twisting onto her back, she saw another grate above her head, behind the guard.

Ready? she sent.

Ready, Mender replied.

Be careful, Ethan added.

She pressed her palms to the metal grille above her head and began to stand, carefully opening the grate as she rose. She was halfway up when the hinges let out a squeal and the guard whirled, raising his shotgun.

'What the hell?' He took a step towards her. 'Out of there – now!'

'Okay, okay,' she said, keeping her voice calm despite the yawning in her stomach at the sight of the shotgun. *Panic is infectious*, Dad always used to tell her. *When someone's pointing a gun at you*, don't *act jumpy.*

She tipped the grate back on its hinges and climbed out, slow and steady.

'Who are you?' the guard, a young man, demanded. Jet-black hair fell over one eye, but he had a cruel face. 'What the fuck are you doing down there?'

She kept her eyes fixed on his as she glimpsed Mender moving behind him. Despite his gammy leg, the old man could be silent as a ghost when he needed to.

'Routine maintenance,' she ventured hopefully.

The guard stiffened, a look of fear replacing the suspicion on his face.

'Now, don't be doing anything stupid, laddie,' Mender said from somewhere behind him. 'Just stay cool and hand me your piece, nice and easy like, and nobody has to die tonight.'

Sweat stood out on the guard's face. 'I'll shoot the girl,' he said, with enough conviction to tighten Orry's throat.

Mender chuckled.

The guard's brow creased. 'What's so funny?'

'See, son, you're not thinking things through. And that's

fine: a gun in the back tends to do that to a man. So, why not just take a moment and consider: you shoot her, and what am I going to do?'

'Shoot me?'

'And is that what you want? Your guts all steaming on the deck in front of you?'

The guard swallowed.

'No, of course it isn't. Now, I ain't gonna lie to you, we've come for what's behind that door. And you're guarding that door. And your suggestion back there of shooting the girl, well, that does you credit. A lot of hard men would have just folded, right there and then. But you have to ask yourself, son: is this really worth dying over?'

The guard moistened his lips and Orry saw the fight go out of him. 'What will you do to me?'

'Not a thing. We'll just lock you in that room when we're done and be on our way. I could rough you up a little if you like, make it look like you put up a fight.'

The guard hesitated a moment longer, then lowered his gun. Mender stepped into view and took it, and Orry saw the hipflask he was holding in one hand – its cap about the same diameter as a pistol barrel. Relief washed over her as Mender pocketed the flask and pointed the guard's own shotgun at him.

'Don't worry, I wasn't bullshitting you,' he told the man, who was staring at him with wide eyes.

That was intense, Ethan sent.

Glad you enjoyed it, Orry replied. *Can you open the door?*

Sure, give me a minute.

Take your time, she sent drily.

Tyrell appeared from the corner and joined her by the door. He was edgy, almost buzzing. 'Can he open it?'

'Sure, give him a minute.'

He glanced around, then looked back at the door, a solid sheet of metal with a red light glowing by the handle. Tyrell raised himself onto the balls of his feet and back down again.

'What's with you?' she asked. 'Never robbed anyone before?'

He gave her an easy smile. 'When the door opens, you stay here with Mender,' he said. 'I'll go in first.'

She frowned, suddenly suspicious.

'I feel bad,' he explained. 'I said there were no guards – that guy could have killed you.'

Now she was certain he was up to something. 'I'm touched by your concern, but I think I'll be fine.'

A sidelong glance at her, then his eyes returned to the door. 'Suit yourself.' A muscle twitched beneath his stubble.

She heard a metallic *thunk* from within the door and the red light turned green.

Alarms? she asked.

Disabled – I think, Ethan replied.

Filling me with confidence here. Any unpleasant surprises?

No idea. The room's air-gapped; there's no signal going in or out.

She smiled sweetly at Tyrell. 'I've reconsidered. You can go first.'

He frowned and Orry tried not to wince as he gripped the handle and forced it down, pushing the heavy door inwards. He walked inside.

She gave it a few seconds. When there were still no screams, she told Mender to stay with the guard and went after Tyrell. The room was large, the walls lined with hundreds of tubes, each the width of her fist. Many of them were filled with rolled up databranes. There was no Kadiran.

Tyrell was standing at a metal desk in the centre of the room, examining a briefcase, the sort of thing used to transport databranes. This one was empty, but a brane was lying on the desk beside it. He turned as she entered, looking like a child who'd dropped his ice-cone.

'Doesn't look much like a prison to me,' she said.

His desolate expression vanished and he shrugged. 'Maybe we'll have more luck in the next place.'

'I certainly hope so.'

He strode past her and out of the room. Orry stayed a moment to survey the tubes lining the walls. *So much data.* She picked up the databrane from the desk and shook it rigid. It was security locked, with the logo of the Administrate's Science Secretariat at the top. She frowned at that, then folded up the brane and shoved it into a pocket.

'Where next?' she asked Tyrell as she left the room.

'Security centre, level three.'

Mender glared at him. 'There's a fucking security centre? Then why the hell are we wasting our time down here?'

Tyrell rounded on him. 'Hey, I'm just going on what I was told, okay? If you don't like it, go mine your own information.'

'Can we save this for later?' Orry suggested. *Ethan, can you get us to the security centre on level three?*

I can get you there, but that place is definitely *guarded – I'm looking at it now. Four . . . no, wait: three of them. All packing.*

She frowned. *Okay, just direct us to it. I'll figure something out on the way.*

You got it, Sis.

She nodded at Mender, who shoved the white-faced guard through the open door.

'Wait,' the man said. 'Hit me.'

'You sure?' Mender asked.

'Ye—'

Mender's fist slammed into his jaw. The guard dropped, eyes fluttering.

'You enjoyed that, didn't you?' Orry asked as the old man closed the door.

He smiled as he rubbed his knuckles, and glanced longingly at Tyrell.

28

THE STRATAGEM
DISHONOURS US

The security centre was in a more populated area of the super-structure, but Ethan only needed to reroute them twice to avoid running into crew. Orry was worrying about the time this was taking: dawn was approaching and the empty passageways would soon start to fill up.

'Ready?' she asked Tyrell, who nodded and shook out his arms and legs like an actor preparing to go on stage. She rolled her eyes.

Okay, little brother, whenever you're ready.

One sec . . . there.

The light at the side of the heavy door changed from red to green.

'Right behind you,' Tyrell said, and Mender gave her a re-assuring nod, although his face was strained.

She jogged towards the door, slowing to let it slide open, then ran on into the room beyond. As she entered she looked back over her shoulder and giggled like a schoolgirl. The security centre was a wide compartment with cell doors lining the rear wall. Only one of them was closed. The three guards were just where Ethan had said they would be: a woman leaning back in a revolving chair, boots up on a desk, a large man nearby, cleaning his gun, and a second woman dozing on a couch.

The woman behind the desk leaped to her feet as Orry entered, drawing her sidearm in the same move.

'Who the fuck are you?' she demanded, narrowing shrewd eyes. 'How did you get in here?'

Orry let her smile fade a little, then she burst out laughing.

The second guard looked up from his disassembled weapon and rose slowly. He was a big man, the rolled-up sleeves of his khaki T-shirt tight around bulging arm muscles. 'I'll tell you how she got in here,' he said, crossing to the couch. 'Goddamn Hwang didn't lock the door - *again*.' He kicked the sleeping woman on the couch, who jerked awake.

'What the *fuck*, Bannerjee?' she snarled.

'Who are you?' the first guard repeated, coming out from behind her desk to approach Orry.

'Relax, De Falco,' the one called Bannerjee said. 'She's just some drunk slapper.' He walked closer and Hwang raised her middle finger at his departing back.

'Hey!' Orry objected, swaying slightly. 'I'm not a slapper.'

'This isn't fucking funny,' the first guard - De Falco - snarled. 'This is supposed to be a secure area. Fuck's sake, Hwang - tonight of all nights?'

'I didn't—' the woman on the couch began, but then the door hissed open again and Tyrell ran in.

'I know you're in here, Sweetcheeks! Bring that tight arse over—' He stopped abruptly at the sight of De Falco's pistol. 'Oh - hey there, sister. What's up?'

'Hey yourself,' she said coldly. Beside her, Bannerjee seemed to be finding the whole situation hugely amusing.

'Planning on having a good night?' he asked lasciviously.

Tyrell gave him a lopsided smile and walked over to Orry.

De Falco moved to stand in front of her, while Bannerjee loomed over Tyrell. Ethan hadn't mentioned the man's sheer size and now she wondered if Tyrell could handle him. To Orry's surprise, De Falco gave her a lecherous look. *That should make things easier*, she thought, smiling shyly back from beneath lowered lashes. Beside her, Bannerjee was directing a similar look at Tyrell.

'Hwang,' De Falco said, 'lock that fucking door.' She stepped closer to Orry, her gun held more loosely now.

Orry sidestepped out of the line of fire while grabbing the woman's wrist and turned, dragging De Falco in a tight circle as she twisted her wrist back on itself and used it to force her to the deck, all the time keeping the muzzle pointed away from herself.

Beside her, Tyrell was moving too.

She had De Falco face-down and immobilised at her feet now, her grip on the woman's right arm bringing it almost to breaking point. The weapon was still in the woman's right hand, but twisted painfully to point down at her. Orry matched her grip and slipped the pistol from unresisting fingers, checked the safety was off, then pointed it at De Falco's head before glancing over at Tyrell—

—who cannoned into her, knocking her flying and sending the pistol clattering away. He was up again immediately and grinning at her through blood-rimed teeth before launching himself back at Bannerjee.

De Falco jumped up too and lunged at her, but Orry, staying

low to the floor, spun and swept the guard's legs out from under her, sending her crashing onto her back.

Orry glanced around, but the pistol was gone. On the other side of the room, Tyrell was clinging like a monkey to Bannerjee's back, his forearm tight across the big man's windpipe as he sank his teeth into his ear. The giant roared and crashed around, trying to throw his tormentor clear.

Orry grabbed the chair from behind the desk and brought it down on De Falco's head as she tried to stand. The guard dropped and lay still.

Tyrell lost his grip but took a chunk of Bannerjee's ear with him as he tumbled into Hwang, who'd made it off the couch and was reaching for her own gun. Bannerjee touched his damaged ear, stared at the blood on his palm, then started towards Tyrell with a murderous look on his face.

The door hissed open.

'Everybody just calm the *fuck* down,' Mender said, levelling his stolen shotgun at Bannerjee, who stopped dead. 'You, big guy: pick up your pal and get in a cell. You too, lady.'

Breathing heavily, Orry went to stand beside him as Bannerjee helped De Falco up and half-carried her into one of the open cells. Tyrell disentangled himself from Hwang and winked at her as she followed her comrades, glaring.

'You'll never get away with this,' Bannerjee snarled. 'Guzman is going to have your—'

The cell door slammed shut.

'Are you all right?' Orry asked Tyrell, who was probing gingerly inside his mouth with a finger.

He spat blood onto the floor and grinned. 'He was a big fella.'

'He is,' she agreed.

'You know how to handle yourself,' he continued approvingly. 'Nice moves.'

Her answering smile froze at the sound of a vacuum flush from a side corridor.

Oh, shit, Ethan sent, *I might have missed—*

'Don't fucking move!'

An older man had appeared at the entrance to the corridor and was pointing a darklight rifle at them. Mender swung towards him but the rifle hummed and the end of the shotgun vanished in a swirl of particulates.

Mender dropped the ruined weapon and held up his hands.

Wait . . . just wait, Ethan sent, *I've got this – give me a minute.*

The grey-haired man walked into the room and stopped in front of one of the two occupied cells. 'What have you done with them?' he asked.

'Your friends are fine,' Orry reassured him, wondering if he might take a bribe. *No,* she decided reluctantly, *he doesn't look the sort.* 'We put them in there.' She pointed at the cell a couple of doors away from him, but he didn't look round.

'What are you doing here?' he demanded. 'Have you come for the Kadiran?'

She exchanged a glance with Mender and decided bribery was at least worth a shot. After all, what did they have to lose? 'If you let us take him,' she said, 'we'll make it worth your while.'

'How much?' the man asked.

'How much do you want?'

He snorted as if that was the wrong answer. 'Actually, what I want is for you to get into one of these cells. You're pretty much screwed.'

Orry gritted her teeth; she hated an honest man.

Got it! Ethan sent.

The cell door behind the grey-haired man shot open, revealing a pitch-black space beyond. Startled, he began to turn – then let out a squawk as a thick arm reached out of the darkness, clutched him by the throat and jerked him into the cell.

Orry winced as his strangled scream was cut short by a sickening crunch of bone. Blood washed out of the door.

Don't bother to thank me, Ethan sent.

She ignored him and peered inside the cell. 'Hello?' she called, forcing her legs to carry her a few steps closer. She glanced round to see a look of horrified fascination on Tyrell's blood-streaked face. Mender was wearing the same sour expression he always adopted when he didn't have a gun and thought it was her fault.

A massive shape shifted in the darkness and a Kadiran male stepped into the light. The darklight rifle looked like a toy in his giant hands. Orry had only been in the presence of Kadiran once before, and this one filled her with the same primal, bowel-loosening fear. He dwarfed Tyrell, who was a tall man, but the most frightening thing was his face: tiny, lifeless eyes set deep beneath bony brows, a surprisingly fragile-looking mouth protected by a cage of bones. The wide leathery crest crossing his head from earhole to earhole was tattooed with colourful markings.

She got the impression from the alien's posture that killing one human wasn't going to be enough for him.

'I'm Orry Kent,' she said, croaking a little through a suddenly dry throat. 'I'm here to rescue you.'

The monster surveyed her. 'You are not known,' he finally rumbled, and Orry was surprised – not just that he understood her, but that he could respond without a translation device. Very few Kadiran spoke English.

'I'm here to rescue you,' she said insistently. 'Major Irina Yolkina sent me.'

His breath sounded like a bull about to charge. 'Major Irina Yolkina' – he mangled the name badly – 'is not known.' He moved away from the cell, his massive head turning to survey the room.

'We don't have any weapons,' Orry said. 'We're not here to harm you. We let you out.'

'Do not obstruct my path, female.'

Somehow, she made herself remain still as the alien approached her, heading for the exit.

'We have a ship,' Tyrell said.

The Kadiran stopped, as if noticing him for the first time.

'Cordelia Roag is sending a crew for you,' Orry said. 'They'll be here in a few hours. You have to come with us.'

'To what location?'

'Wherever you like.'

'For what purpose?'

'You have information I need, about—' She stopped and glanced at Tyrell, then decided he may as well know everything. 'Information about the plot to kill the Imperator,' she finished.

Tyrell's eyes widened.

'Such information is not known,' the Kadiran said.

'But . . . I thought you knew about that – I was told—'

'Fantastic,' Tyrell commented drily.

She ignored him, her mind whirring. 'You don't know *any-thing* about a plot between the Kadiran and someone in the Ascendancy? Something to do with Cordelia Roag?'

The expression on the alien's broad face altered. 'For what entity or association do you toil?'

It took her a moment to unpack that one. 'I don't work for anyone, really. I just want to stop this . . . whatever it is . . . from happening.'

The Kadiran's expression changed again, together with his posture. *Less aggressive?* Orry thought. She hoped she was right.

'The stratagem dishonours us,' he stated.

Relief filled her. 'So you *do* know something.' She felt like she was getting the hang of this now. 'If it dishonours you, help me stop it.'

He thought for a moment.

'Where is your vessel?'

29

I WON'T SAY THIS AGAIN

'Well this is crap,' Ethan said, staring at the twenty or so heavily armed whalers who were blocking their route to *Dainty Jane*. 'They were *not* there when I disconnected from the security net.'

Orry could see Francisco Guzman standing on the pad with his crew, light glinting from the barrel of a silver-plated revolver as he used it to direct them into the cover provided by cargo crates and loading equipment.

'Your vessel is inaccessible,' the Kadiran stated redundantly, joining her at the door. 'This is a lamentable state.'

She ignored the meaty odour coming off him and concentrated on trying to raise *Jane* with her integuary, with no success.

'We got company,' Mender said from behind her.

'I can see that,' she snapped.

'Not out there – behind—'

He was interrupted by a burst of automatic weapons fire, muzzle-flashes strobing at the far end of the dim corridor they'd just come down. Jets of steam erupted as bullets tore through the wall beside them. Mender dragged Ethan behind him before returning fire with a pistol he'd taken from the security centre.

'We have to get out of here,' Tyrell said.

'You think?' Orry said snarkily. 'That's what they want, to drive us onto Guzman's guns.'

'Well, it's working, isn't it?' he snapped back. 'We're dead if we stay here.'

He ducked as a round ricocheted overhead and buried itself in the Kadiran's darklight rifle. The weapon began sparking alarmingly and the alien hurled it down the corridor with an angry roar.

'Shit,' Orry muttered, trying to think, but there was no time for anything approaching a plan. She just had to hope Guzman didn't want them dead – or rather, he didn't want the Kadiran dead. *That might give us some leverage, at least.* 'Everybody out!' she yelled, pulling her respirator over her face and hitting the door release.

The door swung open and she ran out, ducking left into the cover of a mechanised loader. The others followed the Kadiran, who lumbered along at a fast walking pace. Mender brought up the rear after closing the door and smashing the lock to buy them some time.

'You almost made it!' Guzman yelled cheerily. 'How vexing for you. Now, throw down your weapons and surrender.'

'What are you going to do if we don't?' Orry shouted back. 'Come and get us? I don't think Roag would be very pleased to hear her prisoner was killed in the crossfire.'

Guzman laughed. 'Who are you, really?'

'Me? I'm nobody.'

'Well, Miz Nobody, you're absolutely right. So what's your plan? You can't stay there for ever.'

'He has a point,' Ethan said, adjusting a fabric bag he'd slung across his shoulder. Orry hadn't had time to ask him what was in it.

From the far side of the pad she heard the distinctive whine of *Dainty Jane*'s auxiliary power unit coming online and grinned.

'Get ready to move,' she said. 'I think we're about to get a little help.'

The Kadiran's sensitive ears had evidently heard the sound as well. 'There are other humans aboard your vessel?'

'Not exactly.' She raised her voice. 'Mr Guzman, please pay attention because I'm not going to say this twice: take your men and get out of here before someone gets hurt.'

'*Bor-ing!* You're becoming tiresome, Miz Nobody. Come out of there so I can have my breakfast.'

'Okay – but don't say I didn't warn you!'

Behind Guzman's position, a single eighteen-millimetre point defence turret high on *Dainty Jane*'s curved hull rotated until its multiple barrels were trained on the whalers.

'I'm a reasonable man,' Guzman yelled, apparently unaware of the turret, 'and I happen to like you, so how about this? You give me the alien and I'll let you all go. How does that sou—'

The turret's buzzsaw roar ripped the air and dicore slugs tore through the pad in a neat line just behind the whalers. Guzman dived for cover as his yelling crew scattered, trying to find shelter from the ship's gun without opening themselves up to fire from Orry's band.

Jane fired again, this time carefully targeting the cover, disintegrating crates and containers. A stray round struck a fuel bowser which exploded spectacularly, sending a great jet of orange flame spurting high into the air.

'Go!' Orry yelled, and shoved the others ahead of her towards the ship. The Kadiran thundered along, slow and steady, and Ethan slowed to use his bulk as cover. Tyrell, striding behind them, was holding his stolen pistol casually, searching for targets. A woman squatting by a towering pile of pallets turned and raised her rifle – and Tyrell calmly put a bullet in her leg.

Ahead of Orry, Mender also had his pistol raised and was tracking from side to side, but the whalers were now more concerned with their own survival. She looked for Guzman but he was out of sight, keeping his head down to avoid the slugs whipping through the thick air.

At the familiar rumble of *Dainty Jane*'s engines spooling up, Orry willed the Kadiran to move faster. They were passing between two groups of whalers, but thankfully, they were all more intent on keeping out of *Jane*'s relentless fire than stopping their escape.

They were more than halfway to the ship now.

Orry could see that a number of Guzman's crew had been injured, but from flying splinters rather than direct fire. *Dainty Jane*'s point defence turrets were designed to punch through armoured torpedoes; if the guns had deliberately targeted anyone on the pad there would be very little left of them to identify. Orry could imagine how distressed the ship would be about causing even these collateral injuries. Fortunately, neither Guzman nor his people knew how much *Jane* hated violence. *As long as they believe they're in mortal danger, we've still got a chance*, she thought.

She could hear Guzman raging and threatening as *Dainty Jane*'s cargo ramp lowered. Orry was finally beginning to believe they would make it out of this alive when a group of four men broke cover to their right and charged, firing wildly.

Her first thought was for Ethan, but her brother had already darted to the other side of the Kadiran. He was cradling his bag protectively, sheltering behind the alien's massive frame as the Kadiran turned to face this new threat. *Jane* could be of no help now, Orry realised; the attackers were too close for the ship to risk firing on them.

Tyrell threw himself to the ground and rolled through the bullets sparking off the metal around him, emptying his handgun blindly and finally bringing down one of the men just as the pistol's slide locked open. A blur to Orry's left made her turn: a woman had popped up from behind the smoking remains of the bowser – but *Jane* immediately peppered it and the woman dropped smartly back out of sight.

Orry swung back as Mender fired three quick shots, lifting another of the charging men from his feet.

The remaining two were firing at the Kadiran's legs, trying to bring the huge creature down without actually killing it, and Orry winced as the rounds tore chunks from his natural armour and a thick ichor started to leak out. The Kadiran roared and charged, reaching out a long arm to pluck one of his attackers from the pad. The man screamed in terror, but his voice was instantly cut off as the Kadiran gripped his head with his free hand and twisted. Orry winced at the dull crunch but the Kadiran had already tossed the body casually aside. The whaler's comrade was firing uselessly into the Kadiran's chest; ignoring the fusillade, the arm shot out again, this time in a devastating punch that sent the man cartwheeling off the side of the pad.

Orry grabbed Tyrell's hand, hauled him up and shoved him towards the ramp, where Ethan was standing yelling at the Kadiran to *hurry up!* Mender kept firing as the two of them ran the rest of the way, Orry wincing every time a bullet rang against *Jane*'s hull.

'Get us out of here!' Mender yelled as the ramp began to rise.

'Just what I was thinking,' *Jane* replied, and the ship rose swiftly, making them all stagger.

As she felt the main engines ignite, Orry clutched a brace to stop herself from falling. On the far side of the bay the Kadiran was swaying, ichor wet on his armoured skin. Ethan looked pale, Mender as stoic as ever. Tyrell was staring at her, for once apparently lost for words.

She released a ragged breath and tried to stop her hands from shaking.

30

QUONDAM

'What's your name?' Orry asked the Kadiran, who was swathed in fresh dressings after a prolonged visit to the medbay.

He looked around the crowded galley. 'I am called Industrious-Chronicler-Of-Quondam-Annals.'

'That's a mouthful,' Tyrell said.

'How about we call you Quondam?' Orry suggested.

The Kadiran nodded, a slow, majestic movement. 'I express gratitude for your deed.'

'My deed?'

'The cessation of my captivity.'

'Oh . . . no problem.'

'Happy to help,' Tyrell added.

'So, can you tell me what you know?' Orry asked.

'My knowledge is diverse. Specify.'

This is going to be hard work. 'About the plot – to kill the Imperator Ascendant.'

'The details were unknown to me,' Quondam admitted. 'I knew only of a contact between the human Cordelia Roag and my superior, Installation-Alpha Kills-With-A-Bright-Edge.'

'Why don't you start from the beginning?' Orry said. 'Maybe then we can make some sense of all this.'

'This war,' Quondam began, 'is a dishonourable endeavour. Not all Kadiran support it, but we are forced to fight. The Iron Guard say we must go to war with the humans – we must kill *all* humans – but to what purpose? For their planets, they say. But there are sufficient planets for all. The real reason is something other. The Iron Guard look backwards; they say things were better in the past. This does not reflect the true state. I was a chronicler before the war: I know this to be true. But the Iron Guard, they say fight. Some Kadiran say no, and the Iron Guard kill them. So we all must fight.

'I have not won the right to breed, so I was posted to a communications facility on Kadir. This is where I received a transmission from the human Cordelia Roag. I directed the transmission on to Installation-Alpha Kills-With-A-Bright-Edge, but I was curious: for what reason could a human be sending such a transmission? I examined the transmission's meta-data, but it was encrypted. In consequence, I packaged the data and sent it to a dispatch pod, to travel to Tyr, to my contact in your Seventh Secretariat.'

'Wait, *what?*' Ethan sounded stunned. 'You had a contact in Seven?'

'This statement reflects the true state. Some of us work to bring down the Iron Guard from within. This is not an honour-able action, but we make this sacrifice for the good of Kadir. For this, we have contact with the humans.'

Orry looked from Ethan to Tyrell, then at Mender, who raised his bushy eyebrows, clearly as surprised as she was. 'What happened to the transmission?' she asked.

'The dispatch pod never launched,' Quondam told her. 'Its data package was discovered by the Reverence Division. I knew they would trace it back to me, so I fled Kadir and concealed myself on Morhelion.'

'And you don't know the details of the plot?' Ethan asked. 'You didn't even know it was an assassination attempt?'

'This reflects the true state.'

'Great,' Mender muttered. 'Just great.'

'Is there anything else you can tell us?' Orry asked. 'Anything at all we can use to stop it?'

The Kadiran looked at her. 'I know nothing more, but the transmission was directed to Installation-Alpha Kills-With-A-Bright-Edge: he will know everything.'

'And he's on Kadir,' Orry said heavily.

'This does not reflect the true state. The installation-alpha was promoted. He is now planet-alpha in command of the occupying forces on the human Odessa colony.'

'That's that, then,' Mender said to Orry. 'We'll just have to take this guy back to Tyr and hand him over to your spy friends. Let them sort everything out.'

'We can't do that,' she replied, a heavy feeling in her stomach.

'Why the hell not?'

'Because of what Irina told me: there's a good chance the plot originated not with the Kadiran, but with a traitor highly placed on Tyr who may have agents within the Seventh Secretariat. There's no way to know who to trust, so we can't just hand Quondam over.'

'What other choice do you have?' Tyrell asked. 'Kidnap the commandant of an occupied planet? And even if you do, how do you expect to get him to talk? Torture?'

'Don't be ridiculous.'

'The suggested application of torture would be ineffective,' Quondam said. 'We Kadiran are able to disconnect our pain receptors. We first learned of the concept of torture from humans.'

'See?' Tyrell said. He looked at her pointedly. 'So go on then, what's your grand plan? If you're going to put people in harm's way again, it would be nice to know in advance this time.'

'You can be a real dick sometimes,' Ethan said.

'So I've been told.' Tyrell folded his arms and fixed his eyes on Orry.

'I don't know, all right?' she told him. 'I need time to think. Mender, can you and *Jane* figure out a way to get us down to Odessa's surface without getting vaporised by the Kadiran? Ethan, you're on research. I want to know everything about the place – and especially about Kadiran occupation doctrine and tactics.'

'I have knowledge that might benefit you,' Quondam rumbled. 'There are many who oppose the Iron Guard from within. There will be cells of dissident Kadiran on Odessa.'

'Sounds good.' Orry turned to Tyrell. 'I assume you want us to take you back to your smoker before we collapse?'

'You say that like you expect me to come with you.'

She pressed her lips together, irritated that he'd read her so easily. The man was selfish, untrustworthy, infuriating – but half of her *did* want him to come. She'd be damned if she'd admit it, though.

'Come or don't,' she said, a little too casually. 'It's your choice.'

He grinned at that. 'Then I think I'll stay. Morhelion's about to get very dangerous for me, but I'd still rather take my chances with Guzman and the League than wind up dead with you bunch of lunatics. Pay me what I'm owed and you can drop me back aboard *Zephyr*.'

Her stomach dropped, and not just because he wasn't coming with them. She'd been dreading this moment ever since she'd realised Tyrell hadn't stolen anything for himself from the *Hardhaven Voyager*. Now she was going to have to tell him that she *still* didn't have the money she'd promised him. She could imagine how that would go down.

'Listen—' she began hesitantly.

'This should cover it,' Ethan interrupted, rummaging in the bag he'd been holding so protectively and bringing out the lacquered wooden box from their suite on *Hardhaven Voyager*. He opened it with a flourish to reveal the bottle of green liquid in its silken nest.

Tyrell's eyes widened. 'Is that—?'

'Hundred-year-old Dundurian spicewater,' Mender told him. 'Those little flecks are pure spice paragon.' He grinned approvingly at Ethan. 'Well done, kid – at least one of us was thinking ahead.'

'I looked it up,' her brother explained happily. 'This will more than cover what we owe you.'

Tyrell picked up the bottle almost reverently, running his hands over the intricate twists in the glass.

'Happy now?' Orry asked, trying to pretend she'd known about this the whole time.

He replaced the bottle in its box and carefully closed the lid. 'It'll do, I suppose,' he said grudgingly, though she could tell he was pleased. 'About bloody time, too.'

'Good,' she snapped, feeling her cheeks flush with anger.

*

Orry's anger had cooled by the time they arrived back at *Zephyr* and she felt unaccountably morose as she followed Tyrell into the smoker's cabin.

In contrast, he looked happier than she'd ever seen him. He set the lacquered box on the fold-out table, opened it and removed the bottle of spicewater. 'You have time for a drink before you go?' he asked.

'You're not serious?' she asked, genuinely shocked.

He grasped the cork in his fist and twisted. 'I *never* joke about booze.'

'You realise if you drink it, you won't be able to sell it?' she pointed out carefully.

He replied with a grin. The bottle opened with a hiss. He blew into a mug, emptied a generous measure of spicewater into it and handed it to her. 'Cheers,' he said, before raising the bottle to his lips.

She drank as well – and wondered what all the fuss was about. The peppery liquid made her want to sneeze . . . though she couldn't deny that the warm feeling it left in its wake *was* rather pleasant. She took another mouthful and regarded Tyrell with something approaching affection.

'Are you going to be okay?'

He gave her a lopsided grin. 'You almost sound like you care.'

'I wouldn't go that far.' She smiled to soften her words and had another sip. The stuff was growing on her. 'I should thank you for everything you've done for me.'

'Yes, you should.'

She rolled her eyes. 'I'm serious, Tyrell. Without you I'd probably be in pieces inside one of Sticky Pete's freezers right now.'

'I doubt it – and as jobs go, it certainly had its high points.'

She chuckled. 'It did, didn't it?'

The way he was looking at her made her feel suddenly hot. She drank again to hide her discomposure, and when she'd finished he stepped closer to refill her cup. 'No,' she said quickly, setting it down. 'Thanks, but I really have to go.'

'To save the Imperator,' he said, his face inches from hers.

Her heart was pounding now. 'Someone has to,' she replied, trying for offhand and only partially succeeding.

He said nothing, looking suddenly serious as his smile faded. Then he leaned in and kissed her, and she let him, enjoying the touch of his lips on hers for a few seconds before she pulled away, flustered.

She hurried to the door. 'I – I have to go.'

He was grinning again. 'You said that already.'

She stifled a sudden laugh with her hand. *Rama, how strong is that stuff?*

'Look after yourself, Tyrell.'

'You too. If you're ever back this way, look me up.'

'I might just do that.'

She clambered quickly out of the cabin to see Ethan sitting on *Dainty Jane*'s ramp, tinkering with his node kit.

'Looking a little red there, Sis,' he observed with a knowing smile.

Light-headed from more than just the spicewater, she hurried onto the ship, not even taking the time to punch him as she passed.

There was a rap on the door to Orry's cabin and Mender entered. 'Our course is laid in. Odessa's a big planet – I think we can get down in one piece.'

'Thanks,' she said, not moving from her bed where she'd been lying, thinking about Tyrell. She could feel Mender's eyes on her.

'You all right, girl?'

She turned her head to him. 'Did *Jane* put you up to this?'

'No,' the ship said.

'We were just wondering—' Mender began.

'—*he* was wondering,' *Jane* clarified, and the old man growled.

'—why you're doing this,' he finished. 'Considering how much you hate the Ascendancy and all. I thought you'd be glad to watch it implode.'

'But it won't implode, will it?' she said, still not looking at him. 'If Irina is right, then this has nothing to do with the Kadiran. It's a power-play from within, so when the Imperator is killed the Ascendancy will carry on, just with someone else leading it – someone *worse*. Better the devil you know, I guess.'

She'd been struggling with this very question since Irina's death and she'd come to the realisation that for all his faults, she believed Piotr to be a just man at heart. That had surprised her, but she knew she was generally a good judge of character.

'I told you she'd say that,' *Jane* said.

'Fine,' Mender said. 'As long as you know what you're doing.'

Orry turned to look at him as he opened the door to leave. 'Mender?'

'What?'

'Thanks.'

'For what?'

'For trusting me.'

He produced a rare smile. 'I figure you've saved my life more than once, and you haven't got me killed yet. Just keep it that way.'

The door folded closed after him.

31

OCCUPATION

Orry stopped by the side of the mountain trail to gaze out over the view, filling her lungs with crisp, clean air. Growing up aboard *Bonaventure*, she'd visited more than a hundred worlds, but Odessa was by far the most beautiful of any of them. Native megaflora carpeted the mountain's lower slopes, giving way to an undulating plain of yellow grass broken in places by homesteads, curls of smoke rising lazily from the chimneys of some of them. Obscured by a heat haze in the distance lay the low sprawl of Bel Moritz, the colony's capital city.

She saw Mender stop down the trail ahead of her and mop his brow. 'It's a view,' he grumbled. 'Get over it. It's taken us an hour already – at this rate we'll still be up here come nightfall.'

Using a combination of stealth and inspired flying, *Dainty Jane* had slipped through the gaps between the ships of the Kadiran fleet stationed above Odessa and made her way to this range of low mountains, the Schaefer Massif. The ship had decided this place, around a hundred kilometres from the capital, was a good location to conceal herself and babysit their Kadiran passenger.

Orry grinned down at the old man. 'What's the matter, Mender, don't you like it?'

'I've been to worse places,' he admitted, 'and I've also seen what war can do to a planet like this. Might look nice and peaceful from up here, but I guarantee it won't be so pretty close up.'

Her smile faded as he trudged on.

Ethan passed her, sweating from the unaccustomed exercise. With a last brief glance up at Odessa's three companion planets, hanging like ghostly crescents in the blue sky, she adjusted her pack and set off after him.

The dusty track led eventually to a forest carpeted with seed husks that crunched underfoot. Silver trunks wide enough to cut a tunnel through supported a leafy canopy a hundred metres overhead. Sunlight dappled the forest floor and native wildlife rustled invisibly.

'Are there any natural predators on Odessa?' Orry asked.

'Sure,' Ethan answered breathlessly. 'Some pretty nasty ones, actually. You want me to tell you about them?'

'Maybe later,' she muttered, eyeing the canopy warily, then shivered and hurried on.

The slope they were following became shallower, the gaps between the trees widening, and before long they were facing rolling fields of deep green alpine grass scattered with pretty blue and yellow flowers. A waterfall thundered down a nearby cliff-face, churning a deep pool which turned into a narrow, fast-flowing river of crystal-clear water.

They saw their first colonist half an hour later, a wiry man hanging from a harness two metres up the back of a humanoid agribot, his arms thrust deep inside an open maintenance hatch. A third of the gently sloping field was neatly ploughed and rich, dark soil caked the blades of the giant ploughshare clutched in the bot's frozen hands.

The farmer didn't see them at first; when he did, Orry raised a hand in greeting. He made no response, instead lowering himself to the muddy ground and hurrying to a buggy parked near the wooden fence that bordered the field. When he turned back to watch them approach, he had a hunting rifle cradled in his arms.

'Morning!' Orry called as she drew near. The scent of freshly turned soil was competing with the rusty metallic aroma coming off the bot.

'All right,' the farmer said by way of greeting, studying each of them in turn. 'Help you folks?'

'Beautiful day, isn't it?'

He adjusted his grip on the rifle. 'You come down from the mountain?'

'Yes – wonderful views up there.'

'Where you from?'

'Lascar,' Ethan said, naming a town on the other side of the continent. The farmer narrowed his eyes.

'Flyer trouble,' Orry explained. 'Is there an engineer around here?'

'Bel Moritz,' he said, jerking his head towards a two-track dirt road.

'Is the cityloop still running?' Ethan asked.

'Sure. The kucks are very efficient.' He spat in the dirt.

'Anything we should know?' Orry asked. 'Going into the city?'

He looked at her with suspicion. 'You not have kucks in Lascar?'

'Sure we do.'

'Kind of a stupid question then, don't you think?'

She smiled. 'Sorry to bother you. We'll be on our way.'

The four of them trudged across the muddy field towards the road. As they reached the open gate, the farmer's voice made them turn back.

'Lascar was flattened from orbit two days ago,' he called. 'Nothing left there but craters now.' He replaced his rifle in its long holster and walked back to the bot. 'Might want to get your story straight before you go talking to any kucks.'

'Thanks,' she called back, but he was busy strapping himself back into his maintenance harness.

The countryside became more cultivated as the dirt road turned into a single-lane metalled highway. They were passing homesteads every couple of kilometres now, but apart from the occasional bot toiling in a field, they saw no other people, and many of the fields were untended, their crops left to rot. Litter collected in the deep trenches at the sides of the road or blew tumbling across its white surface.

As morning turned to afternoon they stopped to watch a damaged bot repeating the same sequence of simple actions, harvesting imaginary crops from a bare patch of earth and placing them into a shredded canvas bag fixed to its waist. Scorch marks surrounded a jagged hole in the side of its head and one arm was dangling limply, but still it carried on. Behind the bot stood the blackened shell of a burnt-out farmhouse, melted composite hardened into bubbles on its printed walls.

They reached the cityloop station, a glass dome in the centre of a deserted parking lot, in the middle of the afternoon. A dead cat lay near the ticket machine, its mangy fur crawling with tiny insects. Breathing shallowly against the smell of corruption, Orry bought four singles into the city. The machine thanked her and they ascended to the platform on an escalator.

The capsule arrived five minutes later, heralded by a minute vibration in the platform surface. The doors hissed open, they entered a deserted carriage and were still the only passengers when it set off. The numbers on the wall display cycled quickly up to the speed of sound as the countryside outside became a blur, then, as it started to slow, yellow fields gave way to the grey and green of the suburbs, then the city proper: wide boulevards lined with trees and detached buildings with large windows. Occasionally a building was just missing, like a pulled tooth, leaving only a pile of rubble or twisted composite in its place. There were few vehicles on the roads, and fewer people. As they approached the centre of the city she saw an ugly armoured transport parked across a road, bulky Kadiran breedwarriors looming over human colonists as they stopped and searched them.

The capsule drew alongside the platform and the doors hissed open. Escalators took them back down to street level, which in this case was a large square paved with white flagstones and edged by beautiful three-storey buildings. The square was busy by comparison with the rest of the city, but the colonists all shared the same dull expression of defeat.

There was a heavy Kadiran presence here, particularly around the ornate building dominating one side of the square. Long banners hung down the building's facade, rippling in the breeze.

Barricades protected the entrance, where several breedwar-riors stood guard, supported by a squat armoured walker. They were armed with bulky personal assault cannon far too heavy to be wielded by an unaugmented human, and across each broad back was slung a war-maul, the traditional weapon favoured by the Kadiran for hand-to-hand combat. The mauls were ter-rifying weapons, one side of the brutal sledgehammer head covered in pyramidal protrusions like a meat tenderiser, the other tapering to a vicious spike. Another spike decorated the top of many of the mauls, and no two were exactly the same. These modern-day mauls were made from tempered thermoce-ramics, Ethan had told them, their points tipped with cultured diamond that would penetrate the toughest armour. The display of military-spec hardware violated the square's serene beauty.

'I don't understand,' Ethan said quietly as they gathered around a nearby map of the city. A bullet had shattered the plastic, sprouting a network of cracks across it. 'Since when do the Kadiran leave the human population alive on any of the worlds they conquer? Shouldn't they be eating everyone?'

Orry rolled her eyes. 'That's just a children's story.'

'Based on real incidents,' Mender added.

'A long time ago,' she said.

He frowned at her. 'Why are you defending them?'

She looked around the square. 'Because if the Kadiran really are just the monsters our parents told us horror stories about, then what hope is there for a meaningful peace? Besides, you heard Quondam: not all of them want this. It's these Iron Guard fanatics who've come to power – they're the ones driving this war.'

'So what *do* they want?' Ethan asked, staring at the fluttering banners on the large building, angular white slashes of Kadiran script on a field of black.

She hesitated. Ethan was right: this wasn't what she'd expected a world occupied by the Kadiran to look like. For all her need to believe that the Kadiran and humanity had enough in common to be able to live in peace, the old prejudices were hard to overcome. Part of her had expected death camps and scorched earth; this orderly occupation was unsettling . . . but she was here for a reason; *that* was what she should be concentrating on. The rest could wait.

'It doesn't matter,' she told him. 'Focus on the job.'

An odd expression came over her brother's face.

'What?'

He smiled sadly. 'You sounded just like Dad.'

She stared at him, unable to speak for a moment. 'So,' she said, a little hoarsely, 'we all know what we're doing – I suggest we get on with it. Stay in touch, and *be careful*.'

'Come on, kid,' said Mender, already limping away.

Ethan hurried after him. 'Do you even know where you're going?'

She didn't hear Mender's muttered reply, but smiled as her brother turned briefly back and mimed putting a gun in his mouth and pulling the trigger.

Shading her eyes against the sun reflecting from white stone, she looked around the square.

'Right,' she muttered, 'if I was in the resistance, where would I hang out?'

32

MARK 17

The mech was an older model: a HalseyTech Mark 17. Ethan had never subverted one before, but a quick check of the forums cached in his integuary provided a rootkit that could exploit a vulnerability in its authentication core, as long as it hadn't been patched since he'd last synced his internal storage back on Morhelion.

'You sure about this?' Mender growled, as Ethan shoved him into an alleyway several streets from the Kadiran headquarters. The mech had emerged from one of the building's service entrances several minutes ago and they'd picked it up as soon as it was clear of the cordon. Ethan peered out of the alley to see it was walking steadily towards them, each step marked by a faint pneumatic hiss.

'Relax,' he said, pulling Mender into cover behind a dumpster a little way down the alley, 'this is my jam.'

'Your *jam*?' the old man repeated with disgust, surveying the alley with a professional eye. 'Just make it quick, kid.'

'You don't rush a maestro.'

He gritted his teeth. 'I will shoot you myself, right here.'

Ethan grinned and settled himself on the ground with his back to the alley wall. Once he was comfortable, he closed his eyes and accessed his integuary. As the Mark 17 passed, he hooked its contact field and held his breath as he waited for it to accept his side-loaded ident, a clone of a HalseyTech service engineer. He breathed again as it allowed him past its secondary firewall – with restricted privileges, but that was all he needed to install the rootkit.

Four seconds after first requesting access, Ethan found himself looking through the mech's eyes. He turned the Mark 17's chassis, taking a moment to adjust to its movement, and walked down the alley to the dumpster.

It was strange looking at himself. His body was slumped against the wall next to Mender, looking for all the world like he was unconscious. The old man was squinting suspiciously at him.

'You in there, kid?'

'*A-firm-a-tive,*' Ethan said in a robotic voice, and Mender looked horrified.

'Just shitting you,' he continued normally through the mech's voice box. 'It's all good.'

The old man walked up to him and tapped his face. Peering into his lenses he asked, 'What's it like in there?'

'You've never used telepresence?'

'Not into a bot.'

'You're not missing much – especially in this thing. It's old tech, pretty basic.'

'What do you expect in a cleaner?'

'Fair point. I'd better get on. Look after my body while I'm gone.'

'I'd like to move you somewhere less exposed first.'

'You'll be fine here. I won't be long – just keep an eye out.'

Mender didn't look happy, but said grudgingly, 'Watch yourself, kid.'

'That's *your* job.' Ethan tried to smile, but realised he wasn't built for it. 'Back in a mo, Joe.'

The thing about mechs, Ethan reflected happily as a breedwarrior waved him through the cordon at the rear of the headquarters building without question, *is that nobody really sees them. After all, who's going to suspect a household appliance?*

The service door sent a challenge as he approached but Ethan ignored it, content to let the Mark 17's own systems deal with the handshake. As he entered he called up the building's schematics and noted that before the Kadiran occupation it had been the colony's administrative centre. Many of the rooms were offices, too small to be converted into what he was looking for, but at last he found a larger space that fitted his requirements.

After navigating a series of utilitarian service corridors, he opened a door into an atrium brightly lit by sun streaming through a glass roof and glinting off the plants in large pots dotted among tinkling water features. He was surprised to see both breedwarriors and colonists here. Ethan eyed the uniforms the Kadiran officers were wearing instead of armour, wishing he'd had the time to research the aliens' complex military and social hierarchy more thoroughly. Suddenly aware that the mech had been standing still while he was thinking, he checked his location and moved on. He felt secure within the chassis, invisible, just one service robot among many.

The atrium led deep into the heart of the building and

after a few more minutes he located the area he was looking for.

Bingo.

Whatever the room's original purpose, it was clearly now a makeshift barracks. Large nests made from mounds of fabric covered the floor, divided from each other by rug-like curtains woven with breath-taking skill and intricacy. Only one was occupied, by a Kadiran breedwarrior buried so deeply he was almost invisible, but producing stentorian snoring of such volume that it registered on the mech's vibration sensors.

Ethan moved to the nearest empty nest and spotted a hanger clearly designed to hold a Kadiran uniform, but it was empty, as were the others in the remaining unoccupied nests.

Bugger.

He moved closer to the snoring Kadiran and saw an officer's uniform hanging above him. The one-piece garment's integral nanotech made it look brand-new, as if it had never been worn. He eyed the sleeping breedwarrior nervously, then edged his robot avatar carefully forward until it was near enough to reach for the uniform. The Kadiran snorted and shifted in his nest, one thick arm brushing the mech's leg as it moved. Ethan waited until the alien's breathing had settled again, then lifted the uniform clear and backed away. Bubbling with relief, he turned for the doors.

Got it, he told Mender, concentrating on keeping the mech at its usual pace despite an overwhelming urge to run. *Everything okay out there?*

Fine, kid. Just hurry it up, will you? There could be a patrol along any minute.

You want to swap places?

If I slapped your face real hard out here, would you feel it?

Funny.

I ain't joking.

Ethan bit off his reply and after ensuring no one was about, slipped into an empty office and opened the Mark 17's internal storage compartment. Once he'd removed the sanitation supplies and attachments there was just about enough room for the folded uniform to fit inside.

He re-entered the glass-roofed atrium and was halfway to the exit when an armoured Kadiran guard turned to block his path, barking out a guttural challenge. A second later Ethan's integuary provided a translation.

'Halt!'

He slowed the mech, his heart in his mouth as the guard thudded towards him.

'What is the intention of this action?' the breedwarrior demanded.

Ethan retreated deeper into the mech's substrate, preparing to let the machine act dumb for him, but before he could tell Mender to grab his body and run, the guard shoved the Mark 17 out of the way and stomped past. Ethan twisted the mech just enough that he could see the Kadiran had stopped in front of an elderly colonist carrying a rolled-up databrane.

'I was just taking this to the records room—' the man began, clearly terrified.

'Do not meet my gaze!' the breedwarrior roared, making heads turn across the atrium. 'What action is required of humans when in the proximity of a member of the glorious Hierocracy?'

'Um . . . I—'

'Human filth will remain motionless and avert their eyes to

show proper respect to their superiors!'

'I-I'm sorry,' the man stammered desperately, shrinking away from the heavily armoured alien, 'but I didn't—'

The breedwarrior regarded him with contempt. 'Ignorance does not mitigate.' Swinging his assault cannon, he smashed the barrel into the terrified administrator's face. Ethan winced at the crack of breaking bone and the man shrieked, clutching his nose as blood spurted. He dropped to his knees and the brane he'd been carrying rolled away.

A new Kadiran voice rang out sharply and Ethan saw an officer striding over. The translation kicked in a moment later.

'What are the circumstances of this incident?'

The guard stiffened to attention and saluted. 'This human refused to demonstrate an appropriate level of deference.'

'And you think a physical rebuke is an effective method to instruct humans about our enlightened Kadiran culture?'

'I do, sir!'

'Did you learn nothing in orientation, warrior? The humans are an intractable species. Physical violence is often counter-productive, serving only to increase their resistance.'

'Yes, sir!'

'There is only one way we will win this war, soldier.' In one smooth movement the officer drew his war-maul from across his back and swung it almost casually, driving its back-spike down through the top of the man's head.

All movement in the atrium ceased. Ethan stared dumbly at the blood pouring from the man's nose and mouth. It was like a tap had been turned on inside his head. His body slumped sideways, one foot twitching.

Kid? You okay?

Uh – yeah, sure. Heading back now. Feeling numb, he let the
Mark 17 walk forward again, carrying him out of the atrium
and away. All along the corridors, past endless closed doors, he
couldn't get the image out of his head – the casual brutality of
the death, as if the Kadiran officer had been squashing an insect.
And the blood . . . *so much* blood.

The sight of the cordon ahead of him set his pulse pounding
and he felt both oddly distant and yet very present, but again
the mech was waved through without incident. A short walk
brought him back to the alley.

Mender stepped from behind the dumpster and patted the
mech. 'Good job, kid. Now let's get the hell out of here.'

Ethan experienced a wave of disorientation as he left the
Mark 17 and returned to his body. It took a moment for his
mind to adjust, then he walked over to the mech and retrieved
the wadded-up uniform.

Mender watched him stuff it into his rucksack, a concerned
look on his craggy face. 'Sure you're all right?'

'Can we just go?'

He frowned as Ethan hurried away, then followed him out
of the alley.

33

OUT THE BACK

Orry was the only customer in the coffee shop, one of several in the main square of Bel Moritz. She had taken a seat beneath an awning, a hundred metres from the barricades in front of the Kadiran headquarters. The establishment's lone member of staff, a young waiter, had been watching her since bringing her what had to be one of the worst cups of coffee she had ever tasted.

The coffee had been stone cold for some time now and she was still no closer to coming up with a plan to contact the resistance – if there even was one. *No*, she told herself sternly, *don't be defeatist. There's* always *a resistance.* Her stomach growled and she realised she couldn't remember the last time she'd eaten anything. She gestured to the waiter. Considering she was the only customer, he took his time to come over.

'Do you serve food?' she asked.

'I'll fetch a menu.' Rather than looking at her, his eyes were fixed on the Kadiran headquarters. He returned to the counter.

Orry cast her gaze over the square again, realising something had changed. She'd been too absorbed in her thoughts, but now she saw the few colonists who'd been around had gone.

She looked over at the waiter, who slowly extended a finger and pointed towards the ground – before sinking almost comically out of sight behind the counter.

'Oh shit,' she breathed.

She launched herself from her chair just as a deafening roar assaulted her ears. The ground bucked beneath her and the table struck her on the shoulder as it was tossed away with the rest of the street furniture.

She gritted her teeth as a wave of scalding heat washed over her, then rolled onto her side so she could see the Kadiran headquarters. The armoured walker in front of it was a burning shell, vomiting a thick plume of oily black smoke into the clear blue sky. Kadiran bodies, whole or in parts, lay scattered around the shattered barricade. Some were moving feebly.

The high-pitched whine in her ears faded, giving way to the chatter of small-arms fire. Sparks flickered on the armour of the few remaining breedwarriors, who were shakily taking up defensive positions in front of the broken barricade. In the square, she could see perhaps twenty colonists advancing on the three remaining Kadiran defenders in a loose skirmish line – but despite the disparity in numbers, she knew the colonists were doomed. Their fire was ineffective against the breedwarriors' armour, and as she watched, one of the Kadiran aimed his assault cannon at a charging colonist and pressed the trigger, instantly turning her into a storm of bloody rags.

The same scene was repeated again and again, the resistance fighters cut down before they could get anywhere near the defenders. The attack quickly stalled.

A squeal of tyres diverted her attention from the slaughter to an agricultural pick-up careering out of a side street. A pintle-mounted machine-gun fixed to the rear bed was being crewed by a colonist. As the truck accelerated across the square, the man opened up and heavy rounds clanged off the burning Kadiran walker and chewed holes in the walls of the building behind the defenders.

Another of the Kadiran went down under the relentless fire, but the breedwarrior beside him calmly adjusted his cannon and took aim, smoothly tracking the speeding vehicle before firing. The truck's engine exploded, sending its bonnet spinning high into the air. The vehicle somersaulted and Orry winced as it landed on its roof, crushing the rear gunner.

The mangled wreck slid to a halt, metal screeching as it scarred the white stones of the square, and the remaining colonists broke and ran. The two surviving breedwarriors kept firing, picking off several more of them as they fled.

Time to go.

Dragging herself to her feet, she turned to see the waiter disappearing inside the coffee house. *There's always a resistance*, she thought, and raced after him.

The interior was gloomy after the bright sunlight of the square. A door slammed somewhere deeper within the building and she followed the sound, speeding through an empty kitchen and out of another door to find herself in a broad alley at the rear of the café. The waiter was there, sitting astride a scooter, trying to coax its engine into life. His eyes widened at her sudden arrival. He leaped from the bike, which clattered to the ground as he began to run.

'Wait!' she yelled, dashing after him.

He glanced back and stumbled, almost falling, and Orry flung herself at him, sending them both headfirst into a pile of refuse sacks and empty food crates. As she rolled him onto his back his fist connected with her jaw, cracking her teeth together. He tried to scramble to his feet but she grabbed his legs and brought him down again, and they rolled around in the foul, slippery contents of the burst sacks.

'Please,' she cried, 'I just want to talk to you.' She released him and rose unsteadily to her feet, her jaw aching, and he did the same, eyeing her like a cornered animal. 'Please,' she repeated.

He backed away, chest heaving, his face smeared with eggshells and limp brown leaves. 'Who are you?' he asked, glancing up and down the alley. She could hear the rising wail of an alarm from the direction of the square now.

'I'm looking for the resistance.'

He stared at her, then bent forward and placed his hands on his knees, breathing heavily. His shoulders started shaking and it took her a moment to realise he was laughing.

'What's so funny?'

He straightened and peeled a leaf from his cheek, flicking it towards her. The back of her neck suddenly crawled and she whirled to see a hard-eyed woman in a tactical vest aiming an assault rifle at her. Two men, also armed, were flanking the woman. The right-hand man's sleeve was dark with blood.

'You all right, Hamada?' the woman said, and the waiter nodded, scowling at Orry. 'You want me to off this bitch?'

He thought about this for a moment. 'No,' he said, 'bring her. Let's find out who the hell she is.'

The woman pulled a set of restraints from a pocket. 'Put these on,' she ordered, glancing towards the other end of the alley where a large vehicle had appeared, its engine running. 'And hurry the fuck up.'

34

CRAZY FUCKER

'It fits okay, then?' Ethan asked, as he and Mender checked Quondam over.

'The garment has adjusted to my frame,' the Kadiran answered.

'What type of uniform is it?' Holding a conversation with Quondam was like pulling teeth, but Ethan was very conscious of how dangerous this part of the plan was. It felt wrong to send him off without at least a friendly word.

'The uniform was of insufficient rank for my purposes.'

'Oh. I'm sorry – there wasn't a whole lot of choice.'

'I have modified the garment to suit my purposes. Its acquisition was a critical factor.'

'Um . . .'

'I think he's thanking you,' Mender said.

'Cool.' Ethan grinned. 'So, what's your plan?'

Quondam gazed at him. 'I will commandeer a small transport and enter a significant military installation in order to locate a dissident cell.'

'How will you find a dissident cell?'

'The state is uncertain.'

'Are you even sure there are dissidents here on Odessa?'

'The state is uncertain.'

'O-*kay*.'

'I must depart,' the Kadiran said, and walked away.

Ethan exchanged a bemused look with Mender.

'Ten to one that's the last we see of him,' the old man grunted. 'Crazy fucker.' He glared around the unspoilt valley, bare rocky peaks surrounding a crystal-clear mountain lake, then stumped up the ramp into the ship.

Ethan gazed after the departing alien. 'Good luck!' he called out, but Quondam made no response.

Turning back to the ship, he pulled a folded databrane from his pocket – the one Orry had lifted from *Hardhaven Voyager* – and stared at it with distaste. She'd asked him to go through its contents, but she had no idea what he was supposed to be looking for. He unfolded it as he walked up the ramp and shook it into rigidity. The brane lit up and displayed a security lock.

Ethan smiled. While he didn't relish combing through whatever data the thing contained, cracking its security might at least provide a diverting challenge. He stopped at the top of the ramp and looked back at Quondam. The big Kadiran was trudging down the gravel path past the lake, almost out of sight.

Ethan turned his attention back to the brane.

Well, it's not like I have anything else to do.

35

PARTISAN

'What are you doing on Odessa? Who are you working for?'

Orry squinted into the blinding light, trying to make out her interrogator's features. She was pretty sure it was the woman from the alley but even with her integuary filtering the brightness, she couldn't see a thing; it was like staring into a sun. She looked down again, red afterimages blooming in her vision. The restraints binding her to the chair were painfully tight.

'I'm here to offer you a deal,' she said.

'What kind of deal?'

'I can't tell you that – I have to show you. I want to talk to whoever's in charge.'

'Talk to *me*.'

She shifted slightly to relieve the pressure on her arms, which were tied awkwardly behind her. She had no idea where they were, not even the shape of the room, since the blinding light had replaced the hood she'd been swaddled in since being bundled into the van in Bel Moritz. Orry had never been interrogated before. It was terrifying.

'Are you in command?' she asked.

'Yes.'

'I don't believe you.' She didn't know exactly why, but this woman didn't strike her as a leader.

'We know you're working with the kucks to infiltrate us. Admit it.'

'Don't be ridiculous.'

She flinched at the crack of a palm hitting a table. 'You're a collaborator!' the woman shouted, showing anger for the first time.

'No! I'm here to help. Let me speak to your leader.'

'Tell me why!'

Sweat ran down Orry's face. She was getting nowhere fast. 'Look, we both want the same thing – to strike a blow against the Kadiran. I can help you, but I need your boss to meet someone.'

'Meet who?'

'Someone who can help.'

'Where?'

'Outside the city.'

The woman grunted. 'Somewhere remote, I'm guessing. Do you really think we're just going to walk into your trap?'

'It's *not* a trap!' Orry insisted.

Her head snapped to one side as the woman struck her, the sound brutally loud in the silent room. It took a moment for the pain to come, a burning rush that set the side of her face on fire. Shocked to silence, she tongued her cheek and tasted blood. Her fear cranked up a notch.

'Tell us what you know about the Kadiran,' the woman asked, as if nothing had happened.

Orry glared into the light, tears of pain creating a kaleidoscope. 'I'm not a collaborator,' she said hoarsely.

A muffled scream sounded from somewhere nearby, making

her stiffen.

'Do us all a favour and just talk,' her interrogator said.

'Please,' Orry said, 'I'm telling the truth. How can I convince you?'

A door opened and someone entered. She heard murmuring and some movement, then a man's voice spoke.

'There's no point in maintaining this charade – we have a source inside the Kadiran command unit. They've told us everything.'

Even through her terror, Orry managed to laugh. 'You're full of crap. No one's told you anything because there's *nothing* to tell. I'm not a collaborator. I'm here to help.'

A face thrust into hers, making her recoil, and she realised she was right: it was the woman from the alley. '*Tell us!*' she roared.

'Fuck *off*!' Orry screamed back, bracing herself for another blow, but it never came.

'What's your name?' the man's voice asked eventually.

'Orry.'

'Where are you from?'

'Nowhere, really. I have a ship.'

'What are you doing on Odessa?'

'Like I told *her* – I'm here to help.'

'Who is this person you want me to meet?'

She looked up, seeing only a new silhouette in front of the light. 'You're in charge?'

'I am.' Something in his tone made her believe him.

'Come with me, meet my contact,' she said. 'It's in your best interests. It's not a trap, I swear.'

'Why can't you tell me what this is all about?'

Judging from her experiences so far, Orry could take a good guess at what would happen to her if she told these guys she wanted them to meet a group of breedwarriors.

'I just can't. You have to see it for yourself.'

'Tell me where we're going,' he said.

'I can't do that either.'

'Because there's a company of kucks hiding there,' snarled the woman who'd struck her. The man ignored her.

'Why not?' he asked.

'You think you're the only one worried about being double-crossed?' Orry said.

'Hey, we're the good guys here.' He sounded genuinely offended.

She spat a mouthful of blood onto the floor between them. The burning in her cheek was fading, but her jaw ached. 'Sure you are,' she said.

'Do you know what the Kadiran do to their prisoners?' the woman sneered. 'If it was them who'd caught you, you'd be praying for something as harmless as a friendly slap.'

Orry said nothing, sensing that her interrogator's belligerence was acting in her favour.

'If I go,' the man said, 'I'm taking a full squad.'

'*What?*' the woman objected. 'You can't be—'

'Shut the *fuck* up, Sykes!' he snapped angrily.

'Three men,' Orry said, and was met by silence. 'If it's a trap, what difference does it make? You'll be screwed either way.'

He let out an amused grunt. 'All right: three of us. Armed.'

'Of course,' she said, hiding her relief. 'Just pick people with cool heads.'

'You've caught my interest, but know this: I'll have a gun in your back the whole time. If it turns out you're lying, you'll be the first to die.'

'I'm not lying.'

'Well then, you've got nothing to worry about.'

Shadows rushed in as the light clicked off. As her eyes adjusted to the sudden dimness, Orry felt someone release her restraints. She blinked rapidly, rubbing her chafed wrists.

The man seated in front of her looked more like a college professor than a resistance leader. He wore his long dark hair in a ponytail, only the grey streaks at his temples suggesting he was older than he looked. She twisted her neck to see the woman he'd called Sykes. She was still standing behind her, and Orry could see hatred in her eyes.

Orry stood on shaky legs and turned to face her.

'If you think I'm going to apologise,' Sykes said, 'then keep fucking thinking.'

Orry put all her strength into the punch. Her hand exploded into pain as it connected with Sykes' jaw and the woman rocked back.

Rage clouded her face and she lunged at Orry.

'Sykes!' snapped the man, and she stopped abruptly. 'Our guest owed you that one. Now, off you fuck.'

Sykes scowled at them both, and stalked from the room.

Orry sat back down, rubbing her knuckles. 'Nice people you have working for you.'

'This isn't a tea party. Sykes is a stone killer – we need more like her.' He studied her for a moment. 'You can call me Partisan.'

'If that's what you want.'

'It is. So, when is this meeting of yours?'

'As soon as you can arrange some transport.'

He stared at her for a moment longer, then rose to his feet. 'Things are still pretty hot out there after the attack, but we should be able to get out of the city. Wait here while I sort a few things out.'

36

A VERY ANGRY MAN

'There they are,' Ethan said, watching a swirl of pale dust making its way up the steep trail towards them. He shaded his eyes and looked nervously into the crisp blue sky. A Kadiran gunship had passed over half an hour ago; its white contrail, a thin skein of expanding vapour kilometres above them, was still visible.

'I see them,' Mender grunted. He watched the approaching vehicle for a while, and added, 'Check in again.'

Ethan smiled. *Mender's worried about you, Sis.*

I'm fine, came Orry's immediate reply. *Tell him to worry about what's going to happen when we get there.*

I already am, Mender sent. *I'm thinking I might go up to the cockpit, get on the eighteens in case things go south.*

I hope it won't come to that.

So do I, girl, but there's no harm in it.

I suppose you're right – just don't let them see the turret move.

That would be bad, Ethan agreed.

Mender scowled at him. *I'll do my best,* he sent, then sighed. *Now I have to go back through the goddamn hold.* He limped away.

The Kadiran dissidents are in there, Ethan told Orry, *and they're being . . . difficult.*

Can Quondam keep them in line? Orry asked.

So far. I'm glad you're almost here, though. Quondam got back with them just before dawn and things have been a little tense since.

She stayed silent for a moment. *Ethan, things could go wrong very easily. If they do, I want you to run, okay? Just get out of there, and keep running until we come and find you.*

I hate it when you call me Ethan: you sound so serious.

I am serious.

He grimaced. *Okay, I'll run. Just don't get yourself killed.*

I didn't know you cared.

I don't. I just don't fancy being stuck on a planet full of bloody kucks.

Don't call them that, Orry said sharply.

Why not? Mender does.

Mender is not a good moral compass.

He rolled his eyes. *Fine, whatever. We are at war with them, though – or had you forgotten that?*

No, Ethan, I'm well aware of that. A pause. *We're coming up on your position now. Good luck.*

You too, Sis.

The vehicle was a large off-road buggy, its six balloon tyres eating up the rough mountain track with ease. It pulled up in a cloud of dust and doors swung open above the enormous wheels. A man and a woman clambered down, both armed and wearing tactical vests. The woman approached Ethan and covered him with her assault rifle while her comrade scanned their surroundings.

'Hi,' Ethan said. The woman looked really wound-up, as if she was just looking for an excuse to shoot him. 'Can you point that somewhere else?' he asked, annoyed at the quaver of nerves he heard in his voice. She ignored him.

'Okay,' the man called up to the vehicle.

Orry appeared, followed by a slight man with a black pony-tail. He kept his pistol pointed deliberately at her back as they climbed down and walked over. Ethan resisted the urge to hug her.

'This is my brother, Ethan,' she told the black-haired man. 'Ethan, this is Partisan.'

'I assume we haven't come all this way to meet your brother,' Partisan said.

'No,' she answered, and gave Ethan a nod.

He crossed the dusty ground to the cargo ramp, experiencing a sudden spike of anxiety as he stopped by the airlock's outer door. This was the part of the plan where things could go very wrong indeed. *Okay,* Jane, he sent, biting his lower lip in trepidation. *Open up.*

The door opened.

'Please,' Orry said quickly, moving to stand in front of the three resistance fighters, 'lower your weapons and listen to what they have to say.'

Three hulking figures emerged from the gloom of the airlock, the heavy ramp creaking under their combined weight.

The hard-eyed woman reacted immediately. 'Kucks!' she yelled, dropping to one knee and raising her rifle.

'No!' Orry cried, throwing herself forward.

Ethan's world slowed as the woman fired. Her first shots went wide, one of them zipping close enough to him to feel it pass. The next struck Orry's arm with a meaty thud, twisting her violently round.

He didn't have time to yell. The other fighters' guns were coming up as well, and the two dissident breedwarriors Quondam had brought back with him were reaching for their own weapons. Ethan looked on helplessly, stunned by the speed with which the situation had escalated.

The eighteen-millimetre cannon hanging from *Dainty Jane*'s belly whirred round and burst into life, rippling out a chest-caving series of concussions that tore a metre-wide line across the ground between the opposing groups, showering them both in dirt and chunks of smoking rock. Through ringing ears, Ethan heard Mender's voice from the ship's external speakers.

'Put the guns down, *right now*, motherfuckers, or things will get real unpleasant real fast.'

The cannon rotated rapidly, swinging first towards the Kadiran, then over to the resistance fighters.

'I'd do as he says,' Ethan advised shakily, unable to keep his eyes from Orry, who was on her knees clutching her arm, her hands red with blood. 'He's a very angry man.'

The woman who'd shot his sister adjusted her grip on her rifle and glanced at Partisan. Sweat stood out on the man's forehead as his eyes shifted from the Kadiran to the cannon.

'Put your weapons down,' he said in a tight voice. He laid his gun on the ground beside him. The woman hesitated and for a moment Ethan thought she was going to disobey. Then her comrade tossed his assault rifle and she finally did the same. The turret whipped round to cover the Kadiran.

'You, too,' Mender told them, his voice distorted through the speaker.

Quondam, who was unarmed, barked out a series of the coughing, gurgling screeches Ethan had heard so much of over the past few hours. The two other Kadiran slowly dropped their guns.

'Kid, get your sister to the medbay,' Mender said. 'You lot: stay right there while we see what damage you've done.'

'I'm fine,' Orry said, struggling to her feet. 'I just need a dressing.' Ethan hurried to her and took her weight as she leaned on him. Blood ran feely between her fingers where they covered her wound, trickling down her arm.

Medbay, Mender insisted over the integuary channel. *These bastards won't try anything now – I only wish they would.*

Mender is right, added *Jane. Let me examine you.*

All right, Orry agreed reluctantly. *Just don't shoot anyone until I get back. Or let them shoot each other.* She allowed Ethan to lead her towards the ship.

'Have you put on weight?' he asked as he walked her up the ramp.

'You don't actually believe this bullshit, do you?' Sykes snarled.

Mender adjusted his Fabretti to point at the woman. 'You've all done a passable job of keeping things nice and civil so far,' he said, 'so let's keep it that way.'

Orry remained silent, trying to ignore the ache in her arm as she let the resistance fighters talk. She had explained her plan, ignoring Sykes' evident disgust, but it was up to them now to decide if they wanted to be part of it.

'If they wanted to kill us, they would have,' Partisan pointed out.

'It's not *us* they want,' Sykes shot back. 'They want to tear the heart out of the resistance.'

'Oh, wake up,' Partisan told her wearily. 'The kucks have been here for months and what have we achieved? Blown up a couple of walkers and picked off a handful of their foot soldiers – at the loss of *hundreds* of our own. We're barely holding their attention.'

Sykes stared at him. 'People have *died* – *Amy* died – and you're saying . . . what? That it's all been for nothing?'

'I'm *saying* this is our chance to really hurt those bastards, to make them take us seriously.'

Incredulous, Sykes turned to the other fighter. 'What do you think?'

The man shrugged. 'I agree with Partisan.'

She threw up her hands in angry disbelief and lapsed into a sullen silence.

Orry turned to Quondam. 'What about your guys?'

'We have discussed the matter and are in accord.'

'So they'll do it?'

The Kadiran moved his giant head in what Orry judged to be a gesture of consent. Her knotted muscles relaxed a fraction.

She could hardly believe they had got this far. 'Great. So now we need to discuss the details.'

Late that afternoon, as the resistance fighters were returning to their buggy, Partisan broke off and approached Orry. He glanced around to make sure they weren't overheard, but the two Kadiran dissidents were heading towards their flyer.

'Do you really think this will work?' he asked.

'If we work together – and if you can keep a leash on Sykes,' she replied, 'then yes.'

He smiled. 'I'll make sure our part goes smoothly, but I have one condition.'

'It's a bit late for conditions.'

'Nevertheless, I have one. I could hardly mention it in front of the kucks.'

She narrowed her eyes. 'Go on.'

'The target. Once you're done with him, I want him.'

'What for?'

'Leverage.'

'The Kadiran aren't going to leave Odessa because you have one officer.'

'Maybe not, but we can use him to send a message.'

'How? By killing him? Torturing him?'

His face hardened. 'I appreciate the courage it took to bring us all here, but you don't know a damn thing about what's happening on this world. You can judge me all you like, but until you've seen what I've seen, done what I've had to do, you'll never understand. Now, I've told you my condition. You're not getting our help unless you agree.'

She sighed. Handing the planet-alpha over to the resistance didn't sit well with her, but perhaps she could think of a way out of it before she had to.

'Fine. When we've got everything we need out of him, he's yours.'

'Good.' He held out his hand and she took it. 'I'll see you later – if we're both still in one piece.'

She watched him walk to the buggy and thought about how she had felt when Morven Dyas had raided *Bonaventure* and killed her father. *Bonnie* had been her world. She could understand how Partisan felt.

Quondam appeared beside her. 'Your stratagem appears viable, Orry Kent. Your wound was gained with honour.'

'Thanks. You did a good job convincing your people to help.'

The Kadiran hesitated. 'There is information I have not yet imparted.'

She turned to face him, filled with a sudden, bone-deep weariness. 'Go on.'

'Once you have the intelligence you seek, the planet-alpha must not be harmed. You must allow us to take him. Any other outcome would be dishonourable.'

She closed her eyes for a moment. 'Let me guess: if I don't agree, they won't help?'

'This statement reflects the true state.'

'Wonderful.' *Future Orry is not going to thank me for this.* 'Okay, tell them they can have him when he's told us everything we need to know.'

Quondam gave a Kadiran nod and lumbered away. Behind her, the buggy's engine roared to life. She watched it drive off, Sykes glaring at her from a rear window, and released a deep breath.

'Chin up,' she told herself bleakly. 'We'll probably all be dead tomorrow anyway.'

37

RODIN

The problem with tanglegrass was that it was native to Tyr, so no matter how many genetic tweaks the atomicists made to Lucia Rodin's roses, she still needed to spend every other day weeding out the damned grass to stop it choking them.

Stepping into the flowerbed, she bent and plucked a budding clump from the moist, dark soil. The first colonists had needed to tinker with that too, to get it rich enough to grow their imported seeds, and even tweaked, it still needed a lot of watering in the hot climate of Tyr's northern continent.

Behind her the mower whirred past, leaving a dead straight stripe on the lawn.

Lucia stepped back and surveyed the bed. This was her favourite time of year, when the garden was just bursting into life, filling the air with the scent of roses and mock orange. Even this early in the day, Tyr's sun was beating down, making her back prickle with sweat beneath her frock coat. She considered removing it, then checked her integuary for the time and decided against it.

'You'll get mud on your suit and have to change.' Alexei

observed, arriving from the house with two clinking glasses of iced tea on a tray, which he set carefully on the wooden table beneath the pergola.

'It's fine,' she told him, tossing the clumps of tanglegrass into a weed-filled trug and accepting one of the glasses. Sipping the tea, she surveyed the garden, instantly seeing a dozen jobs she needed to make a start on. 'How's the painting coming?'

When Alexei smiled she could instantly see the handsome young man she'd married so long ago. 'I don't think I'm cut out to be an artist,' he admitted. 'I'm thinking of finding something else to occupy my time.'

She ignored the implicit criticism. 'Like what?'

'Carpentry, perhaps.' He drank some tea.

Birds were singing in the trees at the lower end of the grounds. Lucia loved the birdsong, but she'd never had the time to learn about the different breeds that visited. 'I've been thinking,' she said.

'That's what they pay you for.'

She watched a small bird with bright blue plumage swoop low over the lawn. 'After all this is done, I'd like to spend more time on the garden. A *lot* more time.'

In her peripheral vision she saw him look at her then. A lump rose to her throat.

'That . . . would be nice,' he said, and placed his hand on hers. She squeezed and looked away, back down the lawn.

They sat in comfortable silence as the mower whirred and the birds sang. The ice was melting into the bottom of her empty glass when she heard the flyer coming in from Usk. It landed at the far end of the garden, startling the birds away as it settled onto the grass. Lucia stood and bent to kiss Alexei on the cheek.

'See you sometime tonight.'

'I'm doing Ancerro spiced ham,' he told her. 'I'll leave it in a pot on the stove if you're late again.'

'Sounds wonderful. Thank you.' She straightened her frock coat and walked down the lawn to the flyer. One of the gull-wing doors was already open, a well-built man in a dark suit standing beside it, hands crossed in front of him.

'Morning, Georgi,' Lucia said as she climbed inside. 'How's Lillya doing?'

'Much better, thank you, ma'am. Just a spot of eczema, like you said. The ointment cleared it right up.'

'That's good. My granddaughter had the same thing. The trick is to let the skin breathe.'

She took a seat opposite Nika, who was engrossed in a data-brane. Several more had spilled out of her briefcase and were littering the seat next to her.

'Alexei made me iced tea,' Lucia said, looking back down the garden to where he sat. Nika didn't look up, responding only with a distracted grunt as she scrolled through the brane's contents.

The flyer swayed a little as Georgi climbed into the front and the engines hummed to life. Alexei stood up and waved as they rose smoothly into the air. She watched the garden shrink, then disappear as they banked towards the spires of Usk.

'The interrogation of the raider we captured at Manes has been moved up to ten a.m.,' Nika told her, still scrolling, 'so you'll need to attend via integuary. There's no time to get out to Saabitz Rock after your council meeting.'

Lucia tore her eyes from the window. 'Moved on whose orders?'

'Colonel Zaytsev. He wants to attend personally.'

Lucia preferred to attend interrogations in person, as she did meetings; she could read people far better face-to-face.

'For Rama's sake, *why*? Is he going to attend the interrogation of every single raider who may or may not have information about Cordelia Roag?' Co-operation between Zaytsev's Arbiter Corps and Seventh Secretariat had never been particularly good, but since the Kadiran attack on Tyr, Zaytsev appeared to be determined to dump the blame squarely on Lucia's shoulders. 'Let me speak to him.'

A moment later Nika shunted the call to Lucia's integuary and Arbiter-Colonel Zaytsev's lined face appeared in her field of vision.

'What is it, Lucia? I'm rather busy.'

'Good morning, Vadim. I understand you rescheduled an interrogation I arranged. I would appreciate it if you would change it back so that I can attend in person.'

'Out of the question. The prisoner is in the custody of my arbiters and that slot is the only time I have available today.'

She took a breath. 'He may be in your custody, Vadim, but it was Seventh Secretariat operatives who brought him in. He's *my* prisoner and I need to be present at his interrogation – in person. I have no objections if you want to be there, but *you* must rearrange your schedule, not the other way round.'

'Why can't *you* reschedule? What are you doing that's so important?'

'I'm on my way to meet with the Proximal Council.'

It was difficult not to smile at the stiffening in Zaytsev's features. Her inclusion on the council while he was denied access was like an open wound to him.

'I don't see what that—'

'I shall mention this to the Imperator when I see him,' she interrupted. 'Piotr likes me to keep him informed on the progress of *our* investigation.'

The arbiter narrowed his eyes. 'Perhaps I can move some things around.' The channel cut out and she leaned back in her seat. Why did every little thing have to be a battle? She'd hoped things would be easier now they had a common enemy to fight. *You should know better at your age.* She stared out of the window.

Exempted from the usual traffic restrictions the flyer streaked over the city, heading directly for the palace.

The Imperator's Palace was widely recognised as one of the foremost examples of Post-Expansion Ruuz architecture in the Ascendancy. Lucia thought the rambling collection of towers and domes, dazzling white stone and mirror-like glass was ostentatious, even bordering on vulgar, not that she'd ever voice that opinion. The gardens to the rear of the building were by far its best feature, if too formal for her taste.

Since its inception almost two hundred years ago, the Proximal Council had met in the same room, deep within the hill upon which the palace was constructed. A warren of tunnels and rooms went deep down into the bedrock – even she did not know how far – which had been hardened to withstand even an orbital bombardment.

The lift doors opened: she was the last to arrive, except for the Imperator himself.

The other five members of the council watched her take an empty seat beside Feodor, Sixth Duke of Lowenstaat.

'Nice of you to join us at last,' the young noble commented sourly.

Even at this early hour she could smell the wine on his breath. 'Thank you, Your Grace,' she replied in an even tone, pulling a databrane from her case and shaking it into rigidity before placing it on the table before her.

Seeing she would not be goaded into a reaction, he pouted and looked away.

Milan Larist Soltz, fifth Count of Delf, sitting in his customary position on the right of the Imperator's empty seat, smiled thinly at her handling of the lordling. Feodor was a recent appointment to the council, following the death of the old duke, his father. He was not a popular figure.

From the other side of the Imperator's chair, the Duchess of Goltenberg piped up, 'How is the garden, Lucia?'

She looked up from her brane. 'The tanglegrass is determined to stifle my roses, Your Grace.'

The duchess smiled sympathetically. 'Rootrenders,' she said, 'that's what you need. Little fuckers will eat right through the damned grass and leave the flowers alone. Can't digest non-native matter, d'ye see?'

'Thank you, Milady. I'll certainly give that a try.'

Beside the duchess, Jessica Brookes, President of the Empyrean Development Company, rolled her eyes at the sheer mundanity of gardening talk. Next to her was another empty chair, reserved for First Oversecretary Barsukov, the Administrate's senior civil servant, currently away on a visit to Alecto. The final member of the council, Grand Marshal Solsky, was engrossed in his own databrane; Lucia wondered exactly what he was scrolling through so intently.

They all rose to their feet as a door opened and the Imperator entered. He was a portly man, wearing uniform trousers but no tunic, his shirtsleeves rolled up. Once again, Lucia noted with concern how much the Imperator had aged in the past few months. Dark shadows hung beneath his eyes and his skin, that which wasn't hidden behind his grey walrus moustache and bushy sideburns, was pale and parchment-like.

'Sit, please,' Piotr said, sinking into his chair. 'Let's make this quick, if we can – the bloody trade guild is killing me.' He threw a glowering look at Brookes, who held her hands apart to indicate her helplessness in the matter.

'There is nothing more I can do, Your Excellency,' she said. 'The guild feels the special privileges granted by EDC's charter gives us an unfair advantage—'

'Which they do,' Delf pointed out.

'—over them,' she continued smoothly. 'We've tried lobbying, but the guild won't listen. They say the war is strangling their members' livelihoods.'

'Just bribe the grubby little bastards,' Feodor said, examining his manicured nails. 'You know how greedy merchants are. They'd whore out their daughters if the price was right.' He raised his eyes to look at Brookes and grinned. 'No offence.'

'None taken, Milord,' the EDC president said stiffly. 'Though I seem to recall the fortune you recently inherited is largely dependent upon House Lowenstaat's business interests in the rim.'

'Can we get on?' the Duchess of Goltenberg interjected irritably as Feodor glared at Brookes.

Lucia smiled inwardly; in her experience, nobles never enjoyed being reminded where their fortunes came from.

The Imperator waved his hand in agreement. 'Who would like to begin?' he asked.

'If I may,' Grand Marshal Solsky jumped in, 'during the past few days we have observed some unusual enemy movements. In particular, the Kadiran Fifth Fleet has withdrawn from Mon Audberg and redeployed to the Horcan system.'

'Horcan?' Feodor said. 'Where's that?'

Lucia was frowning. 'In the Kadiran Marches,' she said.

'Why would they withdraw?' Brookes asked. 'Was there an engagement?'

'No engagement,' Solsky said. 'The Kadiran forces far out-numbered our own in Mon Audberg.'

'They're cowards,' Feodor announced. 'That's why they tried that sneak attack last year.' He turned to Delf. 'If it hadn't been for your granddaughter—'

The count's palm slammed onto the table. 'That whelp is *not* my granddaughter!'

A ghost of a smile crossed Feodor's face.

'The Kadiran may be many things,' the duchess pointed out, 'but they are certainly not cowards.'

'I concur,' Solsky agreed. 'The Grand Fleet has suffered sub-stantial losses to the Kadiran. This is the first time we've seen them do anything but push towards the Fountainhead.'

'So what *are* they doing?' Delf asked.

'We are still trying to determine that.'

The Imperator turned to Lucia. 'Your thoughts?'

She considered for a moment. 'If there's one thing we've learned, it's how difficult it is to analyse the intentions of a race so different to ours in culture and motivation. If the Grand

Marshal is willing to share his data with me, Seven will be happy to undertake our own analysis.'

'That's a long-winded way of admitting you don't know anything,' Feodor said with a sneer.

'Give her the data,' the Imperator told Solsky.

'Yes, Excellency. Of course.' The grand marshal did not look happy about it.

The meeting continued, but for all Lucia absorbed everything that was said, smoothing discord and gently steering intentions where she could, her mind kept returning to Solsky's news about the Kadiran withdrawal. Something about that bothered her greatly. She waited impatiently for the talking to draw to a close so that she could properly examine his data.

38

EXTRACTION

Planet-Alpha Kills-With-A-Bright-Edge awoke, his hearts thudding, from another flying dream. He'd been back on Kadir, careering between the squat, broad trees of the blade forest. Naked and unable to control his headlong flight, he could do nothing but watch the razor-leaves as they whipped past. The dreams had become a nightly torment since his arrival on this forsaken world with its low gravity that spring-loaded every step – but he did not think it was the dream that had awoken him tonight.

Lying on his back, he could feel the hard floor through his meagre nest. There were plenty of nesting materials in this house – the humans loved their comfort – which was precisely why he'd used so little. He opened his eyes, keeping the inner membranes drawn for now. There was no sound from the compound – even the cursed insects were silent for once.

Something is wrong.

His membranes flicked open and he struggled into a sitting position, staring at the open windows flanking the glass door to the veranda. Cream curtains billowed in the warm night breeze, allowing the sickly scent of human flora into the room. All was silent.

The distinctive whistle of a mortar shell made his body stiffen; a *crump* came from the compound, followed almost immediately by cries and shouted orders, then there were more whistles and the stutter of one of the heavy plasma guns on the walls was quickly joined by another.

The door crashed open and his two bodyguards burst in.

'Resistance attack, sir,' one of them said as the other strode to the window and tugged back the curtain to peer out. 'Advancing on the walls.'

'How many?'

'*Hundreds.*' The breedwarrior sounded excited and Kills-With-A-Bright-Edge made a note to discipline him when this was over.

The warrior by the window paused to listen to his comm. 'Acknowledged,' he snapped into it, then glanced at his comrade. 'Stay with the planet-alpha,' he said. He went through the door to the veranda, closing it after him.

The shooting was intense now, but still confined to the far side of the compound. The remaining bodyguard fingered his assault cannon and stared at the door, raising the weapon at the sound of a series of shots from right outside.

When the firing stopped, the bodyguard glanced at Kills-With-A-Bright-Edge. 'Wait here, please, Planet-Alpha.' He eased the door open and stepped out after his comrade, the flapping material snagging on his cannon for a moment as he left.

Kills-With-A-Bright-Edge reached for his war-maul, his claws closing around its metre-long haft as another series of shots sounded – closer this time, practically outside the door, and sharp against the background firefight. *A human weapon*, he thought, his crest fanning involuntarily. It grew warm as blood rushed to it, colouring it a menacing red. He hefted his maul, reassured by its familiar weight.

A shadow moved on the other side of the curtain, the movements measured, concise. *Too small for a breedwarrior.* He stepped away from the window. The shadow grew larger as it neared the door and the planet-alpha raised his maul, wondering how much armour the human would be wearing.

He tensed as three quick shots came from outside. A dark splash of blood appeared on the cream material and the human's shadow dropped from sight.

He lowered his maul as a Kadiran stepped into the room. The breedwarrior's face was obscured by a mirrored helmet, but he wore the uniform facings of a formation-alpha in a close-air-support squadron.

'Planet-Alpha,' the newcomer said respectfully, lowering his carbine, 'you must come with me. The compound is about to be overrun.'

'Impossible!'

A huge explosion rocked the building.

'Please, sir. This way.'

A substantial portion of the ceiling dropped onto Kills-With-A-Bright-Edge's head, almost flooring him, and he reconsidered. As he stepped onto the veranda he saw a human body clad in black tactical gear lying on the stone floor. A second mirror-helmeted breedwarrior was standing over the body. Nearby, his two bodyguards lay dead. On the far side of the compound, flames lit the night amid streaks of tracer-fire and the neon flicker of energy weapons. Rage suffused him.

'What is happening?' he demanded, staring at the dead

human.

'The resistance has become organised, sir.' The formation-alpha indicated the human body. 'A snatch squad is coming to acquire you under cover of the attack. Intel found out too late; they sent us in to extract you. An armoured company is right behind us, but we have to get you out of here.'

The planet-alpha's hand trembled on his war-maul. He should have dealt with the resistance scum weeks ago. *This will be their death knell.* Raising the heavy weapon, he brought it down on the dead human's head, crushing his skull flat. Blood washed over the stone flags as the body twitched and jerked. It did little to quell his fury. He turned to the formation-alpha, who was staring at the dead human, his face hidden by the mirrored visor.

'What are you waiting for?' he demanded. 'Let's go.'

The formation-alpha roused himself and gestured for Kills-With-A-Bright-Edge to follow. They hurried across the compound towards a light recon flyer, the other warrior bringing up the rear. As they reached it a flare spiralled up from the compound and descended slowly, bathing the low walls and buildings in an eerie green light.

'After you, sir,' the formation-alpha said, indicating the flyer's open side hatch. He followed him into the rear compartment and sealed the hatch as the pilot climbed into the cockpit. A hammer blow struck the hull as the engines spooled up. Kills-With-A-Bright-Edge found a headset on a rack beside him and put it on as the flyer lifted into the air.

'Strafe the bastard humans a couple of times,' he ordered.

'Can't do that, sir,' the formation-alpha replied. 'If they bring us down we're giving them what they want.'

The planet-alpha considered insisting, then decided against

it. There would be plenty of time for retribution. He would make the humans realise one and for all who was in charge on this shithole of a planet. The thought brought a cold smile to his lips.

Orry couldn't get the image of the dead man on the veranda out of her head. Hamada, the waiter from the coffee shop in Bel Moritz, had volunteered to play dead in front of the planet-alpha in order to lend urgency and authenticity to her plan. Now he was dead for real, and it was her fault.

On the table in front of her in *Dainty Jane*'s cramped galley was a databrane showing the planet-alpha, whose name translated as Kills-With-A-Bright-Edge, seated in the rear of the stolen flyer, barking at Quondam in Kadiran. *Jane* provided an immediate translation.

'What is all this about, Formation-Alpha?' the ship said, relaying the planet-alpha's words. 'What aren't you telling me?'

Orry forced her thoughts away from Hamada; she needed to concentrate on getting the information she needed from Kills-With-A-Bright-Edge so the resistance fighter's death would not be in vain. 'Thanks, *Jane*,' she said, 'keep the translation coming.' She pressed her throat mic. 'Quondam? Just as we rehearsed, please.'

She watched him on the screen. His face was impossible to read behind his mirrored visor, not that she could glean much from Kadiran physiognomy anyway. The feed from the flyer was a high-angle shot from the miniature lens Ethan had rigged in the cabin's overhead. The image was distorted at the edges, but at least the fish-eye effect allowed the whole compartment to remain in shot.

'I am not really a close-air-support officer, sir,' Quondam told the planet-alpha.

She could see the other Kadiran's grip tighten on his war-maul. 'Who are you, then?'

Quondam hesitated. 'I work in the Intelligence Bureau. I have been sent to Odessa to fetch you.'

The ship waited a beat before adding her assessment of his performance. 'Not bad,' she said. 'A little stiff, but he's a convincing liar, for a Kadiran.'

'The attack on the compound,' Kills-With-A-Bright-Edge said, 'was far more ambitious than anything the resistance have attempted before. How did they know where I was?'

'That is part of the reason I am here, sir. Our sources tell us that human Seventh Secretariat operatives and Grand Fleet special forces are on Odessa, embedded within resistance cells to provide training and materiel support.'

'Materiel?' the planet-alpha queried. 'You mean weapons.'

'Yes, and tactics – but that is no longer your concern, sir. I have been tasked with extracting you and returning you to our fleet at the Dagger Nebula.'

'I am in command of this colony. Who will replace me?'

'I do not have that information, sir, but I am assured your successor will do a fine job quelling the resistance.'

Kills-With-A-Bright-Edge was silent for a moment, his hulking frame hunched. Orry thought he looked angry, but then Kadiran always looked angry to her.

'Does the Intelligence Bureau often extract serving officers in such an unconventional manner?' he asked eventually.

She touched her mic. 'Go ahead, Quondam – you're doing well. Reel him in nice and gently.'

'No, sir,' Quondam replied after a pause. 'Your knowledge

makes you an exceptional case.'

'What knowledge?'

'Of a highly compartmentalised operation that targets the human Imperator Ascendant.'

Even Orry could see all expression leave the planet-alpha's face. 'I don't know what you are talking about.'

She resisted the urge to caution Quondam. He was doing fine, and the planet-alpha's reaction was promising – she hadn't even been convinced there *was* an operation.

'Seventh Secretariat have discovered the operation,' Quondam continued. 'We do not know how. Over the past few days they have systematically targeted every senior officer with knowledge of it. We do not believe they gained any useful intelligence from any of the officers.'

'Why not?'

'Because every one of them died rather than be acquired.'

Kills-With-A-Bright-Edge nodded approvingly.

'Which leaves you, sir,' Quondam continued. 'You are one of a very few officers left with intimate knowledge of the plan – and you have senior battlefield experience. The War Council have placed you in overall command of the operation, effective immediately.'

It was a risky strategy, particularly as they knew precisely nothing about the plot. Orry looked at Mender and Ethan, who were also glued to the scene playing out before them.

Mender tapped his ancient timepiece.

'Time pressures,' she prompted.

'It is important to move quickly, sir,' Quondam said. 'We cannot be certain Seventh Secretariat have not discovered enough details about the operation to foil it.'

'Considering the date, that won't be a problem,' Kills-With-A-Bright-Edge said. 'Unless the Imperator's itinerary has changed. Has it?'

'Tell him no,' Orry said.

'Not to our knowledge, sir.'

The planet-alpha nodded slowly, thinking. 'Is everything in place?'

'Sir?'

'The assault ship?' Kills-With-A-Bright-Edge said impatiently. 'The strike teams? Warships to deal with the Imperator's vessel?'

'Yes,' Orry said, and heard Quondam echo her.

'Orry,' *Jane* interrupted, 'the flyer's systems indicate two incoming vessels: Kadiran gunships. Five minutes from intercept.'

'I'll get us airborne,' Mender said, heading for the rungs up to the cockpit.

'I'll come with you,' Ethan said, hurrying after him.

'Quondam,' she said, 'we need to hurry this up. Ask him *where* it's going to happen.'

The Kadiran remained silent.

'Do it, please.'

Quondam shifted uncomfortably. 'Planet-Alpha, can I ask where the assassination will take place?'

Kills-With-A-Bright-Edge raised his head to stare at him with an odd expression. 'Assassination? That idea was rejected right at the start. It was felt that the Imperator would be more valuable to the Hierocracy alive, as a bargaining chip.' He snorted, making his feelings about that decision quite clear. 'The assault team do know they're going into the asteroid to *acquire* and not kill him, don't they?'

Orry thought fast. 'Tell him you're sure they do know. Say you haven't been properly briefed on the operation.' Quondam relayed her words.

'Three minutes to intercept,' *Jane* added, 'and we are still five minutes away.'

We're running out of time. 'Try again,' she told Quondam urgently. 'Suggest it might be useful if he gives you more details about the assault.'

'Perhaps it would be useful if you filled me in, sir,' Quondam said obediently. 'That way I can confirm that all necessary preparations have been made.'

The planet-alpha gazed at his reflection in Quondam's visor. 'What is your security clearance?'

Quondam said nothing.

'You must know some clearances,' Orry said quickly, 'just lie. Name a high one.'

'Diamond Six,' Quondam said.

She waited as the planet-alpha regarded him, his expression unreadable. When he finally nodded, she let out her breath.

'According to the intel we received,' Kills-With-A-Bright-Edge said, 'the Imperator will be visiting an asteroid habitat designated *Holbein's Folly* in the Mephiston system. He takes the same trip every year on the same day, always incognito, with only a small personal bodyguard. Security is predicated on nobody knowing about the visit. Apparently it is a major headache for his security team, but he insists nonetheless.'

'Why does he go there?' Quondam asked, echoing Orry's thoughts.

'The intel package did not specify that information,' the

planet-alpha said.

'When is the next visit?'

Kills-With-A-Bright-Edge opened his mouth, then appeared to change his mind. 'Remove your helmet,' he ordered.

Shit. Orry's finger hovered over her throat mic. 'We'll have to risk it,' she said.

They had discussed this. The planet-alpha had commanded the communications facility on Kadir to which Quondam had been assigned. They had never worked together directly, but it was still possible that Kills-With-A-Bright-Edge would recognise him. There had been a lot of staff at the facility, however, so Orry had deemed it an acceptable risk. The biggest problem she could envisage – and the reason she was staring so hard at the image from the flyer – was if the planet-alpha had been specifically briefed on Quondam's treason and subsequent flight to Mor-helion. That kind of thing tended to commit a face to memory.

Moving slowly, Quondam reached up and removed his helmet.

Kills-With-A-Bright-Edge frowned. 'You look familiar. Have we served together?'

'Never, sir. I would remember.'

'Good,' Orry whispered, eyes fixed on the planet-alpha's face. She wondered if there was an integuary routine that would allow her to read Kadiran faces like she could humans; she felt blind without the additional input. As it happened, she didn't need a routine to see the change in his expression.

'Look out!' she cried into the mic, but Quondam had seen it too.

The planet-alpha's war-maul swept up in an arc intended to puncture Quondam's belly, spilling his guts, but Quondam shifted and the diamond point of the maul's back-spike scraped across his armoured hip, shaving a node of cartilage from the protrusions there but doing no more damage. Stepping inside his attacker's reach, Quondam hammered the planet-alpha with a combination of powerful blows that drove him back against the bulkhead. The picture juddered with the impact and Orry, worried they might lose the transmission.

Kills-With-A-Bright-Edge shortened his maul and tried to jab the top-spike forward, but Quondam stamped on his forearm.

'Orry,' *Jane* announced, 'the lead Kadiran gunship is ordering our pilot to land.'

She didn't take her eyes off the brane. 'Tell him to stall them until we get there.'

'They are very insistent.'

'Just tell him, please!'

On the screen, the planet-alpha was back on his feet and the two Kadiran were trading blows, each of which would have killed a human. The picture jumped and broke into coloured squares before giving out entirely.

'*Jane*? What's happened?' she demanded.

'One of the gunships has fired on the flyer.'

'*What*? But they must know their alpha's on board.'

'Kadiran tend to display zero tolerance towards this kind of situation,' *Jane* said evenly. 'At least they only targeted one of the engines. The flyer has made a forced landing. I have lost contact with the pilot.'

Orry pressed her throat mic. 'Quondam? Quondam!'

There was no reply.

39

COMPLICATIONS

Dainty Jane streaked towards the grounded flyer, so low that the curve of her lower hull barely cleared the treetops. Hooked into the ship's external lenses, Orry could see one of the Kadiran gunships on the ground near the crumpled wreckage of the flyer while the other circled the crash site.

Mender popped *Jane* up at the last possible moment, the ship shuddering as the mass driver under her nose spat hypersonic slugs at the circling gunship, which broke apart in seconds and dropped to the rocky ground as chunks of burning wreckage.

On the ground, the fire-team of three breedwarriors who were approaching the downed flyer turned and raced back to their own vessel. One of them paused briefly to shoot ineffectually at *Dainty Jane* as she screeched overhead, then took to his heels as Mender threw the ship into a tight turn.

The mass driver spat again, throwing up clods of earth and rock as it stitched a line across the clearing to the gunship. A mushroom of orange flame belched from the shattered craft, tossing the breedwarriors away like ragdolls. They landed hard and lay still.

Two minutes later *Dainty Jane* settled to the ground, creaking as her struts took her full weight. Orry slammed her palm on the ramp release, shifting nervously as she waited for it to lower. She turned at a sound from behind her to see Ethan run into the cargo bay, clutching a carbine.

Mender, are those three breedwarriors still on the ground? she asked.

Two of them are starting to move, he replied. *Don't worry, I'm on it.*

No more killing unless you have to.

Sure, whatever.

Her boots clanged on the ramp as she ran out of the ship, coughing as the stink of the burning gunship caught in her throat. She and Ethan raced over to the remains of Quondam's flyer and followed the luminous symbols that she assumed were the Kadiran version of arrows to the emergency hatch release.

Orry yanked the handle down with all her strength, but the hatch ground open only a few centimetres before jamming. The frame was hopelessly buckled. She put her eye to the gap but could see only darkness inside the flyer. Her heart in her mouth, she called, 'Quondam?'

A guttural Kadiran cough. 'I am here.'

Relief flooded her. 'Cutting gear,' she told Ethan.

'On it.' He dashed away.

Orry, sent *Jane, I am detecting more Kadiran vessels inbound – too many for us to defeat. Six minutes.*

Acknowledged. She turned back to the hatch. 'Quondam, what's the status of the planet-alpha?'

'The crash has rendered him unconscious.'

'Are you hurt?'

'My injuries are not critical.'

She stepped back and surveyed the crumpled vessel. The

stern was a blackened ruin with a jagged hole in one of the engines where the missile had struck. She clambered up to the shattered cockpit canopy and peered in at the Kadiran pilot, one of the two dissidents Quondam had brought to the meeting. He was clearly dead: his head had been almost completely severed by a long shard from the canopy.

'Quondam,' she called, 'can you open the internal hatch to the cockpit?'

'I will attempt to do so.'

She reached through the hole in the canopy for its release lever and the bulbous frame sprang open just far enough for her to get her hands under it and heave it up the rest of the way. She tried not to look at the dead pilot as she squeezed behind his seat and crouched in front of the hatch to the rear compartment.

'Quondam!' she yelled, banging on it.

'The hatch is jammed,' came the muffled reply, and something thudded against the other side. The hatch shifted a centimetre and then, as the thudding repeated, a couple more.

Orry braced her back against the pilot's seat and gave the hatch a hefty kick. Pain shot up her shin, but the metal did move a little more. She tried again, and now eight clawed Kadiran fingers appeared through the gap they'd made and gripped the edge. Quondam heaved and the hatch shifted, making Orry shudder at the thought of the strength in those alien muscles – and then the metal gave way enough for the hatch to spring open, revealing Quondam, dark ichor oozing from a ragged tear in his crest.

'We have to hurry,' she told him.

He vanished into the rear compartment and reappeared

a moment later with the planet-alpha's unconscious body. Between them, they managed to haul the Kadiran out of the cockpit and onto the scorched earth beside the flyer, just as Ethan appeared lugging a thermic cutting torch.

Seeing Quondam and the planet-alpha, he sighed and started dragging the heavy equipment back to *Dainty Jane*. Quondam hoisted the planet-alpha onto his shoulders and staggered after him.

One minute until the Kadiran ships arrive, Jane informed them as they reached the top of the ramp.

Get in, quick, Mender ordered, and the ship lurched upwards before the ramp was fully closed.

Orry crouched beside the planet-alpha lying on the deck of the cargo bay. 'How bad is he hurt? Is he going to wake up?'

Quondam ran his hands over his fellow Kadiran's head and neck, then sat back on his haunches. 'The state is uncertain.'

She examined Quondam, noticing several other wounds on his body. 'Let's get you to the medbay,' she told him. 'Ethan will watch this one.'

'I will?' He didn't look too happy at the prospect. 'What if he wakes up?'

'You have a gun, don't you? Look, we *want* him to wake up. Quondam did brilliantly' – she patted the Kadiran's leathery arm – 'but we only know *where* the attack on the Imperator is going to happen, not *when*.'

'And you think he's going to tell us that now he knows Quondam was lying? Isn't knowing *where* it's going to happen enough? Shouldn't we warn someone?'

'Warn who? Irina told me to trust *no one* – she said this conspiracy goes right to the top.'

'Then we need to go to the asteroid ourselves,' Ethan said, 'and warn the Imperator in person.'

She realised he was right. They didn't have time to waste trying to get anything else out of the planet-alpha.

'All right,' she said, 'we'll go and talk to Piotr.'

Quondam's bulk shifted beside her. 'You will deliver the planet-alpha to my comrades first,' he rumbled.

'What does he mean?' Ethan asked.

'Quondam—' she began, then stopped. How could she explain to him that she'd made a promise that was impossible to keep? How would he react? She eyed him nervously, knowing that she had no choice but to tell him the truth; she owed him that much at least.

Best to just get it over with.

'I'm not going to be able to give the planet-alpha to your friends,' she said bluntly.

He was silent for a moment, his torn crest rippling. 'I do not understand.'

She drew a breath, horribly aware of his sheer size. 'Things have changed. We have to warn the Imperator *now*, or all this will have been for nothing.'

'What has changed?'

She glanced at Ethan for help, but he looked as confused as the Kadiran. *That's what you get for keeping things to yourself,* she told herself. 'Things . . .' she said weakly.

'Nothing has changed,' Quondam stated. 'You will fulfil your promise.'

'Sis?' Ethan said uncertainly.

'You don't understand,' she said, thoroughly miserable. 'I had to say yes, or none of this would have happened.'

Ethan was looking worried now. 'Yes to what?'

She stared at her boots, then forced herself to look at them both. 'Partisan wanted the planet-alpha as well as you,' she told Quondam. 'I told you both you could have him when this was over. I'm sorry, but there was nothing else I could do!'

Ethan looked nervously at Quondam, who remained silent.

'Did you understand what I just said?' Orry asked.

'I understand.'

'Then please say something.'

His little eyes regarded her. 'Dishonourable actions will often result in such situations. The true test is how you choose to resolve it.'

'What does *that* mean?'

He turned away, towards the medbay. 'I know there is honour in you, Aurelia Kent.'

Ethan shot her a disappointed look and hurried after him.

Orry watched them disappear in the direction of the medbay, feeling just like she used to whenever her father had played the guilt card over something she'd done.

'Well, *shit*,' she said eventually.

Dawn was as beautiful as everything else on Odessa: twin suns hanging low above the mountains, casting a soft golden glow that set the snow-laden peaks on fire and sparkled on the clear water of the nearby tarn.

Dainty Jane sat beside the lake in a natural bowl surrounded by bare rock. The two groups gathered in front of her cargo ramp were eyeing each other warily. There were more Kadiran dissidents than last time, and more resistance fighters. Everyone was armed.

Orry couldn't quite believe she was doing this.

'We had a deal,' Partisan said, his face clouded with anger, and the women and men behind him growled in agreement.

Orry looked down at him from halfway up the ramp, in front of the planet-alpha's slumped body. Mender and Ethan, standing nearby, were letting her do the talking. *As usual*, she thought bitterly.

'I'm sorry,' she said, 'but I still need him.'

'He killed Hamada – that wasn't supposed to happen.'

'No,' she said, regret twisting her chest, 'it wasn't, and I'm truly sorry it did.'

One of the Kadiran dissidents stepped forward. 'Our comrade was lost also. Honour requires the planet-alpha be relinquished to *us*.'

Orry held up her hands, trying to stop the rumbles of discontent coming from both groups. 'I said I would hand over the planet-alpha once I had all the information I needed from him,' she announced, 'but I haven't yet got that. There's much more I need to learn—'

'You told us *both* we could have him,' Sykes interrupted, 'and that makes you a lying bitch!'

Orry straightened her back. 'You have to believe me when I say that this is more important than any single colony.'

'Bullshit!' Sykes yelled, and Partisan, looking as furious as his lieutenant, stepped forward.

'Secure the kuck commandant,' he ordered his people, and a pair of colonists started towards *Dainty Jane*.

One of the Kadiran dissidents moved forward at the same time. 'The planet-alpha was promised to us,' he rumbled through his translator. 'Any other course of action is unacceptable.'

Orry stepped back, straddling one of the unconscious alpha's legs. In front of the ship, humans and breedwarriors were facing off, weapons coming up. 'Stop this!' she yelled. 'Hasn't there been enough killing? You all want the same thing – so let's talk—'

But *everyone* was ignoring her now. She glanced at Mender, feeling things start to unravel as Partisan's two soldiers raised their weapons and stepped into the path of the Kadiran dissident coming to get his planet-alpha.

'We're taking him,' Partisan informed the Kadiran officer, who was reaching for his war-maul. 'Don't do anything stupid.'

Beside her, Mender was watching the scene through narrowed eyes, his hand on the butt of his Fabretti.

The Kadiran's hand closed on his weapon and the two humans in front of him shifted nervously, fingers tense on triggers.

'Don't do it,' Partisan warned. 'He's ours.'

The Kadiran appeared to consider. 'This state is unsatisfactory,' he announced after a moment's thought.

'No!' Orry yelled, moving forward, then stumbled as something caught at her ankle. Glancing down, she saw the planet-alpha's clawed hand had closed around her leg.

With a terrifying cry he rose and with his other hand, gripped her by the throat and drew her to his chest. She choked, clawing ineffectually at his iron grip. Her head felt as if it was about to explode, her lungs were heaving for air. Her throat was burning, her vision dimming.

She could make out shouting but it sounded hollow, as if she were underwater. Shadow-people moved like spectres at the bottom of the ramp. She thought of Ethan: who would look after him after she was gone? Would he even live through this? Would any of them?

A dull thud like an explosion sounded from somewhere behind her, loud enough to break through the roar in her ears, and suddenly the steel band around her throat released.

She fell to the ground, gasping as sweet, cold air rushed down her throat, searing at first, then soothing as it filled her desperate lungs. She coughed, retched, retched again until her vision finally started to clear.

Trying to ignore the pain in her neck, she looked around.

The planet-alpha was lying on the ramp behind her. Half his head was missing. Mender was standing over him, smoke curling from the huge barrel of the Fabretti. His look of concern faded a little when he saw she was moving. He rolled her eyes at her, as if to suggest that she should have known better. *Maybe he has a point.*

There was still a lot of shouting, she realised as her senses returned: someone was yelling to lay down weapons; barks and grunts in Kadiran she imagined meant much the same thing. She rose unsteadily and tried to call out, but all she could manage was a hoarse croak.

Everyone looked up as a crack like thunder rolled across the mountains, followed by several more. High above them, the blue sky was suddenly crisscrossed with white contrails as a flurry of needle-thin black lines streaked towards the ground from high in the atmosphere and disappeared behind the mountains.

Seconds later the ground shook, a tremor that caused ripples across the lake.

Jane, *what's going on?*

The ship sounded calm. *Ascendancy warships have entered the upper atmosphere*, she sent. *Dozens of them. They are rodding Bel Moritz and other major settlements, likely in preparation for a ground assault.*

'What is happening?' Quondam asked, shading his eyes as he stared into the sky. Orry could see flashes up there now, and more black streaks falling.

'It's the Grand Fleet,' she croaked in reply. 'I think the Imperator wants his planet back.'

40

MEDEVAC

'I'm picking up a distress call,' *Jane* announced, 'from Bel Moritz.'

Mender was keeping the ship low and aiming for the base of a narrow corridor of airspace that *Jane* assured them would enable her to enter orbit without being detected by the Ascendancy fleet.

'Let's hear it,' Orry said, wincing as the words burned her bruised throat. She applied another shot of the analgesic spray she'd picked up from the medbay and the pain eased.

A woman's voice, shrill with fear, filled the cockpit. In the background, Orry could hear explosions and the rattle and crack of gunfire.

'This is Memorial Hospital – if anyone can hear this, please help us! They said they'd come back to evacuate the rest of us but now the roads are blocked. We have patients here and no way out of the city. If anyone can hear this, please assist. I repeat: this is Memorial Hospital—'

'That's enough,' Mender growled.

'We have to help them,' Orry said.

He groaned. 'No, not this time. It's none of our goddamned business.'

She said nothing, just waiting until he glanced uncomfortably at her, as she knew he would.

'I said *no*, girl. Don't go giving me those eyes of yours either – it won't work.' He looked angrily at the control panel. 'I should never have picked up your scrawny ass in the first place.'

She hooked the navigation core and accessed local charts. 'Look,' she said, 'the hospital's on the edge of the city. We can be there in five minutes, land on the roof and fill the hold with people.'

'And then what?'

'And then . . . we'll take them to the fleet. That way they won't shoot us down.'

'They won't shoot us down anyway if we use this corridor.'

'I calculate a seventy-six per cent chance of survival,' *Jane* said.

'There you go,' Mender said, then faltered. 'Wait, what? *Seventy-six?*'

'It's just an estimate,' the ship told him helpfully.

'Mender,' Orry said, touching his arm, 'the city's being flattened. We have to help.'

He cursed again. 'Goddamn tree-hugging do-gooders. All I want is a quiet life . . .' The rest of his muttered imprecations were lost under the screech of *Dainty Jane*'s engines as he hauled the ship around and pointed her towards the city.

Orry grinned.

Her good humour vanished as they approached Bel Moritz. The beautiful city was broken, plumes of black smoke rising from craters filled with collapsed buildings, trees aflame like giant torches. Kadiran gunships rumbled above the rooftops, exchanging fire with Ascendancy drones as Grand Fleet dropships streaked down, the flares of braking thrusters scorching the roads where they landed.

Orry watched assault troopers spilling out of one dropship, only to be cut down by a Kadiran armoured unit concealed in a nearby building. Seconds later a tungsten rod struck the building from orbit and brought the whole structure down on the artillery piece. A cloud of dirty grey dust rolled over the scene.

'There,' she said, leaning forward in her acceleration shell to point at a large white building surrounded by rolling lawns disfigured by wide brown scars. The burning wreckage of an armoured vehicle was blocking the approach road. 'Put us down on the roof.' She pointed at the broad landing pad occupying the top of the hospital and ran for the freight ramp.

As Mender expertly set *Dainty Jane* down, Orry peered out from the lowered ramp, her arm wrapped around a cargo strap to steady her.

A physick ran over, her black coat flapping in the down-thrust of *Jane*'s rumbling engines. 'You got our message,' she yelled. 'Thank Piotr!'

'Glad to help,' Orry told her.

'Are there more ships coming?'

'I don't know.'

The woman's face fell. 'How many can you take?'

'Let's see, shall we? Start loading them.'

The physick hurried away and before long a stream of wheel-chairs and walking wounded began to cross the roof to the ramp.

The medbay, cabins and hold filled up quickly and Ethan started directing the more mobile patients first into the galley, then into the observation blister.

Finally the exodus began to ease and Orry felt a surge of relief, thinking they would just about be able to fit everyone in. But as the last dozen walking wounded shuffled towards the ramp, gunfire rang out from the edge of the rooftop and a series of metallic *clangs* reverberated off *Jane*'s hull.

The remaining patients threw themselves to the ground, screaming as a contingent of breedwarriors appeared on the far side of the roof and began exchanging fire with a squad of assault troopers somewhere in the hospital gardens below. The Kadiran appeared to have no direct interest in *Dainty Jane* or the patients – *for now*, Orry thought – but they were caught in the deadly crossfire between the opposing forces.

When the breedwarriors spread out, skirting the roof's low parapet as they tried for a better position to fire down on the Ascendancy troopers, Orry beckoned the nearest patients to get up the ramp and into the crowded hold. Five more got inside before increasingly savage gunfire announced the arrival of another squad of Ascendancy assault troopers, who burst from a door onto the roof. As some of the Kadiran turned to face this new threat, the fire from below increased in intensity. A drone joined the action, the remote gun platform rising from the grounds to pour fire onto the beleaguered warriors, who fell one by one.

At last only a single massive specimen, his matt black armour daubed with white paint, remained standing. The Kadiran tossed aside his empty cannon, drew his war-maul from his back and opening his powerful arms and thrusting out his chest, bellowed a challenge. Orry watched in fascinated horror as he charged the troopers on the roof, ignoring the rounds slamming into armour and flesh and the flickering darklight beams that left holes wherever they touched.

The breedwarrior staggered, dropped to his knees, then rallied, managing to rise briefly until a fresh flurry of rounds brought him down again to lie face-first on the dusty roof. His shoulders rose and fell as his shallow breaths caught in his throat.

A sergeant approached the fallen warrior. She stared down at him, then shifted her rifle almost casually until the muzzle was resting on the back of the Kadiran's helmet.

'Sergeant!' Orry cried, running over. Guns came up to cover her, but the sergeant didn't react other than to turn her head. Her young face was deeply lined, particularly around the eyes, which held a deadness that chilled Orry.

'Help you, miz?'

'That warrior is wounded. What are you going to do to him?'

'Just what it would have done to me, and you, and all these folks here, given half a chance.'

Her tone held such certainty that Orry faltered, feeling like a child challenging an adult. She continued anyway, 'What difference does that make? They commit atrocities so we do the same – is that how it works now?'

The sergeant spat on the ground, then lifted her rifle from the Kadiran's neck and rested it over her shoulder as she turned to face Orry. 'Who the hell are you?'

'We're evacuating the wounded.'

'Best you get back to your job then, miz, let me do mine.'

At their feet, the Kadiran's breaths were becoming more laboured. Muscles moved beneath torn flesh.

'You're a soldier, Sergeant, not a murderer.'

'It's a fucking kuck. They invaded this world. They invaded the *Ascendancy*.'

'You can't just *execute* him. He's your prisoner. He needs medical attention.'

Her face hardened. 'Who's gonna stop me?'

A shouted warning from one of the other troopers came too late. The Kadiran's maul swung up, its back-spike driving into the sergeant's stomach. She let out a screech of agony and fell back, clutching the wound as blood gushed out. Then the Kadiran was on his feet, his war-maul swinging. Orry threw herself aside as the hammerhead whistled past her ear. She landed hard, but rolled, seeing the warrior stagger forward into the crowd of patients. His powerful arms swept the fearsome weapon left and right, hospital gowns blooming red as he crushed already injured bodies. The Kadiran keened as he killed, the wet sound of his butcher's work rising over the panicked screams of his victims.

The troopers opened fire again, tearing him apart, until his mangled remains fell in the centre of a circle of pulped, twitching meat.

Orry stared at the carnage, a sharp taste in the back of her throat.

The moment he was down, hospital staff hurried to help the survivors while the troopers' medic raced to the sergeant. She was curled into a bloody ball, her hands clutching her stomach as she moaned. After a brief exchange of words with the medic, a wiry trooper with a corporal's stripe on his chest armour strode over to Orry, his face contorted with rage.

'Is this what you fucking wanted?' he spat.

She guessed it was taking all his self-control not to strike her. She couldn't blame him.

'This is our *third* combat drop - this is what these fuckers *do*. Every fucking chance they get.' He swept his rifle across the bloody mess, ending up with it pointing at the sergeant. '*We* know that – *she* knew that.'

'I—' Orry began.

'Stow it! You're gonna evac the sarge and you'd better make goddamn sure she stays alive. You read me?'

Orry nodded mutely, stunned.

'Where are you taking these people?'

'I don't know exactly. I thought one of your ships—'

'Take them to the flagship, *Gratitude*.'

'Will they let us aboard?'

'Tell them you're a civilian evac – any problems, say you have the sarge aboard.' He thrust something into Orry's hand: a metal dog-tag, blood pooling in its stamped letters. 'That's her name and serial number.'

Orry stared at it, the sergeant's blood wet on her hand. *Ling, Emilia J. RH Positive. 09-342513-56.*

'Thank you,' she said.

The corporal shoved her hard in the chest, sending her staggering back towards *Dainty Jane*. 'She's a good person. Don't let her die.'

'I won't.'

The medic and another trooper passed Orry, carrying Sergeant Ling between them. They disappeared up the ramp, then ran back down to re-join their squad.

'What are you waiting for?' the corporal snarled. 'Get the fuck out of here.'

Orry turned and fled up the ramp and into the hold. As the airlock closed behind her she had to step over and around the crammed-in patients to get to the ladder up to the galley. She finally made it to the cockpit, where Mender was completing the pre-launch checks as Quondam sat silently in one of the rear shells.

'We're overloaded,' he said as she strapped herself in.

'Can we take off?'

'Just about.'

'Then let's go.'

He glanced at her. 'Warn them.'

She hooked the general systems core and sounded the klaxon, cycling through the external lenses to make sure there was no one too close to the nacelles.

'Clear?' Mender asked.

'Clear.'

'Lifting.'

Dainty Jane rose ponderously into the air, wallowing as she turned, gaining speed slowly as Mender kept the nacelles almost fully down, struggling to keep the overloaded ship in the air.

'Better pray we don't run into any Kadiran ships,' he muttered, fighting with the controls. 'If we have to manoeuvre, we're shafted.'

She didn't reply but kept watching through the stern lenses as the hospital shrank away below them. She zoomed in on the fallen Kadiran lying in the centre of a circle of dead patients.

Dead because of me.

She felt sick. She'd been so sure she was doing the right thing – and look what had happened. She thought of Sergeant Ling, bleeding out in the hold, and when she looked down at her bloodstained hands, she saw they were shaking.

41

GRATITUDE

Gratitude was a heavy cruiser, according to *Dainty Jane*'s data core. The huge ship was in geosynchronous orbit over Bel Moritz, hanging above Odessa's curve and surrounded by the Ascendancy task force she commanded. Orry recognised frigates and destroyers and *Jane* pointed out the blocky shapes of assault ships and troop carriers, but *Gratitude*, a five-hundred-metre-long wedge of distilled aggression, dwarfed them all.

Dainty Jane had made orbit without attracting any unwanted attention, but now they had no choice but to announce themselves.

'Where are all the Kadiran ships?' Ethan asked, arriving from the hold. He had blood on his T-shirt and a distant look in his eyes that Orry didn't like.

'That's exactly what I'm thinking, kid.' Mender was looking grimmer than usual, too. 'Better get on to that cruiser, girl, before they find us.'

She eyed the distant warship disgorging a steady stream of dropships towards the planet's surface and activated the comm. 'Ascendancy cruiser *Gratitude*, merchant *Dainty Jane*.'

The response came back immediately. '*Dainty Jane, Gratitude*. Do not approach any closer or you will be fired upon. Acknowledge.'

She glanced at Mender. 'Not very friendly, are they?'

'Did you expect anything else?'

She tried again. '*Gratitude*, we are carrying civilian wounded from the fighting in Bel Moritz. They require urgent medical attention. Request vectors to a landing bay and med teams to receive casualties.'

'Negative, *Dainty Jane*. Change course immediately or we will open fire.'

'Wait!' She fumbled with the dog-tag, rubbing the blood from it with her thumb. 'We have one of your troopers on board, in critical condition: a Sergeant Ling.' She read off the serial number. 'That makes us a medevac.'

A pause. 'Wait one, *Dainty Jane*.'

'Will they go for it?' Ethan asked worriedly.

She met Mender's eye, but he didn't look hopeful.

'*Dainty Jane*, permission to dock is denied. I say again, permission is denied. You have ten seconds to change course. Expedite.'

'Piotr's withered balls,' Mender muttered, pulling back on the yoke.

'Leave those controls alone!' she snapped at him, filled with sudden fury. '*Jane*, send those bastards a feed from the hold.' She activated the comm again. 'Now you listen to me, *Gratitude*. These people are going to die without your help. It's your bloody fault they're in this mess and it's your duty to provide assistance. We are no threat to you and we are going to land, with permission or without. If you want to blow up a ship full of wounded civilians, then you go right ahead . . . and I'll see you in hell!'

Mender regarded her with a sour expression. '"I'll see you in hell?" Kind of a cliché, don't you think?'

She managed half a smile, her anger already collapsing into a sick fear. 'What can I say? I just went with it.'

'I really hope they don't end up being your last words.' He looked out at the approaching cruiser. 'Kind of embarrassing if they are.'

'I hope so too.'

He held his course as she watched the seconds tick by. Ethan came to stand beside her, white-faced, his jaw set. She felt his hand on her shoulder and reached up to squeeze it. Ten seconds took an age to pass, but when they had, *Dainty Jane* was still in one piece.

Another half a minute crawled by. *Gratitude* was growing larger all the time.

When the comm finally burst into life, Orry actually jumped.

'*Dainty Jane, Gratitude*, you are cleared to land in Bay Six, that's on the starboard side. Medical personnel will be waiting. Proceed directly to the landing bay. You try anything, you're toast. Acknowledge.'

'Directly to Bay Six, starboard side, no funny business. Thanks, *Gratitude*.'

'Have a nice day.'

'Smart arse,' Orry muttered, closing the channel. She sank back into the gel of her couch and grinned wearily at Ethan and Mender.

The old man shook his head. 'One of these days this shit you keep pulling will come back to bite you.'

She reached over to pat his arm. 'Oh, Mender, you *do* care.'

'Just worried it'll bite me too.'

*

A large team of medics were waiting in the landing bay as

promised, together with a full squad of auxiliaries. Orry, first down the ramp, was met by an auxiliary under-lieutenant whose skin was so dark it was almost blue.

'You have a wounded trooper?' he asked, his voice oddly soft-spoken for a soldier.

'Yes, top of the ramp. About forty civilians too.'

The lieutenant made a gesture and medics and auxiliaries clanged up the ramp. Orry thought of Quondam, up in the cockpit, and prayed Mender would be able to keep the Kadiran away from prying eyes.

'Under-Lieutenant,' she said urgently, 'I need to speak to your commanding officer at once.'

If the request surprised him, he didn't show it. 'Lieutenant Maxwell? Why?'

'No, I mean whoever is in command of' – she swept her hand through the air, encompassing the entire bay – 'all this.'

'You mean in command of the ship?'

'I mean in command of *all* the ships.'

He frowned. 'Counter-Admiral Vetochkina is a little busy liberating a planet at the moment, miz.'

Orry sighed and activated Irina's ring. 'I'd like to see her *now*, please.'

The lieutenant glanced at the Imperator's Seal, his face puzzled. 'Like I said, the admiral doesn't have time to—'

Oh, for pity's sake. 'Don't you know what this is?'

'It's a ring.'

She was at a loss. *What's the point of having this damn thing if no one—*

'Let me see that.'

The portly fleet medic approaching looked young to be

wearing the sword and star of a second-captain, but he had a clear air of command about him and his salute was impeccable. 'Captain Telemann, at your service.'

Orry offered her hand and Telemann studied the ring before regarding her with something approaching awe.

'What is *wrong* with you, Lieutenant? Have this woman escorted to the ops room immediately.'

'But—'

'*Now*, Under-Lieutenant!'

The junior officer snapped to attention. 'Aye aye, sir! Private Kier, escort our guest to operations. Offer them Captain Telemann's compliments and request a meeting with the admiral – *immediately*.'

The fresh-faced auxiliary gave a crisp salute and turned to Orry. With her pretty features and big brown eyes, she looked like she would be more at home in a prom dress than her composite-ceramic armour. 'This way, miz,' she said.

Orry thanked the officers and followed her guide.

Gratitude's operations room, following standard Grand Fleet doctrine, was located deep in the cruiser's heart, a metal cave darkened by rubbery anti-spalling compound on the bulkheads, faces cast pallid in the light of screens. A large holographic display filling the centre of the space showed the uppermost segment of Odessa looking like the sheared-off top of an egg.

Private Kier halted just inside the door.

'What's the matter?' Orry whispered, unwilling to break the focused calm of the room.

Kier adjusted her helmet. She was sweating. 'I thought I was lucky not to be going down to the bloody surface,' she griped quietly. 'Having my guts pulled out by a kuck seems like a pretty good option right about now.' She gave a humourless laugh and marched over to the cluster of senior officers gathered around the central display. Standing rigidly at attention, she snapped off a salute.

'Admiral Vetochkina, ma'am?'

A gaunt woman with fine, close-cropped white hair turned to her, frowning with irritation. Her skin looked waxy in the artificial light.

'What is it, Private?'

'Second-Captain Telemann's compliments, and would you spare this woman a few moments?' Kier's voice sounded robotic.

Counter-Admiral Vetochkina shifted her frown to Orry, but to her credit, did not waste time questioning Telemann's judgement. Orry suspected that might come later.

'Well?'

A tremor ran through the cruiser as more rods were despatched towards the surface. On the central display Orry could see mushroom clouds rising from an earlier salvo. Bel Moritz was in ruins.

She balled her fists. 'What the hell do you think you're playing at?' she demanded, causing every head in the ops room to turn. 'There are *civilians* dying down there!'

Vetochkina regarded her without expression. 'And you are?'

'I'm the person who just flew a shipload of wounded people off a hospital roof.'

'Ah, yes. You're lucky to be here.'

'*Lucky?*'

A first-captain with oiled whiskers glistening above a broad shovel of a beard gestured at Kier, who was staring stiffly ahead.

'Private, get this woman out of here. *Now.*'

Orry held up Irina's ring and the first-captain's mouth dropped open.

Counter-Admiral Vetochkina pursed her lips in irritation. 'Where did you get that?'

Orry smiled coldly. 'No, I don't think that's how this works, is it, Admiral?'

Vetochkina's eyes were like ice. 'What do you want?'

'Your fleet.'

The admiral blinked. 'For what purpose?' she asked.

'I don't believe I need to tell you that.'

That produced a thin smile. 'We are in the middle of liberating a colony. If you think I am going to pull out without a damned good reason, then you are very much mistaken, young lady. I don't care how many rings you show me.'

Orry had expected as much. 'Is there somewhere we can talk privately?'

The bearded first-captain stepped forward, blustering, 'Now wait one damned—'

Vetochkina waved him to silence. 'Continue the assault. This won't take long.' She gestured towards a door between two banks of monitors.

The door opened at their approach, revealing a compact compartment with the obligatory glass tea dispenser steaming on a desk.

The admiral didn't sit but simply folded her arms and waited.

'I have evidence of a plot to assassinate the Imperator Ascendant,' Orry said. 'I need you to retask your fleet and immediately proceed to a location I will give you.'

Vetochkina snorted. 'Impossible. We're in the middle of

operations.'

As far as Orry was concerned, stopping the bombardment was a bonus. 'Make it happen,' she said.

The older woman looked disgusted. 'Who are you?'

'My name is Aurelia Katerina Kent.'

A flicker of recognition crossed the admiral's cold face and Orry waited to see if the admission would help or hinder her. Six months earlier she'd saved the Imperator and Tyr, the Ascendancy's capital world, from destruction, along with the entire Home Fleet. Despite her actions, she knew many Grand Fleet officers considered her a criminal for also destroying the weapon they could have used to wreak untold destruction on their Kadiran enemy.

'We have troops on the ground, Miz Kent,' Vetochkina pointed out. 'Even if I recalled them immediately it would take at least eight hours to get them back to their ships. Surely you're not asking me to abandon thousands of troopers and auxiliaries without support?'

Orry bit off a curse. 'What about warships? You must have some you can spare?'

'This task force is woefully under-strength as it is – and you want me to weaken it further? We're expecting a Kadiran counter-attack at any time.'

'So you won't help,' Orry stated.

The admiral grimaced. 'I *can't* help – it's a matter of logistics. Besides, this world is of strategic significance and if we fail to retake it, the consequences will be dire.'

'What about the consequences if the Imperator dies?'

Vetochkina considered this. 'You're certain this plot is a

credible threat?'

'Absolutely.'

The admiral unfolded her arms and leaned against her desk. Another salvo shook the cruiser as she thought, but after a few moments, she repeated, 'I'm sorry. I can't help you.'

Swallowing her frustration, Orry forced herself to speak calmly. 'You can't spare even a single ship?'

'I have more than ten thousand souls under my command. I will not put them at any more risk, not even for the Imperator. When is this assassination attempt due to take place?'

'Soon.'

'*Soon?* What does that mean?'

'It means *soon*!' Orry could hear her voice rising with her frustration. 'It could be happening while we waste time arguing – that's why we have to go, now!'

'But it might not happen until tomorrow? Or next week?' The admiral's voice was measured and Orry felt foolish.

She got a grip on her anger. 'We can't afford to take that risk,' she said.

'Well, you have no choice, do you, because I am *not* abandoning my people.'

Orry realised Vetochkina wouldn't be moved. *I don't have time for this crap*. She turned on her heel and strode away.

'What are you doing?' For the first time, the admiral sounded surprised.

'I'm going to warn the Imperator.'

'Alone?'

'Evidently.'

Vetochkina raised her voice a little. 'Miz Kent?'

Orry paused at the door. 'Yes?'

The admiral was looking oddly at her. 'I'm sorry I can't be of more assistance. Good luck.'

42

HOLBEIN'S FOLLY

'*Holbein's Folly?*' Mender said, searching the clutter on top of his instrument panel for the pre-collapse checklist. 'As in *Rudolf Holbein?*'

'That's correct,' *Jane* replied.

'I know that story.'

'Wasn't he some kind of early pioneer?' Ethan asked.

Mender rolled his eyes. 'What the hell do they teach you kids these days?'

'Dad taught us,' Orry said defensively. 'He did his best selecting the auto-didactic modules, but between all the scams we were running there were . . . gaps.'

'Rudolf Holbein was a Russo-Prussian entrepreneur and media mogul,' *Jane* informed them. 'He was influential in the latter years of the Ruuz Empire on Earth, in the late 22nd and early 23rd centuries, pre-Ascendancy calendar. When the empire fell and the Chinese moved in, millions of Ruuz fled the persecution. Holbein was one of the richest men in the world; his global interests protected much of his fortune from the Chinese.'

'This was back before they developed the postselection drive,'

Mender broke in, 'when we were still sending out generation ships. Holbein spent all his damned money converting a hollowed-out asteroid into a colony ship. He called it *Holbein's Conveyor* – it was only years later that everyone started calling it *Holbein's Folly*.'

'He populated it with tens of thousands of displaced Ruuz aristocrats and set off,' *Jane* continued. 'The year after their departure, the first Departed ruins were discovered. The partially intact data core unearthed by the archaeologists set drive research off in an entirely new direction – the first postselection drive was operational just ten years later.'

Ethan whistled. 'Talk about bad timing! So how long was the asteroid's voyage?'

'One hundred and forty years.'

'Rama . . .'

'A brave venture,' Quondam rumbled solemnly.

But Mender was chuckling. 'That's not all. Once they got to where they were going, it turned out to be a shithole, barely capable of sustaining life. They called it Sanctuary, and the poor bastards were there for twenty years before an EDC survey ship finally found them and told them about the postselection drive and the Fountainhead. I'd have given anything to have seen the look on their chinless Ruuz faces!'

Orry tried to imagine how the colonists must have felt, growing up in a sealed asteroid, being told stories of how their ancestors had fled genocide on Earth in a brave attempt to colonise the stars, and then finding out it was all for nothing – that while they had been drifting through space for decades, a vast human empire had been forged. It was almost enough to make her feel sorry for the Ruuz.

Almost.

It still doesn't excuse what Piotr and the rest of them have done since, she told herself firmly.

'What does this have to do with the Imperator?' Ethan asked.

'The Ruuz colonists from Sanctuary were resettled on Tyr,' *Jane* said, 'and their descendants went on to form the noble houses that prop up the Ascendancy.'

'Could the Imperator have been born on the asteroid?' Ethan asked. 'Is that why he comes here every year?'

'He's too young, surely?' Orry said.

'Yes,' *Jane* agreed, 'the first record of Piotr Lvov dates back a little over two hundred years. He rose to political prominence after the first Kadiran War and the Withdrawal and went on to found the Ascendancy. Sanctuary was settled about eighty years before that, so if he was actually born on *Holbein's Folly*, that would make him more than three hundred years old.'

'How old is he?' Ethan asked.

'Around two hundred and thirty,' *Jane* answered. 'No one knows for sure, but the Imperator has already lived decades longer than is expected, even for a wealthy Ruuz living in the Fountainhead, with access to all the latest gene treatments.'

Ethan looked thoughtful. 'So why *does* he visit the asteroid?'

'Why don't we go and ask him?' Mender suggested, and tossed Orry the checklist.

'I'm picking up a ship a hundred thousand miles out from the asteroid,' *Jane* said, a few seconds after they appeared in the Mephiston system.

Orry was swallowing hard, still trying to avoid throwing up after the collapse, not helped by being able to hear Ethan filling his own sick-bag in the galley below. She took a deep breath and asked, 'What sort of ship?'

Jane's momentary hesitation spoke volumes. 'It looks like a class of Ascendancy frigate . . . one that is not listed in my data core.'

Orry and Mender exchanged a look: *Dainty Jane*'s data core should contain every registered vessel in Ascendancy space.

'They're altering course to intercept us, putting on speed.'

Orry hooked the sensor core and watched the other ship approach. Mass-inversion drives were glowing blue at her stern.

'Oh dear,' *Jane* said. 'They're powering weapons.'

'Shit,' Mender growled, pulling the ship into a tight turn.

'Hail them please, *Jane*,' Orry said.

'Channel open.'

'Ascendancy frigate, this is merchant *Dainty Jane*. We are not a threat. Power down your weapons.'

There was a pause while Mender piled on the thrust, sending *Dainty Jane* streaking away from the frigate.

'No response,' *Jane* said.

'Ascendancy frigate, my name is Aurelia Katerina Kent. I am here on behalf of a Seventh Secretariat operative with an urgent warning for the Imperator Ascendant. I know he's here and it is *critical* that I speak to him.'

Mender produced a short laugh. 'You're an optimist, girl, I'll give you that.'

'Weapons are still powered, but the frigate is not firing,' *Jane* reported.

'Yet,' Mender added.

'Should we collapse?' *Jane* asked.

'Yes,' Mender said.

'No,' Orry told the ship, glaring at him.

They waited in tense silence for several minutes, until *Jane* finally spoke.

'Incoming visual transmission.'

Orry turned in her shell. 'Quondam, would you mind waiting with Ethan down in the galley? This is going to be difficult enough without them seeing a Kadiran aboard.'

'I understand,' he rumbled, and squeezed through the hatch out of the cockpit.

'On screen, please, *Jane*,' she said once he was gone, and a monitor in the central comms stack flickered to life.

'I'll be damned,' breathed Mender.

Piotr, Imperator Ascendant and ruler of all human space, stared out at Orry, the hint of a smile twisting up one side of his mouth. He looked older than the last time they'd met, just a few months ago. His bushy moustache lacked its normal sheen and grey stubble sprouted around his sideburns.

The war is taking its toll, Orry thought sadly.

'Miz Kent,' he said, 'and Captain Mender, of course. You do keep surprising me.'

'I must speak with you, sir,' she said. 'Immediately.'

'I believe that is what we are doing.'

'In person.'

The Imperator's pale eyes studied her from the monitor. 'Of course,' he said, and Orry could hear resignation, even sadness, in his voice. 'Come to the asteroid. There's a docking bay.'

'Thank you, sir.'

The screen went blank.

'The frigate has stopped,' *Jane* said. 'Weapons are still powered, though.'

'Turn us around,' Orry told Mender, 'and get us back there

fast.'

Holbein's Folly turned out to be an egg-shaped lump of grey-brown rock pitted with impact craters. *Jane* informed them it was fourteen hundred metres by nine hundred metres at its widest points. As the asteroid filled their field of view, Orry could see twisted metal rising from the surface in places, probably the mangled remains of solar and communication arrays. In the distance she could make out vast engines growing from one end of the rock, but they were as cold and dead as the rest of the asteroid.

'I thought you said this thing ended up at Sanctuary?' Orry asked, watching a crumbling ferroconcrete bunker pass beneath them. 'What's it doing out here?'

'I don't know,' *Jane* answered. 'When the EDC survey vessel discovered the colony, it was close to collapse. The survivors were taken to Tyr, but there is no record of what happened to the asteroid.'

'And what the hell is Piotr doing here – and with just one ship?' Mender added.

'The planet-alpha said the Imperator comes here on the same day every year,' Ethan reminded them, 'so what's that all about?'

Lights illuminated ahead of them, revealing a wide entrance in the asteroid's surface.

'I think we might be about to find out,' Orry said.

They sat in silence while Mender conned them through the huge portal and into a tunnel so large that *Dainty Jane*'s running lights barely reached the metal braces criss-crossing the distant rock walls. It opened onto a vast dock that was blocked at the far end by a grimy metal wall streaked with corrosion. All the darkened landing pads of various sizes cut into the walls of the cavern were deserted but for one, on which rested a sleek shuttle. More lights winked on, beckoning them forwards, and Mender gently guided *Jane* onto the pad. He and Orry ran through the shutdown checklist and the rumble of *Jane*'s drives died away, leaving only the ever-present hum of the ship's systems and the ticking of her hull.

Set into the rock wall ahead of them were a long observation window and a shuttered doorway, which started winding laboriously into the ceiling. A small buggy emerged and rolled across the pad's faded paintwork towards *Dainty Jane*'s freight lock.

'Lower the ramp and let them into the lock,' Orry told *Jane*, before squeezing between the rear two acceleration shells to the ladder. Mender and Ethan followed her down, collecting Quondam from the galley on the way through. When they reached the cargo bay *Jane* opened the airlock's inner door to reveal the buggy parked inside. An attractive young woman wearing a sharp business suit and impeccable make-up climbed out of one of the low seats and approached Orry with a broad smile.

'Miz Kent! I've heard *so* much about you – and it all appears to be true! His Excellency is just *dying* to hear how you found us!'

Orry took the woman's offered hand and they shook.

'I'm so sorry!' she continued, laughing. 'You have no idea who I am, have you? I'm Persephone – Persephone Watkin. I look after the Imperator.'

'Look after him?'

'Make arrangements, deal with the unimportant matters, you know, that sort of thing.'

'Well, this is a very important matter,' Orry said stiffly, feeling like Persephone was handling her. 'I have to see him.'

'Of course, of course – and that's why I'm here. I'm afraid your friends will have to remain on your ship, though. I'm very sorry.' She looked anything but. 'This way, please.'

Orry climbed into the buggy beside her and gave Ethan a reassuring smile as the vehicle's transparent canopy came down. The engine hummed into life and Persephone reversed neatly down the ramp before changing gear and rumbling across the pad, through the doorway from which she'd emerged and into a long tunnel. It stretched out before them, illuminated by the glowing lights lining the rock walls, although many of them were broken. The shutter juddered closed behind them.

'I have to say, we were *very* surprised to see you here,' Persephone said. 'We keep these visits *absolutely* confidential. You've really put the cat amongst the pigeons, so to speak. Heads will roll.' She laughed uncomfortably, looking at Orry. 'So, how did you find out the Imperator was here?'

'No offence, but I'd rather tell him that.'

The woman smiled, although it never reached her eyes. 'Oh, of course – of course!'

The tunnel's rough walls were broken at regular intervals by more shutters with numbers painted on them in peeling white paint.

After a shorter drive than Orry had expected, they passed into a spacious airlock. It took some time to pressurise, but once the red lights set into the walls turned green, Persephone lowered the buggy's canopy. The door in front of them opened and Orry felt moist, scented air on her face.

'I suppose it's no use asking why you've come?' the Imperator's assistant ventured as they drove out of the airlock into what looked to be a continuation of the same tunnel. Orry could understand her curiosity, but she was beginning to find it a bit wearing.

'Nope, sorry,' she said.

Persephone nodded, then indicated a glow up ahead. 'Are you ready?'

'For what?'

The buggy burst out of the tunnel into bright sunlight and for a moment Orry was convinced she was on the surface of a planet, not deep within a mined-out asteroid. Rich foliage surrounded her and the atmosphere was suddenly close and humid. The exotic scent grew stronger. Craning her neck, she could see a bright ball far above the waxy fronds towering on both sides of the road.

'Artificial sun,' Persephone explained. 'It's on a track that runs through the centre of the main habitation cavern – that's where we are now. It disappears beneath the floor at dusk and reappears at dawn. It's set to something called UTC, whatever that is.'

Their emergence from the greenery into a sculpted landscape left Orry speechless. The asteroid's interior shape was clearer here: she could see it rising up on both sides to meet some five hundred metres above her head. The entire surface was covered in a patchwork of fallow fields and coppiced woodland; water flowed between low stone walls and hedgerows tended by robotic figures. Houses were dotted across the landscape. Ahead of them, surrounded by neat rows of gnarled grape vines, stood a stone villa. Red roof tiles shimmered hazily above whitewashed walls.

'I had that same expression when I first saw it, too.'

Orry realised her mouth was hanging open and quickly closed it. 'Was it like this on the voyage out from Earth?'

'No.' Persephone smiled enigmatically. *Getting her own back*, Orry thought.

The buggy jounced along a chalky white lane, passed between two artfully crumbling gateposts and drew up in a dusty yard. Beyond curious now, she followed Persephone across the yard and into the cool of the villa. Her boots squeaked on terracotta tiles as they went through a large main room furnished in a tastefully rustic aesthetic – wicker chairs and tables made from dead vines – to the rear of the building. Persephone stopped outside the only closed door Orry had seen and knocked gently. A moment later she heard the scrape of a key in the lock and the door opened to reveal a mimetic. She shuddered involuntarily, its expressionless ovoid face reminding her of Jericho, the mimetic who had repeatedly tried to kill her not so long ago – but this unit was unarmed and its chassis and slender, graceful limbs were the clinical white of a medical variant. It looked her up and down with a pair of large blue eyes before politely standing aside.

Persephone made no sign of moving, so Orry entered alone and found herself in an airy, spacious bedroom with wide doors thrown open onto a balcony overlooking the vineyard. A surgical bed that clashed with the room's simple décor faced the open doors, its raised back concealing its occupant. The Imperator, sitting beside the bed on a wooden chair, laid down the antique book he was reading and rose to greet her.

'Hello again,' he said.

'Hello, sir.' She looked around the room, her curiosity making her momentarily forget her purpose in coming here.

'So you've discovered my little hidey-hole. Of course, you realise that I must now have you killed.'

Orry laughed, but she couldn't quite stop herself from

glancing nervously at the mimetic.

The Imperator chuckled. 'Come,' he said, beckoning her closer. 'There's someone I want you to meet.'

Feeling a little detached from reality, she walked to the bed, which was occupied by an old woman. Her skin was parchment-fine, rheumy eyes drooping under a few strands of wispy white hair.

The Imperator leaned close. 'Anna,' he said, 'this is Aurelia. She found us.'

The old woman's only response was a strand of saliva leaking from the side of her mouth. He tutted and dabbed it away gently with a cloth.

'She's tired,' he said. 'We should let her rest.' As the mimetic moved to take his place, he led Orry out to the balcony, where a narrow flight of steps led down to the vineyard.

'Beautiful, isn't it?' he said as they strolled between the rows. 'It was the devil of a job to get all this done without anyone finding out.'

She forced her curiosity about Anna and the asteroid aside and started bluntly, 'Sir, the Kadiran are coming here to kill you.'

He stopped. 'Are you sure?'

'Trust me: I would not have come all this way if I wasn't.'

'Talk to me.' He began walking again.

She related the whole story, from their initial encounter with Irina, right through to Counter-Admiral Vetochkina's refusal to assist, trying to ensure she didn't miss out anything important.

He smiled when she showed him the ring. 'Saving my life is becoming something of a habit for you, Aurelia,' he said when she had finished. 'If only everyone in my empire were as loyal as you.'

'What are you going to do?' she asked.

His eyes took on an integuary-glaze for a moment. 'It is already done. The captain of my frigate will despatch a pod to Tyr for help. It's unfortunate, but it appears my little secret must come out.'

'You're not leaving?'

'I'm afraid that isn't an option. Anna is far too frail to be moved.'

'But—'

'You think it's the wrong decision. Would you have me abandon her to the Kadiran?'

'No, but—'

'Save your breath, Aurelia. I will not be persuaded. However, there is no need for you to stay.'

'I've come this far,' she told him. 'I may as well see things out.' Her sudden determination was disconcerting; she hadn't expected to feel so strongly about it.

He studied her, then admitted, 'You never fail to surprise me. What about your crew, though? Your brother?'

'I'll ask them, but I know what they'll say. We could help.'

'Before I met you, I would have laughed at that. Thank you.' He stopped again and turned to look at the villa. 'We should get back. Prepare.'

'Who is she?' Orry asked.

He looked up at the trees and meadows above their heads. 'This place used to be very different. I was born here; did you know that? Anna, too.'

'When?'

'I'd rather not think about that! It was a very long time ago. We were among the last to be born on board. "The chosen generation", they called us. After a hundred and twenty years we would be the ones to finally see our destination.' He smiled wistfully, lost in the past for a moment, then turned to her. 'We were in love, but after we arrived everyone was so busy – there was just no time. We snatched a few hours whenever we could, but I was worried that Anna and I were drifting apart. I was just a surveyor back then and because Sanctuary was lacking most of the basic minerals the colony needed, I was detailed to one of the survey teams being sent to explore the other bodies in the system to search for what was required. I knew I would be gone for three months and I was concerned that Anna would find someone else while I was away. So the night before I was due to leave, I proposed.'

'What did she say?'

He shot her a sidelong glance. 'She said yes, of course! I was quite dashing in my youth.'

Orry grinned, imagining a much younger Piotr. 'I'm sure you were. So she's your wife?'

His face stiffened. 'No ... no, our ship's power plant was damaged by a micro-meteor impact, so we sent a distress signal, but we had no choice but to enter hypersleep until we could be recovered. We didn't know that our signal was too weak: it never reached Sanctuary.' His voice faltered, then he finished, 'I remained in hypersleep for seventy years.'

'You're kidding! How did you get back?'

'The last thing I did before going under was to point the ship towards Sanctuary. It took that long to get within sensor range.'

Orry was riveted. 'What about Anna?'

His face was a mask. 'When I did finally get back, I discovered the whole colony had been resettled on Tyr. I looked for her but records were sketchy – this was just after the First Kadiran War – and I thought she was dead. It was decades before I discovered the truth. And then I discovered that Anna had never given up on me, not even at the point of death. Rather than pass peacefully, she entered suspended animation.'

Orry grimaced. 'Ugh . . . That's horrible.' She turned to look back at the villa, thinking of the aged woman in the hospital bed.

He sighed. 'It was no one's fault. When I did finally track her down – this was long after I became Imperator – she had been asleep for too long and there was nothing left of the girl I knew. So I made this place for her, somewhere for her to live out her final years in peace. I visit her every Earth year, on the anniversary of the day she agreed to marry me. It's . . . painful . . . that she no longer recognises me.'

Orry laid her hand on his arm. He patted it.

'We should get back,' he said after a moment, and led the way in silence between the vines, back to the villa and to Anna.

43

DUMB IDEA

Wyvern, the Imperator's personal frigate, hung motionless relative to the asteroid's dock entrance, ten kilometres out. The dispatch pod she'd released several hours earlier had been about to clear the local gravity well when a pair of Kadiran aggressor vessels collapsed into the system and turned it to a brief flare in the darkness before streaking towards *Wyvern* itself.

Dainty Jane was floating off the frigate's stubby bows, where two drone tenders were attempting to transfer a third torpedo into one of the tubes stippling the curve of *Jane*'s upper hull. It had taken the best part of an hour to load the first two. Looking out through the asteroid's external lenses at the approaching Kadiran aggressors, all sharp edges and bristling weapons, Orry doubted they'd be enough.

As the aggressor vessels drew near to weapons range, *Wyvern* edged away from the asteroid, abandoning her drones, the long torpedo stretching between their suddenly lifeless casings.

God dammit, two won't be enough, Mender sent, echoing Orry's thoughts.

Do you want me to finish loading the third one? Ethan asked him from the villa. *I could take over the drones from here.*

No time, kid. We need to get motoring.

As he spoke, *Dainty Jane*'s drives flared and the ship began to pick up speed, turning to head away from the departing *Wyvern* and into shelter behind the asteroid's concealing bulk.

Be careful, Orry sent. *Both of you.*

You too, replied *Jane*.

Orry turned back to survey the room. The Imperator was sitting between her and Ethan at the wooden dining table in the centre of the villa's main room while Persephone made tea in the kitchen area. Captain Sievers and three of his Imperial Guards, part of the contingent landed by *Wyvern*, were covering the windows. They were clearly uncomfortable about Quondam's looming presence, while the medical mimetic, whose name was Galen, was openly watching the Kadiran. She couldn't really blame them.

The rest of Captain Sievers' squad were busy fortifying the tunnels leading to the asteroid's dock facilities.

As she stared at the databrane stuck to the wall showing a view of *Wyvern* closing on the two Kadiran aggressor vessels, Orry asked, 'How good is *Wyvern*'s captain?'

'He's the best,' the Imperator told her. 'And *Wyvern* is no ordinary frigate.'

'Can he win?'

'One frigate against two aggressors? Oh no, they haven't a hope.' His matter-of-fact tone was chilling.

'Then why are they attacking?'

'What should they do? Run away and abandon their Imperator?'

'But they're all going to die.' The futility of it made her angry.

'That happens in war.' His voice was still unnervingly calm.

Lights sparked in the darkness, the flickering of coherent beams, the flares of torpedo drives, as the three ships manoeuvred. From here it was beautiful, but Orry knew how different a battle was when you were in the middle of it.

Despite the Imperator's misgivings, *Wyvern* appeared to be giving as good as she got. A gout of flame erupted from the rear of one aggressor and the vessel stopped firing, the glow of her drives dying.

'Oh, excellent!' the Imperator exclaimed, clapping his hands. 'Very well played.'

Wyvern twisted and rolled, keeping her main batteries locked onto the remaining aggressor, which left a trail of glittering chaff in her wake. The two ships were closer now, within a thousand kilometres of each other, Orry judged, and the aggressor's heavier loadout was starting to take its toll. Explosions bloomed with increasing frequency across *Wyvern*'s hull and her rate of fire diminished.

Orry noticed the Imperator's eyes had been glazing from time to time during the engagement; this time when they did, *Wyvern* rolled away from the Kadiran ship. Her drives burning bright as stars, she picked up speed. The Kadiran turned to pursue, but before she could close the gap, *Wyvern* vanished.

'She's collapsed away,' she said. 'I thought you said they wouldn't run?'

His face looked strained. 'She put up a valiant fight. She's more valuable now as a messenger.'

'She's gone for help?'

He nodded.

'Will it get here in time?'

'I very much doubt it.'

They all looked back at the screen. The surviving Kadiran ship was powering towards the asteroid, ignoring its stricken comrade, but as they watched, a third Kadiran vessel suddenly winked into existence and immediately matched the aggressor's course. The new arrival had the same distinctive, shard-like architecture of the other Kadiran ships, but it was configured differently, with two bulky assault shuttles fixed to a largely open frame.

'An assault craft,' Quondam rumbled. 'It is time to initiate your plan.'

Orry couldn't take her eyes off the shuttles. She wondered how many breedwarriors each of them could carry and decided she didn't want to know. 'Do you know what to say?' she asked him.

He gave what she now recognised as a Kadiran nod. 'I require a communication device.'

'I am patched into the habitat's comms array,' Galen said. 'I can open a channel to the alien vessels at your convenience.'

Quondam looked at Orry.

'Just speak to the mimetic,' she explained. 'Use him like a microphone.'

The Kadiran thought for a moment. 'Please establish communications,' he told Galen.

'Channel open.'

Quondam barked out a series of guttural phrases and a moment later Orry's integuary began feeding her a translation: 'Attention Kadiran vessels, this is Zealot Exults-In-Obeisance-To-The-Catechisms. You are engaged in a dishonourable and illegal action which is not sanctioned by the War Council. I order you to abort your mission and report to the nearest Reverence Division vessel or facility for re-orientation.'

Ethan caught Orry's eye and mouthed, *Re-orientation?*

She winced at the images the word conjured as they waited for a response.

'Respectful greetings, Zealot,' the Kadiran ship replied. 'I am Vessel-Alpha Rises-With-The-Dawn. Your words confuse me. Our mission is fully sanctioned by the War Council, although due to its covert nature Your Eminence may not be aware of it.'

Quondam drew himself up. 'I am aware of the nature of your mission!' he thundered, rattling the tea glasses on Persephone's tray. 'And I say again: you are engaged in illegal activity to the detriment of Kadir and our war effort. Desist immediately.'

Ethan looked impressed and Orry had to agree: Quondam was turning into a most effective liar.

The Kadiran ship fell silent.

'Do you think they'll go for it?' her brother whispered, but she shushed him.

'Explain the reason for your presence on the human habitat,' the vessel-alpha demanded.

Orry watched Quondam anxiously.

'That is classified. Turn your ships around and leave at once. Do not approach this habitat.'

'What is the reason for your presence there?' the alpha insisted.

'You forget yourself, Vessel-Alpha! How many times must I—'

'They've closed the channel,' Galen said, and Quondam turned to Orry.

'I failed.'

She shrugged it off. 'It was a long shot. Time for something else.' She switched to integuary. *Mender, you're up.*

Didn't work, huh? Told you it was a dumb idea.

She gritted her teeth. *Whenever you're ready.*

Already moving. You realise this isn't gonna work either, don't you? Just do your best.

Always. You'd better get ready for a fight.

Don't worry about us.

He laughed inside her skull. *You think I have time to worry? Now shut up and let me concentrate.* He hesitated. *And don't go getting yourself killed for that fat fuck.*

The 'fat fuck' was watching her. 'What did Captain Mender say?'

'He said to be careful. He doesn't want anything to happen to you.'

The Imperator smiled. 'Of course he did.'

44

FALLING BACK

Mender clenched his teeth inside his acceleration shell as he let the mesomorphic liquid cushion him from *Dainty Jane*'s violent manoeuvres. He tried to ignore the storm of laserlight and flak being flung at them from the Kadiran vessels, instead focusing on targeting the two shuttles fixed to the assault ship's frame. If this was going to work, he would need to be close – suicidally close. The torpedoes *Wyvern* had transferred to *Jane* were powerful, but their evasion systems took a tenth of a second to spin up, and that was too long. At this range their target would destroy them in milliseconds.

This is the second time we've done this since I reeled that damn girl in, he grumbled to *Jane*.

The ship lurched and rolled around a line of tungsten slugs from a quad mass-driver on the assault ship's nose. *Would you rather go back to what it was like before?* she asked. *Just the two of us, drifting through life?*

The cockpit shuddered as her point defence detonated a missile drone a hundred metres from her port nacelle, peppering her hull with fragments of twisted thermoceramic. The assault ship was close now and the barrage was getting more intense.

Peace and quiet or this? Mender scoffed. *No contest.*

Liar.

Something black and light-absorbing streaked past his field of view and he felt an impact somewhere below him. Alarms flashed in his peripheral vision but he had no time for them. *Target the port-side shuttle first*, he told *Jane*.

Her crazed evasive jinking somehow brought the port-side shuttle into his targeting reticule at just the right range. Adding an instinctual adjustment to its guidance he let the first torpedo go—

—and watched it disintegrate before it had travelled much more than its own length from the tube.

Shit! Bring us around.

As the assault ship wheeled jerkily around the cockpit he tried not to think about how he now had to destroy two shuttles with one torpedo. The starboard shuttle rotated into view, but he resisted firing.

Get us closer.

Jane didn't answer, but the shuttle grew until it filled his vision. At the last possible moment he felt the ship begin to turn away and released the last torpedo. The assault ship slid out of view, to be replaced by a field of whirling stars. Beams and slugs whipped past and plunged into a drifting cloud of chaff; *Jane*'s own dispensers added to it with percussive thumps. Mender shifted his view to a rear-facing lens and saw that the torpedo had missed the shuttle and exploded in the framework of support struts above it. He cursed, watching helplessly as the port shuttle detached from the other side of the ship. When its starboard-side twin didn't follow, he zoomed in on the damaged area and realised that the explosion must have jammed one or more of the clamps holding the craft in place. He grunted; it was something at least.

Clusterfuck, as expected, he told Orry. *One of the shuttles is out of action – don't know for how long, though. The other is coming your way.*

One's better than two, she replied. *Are you both okay?*

Jane was still jinking and rolling as they burned away from the Kadiran ships at 10g, but the fire from them was diminishing and neither vessel looked inclined to follow.

Still alive, he sent.

Stay that way.

He eyed the Kadiran shuttle as it headed into the dock.

You too, girl.

Orry had first come across the Imperial Guard at the Imperator's Palace on Tyr, but the eight men and women huddled in the rock-walled tunnel with her looked a long way from the pristine, polished ceremonial soldiers she'd seen then. Captain Sievers and two of his Guards had remained in the villa with the Imperator, but Orry and Quondam had elected to join the rest of the soldiers to help delay the Kadiran advance and buy some time.

The eight Guards had exchanged their dark green dress uniforms and polished breastplates for tactical armour and armed themselves with an impressively large variety of weapons. Their faces were grim as they hunkered down behind a makeshift barricade of overturned buggies and empty cargo crates. The looks they were giving Quondam were far from friendly.

'You sure your friend here isn't going to decide he's fighting for the wrong side?' the man beside her said.

'Durov!' snapped the squad's sergeant, a bull of a man named Brenner, from further down the line. 'Stow that shit.'

'Just saying, Sarge: this fucking thing looks strong enough to rip my head off and stuff it up my arse.'

'*I'll* rip your head off if you don't shut your mouth.'

'Human connective tissue is quite resilient,' Quondam rumbled. 'There are more efficient ways to terminate you.'

Durov stared at him.

'He's *kidding*,' Orry said quickly as a couple of the Guards edged away from Quondam. She nudged him, feeling the iron-hard muscles beneath his grey skin. '*Aren't* you?'

'Just . . . kidding,' he confirmed, then, 'A blow to the base of your skull would be quicker.'

Orry rolled her eyes.

Beside Sergeant Brenner, a corporal called Taube was studying a databrane spread out in front of her. She gestured for silence. 'They're approaching the first line,' she said. 'I count twenty-four breedwarriors. Looks like they didn't leave any back at the shuttle, not even a pilot.'

Orry looked at their tiny band in dismay, then hooked the surveillance substrate and watched the Kadiran force making its way along the wide tunnel she'd driven down with Persephone. They'd set up their barricade on the pressurised side of the airlock so they wouldn't have to wear suits or worry about breaches. Ethan had sealed the lock; she didn't think that would delay the Kadiran for long, but even a few minutes might help, especially if *Wyvern* actually made it back to Tyr to find help.

When the leading breedwarriors passed the first ring of explosives, which had been shielded against scans, Corporal Taube flicked off the safety on the detonator in her hand, then waited.

There were too many Kadiran for them all to fit within the kill zone between the three rings of explosives the Guards had prepared, so Taube waited until just over half of them were in the zone, the most she reckoned she was going to get, then pressed the red button on top of her detonator.

The shaped charges exploded soundlessly in the airless tunnel, shaking the rock beneath them. When the dust began to clear, Orry saw armoured breedwarriors crawling to their feet. Of the fifteen or so Kadiran caught in the blast, she counted only five remaining on the ground – and three of those were still moving.

'Damn, they're tough sons-of-bitches,' Durov muttered.

'All right, people,' Brenner said as the breedwarriors moved on, leaving their dead and wounded, and reached the other side of the airlock. 'This is it. We are all that stands between the Imperator and those fucking kucks. I'm not dressing it up: if we fall, so does the Ascendancy. Simple as that.' He shifted his gaze until he'd stared deep into the eyes of each of them in turn. 'Today we will bring honour to the Imperial Guard: *For the Ascendancy! For the Imperator!*'

The cry was echoed enthusiastically, which made Orry cringe. She went back to studying the airlock. One of the Kadiran had attached cables to a panel beside the door.

Beside her, Private Durov's fingers were drumming incessantly against his rifle stock. When she glanced at him, she saw he was looking a little green.

'Hey,' she said quietly, 'you okay?'

He glared at her. 'I'm fine.'

'It's okay to be scared.'

'I'm not scared.'

Fear souring her stomach, she forced a smile. 'Well, I'm

shitting myself,' she admitted.

The airlock's door opened, the Kadiran force entered and one of them immediately started work on the inner door: the only thing that now separated them from the Guards.

They've overridden the locking protocols, Ethan informed her. *There's nothing I can do.*

The airlock door shot upwards . . . and Orry's world turned to Hell.

The noise of the Guards' weapons deafened her as the airlock became a killing field filled with pulsing energy and metal projectiles. She heard Durov screaming insults, his darklight rifle flickering – until the Kadiran started to return fire and his head vanished, spattering her face with warm droplets.

She felt someone drag her down behind the barricade: Quondam, who was keeping his body hunched low as rounds rang on the overturned buggy in front of them.

'Thanks,' she managed.

Another Guard fell, clutching at her neck as blood soaked the dust of the tunnel floor. Orry peered through a crack between two cargo containers and watched breedwarriors pouring out of the airlock.

Two more Guards were down, she saw, one squirming as a medic worked on the ragged stump of his arm, another staring at Orry with sightless eyes. Only the small scorch mark on the front of her helmet showed where she'd been hit.

There was only a handful of Kadiran casualties. The rest – an awful lot of them – were advancing on the barricade.

Another Guard fell, his screams rising over the storm of gunfire as he clawed at a face blackened and raw from an energy weapon. Keeping low behind the barricade, Orry ran to Sergeant

Brenner.

'We have to fall back!' she yelled over the howl of his rotary cannon, but he shook his head wildly.

'*We hold!*' he roared at her, then directed his rage at the enemy and screamed, '*For the Imperator!*'

A breedwarrior leaped onto the barricade just metres from them, Brenner adjusted his aim and the Kadiran jerked as the rounds bored through both artificial and natural armour and into the soft flesh beneath. He dropped out of sight but another warrior immediately appeared on the sergeant's other side, wielding a war-maul. Before Orry could warn him, the hammer had come down with such brutal force it crushed Brenner's head down into his chest. The Kadiran recovered the huge weapon effortlessly and scrambled over the barricade, his eyes fixed on her as she backed away.

With a keening cry, Quondam slammed into the breed-warrior's side, driving him onto the forklift prongs of a nearby loader, which punched through the side of his armour and deep into his chest. The Kadiran howled, clutching the metal that pierced him, but Quondam had already scooped up the fallen war-maul. His powerful muscles flexed as he swung the weapon and drove its back-spike up through the bottom of the pinned warrior's chin and into his brain. The breedwarrior stopped struggling.

Quondam turned to Orry. 'We must go.'

She grabbed Corporal Taube. 'They're slaughtering us – we have to retreat!'

Taube looked like someone coming back from somewhere very far away. She looked around.

'Brenner's dead,' Orry yelled, trying to make her understand.

'We have to fall back to the villa now!'

'We're the Imperial Guard,' Taube reminded her, her voice hollow. 'We don't retreat.'

'We don't have time to discuss this! They want the Imperator alive, so if we can get to the villa we'll have at least half a chance—'

The corporal interrupted her. 'You're right,' she said, and stepped back from the barricade. A Kadiran reared up on her left, but an explosion bloomed on the warrior's chest and he was thrown back.

'Fall back to the villa!' Taube yelled, gesturing frantically, but the surviving Guards didn't need to be told twice. Orry was shocked to see that only two others had survived, but they fell back in good order, firing as they did so.

The breedwarriors had already started swarming the barricade and climbing up the other side to fire at the retreating enemy when, abruptly, the lights in the tunnel went out.

'Run!' Orry yelled redundantly, her leg muscles burning as they all pelted towards the arch of light at the far end.

Laserlight flickered around them and rounds began smacking into the rock. She waited for the searing pain of a hit or the scream of someone nearby, but somehow neither came and suddenly she was emerging into the artificial sunlight. She swerved to the right, Quondam pounding along beside her, focusing on making it through the trees to the villa. She could see Corporal Taube and the two surviving Guards through the trees as she ran, their reactive camouflage not quite keeping up with the rapidly changing environment.

The chatter of gunfire sounded behind them and Orry risked a desperate glance over her shoulder. Breedwarriors were already spilling from the tunnel entrance. Lasers strobed, burning holes through the trees and slicing branches clean off.

One of the troopers fell with a cry. Taube stopped, but when Orry slowed too, the corporal waved her on. 'Get to the villa – protect the Imperator!'

Quondam grabbed Orry's arm. Bile filling her throat, her lungs aching, he tugged her onwards, while Taube raised her weapon and began firing at the approaching Kadiran, covering their escape.

They broke out of the trees, their boots now biting into the soft ground, and there was the villa up ahead, nestled in its cocoon of vines. To her right, Orry saw the last Guard drop down behind a low stone wall and began shooting into the trees. Bullets raised splinters from the stones and the heat of a laser flashed past her face.

The front door opened, Captain Sievers emerged with two Guards and laid down covering fire.

'The others?' Sievers demanded as Orry and Quondam raced past and threw themselves down beside him.

'Dead, mostly,' she gasped. 'Taube and two more are still out there but one's wounded.'

The low wall among the vines exploded in a ball of flame. The Kadiran advanced in a long line from the trees, at least a dozen of them, firing as they came. One of the beams sliced across the Guard standing beside Orry, neatly severing his head and shoulder from his body.

'Get inside,' Sievers ordered, but Orry was already moving. The other Guard had turned to follow her – and then the woman was gone, in her place a quivering mound of meat and bone. Sievers stopped and stared, white-faced – before a bullet glanced off his armour and brought him back to reality. He tumbled through the door and slammed it after him.

They found Ethan and Persephone with the Imperator. They hadn't been idle; every stick of furniture in the place had been stacked in front of the windows, then draped with all the spare pieces of body armour they could find, turning the room into a makeshift redoubt. Ethan was sitting on the floor, eyes glazed; Orry guessed he was watching the firefight through the asteroid's network of lenses. Persephone, crouching beside him, looked terrified.

The Imperator stood in the centre of the room, wearing a grim smile. 'I take it things are going about as well as we expected?' he said calmly.

'I'm afraid so, Your Excellency.' Captain Sievers hurried to take up his position behind the upended dining room table and pushed his barrel into a loophole burned through the wood.

Orry picked her own spot at an adjacent window. Through her loophole she could see three breedwarriors hunkered down behind a wall a hundred metres away.

'Perhaps you should give me a gun,' the Imperator said. He walked over to stand behind Sievers.

'Please get behind cover, Excellency,' the captain said tightly, but when the Imperator just held out a hand, he gritted his teeth and gave him his sidearm.

'Where do you want me?'

The captain glanced around the room before gesturing to a window near Orry. 'There, if you please, Excellency. And both of you: we need to conserve ammunition. We're running low.'

'Capital!' The Imperator ran to his assigned position, grinning at Orry, and she managed a strained smile in return.

'They've surrounded the building,' Ethan reported. 'I count twelve of them.'

'What about Anna's room?' Orry asked. They had three sides of the villa covered; Anna's bedroom formed the fourth wall.

'We barricaded the balcony doors in there,' the Imperator told her, 'and Galen's with her.'

'Your mimetic? What if the Kadiran try to force their way in?'

'Then Rama help them, eh, Sievers?' He chuckled.

Orry frowned, but a guttural, amplified voice from outside interrupted them.

Quondam translated. 'He announces that he is Unit-Alpha Costumed-In-The-Skin-Of-The-Vanquished, of the Special Operations Legion. We are to deliver the Imperator or ... or you will be ceremonially consumed.' The Kadiran shook his giant head in evident disgust. 'The unit-alpha has given us one minute to comply.'

From the back of the room, Persephone started whimpering.

'Should I reply?' Quondam asked.

The silence that filled the room was broken only by Persephone's sobs.

'Allow me,' Sievers said, then shattered his window with his rifle. 'Go fuck yourselves!' he roared through it.

Persephone screamed as the breedwarriors responded, slugs and beams punching through the blocked windows and closed door.

Orry ducked instinctively, then forced her head back up and sighted along her barrel. She fired the recoilless weapon and saw a puff of stone dust rise near one of the Kadiran. The breedwarrior adjusted his aim and fired straight back; the stream of slugs battered the barricade in front of her, driving her to the floor.

'Keep firing!' Sievers yelled over the din, 'but pick your targets. Keep their heads down.'

Orry gritted her teeth and did as he ordered, watching via the integuary link to her weapon as the remaining ammunition counted inexorably down towards zero.

45

A BALLET OF BLADES

'Lucia would have an embolism if she could see me now,' the Imperator said, ducking forward to empty the last of his magazine out of the window before pulling back to reload. He sounded happier than Orry had ever heard him.

'Who?' she yelled over the noise of the Kadiran advance. Their firing was sporadic, and targeted. She guessed they didn't want to risk killing the Imperator so instead, they were focusing on keeping the defenders' heads down until they could assault the building.

'More bullets!' the Imperator cried, and Sievers obediently fished a magazine from his belt and tossed it over.

'That's the last one, Excellency. Make it count.'

He slapped it into his weapon and worked the action. 'Lucia Rodin,' he explained to Orry, 'is head of my security, among other things. A very capable woman. Your friend Irina worked for her.' He raised the sidearm, fired several short bursts and a Kadiran fell. It was a drop in the ocean, but he looked delighted. 'That's the ticket—'

He spun away from the window, his weapon sailing across the room, and dropped to one knee.

Orry ran to him, ducking the splinters flying everywhere as the Kadiran weapons chewed up their wooden barricades. The Imperator was clutching his shoulder.

'Is it bad?' she asked. Blood was spreading around his hand.

Captain Sievers ran over and knelt beside the Imperator, but Persephone didn't move, just huddled against the wall in the far corner, her arms wrapped round her knees and perfect make-up streaked with tears.

Examining the Imperator's wound, the captain muttered, 'We can't hold this position.' He looked around the room and announced, 'We have to fall back.'

Orry felt like she'd been doing nothing else since the Kadiran landed. 'But there's nowhere left to go—'

He pointed towards Anna's bedroom. 'They want His Excellency alive. If we barricade ourselves in there they won't risk shooting their way in – it will buy us time for help to get here.'

If help is even coming. But she kept the thought to herself. 'Ethan,' she said instead, 'help me, will you?'

He crawled over to her, wincing at the rounds bursting through the windows above his head, and together they hoisted the Imperator up and helped him stagger into the bedroom. As they lowered him into a chair, Persephone crawled in after them, flinching at every shot. The medical mimetic immediately shooed them away from the Imperator, tutting as it examined his wound.

A crash made Orry whirl but it was only Quondam, effortlessly upending a heavy wardrobe across the door to the main room, barricading them all inside.

'You really think this will work?' she asked Sievers.

He ignored her and turned to Ethan. 'I need eyes on the rest of the house,' he said curtly. 'Make it happen.'

Orry went to check on the Imperator. 'How is he?' she asked, looking at the Imperator's lolling head with dismay.

'I have administered a local anaesthetic and a mild sedative for the shock.' Galen straightened and held out a plug of mis-shapen metal between pincer-like digits. The bullet clinked into a dish and the robot's fingers resumed a more normal shape. The mimetic busied itself applying a microbial dressing. 'He requires further treatment.'

'Can you do it here?'

'I cannot.'

Ethan pointed at the databrane fixed to the wall and announced, 'Okay, we have feeds from the house.' The screen was now divided into nine, each showing an image of the villa from a different angle. As Orry watched, the front door burst open and two breed-warriors piled in, weapons tracking for threats. The same thing was happening at the back door, and both incursion teams were followed by more Kadiran, who swiftly cleared the main room.

A guttural voice sounded through the barricaded door.

'The unit-alpha is giving us one final chance to deliver the Imperator,' Quondam translated.

Orry looked at the grim faces around her. Persephone was gnawing at her no longer perfectly manicured fingernail as she stared at the door, a look of absolute terror on her face. The Imperator raised his head, looking groggy, and touched Galen's arm. He murmured a few words and Galen inclined its head, then walked to the barricaded door. The Imperator's hand dropped and he winced with pain.

'What the hell are you doing?' Captain Sievers demanded as the mimetic pulled the wardrobe aside as if it weighed nothing at all.

'Replace this barricade when I have left,' Galen instructed him, and when Sievers glanced at the Imperator, he waved a weary hand in consent.

The mimetic barked out a string of guttural Kadiran.

'It tells them the Imperator is coming out,' Quondam explained. 'Its accent is very good.'

Galen stepped out of the room and closed the door quietly behind itself. The roars started immediately and Orry heard a shot from outside, then several more. She flung herself to the floor with everyone else as bullets punched through the door and ricocheted from the back of Anna's bed. Then the keening began.

Crawling behind a chair, she glanced up at the brane on the wall. She could see Galen, dancing around the breedwarriors, its breath-taking speed making the Kadiran look as if they were moving in slow motion. The mimetic's hands and feet had transformed into long blades that glittered as it vaulted and spun; they were never still as they found impossibly narrow gaps in Kadiran armour, severing a tendon here, an artery there.

Bodies twitched on the ground, ichor pooling, until the breedwarriors threw down their guns and drew their war-mauls: this was now a *personal* matter.

And still Galen danced. *Like liquid metal*, Orry thought, sitting up to see better. The mimetic was almost *flowing* around the room, its passage marked by sprays of the dark ichor that was Kadiran blood.

A war-maul finally caught the mimetic's leg and the breedwarrior wielding it twisted and tore the limb off below the knee, sending Galen tumbling to the floor ... where it rolled – and then sprang up to dispatch another Kadiran before it caught a hammer to the chest that sent it crashing so hard into a thick beam that the wood cracked under the impact. The next Kadiran to reach it died with a blade inserted neatly into his neck, but the last surviving breedwarrior managed to bring his maul down in a devastating blow that crushed the mimetic's head almost flat. Galen stopped moving instantly, but still the war-maul rose and fell in a frenzy, dismembering the robot.

'Protect the Imperator,' Captain Sievers said, flinging open the door and running out, emptying his last rounds straight into the breedwarrior's back. The huge creature staggered, but recovered himself and turned to glare menacingly at his attacker.

Orry saw a swathe of pale leather draped across his chest and squinted to make out the image painted on it. Her stomach turned over as she realised the picture was a *tattoo*, and her perception suddenly shifted: the leather was human skin. This must be the unit-alpha who'd demanded their surrender.

Sievers backed away at the warrior's approach and Orry winced as the war-maul smashed into his side and flung him across the room, where he lay in a broken heap. The breed-warrior moved towards the bedroom, but Quondam had lumbered past Orry and now stood in the open door to block the entrance. He stooped to pick up a fallen war-maul.

The unit-alpha regarded him curiously for a moment, but he said nothing, just lunged, bringing his weapon down in a crushing overhead blow.

Quondam was driven to one knee, barely managing to block it. He responded by sweeping his maul at the unit-alpha's legs – but the warrior just stepped clear and effortlessly stabbed down with his top-spike, piercing Quondam's arm.

Roaring in pain, Quondam swung his maul up, catching

the unit-alpha's helmet and tearing it away to expose the face beneath. Orry could see Quondam must have been badly hurt, because he was clearly weakening, but still he tried to strike again – and this time the alpha caught his maul by the haft and almost effortlessly, twisted it from his grasp.

Quondam staggered to his feet, backing away as the unit-alpha caught his leg. The trunk-like limb buckled and Quondam fell at his opponent's feet, unable to rise. The alpha raised his maul to finish him.

'No!' Orry was already firing, but her rounds buried themselves harmlessly in the breedwarrior's armour. He rounded on her, leaving Quondam, and she retreated. Terrified, she fired another short burst – and saw her remaining ammunition reach zero. A query from the weapon appeared in her peripheral vision: did she wish to insert a fresh magazine or deploy the integral bayonet? She felt the wall pressing into her back.

There's nowhere left to go. As the unit-alpha bore down on her she ordered the rifle to deploy bayonet and when the long blade flicked into position from under its barrel she waved it pathetically at the oncoming monster.

The unit-alpha made a rumbling, choking sound she recognised as laughter and slowed its advance, as if relishing her fear.

She stared at the Kadiran's face, thinking how similar it looked to Quondam, just with more scars and a larger crest. The soft tendrils around the alpha's nostrils fluttered and without thinking, she ran forward and thrust her rifle into its exposed face. The bayonet's long blade sank deep into his nose aperture and the warrior howled, stumbling backwards, wrenching the rifle from her grasp. His war-maul thudded to the floor as he crashed around the room, clawing at the rifle sticking out of his face.

With what must have been a Herculean effort, Quondam heaved his injured body into the breedwarrior's path. The unit-alpha tripped over him and plunged face-first to the ground, making the room shudder under the impact—

—and Orry's bayonet burst out of the back of his skull.

The villa fell suddenly silent.

'You killed it,' Persephone said quietly, coming out of the bedroom with Ethan. A smile crept hesitantly onto her face. 'They're all dead.' She planted a delighted kiss on Ethan's cheek and hugged him tight.

The look on her little brother's face made Orry burst out laughing, a ragged sound in the shattered room, close to hysteria.

'Captain Sievers is dead,' Quondam said, and the laughter congealed in her throat, making her want to throw up.

Persephone released Ethan and crossed slowly to Sievers' crumpled remains, where she crouched to close his eyes. Orry wanted to say something, but she couldn't; any words would be hollow. Instead, she went to Quondam's side.

'Can you walk?'

'My leg is broken. The unit-alpha was a skilled opponent.'

She looked at the carnage. 'He was. Thank you.'

The Kadiran gazed at her, his small eyes blinking languidly. 'You vanquished him. *You:* a human female.'

'It was a joint effort,' she said, choosing not to take offence.

'It is fortunate that Kadiran females are not like you.'

Orry had heard how things were for females in the Kadiran Hierocracy. 'I've never been to one of your worlds,' she said, a little tartly, 'but you know what? I'd lay odds your females are *exactly* like me. One day you'll find that out – and when you do, I'd like to be there to see it.'

Quondam's massive shoulders began to shudder and for a moment Orry thought something was wrong. Then she realised the Kadiran was laughing.

You still alive, girl? Mender asked suddenly, his voice in her head startling her.

For now, she confirmed shakily. *What's going on out there?*

They're clearing the wreckage around the second shuttle. I reckon you have about fifteen minutes before round two.

She looked at the exhausted, smiling faces in front of her and thought about another twenty-four breedwarriors descending on them. A crushing weight settled on her, as if the asteroid's gravity had suddenly doubled.

Thanks, she sent. *I'll let them know.*

46

COMBAT COLLAPSE

Orry slumped on the floor beside Ethan, feeling like she'd had every last bit of energy sucked out of her. Their backs were pressed against the rough-plastered wall as they waited for the second Kadiran shuttle to arrive.

'Oh, by the way, I cracked that brane you stole on Morhelion,' Ethan said, breaking the long silence.

'Yeah?' *Hardhaven Voyager* was a distant memory after everything that had happened since. In their current predicament, it was difficult to summon any interest – but if it kept Ethan's mind off what was coming for them, even for a few minutes, it would be worth it. 'Find anything interesting?' she asked, trying to inject something like enthusiasm into her voice, but he clearly felt the same way.

'Somehow it doesn't feel very important right now, does it?' The humourless laugh was very unlike him.

She nudged him. 'Tell me anyway.'

When he turned to her she saw her own exhaustion echoed in his face, but there was something else. When he started speaking, she realised what it was. Disgust. 'They know,' he said. 'About the leviathans being sentient, I mean – the Whaling League *and* EDC. That brane? It's a report commissioned by the Science Secretariat and conducted by the Halstaad-Mirnov Institute – you know, the exo-biology place where Professor Rasmussen works? It recommends the immediate cessation of whaling and a demand for Morhelion to be declared a planet of Special Scientific Interest – and they don't grant PSSIs lightly.'

Orry looked away, feeling sick to her stomach. Then a thought struck her. She turned back to Ethan. 'So why did Guzman have it? Why didn't he just destroy the whole damn report?' She thought for a moment, grateful for the distraction. 'When was it conducted?'

'About fifteen years ago.'

Her brow furrowed. 'Didn't Tyrell say Guzman's been running the League for fifteen years?'

'You think he's using it as leverage to stay in power? If they try to oust him, the report gets released and the whole sick enterprise comes tumbling down around *all* their ears?'

'Well, he certainly struck me as that sort.'

'So what do we do now?' Ethan asked.

She gazed around the room at the weary faces. 'Well, one crisis at a time. Let's get out of this in one piece first, shall we?'

He smiled thinly and turned away.

A few minutes later, the Imperator, who'd returned to his seat next to Anna's bed, beckoned Orry over. She hauled herself painfully to her feet, hobbled over and sank gratefully into the chair beside him when he patted the cushion.

She could smell the anti-microbial dressing on his chest; if the wound was hurting, he was doing a very good job of pretending otherwise.

'I'm sorry about your mimetic,' she told him.

'It's funny how one becomes attached to the most unlikely of things,' he said quietly. 'We often talked while Anna slept. He was a good companion for her.'

'He was a bodyguard as well as her doctor?'

'It was a good fit. Killing and healing are two sides of the same coin. I never thanked you properly for what you did, Aurelia, by coming here to warn me.'

'Thank me when we get out of here.'

He looked at her then, his eyes bright in his wrinkled old face. 'The second shuttle will be here soon, so I rather think I should do it now.'

She smiled, but said nothing.

'I know you're not interested in titles or money,' he continued, 'so what *would* you accept as a reward?'

'Between now and when we die?'

It was his turn to smile. 'Indulge me.'

She blew out her cheeks. 'That's a big question.' She thought for a moment, then grimaced.

'You've thought of something. What is it?'

She hesitated, but he solemnly held up a hand – unable to stop himself wincing at the pain this time – and announced, 'I promise not to have you executed.'

She chuckled. *What the hell . . .* 'Well,' she started, then took a deep breath and stated bluntly, 'I think you're pretty shitty to a lot of your subjects. I'd like you to treat them better.'

He stared at her, his face unreadable. 'Running the Ascendancy isn't an easy job,' he said at last. 'Perhaps you think you could do better?'

'I didn't say that. I just think you're so concerned with looking after your Ruuz cronies in the Fountainhead that you don't have a clue what's happening on half the worlds you govern.'

'I'm briefed regularly – and you must know there are *hundreds* of colonies in the Ascendancy. Surely you don't expect me to micro-manage every one?'

'But you could prioritise, spend more time on those that really need it.'

The Imperator was beginning to look irritated. 'I think you're making things out to be far worse than they are.'

She grimaced. 'Believe me, I'm not.'

He started at her a moment, then gave a quizzical smile. 'Very well, Aurelia: give me an example. Where would you start?'

'How about Morhelion?'

His brow furrowed. 'The place that exports all that leather? What about it?'

'I spent some time there recently. I guess you weren't aware that the leather comes from an indigenous species? A *sentient* indigenous species.'

'Nonsense,' he said brusquely. 'We have laws against that sort of thing. The Company would never engage in such activities.'

'EDC have been working with the local Whaling League for *decades* to cover it up – and the League treats *your subjects* there like crap – and guess what? No one does a damn thing about it.'

'Those are very serious allegations, young lady. Do you have evidence to back them up?'

'Yes.'

He cleared his throat gruffly. 'In that case I will have someone look into it. Assuming I am still alive to do so.'

'Thank you,' she said, but she was on a roll now. 'But Morhelion's just one example. There are *dozens* of worlds out on the rim where *your* people are little more than slaves – they're exploited by criminals or by the Company, because the Grand Fleet and the arbiters are too far away or just don't care enough to enforce the law. And yes, I know, because I've been to enough of them.'

'I take your point,' the Imperator said, 'but power is a fragile thing: I have to devote time to the Fountainhead systems, because that's where the Great Houses are. If I don't keep the barons happy, the Ascendancy will fracture – and I will not have everything I've built destroyed by civil war.'

'Well it was one of *your* barons who arranged this little surprise for you,' she pointed out, 'so I would say it's going that way, whether you like it or not.'

He rubbed his forehead wearily. 'That does rather seem to be the case, doesn't it? All right, so let's assume we survive the next few hours. How would you deal with the barons?'

'You need to clip their wings. They have too much power.'

'They have armies.'

'So take them away.'

He laughed. 'Just like that? You have no idea.'

She shrugged. 'Where are these armies?'

'On Tyr and the other Fountainhead worlds, mostly.'

She stared at him. 'But we're at war – why aren't they fighting?'

'They're protecting their homeworlds.'

Orry snorted. 'You're Imperator! So create a new law. You can do that, can't you? Make every baron with an army send it in defence of the Ascendancy, and anyone who refuses, charge them with treason. If they comply, their power is gone, and if they don't, you can have them arrested.'

'Interesting. Lucia did suggest something similar when the

Kadiran attacked, but the view among the members of my council was that it would be too provocative a move; they didn't think we should be risking internal division while we're at war.'

'What you mean is, you're too scared to stand up to them.'

His face hardened. 'Careful, Miz Kent.'

She pressed on regardless. 'But now one of them has tried to kill you: that kind of changes things, don't you think?'

He sighed. 'Yes, I rather think it does. Thank you, Aurelia, I will consider your counsel.'

Ethan cleared his throat.

Everyone turned to him.

'Uh, Your – er – Excellency, sir? I think I might have a way to stop that shuttle.'

The Imperator blinked, then smiled warmly. 'What would I do without the children of Katerina Soltz?'

The torpedo abandoned by *Wyvern* before it could be loaded into *Dainty Jane*'s tubes was floating halfway between the Kadiran assault ship and the dock, being guided by the slightest of nudges from its drones.

That's it, kid, Mender sent, *nice and easy. If I can't pick up the movement, the kucks definitely won't.*

Ethan stayed silent, but Orry could sense his irritation. As they watched, the Kadiran shuttle released from its cradle with a silent puff of gas. When it was clear of the assault ship, its main drive ignited and it turned towards the asteroid's dock.

How close does that thing have to be? she asked.

Not very, Mender sent back. *That torpedo is designed to cripple a*

*frigate or destroyer – we don't have to destroy the shuttle, just damage it
enough so they can't dock.*

Sounds do-able, for once. How much further?

The old man was silent for a moment. *I'd stop right where
you are, kid. With a bit of luck they'll think it's just another chunk of
wreckage until it's too late.*

Ethan applied a touch of braking thrust until the torpedo
was stationary relative to the dock entrance and a little to one
side of the shuttle's projected course.

Good job, kid. This was a smart idea.

Orry opened her eyes to see Ethan grinning.

'Everything ready?' the Imperator asked. He sounded weaker
every time he spoke; sweat was pouring down his face.

'The torpedo's in place. We just have to hope they don't
detect it.'

'Is that likely?'

Ethan replied, 'I've shut the torpedo's systems down,
everything but a line in for Mender to detonate it. It's a tube of
black metal again a black asteroid in the black of space. I'd say
the odds are good.'

His confidence made Orry wince, but she told herself not to
be so superstitious. Closing her eyes, she hooked the asteroid's
external lenses again and watched the shuttle's approach. Even
through her immersion she could feel the tension in the room.
After an initial burn the craft's drive shut down and the pilot
let momentum carry the blocky vessel towards the dock. Just
before the halfway point, vernier thrusters fired, the shuttle
somersaulted until its stern was facing the asteroid and the drive
ignited again in a braking burn. She held her breath as its course
took it closer to the torpedo that was lurking in the darkness.

A turret in the shuttle's belly rotated and four tiny lights strobed. For a second nothing happened, then the scene was washed out in a fierce white light as the torpedo exploded.

The shuttle sailed past the expanding cloud of particulates, completely unharmed.

'I guess they saw it,' she said numbly, back in the room.

A muscle twitched in the Imperator's jaw. 'Then we can expect company very soon.'

'Oh no,' Ethan breathed, the dullness of his eyes showing that he was still hooked into the externals. 'What is he *doing*?'

Orry looked outside and felt her chest tighten as she saw *Dainty Jane* streaking towards the shuttle, her guns blazing.

Watch that turret! Mender sent, but *Jane* was way ahead of him. He swayed a little in his shell as the four lines of tungsten slugs flashed past the ship, then slewed the forward cannon to target the threat.

The other Kadiran vessels are firing, the ship told him. *Our odds of surviving this engagement are . . . not good.*

We don't have to survive. We just have to total that fucker. He sent a stream of slugs at the craft's engines, grunting with satisfaction as the blue glow flickered and died.

Orry would not want us to die for her, Jane observed.

You want to leave her?

I didn't say that.

Then shut up and fly.

A hammer-blow struck the ship, setting damage alerts flashing in his peripheral vision, but they continued whirling wildly towards the asteroid.

Unable to complete its braking burn, the Kadiran shuttle was firing its verniers.

Mender tried to move his cannon but it was jammed and grinding against a plate of armour half torn from *Jane*'s hull. He cursed and cycled through the other weapons, but none of them had the range he needed. The shuttle's main drive lit again, slowing its approach to the dock.

A cold sense of purpose came over him. *Ram them*, he ordered.

I don't think—

Ram them!

Jane sighed.

An explosion rocked the cockpit and Mender's integuary link cut out. A moment later his acceleration shell snapped open, venting its fluid over the deck. He vomited up the breathable liquid and scraped more of it from his eyes before peering around the darkened cockpit. Alarms were blaring all over the place.

At last the red emergency lights kicked in.

'My powerplant is damaged,' *Jane* told him. 'I'm working on it.'

'Where the hell are we?' he asked, trying to work out their position.

'Coasting roughly parallel to the asteroid, about ten kilometres out.'

Through the canopy, Mender could see the shuttle nearing the dock entrance. He looked out of the other side of the cockpit and saw the Kadiran aggressor vessel's main guns were still rotating, about to lock on to *Dainty Jane*.

He fished a cheroot from the packet next to his panel, lit it and blew out a stream of sweet-smelling vapour. 'Can't even talk to the girl,' he muttered.

'What would you say?'

He grunted, watching the Kadiran battery swing into position. 'Shit,' he said, 'I don't know.'

But the battery kept turning, passing *Dainty Jane*, and Mender
realised the aggressor vessel's verniers were rotating her end over
end as her main drives flared.

'*She's getting underway*,' he said out loud – and beside her, the
empty frame of the assault ship was doing the same.

He stood and stared past the Kadiran ships, squinting into
the starscape and wishing the external lenses were working.

Some of the stars were moving.

The aggressor deployed chaff as streaks of light started to
whip past her, then her main batteries began to fire. One of
the incoming beams struck her flank, scoring a deep line in the
armour.

Jane's cockpit lights suddenly came back on and the ship
filled with her familiar hum. Mender immediately hooked the
external lenses and sank slowly into his couch. Arrayed in front
of the Kadiran vessels were a dozen ships, headed by a heavy
cruiser and her escorts.

He didn't need *Jane*'s data core to tag the cruiser's name.

'*Gratitude*,' Mender muttered. 'Well, I'll be damned.'

The Kadiran ships were accelerating on a line away from the
asteroid and Vetochkina's taskforce, racing to get to a collapse
point.

Mender gauged the distance to the Ascendancy ships. 'Looks
like they're gonna make it, goddamn it,' he muttered, just as,
in the volume of space ahead of the fleeing Kadiran vessels, a

single frigate blinked into existence.

Wyvern.

'Gutsy move,' Mender muttered, 'but those two will roll right over her.'

Without slowing, the Kadiran ships turned their weapons on *Wyvern.*

Behind the little starship, the stars warped.

'Piotr's puckered ringpiece . . .' Mender breathed, as an entire battle fleet collapsed into existence behind *Wyvern*, a wall of steel in front of the fleeing Kadiran vessels.

It was a combat collapse, and no less than three capital ships immediately unleashed the full force of their main batteries on the enemy, transforming them instantly to superheated gas.

Mender tore his eyes from the fleet to look for the shuttle, which was now hanging motionless a kilometre from the dock and making no attempt to escape.

He drew deeply on his cheroot.

'Well,' he said, with a rare grin, 'that I did *not* expect.'

47

ALLIES

Orry had to keep telling herself that she was in *Wyvern*'s sickbay, not a seven-star hotel on Tyr, but every stateroom in the Imperator's suite looked like this. She wondered what had been sacrificed in the frigate to make room for this bubble of luxury. If Counter-Admiral Vetochkina felt the same way as she stood beside Orry, she wasn't giving anything away.

'I did realise the seal was genuine, Your Excellency,' the admiral said stiffly.

'And yet you chose to ignore it.' The Imperator regarded her coldly from his sickbed. He was still dreadfully weak, but he was hiding it well, Orry thought.

'I have no excuse, Excellency.'

Orry frowned at that.

'This displays a distinct lack of judgement on your part, Vetochkina. It makes me wonder whether a mistake was made in appointing you to senior command.'

A muscle twitched in the admiral's jaw. 'Yes, Excellency.'

Orry stared at her, waiting for her to defend herself, but it was clear she wasn't planning to say anything else.

'Actually, I think Admiral Vetochkina acted entirely correctly,' she found herself telling the Imperator. The admiral turned her head to look at her, clearly as surprised as Orry was.

The Imperator gestured for her to continue.

Orry didn't think the admiral had noticed the faint smile that had momentarily graced his face. 'Counter-Admiral Vetochkina explained to me that she was fully engaged in the operation to liberate Odessa. Had she done as I asked, it would have caused the loss of thousands of personnel and the failure of the operation. She's guilty of nothing more than doing her duty.'

His smile faded. 'Her duty is to her Imperator.'

'At the time I had no way of knowing *when* the Kadiran would act,' Orry explained. 'Admiral Vetochkina chose to prevent the certain death or capture of her people over the *possibility* of an attempt on your life.'

'You almost died too,' the Imperator pointed out. 'And your brother and friends.'

'But we're *not* dead, are we? For what it's worth, I think the admiral is just the kind of senior officer you need.'

'And this advice is based on your extensive military experience,' he commented with a straight face.

Orry smiled sweetly.

The Imperator looked thoughtfully at Vetochkina. 'It appears you have an ally, Admiral, and fortunately for you, one whose judgement I value. And you did come in the end. Better late than never, I suppose.'

Vetochkina blinked. 'Yes, Excellency. Thank you, sir.' Her eyes flicked back to Orry for a moment.

'In future, however, you will obey Miz Kent's orders as if I myself am speaking, whether she has a damned ring or not. Do you understand?'

Vetochkina hesitated, then said, 'I understand, Excellency.'

Orry thought she had misheard. *It must be his meds*, she thought, trying to hide a sudden feeling of discomfort.

'Now get out, both of you,' the Imperator said, not unkindly. 'It sounds like the only way to save me is to slice me open. Sheer barbarism!'

Orry followed the admiral into the passageway outside, then held the door open for the Imperator's personal surgeon, a kindly-looking man who affected an antique pair of half-moon spectacles. He gave her an odd look as he thanked her. The guard stationed outside sickbay saluted smartly as they passed.

'Why?' Vetochkina asked as they walked down the passageway.

Orry looked at her. 'Why what?'

The admiral stopped. 'You saved my career in there – and after I treated you so poorly. Why?'

'I just told the truth,' Orry said. 'You weren't sticking up for yourself, so I thought I'd better.'

The older woman looked incredulous. 'You have no idea what's going on, do you?'

'Erm . . . no?'

'The Imperator Ascendant just ordered *me*, an admiral in command of enough firepower to retake a colony, to obey *your* orders.'

'Yeah, that was kind of out of the blue. I put it down to his meds.'

'You've saved his life *twice* now – not to mention the lives of everyone on Tyr.'

Orry hadn't thought of it like that, but it wasn't like she'd had a lot of choice, after all. 'I guess.'

'Mother of Rama! You told me yourself: someone is plotting to kill him – one of his own! – and they damn near succeeded. But you saved him. *Again*. And you almost died doing it. He trusts you. Hell, *I* trust you.'

'Look, I didn't ask for any of this, okay?' Orry was getting hot under the collar. 'I just want a quiet life – I don't *want* the Imperator's ear.'

The admiral laughed out loud and put a hand on Orry's shoulder. 'Don't you see? That makes it even more perfect: *everyone* close to him wants *something*: money, power, land, influence – but not you, oh no, you just want to be left alone.' Her tone softened a little. 'There's a theory – not one that's very popular in the Fountainhead – that the only people who should be permitted power are those who don't want it.'

'But I *don't* want it,' Orry said, sounding a little desperate now. 'I *really* don't want it!'

'But you *have* it. You have a fleet under your command now.'

'He didn't mean it like that—'

'I think he did.'

'He'll wake up in the morning and change his mind.'

Admiral Vetochkina smiled thinly and started walking again. 'We'll see.'

'I don't want your damned fleet!' Orry called after her. 'You're twisting his words.' A passing officer looked strangely at her and she hurried after the admiral.

'What changed your mind?' she asked, her mind still whirling. 'About coming here? What happened on Odessa?'

'There was no need to stay there. The Kadiran pulled out.'

'They did *what*? What about their fleet?'

'Gone.'

'Without a fight? Why?'

The admiral shrugged. 'I have no idea. I left engineers and medics with a couple of battalions to guard them and came here at full speed.'

'Aren't you worried they'll come back? The Kadiran? They might have gone to get reinforcements.'

'I don't think so. We've been seeing the same thing happen all over, on every front. The Kadiran are withdrawing – they're abandoning their gains and refusing to engage our forces.'

She stopped at the entrance to *Wyvern*'s landing bay and turned to Orry. 'You might not want what the Imperator is offering you, but for what it's worth, I think he's dead right. If you need anything, I'll do my best to accommodate you.'

Her brown eyes stared into Orry's for a moment, then she saluted briskly and was gone.

Orry stared dumbly at the airlock door, feeling suddenly freighted with dread and unable to work out why.

I need some sleep.

Turning away, she went to find her cabin.

She woke five hours later in the unfamiliar stateroom, feeling like she'd hardly slept despite the softness of the bed. After listening to the noise of a pump whirring somewhere behind her head for what felt like an eternity, Orry rose and got dressed.

Wyvern was in her night cycle, the sounds of the ship muted as she wandered through the red-lit passageways, pondering the Kadiran withdrawal. She badly wanted to talk to Quondam about it, but he was on *Dainty Jane* with the others and she didn't want to leave *Wyvern* until she was sure the Imperator was out of danger.

She stopped, frowning, and turned to get her bearings. No, she was right: the sickbay was up ahead – but there was no guard on the door.

Is the Imperator back in his stateroom already?

But she'd just passed it and there was no guard stationed there, either. Puzzled, she approached the sickbay door and found it unlocked. Suddenly worried, she hit the panel by the door.

Persephone Watkin whirled round as the door hissed open. She was standing beside the Imperator's bed, holding a syringe filled with yellowish fluid. She smiled, but not before Orry had noticed a flicker of panic, quickly suppressed.

'Couldn't sleep?' Persephone asked lightly.

'What are you doing here?' Orry demanded.

Persephone stepped away from the bed, holding up the syringe. 'Chief Physick Fischer asked me to add this to the Imperator's line.'

'Oh yeah?' Orry tried to keep her own voice even. 'What is it?'

'A nanobiotic supplement, I think – to be honest, I didn't really understand.'

'Where's the guard who should be outside?'

'Oh, isn't she there? She was when I came in.'

She was a good liar, but Orry had been trained to spot them by the best; no one had been better at reading people than her father. She was about to call bullshit when it occurred to her that if Persephone really was trying to finish what the Kadiran had started, she might not be the woman she appeared to be – and that could mean Orry was in real danger. She considered using her integuary to call for help, but she hadn't been added to any of *Wyvern*'s command channels, and in any case, Persephone would be sure to notice.

'There's no one there now,' Orry said, backing away. 'I'd better go and get someone.'

'No!' Persephone said quickly, and then, more calmly, 'I'm sure she'll be back in a minute. I don't want to get anyone into trouble.'

Orry eyed her. Sweat was beading on Persephone's top lip and her breathing was shallow and fast. She looked nothing like a trained assassin. For a moment she wondered if the woman's story might even be true – then Persephone's nerve broke and she bolted for the door.

Orry shoulder-barged her into a wall of shelves, bringing the whole structure down in a horrendous cacophony of crashing glass, but Persephone had already scrambled to her feet and was holding the syringe like a dagger.

'Get out of my way,' she pleaded.

Orry couldn't take her eyes off the bead of liquid gathered at the tip of the long needle. 'Don't be stupid,' she said. 'You're on a warship – there's nowhere for you to go. Put down the syringe.'

She positioned herself between Persephone and the exit.

'Get out of my way!' There were tears in her eyes now.

'No.'

Persephone moaned, 'I didn't want *any* of this – and now he's going to send those *awful* pictures to everyone . . . my friends . . . my mother, my *father*—'

'Who is?' Orry asked. 'Who made you do this?'

Persephone was shaking now, tears filling her eyes. 'That bastard D-Delf – h-he found the p-pictures and he made me tell him about Anna, the asteroid, *everything*. He t-told me . . .' She choked on her words, then managed, 'If the attack failed, he said I had to finish the old man off myself.' She was sobbing now, the tears streaming down her face, the syringe almost forgotten. 'Oh Rama, what have I done?'

Orry could hardly breathe. *The Count of Delf is behind all this? My grandfather?*

She filed the revelation away; this was not the time to think about it. 'It's okay,' she said calmly, stepping towards the sobbing woman. 'Everything is going to be fine. Just put down the syringe, okay?'

Persephone's eyes drifted down to the needle. She was looking at it as if someone else was holding it – and Orry realised a moment too late what was about to happen.

'No!' she yelled, surging forward as Persephone slipped the needle into her own neck and pushed the plunger home. Orry caught her as she crumpled to the deck, the needle still in her flesh. Persephone started convulsing, the syringe bouncing up and down at her throat.

She yanked it out and hurled it away, trying to hold Persephone as she spasmed. Pink foam was already frothing at her mouth, her eyes rolling back in her head.

'Help!' Orry screamed. '*Help in here!*'

But the convulsions were slacking off now and Persephone's breathing was shallow. Too late, Orry heard the sound of running boots outside and the door hissed open to reveal a guard, his eyes wide as he looked from her to the Imperator.

'Don't just bloody stand there!' she yelled at him. 'Get a physick in here!'

As the guard's eyes glazed, Persephone clutched Orry's arm and a look of terror crossed her face – then her features went slack.

'Medic's on his way,' the guard said, crossing to the Imperator's bed and staring down at him.

She slumped back and gently closed Persephone's eyes.

'There's no rush,' she told him bleakly.

Orry sat on the edge of the bed, staring at the imprints her boots had left in the deep-pile carpet. She looked up at a gentle tap on the door. 'Open,' she said.

A woman stood at the threshold, her charcoal-grey frock coat unadorned with buttons or braid. Her chestnut hair was cut in a style a little too young for her face.

'Good morning, Miz Kent. My name is Lucia Rodin. May I come in?'

It took Orry a moment to realise why the name was familiar. Brushing Irina's ring with her fingers, she stood. 'Please.'

The woman's eyes dropped to the ring, then she stepped into the stateroom.

'I've heard so very much about you,' she said, extending her hand. 'Please call me Lucia.'

Orry took it automatically, feeling Lucia's palm soft against her own.

The older woman smoothly turned her wrist to examine the ring before releasing her. 'I understand Irina is dead?'

Orry nodded, oddly cowed by the sense of cool competence coming off Lucia, but something about her made her feel like everything was going to be all right. The last time she had felt like that was with her father. It was unsettling.

'She died on Morhelion.' She removed the ring and handed it to Lucia, who pocketed it with a tired smile before gesturing to the table set with six dining chairs. 'Shall we sit? Then perhaps you could start at the beginning.'

Orry sat down. 'Um, I don't mean to be rude, but who are you exactly?'

'Just a humble servant of the Ascendancy, although I am fortunate enough to hold a little influence.'

'The Imperator said Irina worked for you, and Irina was with Seventh Secretariat, so does that mean you run Seven?'

A faint smile. 'Details of Seventh Secretariat personnel are classified, for good reason. Why don't you bring me up to speed? The Imperator and I talked briefly before his operation, but I'd like to hear it from you. *Every* detail.'

Orry told her, leaving nothing out. When she was finished, her throat was dry.

Lucia watched her quizzically as she got up to get some water. 'You are a remarkable young woman, Miz Kent.'

'So people keep telling me.' She sipped at a bulb of sparkling water, managing to spill some of it down the front of her flight suit. She brushed the drops off, annoyed at her clumsiness. 'I'm really not.'

'Permit me to disagree. It is a shame Miz Watkin chose to take her life, although possibly the most sensible course of action for her.'

'What are you going to do about Delf?' Orry asked.

'That is the question, isn't it?'

'What question? He plotted with the Kadiran to kill the Imperator and take his place. Just arrest him for treason.'

'Your grandfather is the second most powerful man in the Ascendancy. If I were to arrest him, I rather suspect his legal team would ask to see some proof. Sadly, they would have a point. Do you have any evidence of his involvement in this plot?'

'But Persephone—'

'Is dead. And in any case it would be her word against his.'

'Quondam could testify.'

'Your pet Kadiran? Testify against a Count – a pureblood Ruuz? A member of the Proximal Council?'

Orry thought hard. 'Shit.'

'Precisely.'

'So forget arresting him. Can't you just, you know, *deal* with him?'

The look Lucia gave Orry made her squirm. 'You're talking about – what? Killing him? Making him disappear?'

Orry's cheeks grew warm. 'Why not? We know he did it.'

'Putting aside the question of due process, did you not hear me when I said that Delf is second only to the Imperator? He leads the Proximal Council. He is allied with the heads of half of the most powerful Houses and probably has enough dirt on the rest that they would never dare to oppose him. He's been angling to be named successor for decades, but the Imperator dislikes him.' She smiled. 'In fact, he once said he'd rather hand his empire to a Sabinian goatherd. So Delf is too powerful to "deal with". Any move against him without ironclad proof of his treason would plunge the Ascendancy into civil war, which makes him, for now at least, untouchable.'

Orry sipped at her water, turning the problem over in her head. 'These allies of his – what would they do if they found out the truth? That he plotted with the Kadiran to kill the Imperator.'

'We just established that we don't have any proof.'

'Forget the proof for the moment. *Hypothetically*, what would they do if he were exposed?'

'Delf would be finished. His friends would desert him and his enemies would move against him. But *not without proof.*'

Orry started pacing, a familiar nervous excitement building within her. 'Do you think Delf knows his plan has failed?'

'I doubt it. No pods have been dispatched since the fleet arrived. This whole operation is being conducted under the strictest security protocols.'

'Then I think I might have an idea.' She stopped and turned to Lucia with a grin. 'Tell me, does Seventh Secretariat have access to a face-changer?'

48

DUPLICATE

Nightfall in Tyr's northern continent did little to relieve the sticky heat of the day. Sweat ran down Orry's back as she glanced nervously about, waiting for a guard or a security drone to appear around the corner of the mansion. Her boots sank into soft soil as she peered through a large sash window into the Count of Delf's private study.

Hurry up! she sent.

All right, all right, Ethan replied, *keep your hair on. Oh wait, it's not your hair though, is it?*

Orry touched the long ponytail hanging over one shoulder and grimaced.

A faint *click* sounded from the window. *It's open,* Ethan informed her. The window slid smoothly upwards at her touch. After a final look around the grounds, she hoisted herself up and clambered inside.

The study was two storeys high with an ornate cast-iron balcony running around the upper level. Like the rest of the Delf mansion, the room looked pretty much as it must have done in its prime, back on Earth so many centuries ago. The dark wood panelling was inset with red leather panels and a vast mirror above a stone fireplace made the room look even larger. There was a pair of leather sofas by the hearth, a writing desk and wing-backed chairs. The shelves on the walls were filled with ornaments and a few leather-bound volumes that made Orry think of Konstantin, Delf's grandson and her shit of a cousin – not that she'd known that when he'd been murdered as a result of her last visit to her grandfather's house.

Reluctantly, she crossed to the large mirror, keeping her eyes fixed on the hearth beneath it. Steeling herself, she raised her eyes—

—and saw Cordelia Roag staring back at her. Orry tilted her head to one side, then the other, raised a hand, blew herself a kiss. The likeness was uncanny – and deeply disturbing. Predictably, Seventh Secretariat tech was state-of-the-art.

The sooner her own features were restored, the happier she would be.

Turning away from the mirror, her eyes drifted to the balcony, searching for any sign of the nook. Ethan had uncovered that little architectural nugget during the prep for their previous scam here, but they hadn't needed to use it during the book game. Even knowing where the concealed door was, she couldn't spot it. Instead, she returned her attention to the lower level.

Where is he? she asked, selecting a wing-backed chair facing the door. She sat and practised crossing and uncrossing her legs a few times, trying to remember exactly how Roag sat. Not for the first time, she wondered whether Cordelia Roag would really do something as melodramatic as appearing unannounced in Delf's study. Orry rather thought she would.

I don't have eyes on him at the moment, Ethan told her.

What? *Where is he?*

In his private chambers: there are no lenses in there. I have a heat source though – two, actually.

Who's the other one?

Can't tell. Probably a servant.

Or his new major-domo? Orry remembered Madam Costanza, Delf's former major-domo, all too well, and those cold eyes looking down on her with such utter *disdain*. The woman had been publicly hanged several months ago for her part in Konstantin's murder and the plot to destroy Tyr. Orry hadn't bothered watching the feed.

No, he's at the residence in Usk, Ethan said. *Lucia's people are keeping an eye on him.*

Good – although that was news to Orry, and it unnerved her; it was the sort of thing she should know. But this plan had been put together so quickly, she'd had barely enough time to grasp her own part in it. She liked complete control, but she supposed if she had to delegate, she couldn't hope for anyone more capable than Lucia Rodin. Under any other circumstances the fact that her little brother was calling the head of the most powerful intelligence agency in the Ascendancy by her first name would have made Orry smile, but now it just underlined how many interlocking cogs were turning beyond her sight. It would take only one of them to fall out of position to bring the whole finely balanced mechanism to a grinding and bloody halt – and she was the one who'd be caught right in the middle of it.

Hold on, Ethan sent, *the heat signatures are moving. Should be visible any moment . . . now.*

A moment's silence.

Oh shit.

What is it? she asked, alarmed; Ethan rarely swore in front of her. *Ethan?*

Sis, you need to get the hell out of there. Right now.

What are you talking about? Who's he with?

Orry could hear Ethan's fear and hatred rendered in his voice. *Cordelia Roag.*

She leaped to her feet, turning instinctively to the mirror over the mantel. Roag's face stared back at her again.

They're heading your way. Move it!

She cast about, looking first at the window, then at the pair of facing sofas in front of the fireplace.

They're right outside—

The door handle turned, Orry crossed the room in two strides and dived over the sofa furthest from the door, landing in a heap on a thick rug behind it. She heard the door open then close, and steps sounded on polished floorboards until they were once again muffled by carpet.

'You can wait in here until they're gone,' she heard Delf say.

'But Lucia is *so* keen to meet me.'

Roag's sneering voice brought forth a rancid slick of memories.

Delf chuckled, something Orry could not have imagined him doing. 'Once I am Imperator, Lucia Rodin will no longer be a problem.'

'You're very sure of yourself. She could be coming to arrest you.'

'If she were coming to arrest me, she would hardly bring the entire Proximal Council with her. No, this is it – I *feel* it.'

'We've had no word from the Kadiran, or from Piotr's slut

assistant.'

'Stop worrying, Cordelia. This is it, I tell you. Finally, my destiny will be fulfilled.' The squeak of a cork being removed from a bottle. 'Brandy?'

'Why not?'

Orry listened to them drink, trying to quell her terror.

'Just so you know,' Roag continued, 'if Rodin *is* here to arrest you, I'll be gone.'

'I wouldn't expect anything less from you, my dear. But you needn't worry.' A tap on the door made Orry jump. 'Come!' Delf called.

'Madam Lucia Rodin is waiting in the library, Milord.' The measured tone suggested a mimetic. 'She is with the members of the Proximal Council.'

'Thank you, Hector. I'll be there directly.'

'Yes, Milord.'

Delf waited for the door to close. 'To the future,' he said, and Orry heard the clink of glasses. 'Wait here. This shouldn't take long.'

'I hope not,' Roag said drily.

The sound of steps was followed by the door closing.

'Piotr's withered fucking balls,' Roag muttered and took a slurp of her brandy.

What are you going to do? Ethan asked.

You just keep an eye on Rodin and the others, Orry told him. *Don't worry about me.*

All right, he said hesitantly.

Orry listened as Roag began to walk around the room. By lowering herself silently onto her belly, she could see the woman's boots. She was pacing the study, pausing to examine items that caught her interest. Orry glanced up at a shelf above her hiding place and her eyes settled on a bronze statuette of an eagle. When she looked back, Roag was studying a golden carriage clock.

Orry rose swiftly and silently to her feet, grabbed the heavy statuette and sank back down again just as Roag replaced the clock and moved in her direction.

She moved to the next set of shelves and Orry slowed her breathing even more. The eagle's bronze feathers were digging painfully into her palm and she forced herself to relax her grip a little. She couldn't risk getting back on the floor for a look. *Use your ears*, she told herself.

Roag was close now, close enough for Orry to smell the musky perfume she remembered. She hefted the eagle, ears straining.

A step.

Another.

She rose and turned smoothly, holding the eagle high with both arms. Roag was right there, about to come around the side of the sofa. The woman stopped abruptly, her eyes widening, and Orry wondered what it was like to be suddenly confronted by a duplicate of yourself, rising from nowhere and wielding a bronze eagle.

'Hi!' she said, hearing Cordelia Roag's voice coming from her own mouth. She let out a grunting shriek as she swung the statuette, and felt a savage satisfaction as it connected with the side of Roag's skull. The woman collapsed without a sound and landed at Orry's feet.

She stepped back, raising the eagle again, but when she rolled Roag onto her back with her foot she could see the woman's face was slack, her eyes closed. Blood matted her hair, but her chest was rising and falling.

Still alive. She didn't know how she felt about that.

She lowered the eagle and let it drop with a thud.

With trembling hands, she began to undress.

49

ADMISSION

Lucia's integuary was useless in this situation. Her fellow members of the Proximal Council all had brainware too, subtly micromanaging their skin response, facial and vocal cues and any number of other metrics to foil the deception-detection routines she was running. If she wanted to discover which council members were involved in Delf's plot, she would have to depend on good old-fashioned methods, like reading their faces and body language. She was skilled at it – she'd been doing it for long enough, ever since she trained as a young arbiter – but her subjects today, political animals raised in a world of Great Houses, were particularly challenging. They tolerated Lucia rather than accepted her. Hiding their true feelings was as natural to them as breathing.

'This really is intolerable, Madam,' Feodor, Sixth Duke of Lowenstaat said. 'You drag us all out here – and then we are kept waiting by Delf? I for one have better things to be doing.'

Like humping your stepmother, Lucia reflected, but said nothing.

'Oh, do be quiet, young man,' the Duchess of Goltenberg said. 'What is this about, Lucia?' She glanced at the pair of

Imperial Guards stationed at the drawing room door. 'It's the Imperator, isn't it? What's happened?'

Lucia gave a neutral smile. 'Let's wait for His Grace, shall we?'

As if on cue, Milan Larist Soltz entered, accompanied by a mimetic butler. Lucia knew the Count of Delf usually favoured human help over robots, both as a sign of his immense wealth, and also because it was no fun bullying a machine. Lately, though, he had replaced nearly all of his staff with mimetics. Robots didn't eavesdrop, she supposed.

'My Lords,' Delf said, with a slight bow, 'Ladies. You are welcome, of course, but I must confess I am somewhat at a loss as to why you have come.'

'Ask the spymaster,' Feodor said crossly.

Delf looked more expectant than curious when he turned to her. *Of course he is*, Lucia thought. *He expects me to tell him Piotr is dead and he is the new Imperator.*

'Your Grace, would you please ask your mimetic to leave us?'

'Get out, Hector.'

'Yes, Milord.'

She waited for the machine to close the door behind it before saying, 'Earlier today I received grave news. It is my sad duty to inform you that our beloved Imperator Ascendant, Piotr, is dead.'

She studied their reactions carefully, but learned nothing: shock and dismay mostly, mixed with fear. Holding up a hand for silence, she continued, 'We are still collating the full details of what happened and a report will be provided to you at the earliest opportunity, but after an initial investigation I am satisfied that he is truly gone. The important thing now is to see to the succession. The Ascendancy is at war and I'm sure you will all agree that the last thing we need is any period of uncertainty at this turbulent time.'

'Did he name an heir?' Grand Marshal Solsky asked sharply.

'He did.' She let the silence stretch out, enjoying the moment, contrived as it was.

'Well?' Feodor snapped.

'The Imperator named Milan Larist Soltz, Count of Delf, as his successor. I trust none of you will besmirch his memory by contesting the decision.' She met each of their gazes one by one, and one by one each of them nodded. 'Good, then it is settled. We will make the announcement in the morning.'

She turned to Delf, who was looking solemn. 'May I be the first to congratulate you . . . Excellency.' She bowed deeply and saw the other members of the council do the same.

'Please, please,' he said magnanimously, motioning for them to rise. 'We are all friends here and I hope will continue to be so.' His eyes lingered on Lucia. 'I am both humbled and delighted that the Imperator thought fit to name me as his successor. Of course, I can never hope to fill his shoes, but I will promise to do my best to build on his tireless work and lead our empire to even greater heights.'

Those carefully neutral looks again, Lucia thought, and wondered how many of the people standing in the room would still be on the council – or indeed, still breathing – in a week's time, if Delf's succession had not been a fiction.

'Your Excellency,' she said, 'we must return you to the palace to make preparations for tomorrow's announcement.'

'Of course,' Delf replied. 'Will you forgive me for a moment while I attend to a few household matters first? Please, help yourselves to refreshments while you wait.'

Lucia watched the count leave and had to resist the urge to check in with Ethan. The boy impressed her almost as much as his sister did. Sure enough, his voice sounded immediately on their private channel: *We're on. Delf's heading back to his study. Are you both ready?*

Ready, Orry confirmed.

Lucia wondered what she had done with the real Roag.

Give me a moment, she sent, and clapped her hands to cut through the buzz of alliances already being reforged. 'Please,' she said quietly but firmly, 'I need you all to do exactly as I say, in complete silence and without question.'

'What on Tyr are you blithering about?' Feodor snarled.

'I am not speaking to you now as a member of the Proximal Council but as head of Seventh Secretariat. The future of the Ascendancy rests upon your *absolute* silence and obedience for the next few minutes.'

The council members exchanged uncomfortable glances, but there were no objections. Lucia crossed to the corner of the room and searched for the door.

To your left, Ethan told her. *More . . . more . . . there! Push it.*

Her hand was resting on an oak panel that looked identical to all the others. She pressed her palm against the smooth wood and pushed. There was a soft *click* and a section of the panelling sprang open a few centimetres. She hooked her fingers around it and pulled the concealed door open.

'What are you doing?' Jessica Brookes asked.

She turned back to them and whispered, 'Follow me, please. And remember: *absolute* silence.'

She led the procession into a short passage running between the walls of two rooms, up a narrow spiral staircase and along another passage which opened into a room with a door at the far end.

Remove the panel, Ethan told her as she approached the door and Lucia gripped the handle in its upper half and pulled.

After some initial resistance, a circle of wood came free to reveal a hole the width of a spread hand, partially obscured on the other side by a row of books. Over the tops of the books she could make out parts of Delf's study. The count's voice immediately floated up from below them.

Lucia pressed a finger to her lips as the council members started listening avidly at the hole.

Milan Larist Soltz was a man who rarely let his emotions show, but as he re-entered the study Orry could see he was struggling to contain himself. Excitement almost writhed beneath his pallid skin as he crossed to the drinks cabinet and poured himself a generous measure of brandy.

He's going to see right through me, she thought, suddenly convinced that the whole plan was ridiculous. She was wearing the real Cordelia Roag's clothes and had adjusted her new hair to match, but still . . .

Delf tossed his drink back in one and shuddered, then turned to her with a thin smile. 'Aren't you going to ask how it went?'

He was looking right at her and clearly suspected nothing, which steadied her. She remained seated on the sofa, horribly aware of Roag's unconscious body slumped behind it – if he walked just a couple of steps in the wrong direction he would see her. She found she was clutching the sofa's arm and forced her hand to relax.

We're in position, Lucia told her.

'How did it go?' Orry asked, hearing the modulator implanted in her throat perfectly mimicking Roag's voice.

His answering smile made her skin crawl. 'He's dead – and the old goat actually named me his successor!'

'He did?' Orry was picturing Roag now, remembering the times she had met the woman. She pulled on Roag's persona like a cloak.

'Perhaps the Imperator wasn't as short-sighted as I thought,' Delf pondered, then frowned. 'It is odd, though.'

'At the end of the day he wanted what was best for the Ascendancy,' she said. 'Even he could see that you were the best choice to take the reins . . .'

Delf nodded slowly.

'. . . *Excellency*,' Orry finished, giving the word a touch of irony.

His smile returned. 'You know, it's droll,' he said, stepping closer.

'What is?'

'All the time we spent planning what we'd do to gain power once he was dead – and he just hands it to me on a plate.'

She stood to head him off. 'Who gives a shit? You got what you wanted – it's what this whole thing was about.'

'Yes.' She wanted him to say more but he turned away and started for the door. 'Anyway, you'd better get offworld for a while. I'll send for you as soon as I can.'

'Wait!' she said, a little too shrilly for Roag, and he turned, his eyes narrowing.

Orry realised she had absolutely no idea what to say next. *You're out of time*, she realised. *It's now or never.* 'How do I know you won't throw me to the wolves?' she asked.

He looked disappointed. 'Cordelia,' he chided, 'I expected more of you. If this is your clumsy way of telling me you have a pile of evidence hidden somewhere, primed for release should anything untoward befall you, then I can assure you that I had always assumed as much. I am a Soltz and I will not break my word. Besides, you might be useful to me again in the future.' He stepped closer, his smile fading. 'Just be sure your evidence is kept *very* safe – and don't even *think* of using it as leverage. I intend to honour our agreement in full. You will have more power than you could ever dream of.'

She could sense his desire to leave. *Time to go all in.*

'I'd better,' she told him, then ploughed on, choosing her words carefully. 'I conspired with the Kadiran to murder the Imperator so you could take his place – *under your direct instructions*. You owe me.'

She waited, hardly breathing, as his pale face coloured with anger. He took a step towards her, one long finger raised.

'Never,' he hissed, 'speak of that again.'

Silence fell.

Keep pushing, Lucia told her. *We need more. We need him to say the words.*

'I may have been the go-between,' Orry said, 'but this was *your* idea: it was *you* who blackmailed his slut of an assistant into giving you Piotr's schedule. *You* told me to leak it to the Kadiran. *You* made a deal with them to kill him.'

'What do you want?' Delf snarled. 'More money?'

'I want to hear you say it. Just once, I want to hear one of you Ruuz bastards accept responsibility and not try to squirm out of it – even if it's just to me.'

His expression changed. 'Why, Cordelia, I never realised you had such a chip on your shoulder. Beneath that shell lies a soft and vulnerable woman – no wonder you never let anyone see it.'

'Say it,' she hissed.

'Fine. Of course I did it – you know that. Happy now? Yes, *I* gave the Kadiran everything they needed to kill the old bastard.'

She just stared at him, hardly able to believe it had worked.

'What?' he asked.

He whirled at a crash from the balcony to see a florid, heavyset man in uniform bursting through a concealed door.

'Traitor!' the man roared, pointing a shaking finger at the count. Behind him other people, all white-faced with shock, were emerging. Lucia, wearing a strained smile, brought up the rear.

Delf staggered backwards, then turned to stare at Orry.

'Hello, Grandfather,' she said.

He blinked – then his eyes widened in disbelief. 'No,' he breathed, turning back to the balcony. '*No!*'

'You'll hang for this, you bastard!' snarled the florid man. Orry had seen him on newscasts, making interminable speeches; she thought he was much more effective when he kept his pronouncements short and sweet.

Delf rounded on her, his face twisted with hate. She tensed, certain he was about to launch himself at her, but then the study door burst open and two Imperial Guards entered.

With a visible effort he regained control.

'I don't understand,' a younger man said plaintively from the balcony. His accent was like cut-glass. 'Is the Imperator dead or not?'

'The Imperator is alive and well,' Lucia said, 'despite the count's best efforts. I apologise for the subterfuge, but it was critical that you heard the truth from his own lips.' She gripped the balcony rail and addressed Delf. 'Milan Larist Soltz, in the name of the Imperator I arrest you for treason – specifically, conspiring with an enemy of the Ascendancy in time of war to take the life of the Imperator Ascendant.' She turned to the Imperial Guards. 'Take him away.'

Delf's habitual expression of arrogance was firmly back in place as the Guards approached him.

It might just be a mask to hide his inner turmoil, but the disdain still angered Orry. 'All this' – she gestured around the opulent study and the mansion surrounding it – 'and you still want more. Someone like you will never be satisfied, even as Imperator. I feel sorry for you.'

He stared at her for a moment, then smiled.

'What's so bloody funny?' she demanded.

'You are, Aurelia. The accidental spawn of a common criminal, a man who turned my own daughter against me, who manipulated and seduced her before tossing her aside when she needed him the most. I never thought there was anything of the Soltz in you, but you have proven me wrong.' He shrugged his arm free of the Guard who was trying to put restraints on him and stepped closer to her. 'What you've done to me today is worthy of our ancestors. I'm proud of you . . . *Granddaughter*.'

His face blurred as tears filled her eyes. He began to turn away, still wearing that straight-razor smile, then paused. 'Your mother, though?' he said thoughtfully. 'Perhaps not so much.' He obediently held his wrists out to the Guard.

Orry wanted to scream into his face that he was wrong, that she was *nothing* like him, but the words wouldn't come, for she was suddenly choked with grief. She dashed the tears from her eyes, furious that she'd let him provoke such a reaction. She drew a steadying breath, but as she opened her mouth to speak, a shouted warning from the balcony made her look up.

Lucia was pointing behind her.

She felt something whip past her cheek with a high-pitched squeal that set her teeth on edge. A dark blur flashed across the throat of the first Guard, drawing a line beneath her helmet, but even as the woman's hands rose to her neck, blood was already sheeting down her breastplate. The second Guard staggered and fell on his side, clutching at the fountain of red spurting from his inner thigh.

Orry started to turn but an ice-cold edge pressed into the side of her throat.

'*Don't*,' Cordelia Roag hissed in her ear.

A ringing sound drew Orry's eyes to the balcony. One of the rail's metal spindles had been sliced neatly in two at a steep angle and the young man standing directly behind it was staring down at his shirt in confusion. The glass he was holding tilted, slopping liquid, and fell from his fingers to smash on the ground far below. He plucked at the centre of his chest where a red stain was spreading, then toppled forward, his head bouncing off the rail.

An elderly woman's shout became a gurgling choke and suddenly there was panic on the balcony as everyone but Lucia tried to cram back through the concealed door at once.

'Kill Rodin!' Delf ordered, suddenly back in charge.

'I can't,' Roag said calmly, 'it's a blade-drone, fully autonomous. We need to leave.'

Delf stooped over the Guard choking at his feet, kicked her arm aside and wrenched her sidearm from its holster. He aimed up at Lucia and fired, raising sparks from the railing as she ducked. He fired again but she was already gone; another man at the far end of the balcony died in her place.

Roag shoved Orry forward, the blade nicking her skin. She could smell the Guards' blood now, tinny in her nose and throat.

'It's over,' Roag told Delf. 'We need to regroup.'

He nodded, his usually pale face flushed, and his cold eyes fell on Orry.

'You want to kill her?' Roag asked.

He was clearly tempted, given the way his long fingers were flexing around the pistol's grip, but after a moment's thought he shook his head. 'No, we'll take her.'

Orry put aside her fear and shock, knowing she would rather die than fall into Roag's hands again. She lunged at Delf, reaching for the pistol, but rather than slicing into her flesh, Roag's blade left her throat. The count was stepping backwards, startled by her unexpected attack, but Orry already had her hands on the gun and was turning her shoulder into his chest, ready to wrench it from his grip, when a blinding pain split her skull and the floor came up to meet her. She tried to open her eyes, but the room was suddenly dim.

'*You'll have to do a lot better than that, bitch.*'

She felt herself being rolled roughly onto her back and stared through fluttering eyelids at Roag's face looming large and distorted.

The face vanished into blackness.

50

A GREATER THREAT

Living the life she did, the possibility of imprisonment was always at the back of Orry's mind. She supposed it was testament to her father's caution that she had never seen the inside of a cell until after his death. Since then, unfortunately, she had experienced several. She clearly still had a lot to learn.

This cell was on a ship, that much was obvious from the acceleration tank fixed to one bulkhead. When she had awakened three days ago on the cell's narrow bunk, nursing the mother of all headaches and with a mouth as dry as a saltsea snake, she knew immediately that she'd been in that tank. The mesophase gel never evaporated fully from your skin, leaving a chalky residue that was as unmistakeable as it was unpleasant. She longed for a shower.

The acceleration since then had been at a constant 1g and her initial terror had turned to a nauseating tension that bubbled beneath the boredom, only to crawl up her throat the moment the cell door opened. Three times a day a server bot came into the cell with a bowl of bland but nutritious food. Orry had been wary about touching it at first – she'd suffered from Roag's particular brand of hospitality once before – but she could see no reason for Roag to tamper with the food, not when she was already at the woman's mercy.

When the door opened this time it was not the server that entered, but a solid, dark-skinned man covered in inky-black tattoos. He regarded Orry, his eyes cold. There'd be no help from that quarter. 'Boss wants to see you.' He gestured with a stubby pistol daubed in luminous orange and green paint.

Another of Roag's crew was waiting in the passageway, this one armed with a multi-load shotgun. She wore a similar mismatch of clothing as the man with the luminous gun, knives and pouches strung from mil-spec belts and webbing. *Space pirate chic*, Ethan always called it. The woman eyed Orry sourly and set off down the passageway, her partner bringing up the rear.

'Are we aboard *Scintilla*?' Orry asked.

'Shut up,' the woman grunted.

She was sure they were. *Scintilla* was Roag's personal commerce raider, an Eristani clipper that had once transported luxury goods and Ruuz nobles between the seven systems of the Fountainhead. The signs were still to be seen in the decorative panels on the bulkheads and the lack of exposed pipes and conduits.

Scintilla hadn't been designed as a warship, so her bridge was a transparent bubble sprouting from the upper deck. Orry assumed Roag had also fitted out a command centre deep within the ship, from where she could conduct combat operations without fear of being vented into space. Through the panoramic windows she could see the drive-lights of dozens of other ships; she really wished she could hook *Scintilla*'s lenses for a closer look.

Roag and Delf turned away from the stars as her escort cleared his throat, but rather than the gloating triumph she'd expected to see on their faces, there were strained lines of worry.

Orry folded her arms and waited, damned if she would let her fear show.

Roag smiled at that. 'I know you're scared, Aurelia, you're too smart not to be. But I congratulate you on an almost convincing show of defiance.'

'Why am I here?' Orry asked. 'So you can torture me?'

'I won't deny the notion is appealing; you've caused me no end of trouble. But no, this is not the time to indulge myself.'

'Why, then?'

'Your presence has been requested.'

'By who?'

'The Kadiran.'

Delf's face twitched at the word.

Orry looked out at the blade-like ships surrounding them. 'You ran to them for protection.'

'It seemed to be the prudent thing to do,' Roag confirmed.

'And they want to see me? Why?'

Roag and Delf exchanged a glance. 'I have no idea,' Roag said lightly, but there was a tension beneath her words.

'I imagine they will want to make an example of you,' Delf said, but his attempt to imbue his words with relish sounded feeble. He was scared – they both were.

'I think it might be best for all of us if we just left,' Orry said. 'It could be that we've *all* outlived our usefulness.'

'Speak for yourself,' her grandfather spat. 'I still have *enormous* support within the Fountainhead. With Kadiran backing I could—'

'Oh, *do* shut up,' Roag said quietly, and something in her tone stopped Delf's response before he uttered it. Colour was rising to his pale cheeks as she addressed Orry. 'I have to say I agree with you – but it's too late to leave. A Kadiran gunboat docked a few minutes ago.'

The doors to the bridge folded silently open and a formidable group of breedwarriors entered and spread out until they were covering Roag's crew. A Kadiran alpha flanked by two guards followed them in and stopped in front of Orry.

Reaching up, he removed his helmet and spoke, a series of harsh guttural barks. A moment later her integuary provided a translation.

'The Imperator holds you in esteem?'

The unexpected question threw her. 'Excuse me?'

A crease of irritation formed in the Kadiran's crest. 'You have influence over the Imperator? He will listen to your counsel?'

Oh. 'I wouldn't go that far,' she said cautiously. 'Why do you ask?'

'We wish you to convey a message to him.'

For the first time since awaking in her cell, Orry felt a tiny sliver of hope.

'This woman is my prisoner,' Roag objected, taking a step forward.

Instantly half the Kadiran weapons in the room were turned on her. The rest remained covering her helpless crew.

Roag stopped and held her hands up in surrender, although the weapons remained trained on her.

'Reimbursement will be provided for her loss,' the alpha said, but Roag grimaced.

'That's not the point. She's the reason our plan to kill the

Imperator failed. She's undermined your operation – she's destroyed *months* of work. At best she's prolonged the war, which will cost thousands of Kadiran lives. At worst, she may even have put your ultimate victory in doubt.'

Good speech, Orry thought, *pitched perfectly at the Kadiran mindset*. She was even a little impressed – but the alpha made a dismissive motion.

'You will convey a message to the Imperator,' he informed Orry. She glanced at Roag, enjoying the sight of her glowering with rage at being ignored.

'Uh, okay. What is it?'

'The Kadiran Hierocracy desires an immediate end to hostilities between us.'

The sliver of hope vanished. 'Why do you need me to tell him that?' Orry said coldly. 'You must have diplomatic channels.'

'Diplomatic channels have failed. After recent events it appears the Imperator is disinclined to believe our desire for peace is genuine.'

'After you plotted to kill him, you mean.'

'This statement reflects the true state.'

'So you thought you'd use me to bait the next trap?'

If she was reading the Kadiran features correctly, the alpha looked puzzled. 'You believe this is a ploy?'

'Isn't it?'

'It is a genuine offer. This conflict cannot continue.'

'Prove it.'

'Clarify.'

'Prove it's not another trick.'

He considered for a moment, then barked out what she guessed must be orders, because the breedwarriors instantly moved to disarm the thoroughly cowed bridge crew. None of them were inclined to resist. The Kadiran charged with relieving Roag of her weapons ignored her impressive stream of curses and quickly stripped her of her considerable personal armoury.

At a motion from the alpha, he dragged Roag forward, barely noticing her ineffectual thrashing against his powerful grip.

'This one is now your prisoner,' the alpha said. 'Give the order and my warrior will pull her head from her body.'

Roag's struggles stopped abruptly as the breedwarrior gripped her beneath the chin and pulled her head back.

'Stop it!' Orry shouted, feeling sick to her stomach.

The alpha gestured at the warrior, who let go of Roag's chin. She was white with fear.

'Is *this* supposed to convince me?' Orry asked. 'Cordelia Roag is nothing to you. You wouldn't think twice before killing her if it gained you an advantage.'

The alpha was clearly running out of patience. 'You will specify an action that will convince you.'

'Tell me why you want peace.'

He hesitated, then announced, 'There is a greater threat – to both our civilisations. We must work together to defeat it.'

It was difficult to judge from the inflection her integuary gave his words, but Orry thought she could hear fear in the alpha's voice. She thought of the sudden Kadiran withdrawal from Odessa and the other fronts she'd been told about and felt a sudden chill.

'What kind of threat?' she asked.

The alpha opened his mouth to answer, then held up a clawed hand. Orry realised he was listening to whatever the Kadiran equivalent of an integuary was.

'I urge you to believe my words,' he told her. 'The fate of us all rests with you.'

Before she could decide, he turned and pointed through the window. 'No time remains to us,' he said. 'The Imperator must hold you in high esteem indeed. He has sent a battle fleet to retrieve you.'

Now she could see lights winking into existence beyond the Kadiran force: a mass of Grand Fleet warships were collapsing into the immediate vicinity. She expected the Kadiran vessels to immediately start manoeuvring to engage, but the ships continued on their original courses.

'We will not fire,' the alpha explained, 'even to defend ourselves. Will that satisfy you that I speak the truth?'

It was the look of terror on Delf's face that finally convinced Orry this really was happening and not some elaborate ploy of Cordelia Roag's.

'The Ascendancy fleet is signalling,' one of Roag's bridge crew announced nervously.

'Let's hear it,' Orry said, and with only the briefest glance at Roag, the crewman obeyed.

'—deadly force. I say again, by command of Piotr, Imperator Ascendant, Kadiran forces are instructed to immediately surrender Aurelia Katerina Kent, the traitor Milan Larist Soltz and the criminal known as Cordelia Roag. You have five minutes to comply. Any aggressive action will be met with deadly force.'

The alpha watched her expectantly.

'Open a channel,' Orry told the crewman, and when he did, she said clearly, 'Ascendancy fleet, this is Aurelia Kent. Do *not* fire on any Kadiran vessels. I need to speak to whoever is in command.'

She was about to repeat her transmission when Lucia Rodin replied, 'There are a number of people here very relieved to hear your voice. Captain Mender actually appears to be smiling. He wants me to ask you if Roag has offered you any unguan fruit.'

Orry couldn't stop the grin that spread across her face. 'Nice of you to come and find me. And I'm happy to reassure you that no one is currently holding a gun to my head.'

'Then I don't quite understand,' Lucia said. 'Is Roag there?'

'And Delf.'

'So how is it that you're no longer their prisoner?'

Orry glanced at the alpha. 'Events have taken an ... unexpected turn here. I have a message for the Imperator.'

'A message? From whom?'

'From the Kadiran. If what they tell me is true, we may have more to worry about than the war.'

51

ARTICLE 2

For such a vast construction, *Hardhaven Voyager* could really move when it needed to. Francisco Guzman stood at the very front of the superstructure on a jutting balcony he'd had installed precisely for occasions like this. The aether whipped his long hair back above his respirator and goggles as the processing platform forged onwards, outstripped only by the swiftest of the whaling flotilla.

'This is what it's all about!' he cried, feeling twenty again. 'The fucking *chase*, Rayne! You feel it?'

He spared the woman a brief glance, but her pinch-faced expression of discomfort made him wish he hadn't bothered. *Fucking prims*. How could someone like Rayne *ever* understand? Those bastards had everything handed to them. This sour bitch had never conned a smoker so close to a drifter you could see the gases coalescing off its hide. She had never felt the pure rush of letting a harpoon go, of hearing that primaeval *hoot* of pain as it sank home. The closest Rayne had ever got to flensing flesh from hide was cutting up her evening meal.

'Come on, you bastards!' he roared, leaning over the rail. 'Cable me a big 'un!'

Those whalers thronging the processing floor close enough to hear him turned grinning faces up and gave a ragged cheer. These *are my people*, Guzman thought, *not those backstabbing, necktie-wearing pricks in the boardroom.*

Far ahead, he glimpsed a shadow moving beneath the aether. 'Hard away there, lads,' he shouted. 'She rises—!' He was pleased the years had not dulled his skills.

The flotilla shifted course slightly to head for the shadow, clouds of oily black smoke gouting from some of the smaller smokers as they red-lined their engines to draw ahead. Guzman looked on approvingly, remembering the days he'd done the very same thing.

The shadow was definitely rising, becoming more tangible as it neared the surface. Guzman stared, then frowned, and raising his monocular, zoomed in. His breath caught as he realised this was a vast specimen, perhaps the largest he'd ever seen – but there was something different about this drifter, something not quite . . .

It breached – but the hugely long metallic shape was clearly no leviathan. He lowered the monocular and stared dumbly at the vast craft rising gracefully from the aether, multicoloured streamers of gas pouring from bristling weapons like dry ice.

Beside him, Rayne breathed, 'What the *fuck*?'

Some of the smaller smokers, too intent or too stupid to realise that the thing in front of them wasn't a drifter, had released a flurry of harpoons which were all clattering harmlessly off the ship's hull. One of the craft, its pontoon engine aflame from the effort of drawing ahead of the pack, was unable to stop or turn in time; it slammed into the ship's side, half-flattening itself like a tin can before tumbling into the depths.

Guzman jumped as every speaker on the platform burst into life.

'This is Ascendancy cruiser *Gratitude*. You are engaged in the illegal hunting of an exotic species as defined by Article 2 of the Xeno Rights Act. Cease operations immediately and prepare to receive inspection teams.'

Rayne clutched Guzman's arm. 'Francisco – what are we going to *do*?'

He shook off her hand and stared at the enormous warship. Before he could begin to formulate his response, two of the larger smokers turned tail and fled. One of the turrets on the side of the Ascendancy cruiser swivelled almost lazily and spat four times.

The escaping smokers erupted into balls of flame.

His mouth turned dry as he watched tiny figures leaping from the decks, trying to escape the flames, just moments before the vessels fell apart and spiralled into the depths after them. Armed cutters were launching from the cruiser now. Six of the largest were headed directly for his platform, together with another ship that he knew all too well.

His jaw tightened and he turned to leave the balcony.

'Where are you going?' Rayne asked. The tremble in her voice made him despise her even more.

'I'm going to greet our guests,' he said coldly.

'Do you think I should go with you?'

'Do as you like, Rayne. I really couldn't give a shit any more.'

*

Orry spotted Guzman as *Dainty Jane* circled the platform's superstructure. 'There,' she said, pointing at the same pad they'd landed on last time they were here.

Jane touched down with a jolt and the ramp lowered to disgorge her cargo of auxiliaries, who spread out to secure the pad. Orry dutifully waited for the all-clear before leaving the ship herself, though it was pretty obvious that all the fight had been scared out of the whalers.

Guzman walked over to meet Orry and her companions, Rayne following on behind, looking scared. Beyond the circle of troops at the edge of the pad, *Hardhaven Voyager*'s crew were looking on equally anxiously.

'Miz Nobody. I wish I could say it was a pleasure to see you again.'

'Likewise.'

'I see you've been telling tales out of school.' He glanced at *Jane*'s other passengers and blanched as his eyes fell on Quondam, towering above Ethan beside him. 'It appears I misjudged you. You have powerful friends.'

'You're finished here, Guzman,' she said with satisfaction. 'You and your little club. By order of the Imperator, the Whaling League is hereby disbanded and all its assets confiscated. The same goes for the personal fortunes of anybody who has made their money through the illegal hunting of a sentient species. You two' – she swept her eyes across him and Notable Rayne, not bothering to hide her disgust – 'and the rest of the nabobs are under arrest.'

'This is ridiculous,' he protested. 'No proof has ever been published demonstrating the drifters are sentient—'

She looked at him coldly. 'Not *published*, no.' She pulled out the databrane and unfurled it.

Guzman swallowed at the sight of it.

'How many of these studies have you repressed?' she asked.

'I'm not saying anything until I see legal counsel.'

'Why am I not surprised?'

His eyes were blazing. 'You *stole* that document – it won't be admissible—'

She grinned. 'It doesn't need to be. Members of the Administrate's Science Secretariat are conducting their own study, starting immediately. Based on this' – she furled up the brane and tucked it securely into a pocket – 'I don't think the results will come as any great surprise, do you?'

Guzman looked ready to throttle her. 'Are you pleased with yourself? Without the League and the money we bring in from offworld, Morhelion will die. That will be on *your* head—'

'Not exactly true,' said the man standing beside Orry, who'd remained silent so far. 'Permit me to introduce myself. I am Niru Qin, president of the Empyrean Development Company.' He turned and beckoned and the harlequin scooper Dando Kink stepped forward, accompanied by a woman whose extravagant style of dress made his own look positively tame. 'After meeting with representatives of the scooper community, it appears that Morhelion does in fact have a great deal to offer the Ascendancy – more than enough to replace the regrettable trade in aeriform leviathan products.'

'*You* knew the damned things were sentient!' Guzman hissed furiously. 'EDC are as guilty as we are—'

'Whatever knowledge my *predecessor* may have been party to,' Qin broke in smoothly, 'has unfortunately died with her. A full investigation is underway and you may expect to form a substantial part of it.'

Frankly, Orry didn't trust Qin to run EDC any more honestly than Jessica Brookes had – but she *was* confident that EDC's dealings with Morhelion would be scrupulously fair from now on. The Imperator had been at pains to make that very clear.

'Scoopers?' Guzman scoffed. 'What have they got except a couple of tanks' worth of abyssal gases?'

Qin opened his mouth to reply but Orry cut in. Gesturing at Dando's eccentric companion, she said, 'This is Gossamer Vale from the deep rig *Non Sequitur*. She's a whale-whisperer.'

'Ridiculous,' Guzman snarled. 'That's nothing but scooper mumbo-jumbo.'

'Perhaps you shouldn't be so dismissive of scooper culture,' Qin smoothly took back control. 'Miz Vale has been kind enough to demonstrate the connection she has with the leviathans. In return for an end to the hunting, they are prepared to bring up and disgorge specific cargoes of abyssal gases.'

'Bullshit!'

'It actually doesn't matter what *you* think,' Orry told him. 'What does matter is that President Qin here believes it.'

'Which I do,' Qin confirmed.

A new voice spoke up from the mass of whalers surrounding them. 'So the scoopers will get rich – what're the rest of us supposed to do?'

Orry scanned the crowd until she spotted the speaker, a giant figure standing a head taller than his fellows. It took her a moment to place him, then she had it: Lindqvist, Tyrell's mate from Spumehead. She summoned one of the auxiliaries, who went to lead him through the cordon.

'This is Second Oversecretary Eichel,' Orry told him, waving forward another of *Dainty Jane*'s distinguished passengers. This woman appeared to be far more interested in her surroundings and the complicated-looking device in her hand than in Orry, but she did at least look up at the mention of her name. As she shuffled over, Orry said, 'She has oversight of the scientific budget for the entire Ascendancy.'

From the way Lindqvist was looking down at the over-secretary, he wasn't impressed, and judging by the rumblings of discontent from the crowd, nor were they – but before she could try to calm things down, Second Oversecretary Eichel was speaking.

'A fascinating world you have here,' she began. 'Before leaving Tyr I had the honour to meet personally with the Imperator Ascendant. He impressed upon me the importance of con-ducting an extensive study of aeriform leviathans.'

Orry smiled at that; when the Imperator had offered her a reward, he had clearly not been expecting her to request this.

'And how does that help *us*?' Lindqvist repeated, and his question was quickly echoed by the crowd.

'The Imperator has released a *substantial* sum to fund the research programme, for we will naturally require a very large number of new staff. We need to build and fit out new research stations, to crew and supply them and assist with the research efforts. We will also need to invest heavily in habitat regeneration and implement new planet-wide infrastructure to support our work. There will be plenty of work for those who want it.'

'*Science*,' Lindqvist said slowly, as if the word had left a bad taste in his mouth. 'What do *we* know about science?'

'About as much as me, you stubborn great bollock,' Vance Tyrell said loudly, pushing his way to the front of the assorted dignitaries, 'but they've gone and made me' – he turned to the oversecretary – 'what is it again?'

'Indigenous labour-pool liaison.'

'Yeah, that,' he said with a grin. 'This? This the real deal. You'll all make more than you ever did whaling, and with a much-reduced risk of dying horribly.'

Lindqvist looked suspiciously at him, then a grin spread slowly over his face and he began to laugh, softly at first, then with more gusto. 'Handsome Vance Tyrell: always falls on his feet. So you'll see we get our fair share of all this Ruuz money – is that what you're saying?'

'Exactly, my friend! We Morhelians have to stick together.' Tyrell pounded him enthusiastically on the back and Orry saw a few greedy smiles break out among the assembled whalers.

Lucia Rodin, who was standing next to Counter-Admiral Vetochkina, caught Orry's eye and gave a small smile of approval. Orry had her doubts about Tyrell, but if anyone could convince the whalers to buy into this new world, it was him – if only because of the numerous backhanders he would be expecting, some at least of which he'd be sharing around. Tyrell was going to be popular *and* rich, for a change.

But while Lindqvist and at least some of the whalers were halfway to being convinced, she could still hear growing rumbles of discontent from many of the others. The auxiliaries, outnumbered as they were, watched the crowd nervously.

Admiral Vetochkina stepped forward. 'This is *not* a discussion,' she stated, loudly and clearly. 'This colony's economy has been based on an illegal and morally indefensible trade for *centuries*. Reform *is* coming, and it *will* improve your quality of life. However, any of you unwilling to embrace the new world will be welcome as volunteers in the Grand Fleet or any other branch of the Ascendancy forces. Following the recent cessation of hostilities with the Kadiran Hierocracy, the Imperator Ascendant has approved the Universal Defence Ordinance, which renders all Ascendancy citizens of qualifying age subject to a lottery draft for a term of service of not less than two years, standard. As volunteers you will receive certain privileges that draftees will not, such as choosing which branch to serve in – subject to approval.'

Orry listened to the words with growing horror; this was the first she'd heard of any *Universal Defence Ordinance*. The Ascendancy hadn't once resorted to conscription in its two-hundred-year history, not even during the first Kadiran War. She opened her mouth, but felt Lucia's hand on her arm.

Vetochkina was staring coldly at the whalers, daring them to protest further. No one did, but Orry could see the discontent on a lot of faces.

'A regrettable move, but entirely necessary,' Lucia told her quietly. 'The Imperator thought long and hard before agreeing to it, but the intelligence provided by the Kadiran at the peace summit was . . . alarming.'

Vetochkina was taking control now, waving auxiliaries towards Guzman and Rayne; no one was paying attention to her and Lucia.

Orry had neither rank nor real power in the Ascendancy, but the fact that she hadn't been permitted to attend the private summit still rankled. 'Are you going to tell me what the Kadiran said?' Orry asked quietly. 'On Roag's ship, that alpha talked about a greater threat – so what is it?'

Lucia watched Guzman submit quietly to his restraints, his

face a stiff mask, but Rayne was protesting loudly as her arms were secured behind her back. 'I can't tell you that,' Lucia said. 'I'm sorry.'

She slipped away to speak to Vetochkina and Qin, leaving Orry simmering with resentment. She respected Lucia – more than that, she actually liked the woman – and it hurt that she was being shut out. *Haven't I done enough to earn their trust?*

She turned her attention to Guzman and Rayne and watched with grim satisfaction as they were led away. Rayne was staring numbly at her feet, but Guzman turned to glare defiantly at her. Similar scenes were being repeated all across *Hardhaven Voyager* as nabobs and senior members of the platform's crew were restrained and escorted to the other cutters.

As the craft began to lift from their pads, the distant hoot of a leviathan rolled hauntingly through the aether.

'Hello again, boys.' Orry knew this was a dumb thing to do, but sometimes the risk was worth it.

Marshal Purvis, Sticky Pete and his sons looked like they'd been celebrating in style. She'd found them semi-conscious inside the warehouse, amid piles of empty bottles and wraps of ket-c. The distribution of the League's money had begun and she imagined a lot of Morhelion's upstanding citizens would be spending their first payments like this.

Marshal Purvis was the first of the four men to come to. It took his drug-addled brain a few seconds to recognise her – at which point he reached for the shotgun she'd already removed from his side.

'Fuckin' *bitch*,' he spat, struggling to his feet. He snatched up a bottle by the neck, broke it on the edge of the table and thrust

431

the jagged remains towards her. The noise woke the others, whose bleary eyes went suddenly wide at the sight of her.

'You got a lot of fucking nerve coming back here,' Sticky Pete snarled.

'Not really,' she told him, then waved a warning finger at Purvis, who was advancing on her with the broken bottle. 'I really wouldn't do that, Marshal.'

'Well, you ain't me, *skank*. You have *no idea* who you're—'

He gave a little yelp of fear as Quondam stepped from behind a stack of crates. Grasping the hand holding the bottle, he hoisted Purvis effortlessly into the air. Chairs overturned as the others scrambled desperately away from the Kadiran, only to find their escape blocked by a squad of heavily armed auxiliaries.

'You might have heard about the draft lottery,' Orry said. 'Well, I'm pleased to tell you that your numbers have just come up . . . for a newly formed penal battalion.'

Marshal Purvis whimpered, blood running down his arm where Quondam's giant hand was grinding his fingers into broken glass.

Orry smiled coldly. 'I'm sure you'll have a lot of fun in the service.'

52

HOOK, LINE AND SINKER

Orry felt unaccountably nervous as she entered Tyrell's office. *You're being ridiculous*, she told herself, remembering everything she'd been through over the past weeks. This was different, though. *Then* she'd been playing a part: Orry the grifter. Now she was just plain Orry.

Tyrell didn't look right seated behind a desk. He rose as she entered and she noted his white shirt had been freshly laundered. He held out his arms, inviting an inspection. 'What do you think?'

'You look . . . cleaner.' In truth, she rather thought she preferred the old Tyrell, lounging around in *Zephyr*'s cockpit with a shit-eating grin on his face. 'You're taking this whole job-thing seriously, then?'

'You sound surprised.'

'I am.'

There was the grin. 'So, you here to make sure I don't do a runner?'

'Of course not.' She paused. '*Are* you going to do a runner?'

He came closer. He certainly *looked* happy – this relaxed, almost contented man was not at all what she'd been expecting.

'I admit it's an adjustment,' he told her, 'but actually, yes, I'm fine. Better than fine, in fact. I have a steady income and, more importantly, no one's trying to cut my knackers off.'

'Yet,' she added.

He was right in front of her now and she could feel her heart beating faster. He smelled . . . good. 'Don't forget I recommended you for this post,' she reminded him, keeping her voice hard to mask the quaver. 'Please don't screw it up.'

He reached up and brushed her cheek with his hand. 'Is that the only reason you came to see me?'

'No,' she said, and swallowed. *For pity's sake, get a grip.* 'I came to tell you I'm leaving. Mender's getting itchy feet and we have some money at last.'

'Time for a holiday?'

'Ethan's been banging on about going to Halcyon.'

'I hear it's nice there.' He cupped her face in his hands, his palms rough against her cheeks. 'Are you leaving right away?'

Am I really going to do this?

She realised that she was.

'I have a little time,' she breathed.

He kissed her.

'You look happy,' Ethan commented the following morning as the three of them shared a pre-collapse meal in *Dainty Jane*'s galley. Quondam was there too, not eating but adding the occasional terse comment to the conversation.

Orry felt her cheeks burning. What she'd fully expected to be a total disaster – a few minutes of awkward fumbling followed by bitter nights of regret and self-recrimination, like every other time she'd taken a fancy to someone she'd never see again – had turned out to be anything but. She could imagine herself really falling for Tyrell . . . though of course she would never be naïve enough to actually let that happen.

Although . . . Dad had probably been something like Vance Tyrell when he'd stolen Mum away from the Fountainhead, and somehow they'd made it work.

And the way Tyrell had accepted his new responsibilities? That had surprised her. She'd been suspicious at first that this was another of his games, but he seemed genuinely committed to leaving his old life behind him. She would surely have noticed if he was—

'Orry,' *Jane* said, 'I'm picking up a newsfeed from Hardhaven that I think you should hear.'

What now? 'Thanks, *Jane*. Play it, please.'

A well-spoken voice filled the galley: '—was taken from a storage facility in the early hours of this morning. The whale-stone, seized among the assets of the former Whaling League, was awaiting appraisal, but early estimates place its value in the tens of millions of imperials. Access to the facility was apparently gained using an authorised pass, but details of the owner's identity and position within the new administrative structure have not yet been released—'

'That's enough,' Orry said, staring at her half-eaten bowl of stemhopper chow mein. She laid down her chopsticks, uncertain how she felt.

'You don't think . . . ?' Ethan asked.

Mender chuckled. 'Gotta hand it to the guy. He sure saw you coming, girl. Hook, line and sinker. I knew there was no way he'd take an office job, not without some kind of angle.'

'We don't know it was Tyrell,' she snapped, furious at herself.

A charming smile: was that all it took to turn her into a gullible girl? She realised the others were staring at her and forced a grin that hung awkwardly on her lips. 'All right,' she admitted, 'there's a pretty good chance it was him.'

'Good luck to him,' Mender said. 'I always liked that guy's style. Kind of reminded me of me when I was younger.'

'You wanted to throw him overboard!' Orry objected.

'Eye for the ladies too.'

She stood up. 'Hadn't we better plot the collapse?'

'Plenty of time for that. Finish your grubs.' His smile faded into his customary scowl. 'Rama knows what we'll be eating on bloody Halcyon.'

'You can always stay on *Dainty Jane*,' she snapped, aware that he didn't deserve her anger. Right now she didn't know who she was more pissed off with: Tyrell for playing her, or herself for falling for it.

Mender just shrugged. 'Seems like a waste of money, is all.'

'Did you even *look* at the brochure I sent you?' Ethan asked incredulously. His frown turned into an expression of sudden mock-comprehension. '*I* know what it is: you're worried it'll be so perfect you won't have anything to moan about.' He grinned. 'That's it, isn't it?'

'Wise-ass.'

Orry climbed to the cockpit, leaving them arguing. In truth Halcyon didn't appeal to her much either, but Ethan had been through a lot lately, and at least it would take her mind off Morhelion – and Handsome Vance Tyrell.

The bastard.

ACKNOWLEDGEMENTS

Huge thanks first of all to my publisher and editor, the magnificent Jo Fletcher, and to her fabulous team at JFB, particularly Olivia Mead and Molly Powell. Thanks also to my most excellent agent, Ian Drury.

The writing community as a whole is packed full of wonderful people, many of whom deserve a mention, but I will limit myself on this occasion to lovely and talented blokes Gavin G. Smith, Daniel Godfrey and Guy T. Martland for their kind words.

I would also like to thank my friends for their unwavering enthusiasm and support, particularly (and in alphabetical order) Richard Bish, Ian Cassidy, Sharon Crossman, Richard Eaves, Neil Elliott, Liam Faulkner, Matt Norman, Marek Sroka and Maria Webster. I'm sorry the penguins didn't make the cut, Marek. Their day will surely come.

Finally, and most important of all, love and thanks to my family for providing such a happy home from which to launch myself off to other worlds. I may not always show it ('grumpy' is a word much favoured by my children), but I would be lost without the three of you. Thank you.

Dominic Dulley